MICHAEL CONNELLY

TRUNK MUSIC

An Orion paperback

First published in Great Britain in 1997
by Orion
This paperback edition published in 1997
by Orion Books Ltd,
Orion House, 5 Upper St Martin's Lane,
London WC2H 9EA

An Hachette UK company

Reissued 2007

A CIP catalogue record for this book is available
from the British Library

Typeset at The Spartan Press Ltd,
Lymington, Hants

Printed and bound in Great Britain by
Clays Ltd, St Ives plc

The Orion Publishing Group's policy is to use papers that
are natural, renewable and recyclable products and
made from wood grown in sustainable forests. The logging
and manufacturing processes are expected to conform to
the environmental regulations of the country of origin.

www.orionbooks.co.uk

I

As he drove along Mulholland Drive toward the Cahuenga Pass, Bosch began to hear the music. It came to him in fragments of strings and errant horn sequences, echoing off the brown summer-dried hills and blurred by the white noise of traffic carrying up from the Hollywood Freeway. Nothing he could identify. All he knew was that he was heading toward its source.

He slowed when he saw the cars parked off to the side of a gravel turn-off road. Two detective sedans and a patrol car. Bosch pulled his Caprice in behind them and got out. A single officer in uniform leaned against the fender of the patrol car. Yellow plastic crime-scene tape – the stuff used by the mile in Los Angeles – was strung from the patrol car's sideview mirror across the gravel road to the sign posted on the other side. The sign said, in black-on-white letters that were almost indistinguishable behind the graffiti that covered the sign:

L.A.F.D. FIRE CONTROL
MOUNTAIN FIRE DISTRICT ROAD
NO PUBLIC ADMITTANCE – NO SMOKING!

The patrol cop, a large man with sun-reddened skin and blond bristly hair, straightened up as Bosch approached. The first thing Bosch noted about him other than his size was the baton. It was holstered in a ring on his belt and the

3

business end of the club was marred, the black acrylic paint scratched away to reveal the aluminum beneath. Street fighters wore their battle-scarred stick proudly, as a sign, a not so subtle warning. This cop was a headbanger. No doubt about it. The plate above the cop's breast pocket said his name was Powers. He looked down at Bosch through Ray-Bans, though it was well into dusk and a sky of burnt orange clouds was reflected in his mirrored lenses. It was one of those sundowns that reminded Bosch of the glow the fires of the riots had put in the sky a few years back.

'Harry Bosch,' Powers said with a touch of surprise. 'When did you get back on the table?'

Bosch looked at him a moment before answering. He didn't know Powers but that didn't mean anything. Bosch's story was probably known by every cop in Hollywood Division.

'Just did,' Bosch said.

He didn't make any move to shake hands. You didn't do that at crime scenes.

'First case back in the saddle, huh?'

Bosch took out a cigarette and lit it. It was a direct violation of department policy but it wasn't something he was worried about.

'Something like that.' He changed the subject. 'Who's down there?'

'Edgar and the new one from Pacific, his soul sister.'

'Rider.'

'Whatever.'

Bosch said nothing further about that. He knew what was behind the contempt in the uniform cop's voice. It didn't matter that he knew Kizmin Rider had the gift and was a top-notch investigator. That would mean nothing to Powers, even if Bosch told him it was so. Powers probably saw only one reason why he was still wearing a blue uniform instead of carrying a detective's gold badge: that he was a white man in an era of female and minority hiring

4

and promotion. It was the kind of festering sore better left undisturbed.

Powers apparently registered Bosch's nonresponse as disagreement and went on.

'Anyway, they told me to let Emmy and Sid drive on down when they get here. I guess they're done with the search. So you can drive down instead of walking, I guess.'

It took a second for Bosch to register that Powers was referring to the medical examiner and the Scientific Investigation Division tech. He'd said the names as if they were a couple invited to a picnic.

Bosch stepped out onto the pavement, dropped the half cigarette and made sure he put it out with his shoe. It wouldn't be good to start a brush fire on his first job back with the homicide table.

'I'll walk it,' he said. 'What about Lieutenant Billets?'

'Not here yet.'

Bosch went back to his car and reached in through the open window for his briefcase. He then walked back to Powers.

'You the one who found it?'

'That was me.'

Powers was proud of himself.

'How'd you open it?'

'Keep a slim jim in the car. Opened the door, then popped the trunk.'

'Why?'

'The smell. It was obvious.'

'Wear gloves?'

'Nope. Didn't have any.'

'What did you touch?'

Powers had to think about it for a moment.

'Door handle, the trunk pull. That'd be about it.'

'Did Edgar or Rider take a statement? You write something up?'

'Nothing yet.'

Bosch nodded.

'Listen, Powers, I know you're all proud of yourself, but next time don't open the car, okay? We all want to be detectives but not all of us are. That's how crime scenes get fucked up. And I think you know that.'

Bosch watched the cop's face turn a dark shade of crimson and the skin go tight around his jaw.

'Listen, Bosch,' he said. 'What I know is that if I just called this in as a suspicious vehicle that *smells* like there's a stiff in the trunk, then you people would've said, "What the fuck does Powers know?" and left it there to rot in the sun until there was nothing left of your goddamn crime scene.'

'That might be true but, see, then that would be our fuckup to make. Instead, we've got you fucking us up before we start.'

Powers remained angry but mute. Bosch waited a beat, ready to continue the debate, before dismissing it.

'Can you lift the tape now, please?'

Powers stepped back to the tape. He was about thirty-five, Bosch guessed, and had the long-practiced swagger of a street veteran. In L.A. that swagger came to you quickly, as it had in Vietnam. Powers held the yellow tape up and Bosch walked under. As he passed, the cop said, 'Don't get lost.'

'Good one, Powers. You got me there.'

The fire road was one lane and overgrown at its sides with brush that came as high as Bosch's waist. There was trash and broken glass strewn along the gravel, the trespasser's answer to the sign at the gate. Bosch knew the road was probably a favorite midnight haunt for teenagers from the city below.

The music grew louder as he went further in. But he still could not identify it. About a quarter mile in, he came to a gravel-bedded clearing that he guessed was a staging point for fire-fighting apparatus in the event that a brush fire broke out in the surrounding hills. Today it would serve as a

6

crime scene. On the far side of the clearing Bosch saw a white Rolls-Royce Silver Cloud. Standing near it were his two partners, Rider and Edgar. Rider was sketching the crime scene on a clipboard while Edgar worked with a tape measure and called out measurements. Edgar saw Bosch and gave an acknowledging wave with a latex-gloved hand. He let the tape measure snap back into its case.

'Harry, where you been?'

'Painting,' Bosch said as he walked up. 'I had to get cleaned up and changed, put stuff away.'

As Bosch stepped closer to the edge of the clearing, the view opened below him. They were on a bluff rising above the rear of the Hollywood Bowl. The rounded music shell was down to the left, no more than a quarter mile. And the shell was the source of the music. The L.A. Philharmonic's end-of-the-season Labor Day weekend show. Bosch was looking down at eighteen thousand people in concert seats stretching up the opposite side of the canyon. They were enjoying one of the last Sunday evenings of the summer.

'Jesus,' he said out loud, thinking of the problem.

Edgar and Rider walked over.

'What've we got?' Bosch asked.

Rider answered.

'One in the trunk. White male. Gunshots. We haven't checked him out much further than that. We've been keeping the lid closed. We've got everybody rolling, though.'

Bosch started walking toward the Rolls, going around the charred remnants of an old campfire that had burned in the center of the clearing. The other two followed.

'This okay?' Bosch asked as he got close to the Rolls.

'Yeah, we did the search,' Edgar said. 'Nothing much. Got some leakage under the car. That's about it, though. Cleanest scene I've been at in a while.'

Jerry Edgar, called in from home like everybody else on the team, was wearing blue jeans and a white T-shirt. On the left breast of the shirt was a drawing of a badge and the words LAPD Homicide. As he walked past Bosch, Harry saw that the back of the shirt said Our Day Begins When Your Day Ends. The tight-fitting shirt contrasted sharply with Edgar's dark skin and displayed his heavily muscled upper body as he moved with an athletic grace toward the Rolls. Bosch had worked with him on and off for six years but they had never become close outside of the job. This was the first time it had dawned on Bosch that Edgar actually was an athlete, that he must regularly work out.

It was unusual for Edgar not to be in one of his crisp Nordstrom's suits. But Bosch thought he knew why. His informal dress practically guaranteed he would avoid having to do the dirty work, next-of-kin notification.

They slowed their steps when they got close to the Rolls, as if perhaps whatever was wrong here might be contagious. The car was parked with its rear end facing south and visible to the spectators in the upper levels of the Bowl across the way. Bosch considered their situation again.

'So you want to pull this guy out of there with all those people with their wine and box lunches from the Grill watching?' he asked. 'How do you think that's going to play on the TV tonight?'

'Well,' Edgar replied, 'we thought we'd kind of leave that decision to you, Harry. You being the three.'

Edgar smiled and winked.

'Yeah, right,' Bosch said sarcastically. 'I'm the three.'

Bosch was still getting used to the idea of being a so-called team leader. It had been almost eighteen months since he had officially investigated a homicide, let alone headed up a team of three investigators. He had been assigned to the Hollywood Division burglary table when he returned to work from his involuntary stress leave in January. The detective bureau commander, Lieutenant Grace Billets, had explained that his assignment was a way of gradually easing him back into detective work. He knew that explanation was a lie and that she had been told where

8

to put him, but he took the demotion without complaint. He knew they would come for him eventually.

After eight months of pushing papers and making the occasional burglary arrest, Bosch was called into the CO's office and Billets told him she was making changes. The division's homicide clearance rate had dipped to its lowest point ever. Fewer than half of the killings were cleared. She had taken over command of the bureau nearly a year earlier, and the sharpest decline, she struggled to admit, had come under her own watch. Bosch could have told her that the decline was due in part to her not following the same statistical deceptions practiced by her predecessor, Harvey Pounds, who had always found ways of pumping up the clearance rate, but he kept that to himself. Instead, he sat quietly while Billets laid out her plan.

The first part of the plan was to move Bosch back to the homicide table as of the start of September. A detective named Selby, who barely pulled his weight, would go from homicide to Bosch's slot on the burglary table. Billets would also be adding a young and smart detective transfer she had previously worked with in the Pacific Division detective bureau, Kizmin Rider. Next, and this was the radical part, Billets was changing the traditional pairing of detectives. Instead, the nine homicide detectives assigned to Hollywood would be grouped into three teams of three. Each of the three teams would have a detective third grade in charge. Bosch was a three. He was named team leader of squad one.

The reasoning behind the change was sound – at least on paper. Most homicides are solved in the first forty-eight hours after discovery or they aren't solved at all. Billets wanted more solved so she was going to put more detectives on each one. The part that didn't look so good on paper, especially to the nine detectives, was that previously there had been four pairs of partners working homicide cases. The new changes meant each detective would be working every third case that came up instead of every fourth. It meant more cases, more work, more court time, more overtime, and more stress. Only the overtime was considered a positive. But Billets was tough and didn't care much for the complaints of the detectives. And her new plan quickly won her the obvious nickname.

'Anybody talk to Bullets yet?' Bosch asked.

'I called,' Rider said. 'She was up in Santa Barbara for the weekend. Left a number with the desk. She's coming down early but she's still at least an hour and a half from us. She said she was going to have to drop the hubby off first and would probably just roll to the bureau.'

Bosch nodded and stepped to the rear of the Rolls. He picked up the smell right away. It was faint but it was there, unmistakable. Like no other. He nodded to no one in particular again. He placed his briefcase on the ground, opened it and took a pair of latex gloves from the cardboard box inside. He then closed the case and placed it a few feet behind him and out of the way.

'Okay, let's take a look,' he said while stretching the gloves over his hands. He hated how they felt. 'Let's stand close, we don't want to give the people in the Bowl more of a show than they paid for.'

'It ain't pretty,' Edgar said as he stepped forward.

The three of them stood together at the back end of the Rolls to shield the view from the concertgoers. But Bosch knew that anybody with a decent pair of field glasses would know what was going on. This was L.A.

Before opening the trunk, he noticed the car's personalized license plate. It said TNA. Before he could speak, Edgar answered his unasked question.

'Comes back to TNA Production. On Melrose.'

'T and A?'

'No, the letters, T-N-A, just like on the plate.'

'Where on Melrose?'

Edgar took a notebook out of his pocket and looked

through the page. The address he gave was familiar to Bosch but he couldn't place it. He knew it was down near Paramount, the sprawling studio that took up the entire north side of the fifty-five-hundred block. The big studio was surrounded by smaller production houses and mini-studios. They were like sucker fish that swam around the mouth of the big shark, hoping for the scraps that didn't get sucked in.

'Okay, let's do it.'

He turned his attention back to the trunk. He could see that the lid had been lightly placed down so it would not lock closed. Using one rubber-coated finger, he gently lifted it.

As the trunk was opened, it expelled a sickeningly fetid breath of death. Bosch immediately wished he had a cigarette but those days were through. He knew what a defense lawyer could do with one ash from a cop's smoke at a crime scene. Reasonable doubts were built on less.

He leaned in under the lid to get a close look, careful not to touch the bumper with his pants. The body of a man was in the trunk. His skin was a grayish white and he was expensively dressed in linen pants sharply pressed and cuffed at the bottom, a pale blue shirt with a flowery pattern and a leather sport coat. His feet were bare.

The dead man was on his right side in the fetal position except his wrists were behind him instead of folded against his chest. It appeared to Bosch that his hands had been tied behind him and the bindings then removed, most likely after he was dead. Bosch looked closely and could see a small abrasion on the left wrist, probably caused by the struggle against the bindings. The man's eyes were closed tightly and there was a whitish, almost translucent material dried in the corners of the sockets.

'Kiz, I want you taking notes on appearance.'

'Right.'

Bosch bent further into the trunk. He saw a froth of purged blood had dried in the dead man's mouth and nose.

His hair was caked with blood which had spread over the shoulders and to the trunk mat, coating it with a coagulated pool. He could see the hole in the floor of the trunk through which blood had drained to the gravel below. It was a foot from the victim's head and appeared to be evenly cut in the metal underlining in a spot where the floor mat was folded over. It was not a bullet hole. It was probably a drain or a hole left by a bolt that had vibrated loose and fallen out.

In the mess that was the back of the man's head, Bosch could see two distinct jagged-edged penetrations to the lower rear skull – the occipital protuberance – the scientific name popping easily into his mind. Too many autopsies, he thought. The hair close to the wounds was charred by the gases that explode out of the barrel of a gun. The scalp showed stippling from gunpowder. Point-blank shots. No exit wounds that he could see. Probably twenty-twos, he guessed. They bounce around inside like marbles dropped into an empty jelly jar.

Bosch looked up and saw a small spray of blood splattered on the inside of the trunk lid. He studied the spots for a long moment and then stepped back and straightened up. He appraised the entire view of the trunk now, his mind checking off an imaginary list. Because no blood drips had been found on the access road into the clearing, he had no doubts that the man had been killed here in the trunk. Still, there were other unknowns. Why here? Why no shoes and socks? Why were the bindings taken off the wrists? He put these questions aside for the time being.

'You check for the wallet?' he asked without looking at the two others.

'Not yet,' Edgar replied. 'Recognize him?'

For the first time Bosch looked at the face as a face. There was still fear etched on it. The man had closed his eyes. He had known what was coming. Bosch wondered if the whitish material in the eyes was dried tears.

'No, do you?'

'Nope. It's too messy, anyway.'

Bosch gingerly lifted the back of the leather coat and saw no wallet in the back pockets of the dead man's pants. He then opened the jacket and saw the wallet was there in an inside pocket that carried a Fred Haber men's shop label on it. Bosch could also see a paper folder for an airline ticket in the pocket. With his other hand he reached into the jacket and removed the two items.

'Get the lid,' he said as he backed away.

Edgar closed it over as gently as an undertaker closing a coffin. Bosch then walked over to his briefcase, squatted down and put the two items down on it.

He opened the wallet first. There was a full complement of credit cards in slots on the left side and a driver's license behind a plastic window on the right. The name on the license said Anthony N. Aliso.

'Anthony N. Aliso,' Edgar said. 'Tony for short. TNA. TNA Productions.'

The address was in Hidden Highlands, a tiny enclave off Mulholland in the Hollywood Hills. It was the kind of place that was surrounded by walls and had a guard shack manned twenty-four hours a day, mostly by off-duty or retired LAPD cops. The address went well with the Rolls-Royce.

Bosch opened the billfold section and found a sheaf of currency. Without taking the money out, he counted two one-hundred-dollar bills and nine twenties. He called the amount out so that Rider could make a note of it. Next he opened the airline folder. Inside was the receipt for a one-way ticket on an American Airlines flight departing Las Vegas for LAX at 10:05 Friday night. The name on the ticket matched the driver's license. Bosch checked the back flap of the ticket folder, but there was no sticker or staple indicating that a bag had been checked by the ticket holder. Curious, Bosch left the wallet and the ticket on the case and went to look into the car through the windows.

'No luggage?'

'None,' Rider said.

Bosch went back to the trunk and raised the lid again. Looking in at the body, he hooked a finger up the left sleeve of the jacket and pulled it up. There was a gold Rolex watch on the wrist. The face was encircled with a ring of tiny diamonds.

'Shit.'

Bosch turned around. It was Edgar.

'What?'

'You want me to call OCID?'

'Why?'

'Wop name, no robbery, two in the back of the head. It's a whack job, Harry. We oughta call OCID.'

'Not yet.'

'I'll tell you right now that's what Bullets is gonna wanna do.'

'We'll see.'

Bosch appraised the body again, looking closely at the contorted, bloodied face. Then he closed the lid.

Bosch stepped away from the car and to the edge of the clearing. The spot offered a brilliant view of the city. Looking east across the sprawl of Hollywood, he could easily pick up the spires of downtown in the light haze. He saw the lights of Dodger Stadium were on for the twilight game. The Dodgers were dead even with Colorado with a month to go and Nomo due to pitch the game. Bosch had a ticket in his inside coat pocket. But he knew bringing it along had been wishful thinking. He wouldn't get anywhere near the stadium tonight. He also knew Edgar was right. The killing had all the aspects of a mob hit. The Organized Crime Intelligence Division should be notified – if not to take over the investigation entirely, then at least to offer advice. But Bosch was delaying that notification. It had been a long time since he'd had a case. He didn't want to give it up yet.

He looked back down at the Bowl. It looked like a sellout to him, the crowd seated in an elliptical formation going up the opposite hill. The seating sections furthest away from the music shell were the highest up the hill and at an almost even level with the clearing where the Rolls was parked. Bosch wondered how many of the people were watching him at that moment. Again he thought of the dilemma he faced. He had to get the investigation going. But he knew that if he pulled the body out of the trunk with such an audience watching, there likely would be hell to pay for the bad public relations such a move would cause the city and the department.

Once again Edgar seemed to know his thoughts.

'Hell, Harry, they won't care. At the jazz festival a few years back, there was a couple up on this spot doing the nasty for half an hour. When they were done, they got a standing ovation. Guy stands up buck naked and takes a little bow.'

Bosch looked back at him to see if he was serious.

'I read it in the *Times*. The "Only in L.A." column.'

'Well, Jerry, this is the Philharmonic. It's a different crowd, know what I mean? And I don't want this to end up in "Only in L.A.," okay?'

'Okay, Harry.'

Bosch looked at Rider. She hadn't said much of anything yet.

'What do you think, Kiz?'

'I don't know. You're the three.'

Rider was small, five feet and no more than a hundred pounds with her gun on. She would never have made it before the department relaxed the physical requirements to attract more women. She had light brown skin. Her hair was straightened and kept short. She wore jeans and a pink oxford shirt beneath a black blazer. On her small body, the jacket did not do much to disguise a 9mm Glock 17-holstered on her right hip.

Billets had told him that she had worked with Rider in Pacific. Rider had worked robbery and fraud cases but was called out on occasion to work homicides in which there were overlying financial aspects. Billets had said Rider could break a crime scene down as well as most veteran homicide detectives. She had pulled strings to get Rider's transfer approved but was already resigned to the fact that she wouldn't stay long in the division. Rider was marked for travel. Her double minority status coupled with the facts that she was good at what she did and had a guardian angel – Billets wasn't sure who – at Parker Center practically guaranteed her stay in Hollywood would be short. It was a bit of final seasoning before she headed downtown to the Glass House.

'What about the OPG?' Bosch asked.

'Held up on that,' Rider said. 'Thought we'd be here a while before we moved the car.'

Bosch nodded. It was what he expected her to say. The official police garage was usually last on the call-out list. He was just stalling, trying to make a decision while asking questions he already knew the answers to.

Finally he made his decision on what to do.

'Okay, go ahead and call,' he said. 'Tell them to come now. And tell them to bring a flatbed. Okay? Even if they've got a hook in the neighborhood, make 'em turn around. Tell 'em it's gotta be a flat. There's a phone in my briefcase.'

'Got it,' Rider said.

'Why the flatbed, Harry?' Edgar asked.

Bosch didn't answer.

'We're moving the whole show,' Rider said.

'What?' Edgar said.

Rider went to the briefcase without answering. Bosch held back a smile. She knew what he was doing, and he began to see some of the promise Billets had talked about. He got out a cigarette and lit it. He put the burnt match into the cellophane around the pack and replaced it in the pocket of his coat.

He noticed as he smoked that the sound at the edge of the clearing, where he could look directly down into the Bowl, was much better. After a few moments he was even able to identify the piece being played.

16

'*Sheherazade*,' he said.

'What's that, Harry?' Edgar asked.

'The music. It's called *Sheherazade*. Ever heard it?'

'I'm not sure I'm hearing it now. All the echoes, man.'

Bosch snapped his fingers. Out of the blue a thought had pushed through. In his mind he saw the studio's arched gate, the replica of the Arc de Triomphe in Paris.

'That address on Melrose,' Bosch said. 'That's near Paramount. One of those feeder-fish studios right nearby. I think it's Archway.'

'Yeah? I think you're right.'

Rider walked up then.

'We got a flat on the way,' she said. 'ETA is fifteen. I checked on SID and ME. Also on the way. SID has somebody just wrapped up a home invasion in Nichols Canyon, so they should be right over.'

'Good,' Bosch said. 'Either of you go over the story with the swinging stick, yet?'

'Not since the preliminary,' Edgar said. 'Not our type. Thought we'd leave him for the three.'

The unspoken meaning of this was that Edgar had sensed the racist animosity Powers radiated toward himself and Rider.

'Okay, I'll take him,' Bosch said. 'I want you two to finish the charting, then do another sweep of the immediate area. Take different areas this time.'

He realized he had just told them things he didn't need to tell them.

'Sorry. You know what to do. All I'm saying is let's take this one by the numbers. I've got a feeling it's going eight by ten on us.'

'What about OCID?' Edgar asked.

'I told you, not yet.'

'Eight by ten?' Rider said, a confused expression on her face.

'Eight by ten case,' Edgar told her. 'Celebrity case. Studio case. If that's a hotshot from the industry in the trunk, somebody from Archway, we're going to get some media on this. More than some. A dead guy in the trunk of his Rolls is news. A dead industry guy in the trunk of his Rolls is bigger news.'

'Archway?'

Bosch left them there as Edgar filled her in on the facts of life when it came to murder, the media and the movie business in Hollywood.

Bosch licked his fingers to put the cigarette out and then put it with the used match in the cellophane wrapper. He slowly began walking the quarter mile back to Mulholland, once again searching the gravel road in a back-and-forth manner. But there was so much debris on the gravel and in the nearby brush that it was impossible to know if anything – a cigarette butt, a beer bottle, a used condom – was related to the Rolls or not. The one thing he looked closest for was blood. If there was blood on the road that could be linked to the victim, it could indicate that he was killed elsewhere and left in the clearing. No blood probably meant the killing had taken place right there.

He realized as he made the fruitless search that he was feeling relaxed, maybe even happy. He was back on the beat and following his mission once again. Mindful that the man in the trunk had to have perished for him to feel this way, Bosch quickly wrote that guilt off. The man would have ended up in the trunk whether Bosch had ever made it back to the homicide table or not.

When Bosch got to Mulholland he saw the fire trucks. There were two of them and a battalion of firefighters standing around them, seemingly waiting for something. He lit another cigarette and looked at Powers.

'You've got a problem,' the uniform cop said.

'What?'

Before Powers answered, one of the firefighters stepped up. He wore the white helmet of a battalion chief.

'You in charge?' he asked.

'That's me.'

'Chief Jon Friedman,' he said. 'We've got a problem.'

'That's what I hear.'

'The show down in the Bowl is supposed to end in ninety minutes. After that we've got the fireworks. Problem is this fellow says you got yourself a dead body up there and a crime scene. That's the problem. If we can't get up there to set up a safety position for the fireworks, there isn't going to be any fireworks. We can't allow it. If we're not in position, we could see the whole down slope of these hills go up with one errant missile. Know what I mean?'

Bosch noticed Powers smirking at his dilemma. Bosch ignored him and returned his attention to Friedman.

'Chief, how long do you need to set up?'

'Ten minutes max. We just got to be there before the first one goes up.'

'Ninety minutes?'

'About eighty-five now. There's gonna be a lot of angry people down there if they don't get their fireworks.'

Bosch realized he wasn't as much making decisions as having them made for him.

'Chief, hold here. We'll be out in an hour and fifteen. Don't cancel the show.'

'You sure about that?'

'Count on it.'

'Detective?'

'What, Chief?'

'You're breaking the law with that cigarette.'

He nodded toward the graffiti-covered sign.

'Sorry, Chief.'

Bosch walked out to the road to stamp out the smoke while Friedman headed back to his people to radio in that the show would go on. Bosch realized the danger and caught up to him.

'Chief, you can say the show will go on, but don't put anything out on the air about the body. We don't need the media out here, helicopters swooping over.'

'I gotcha.'

Bosch thanked him and turned his attention to Powers.

'You can't clear a scene in an hour and fifteen,' Powers said. 'The ME isn't even here.'

'Let me worry about that, Powers. You write something up yet?'

'Not yet. Been dealing with these guys. Would've helped if one of you folks had a two-way with you up there.'

'Then why don't you run it down for me from the start.'

'What about them?' Powers asked, nodding in the direction of the clearing. 'Why isn't one of them talking to me? Edgar and Rider?'

'Because they're busy. You want to run it down for me or not?'

'I already told you.'

'From the start, Powers. You told me what you did once you checked the car out. What made you check it?'

'There's nothin' much to tell. I usually make a pass by here each watch, chase away the dirtbags.'

He pointed across Mulholland and up to the crest of the hill. There was a line of houses, most on cantilevers, clinging to the crestline. They looked like mobile homes suspended in air.

'People up there call the station all the time, say they got campfires going down here, beer parties, devil worship, who knows what. Guess it ruins their view. And they don't want nothin' to spoil that million-dollar view. So I come up and sweep out the trash. Mostly bored little pissants from the Valley. Fire Department used to have a lock on the gate here, but a deuce plowed through it. That was six months ago. Takes the city at least a year to repair anything 'round here. Shit, I requisitioned batteries for my Mag three weeks ago and I'm still waiting for them. If I didn't buy them myself, I'd be working the fuckin' night watch without a flashlight. City doesn't care. This ci—'

'So what about the Rolls, Powers? Let's stay on the subject.'

'Yeah, well, I usually make it by after dark, but because of the show in the Bowl I swung by early today. Saw the Rolls then.'

'You came on your own? No complaint from up the hill?'

'No. Today I just cruised it on my own. On account of the show. I figured there might be some trespassers.'

'Were there?'

'A few – people waiting to hear the music. Not the usual crowd, though. That's refined music, I guess you'd call it. I chased 'em out anyway, and when they were gone, the Rolls was what was left. But there was no driver for it.'

'So you checked it out.'

'Yeah, and I know the smell, man. Popped it with the slim and there he was. The stiff. Then I backed out and called the pros.'

There was a note of sarcasm in the way he said the last word. Bosch ignored it.

'The people you chased, you get any names?'

'No, like I told you, I chased them, then noticed that nobody got in and drove away in the Rolls. It was too late by then.'

'What about last night?'

'What about it?'

'Did you make it by here?'

'I was off. I'm on Tuesday–Saturday but I switched with a buddy last night 'cause he had something to do tonight.'

'So then what about Friday night?'

He shook his head.

'Three watch is always busy Friday. I had no time for free cruising and we didn't get a complaint as far as I know . . . so I never made it by.'

'Just chasin' the radio?'

'I had calls backed up on me all night. I didn't even get a ten-seven.'

'No dinner break, that's dedication, Powers.'

'What's that supposed to mean?'

Bosch saw he had made a mistake. Powers was consumed by job frustrations and he had pushed him too far. Powers turned crimson again and slowly took off his Ray-Bans before speaking.

'Let me tell you something, big shot. You got in while the getting was good. The rest of us? We get shit. We – I've been trying for so many years I can't count to get a gold shield and I've got about as much chance of getting one as whoever's in the trunk of that Rolls-Royce. But I'm not laying down. I'm still out here five nights a week chasin' the radio. Says "Protect and Serve" on the car door and I'm doin' it, man. So don't give me any shit about dedication.'

Bosch hesitated until he was sure Powers was done.

'Look, Powers, I didn't mean to give you shit. Okay? You want a cigarette?'

'I don't smoke.'

'Okay, let's try this again.' He waited a beat while Powers put the mirrors back on his eyes and seemed to calm down. 'You always work alone?'

'I'm the Z car.'

Bosch nodded. Zebra unit. An officer of many stripes, meaning he handled a variety of calls, usually trash calls, while cars with two officers abroad handled the hotshots – the prime, possibly dangerous, calls. Zebra worked patrol alone and often had free rein of the entire division. They were in the supervisory level between the sergeants and the grunts who were assigned to patrol geographic slices of the division known as basic car areas.

'How often you chase people outta here?'

'Once or twice a month. Can't say what happens on the other shifts or with the basic cars. But shit calls like this usually go to the Z car.'

'You got any shakes?'

Shakes were three-by-five cards formally called field interview, or FI, cards. Cops filled them out when they stopped suspicious people but did not have enough evidence to arrest them, or when making such an arrest – in this case, for trespassing – would be a waste of time. The American Civil Liberties Union called such stops shakedowns and an abuse of police powers. The name stuck, even with the cops.

'I've got some, yeah, at the station.'

'Good. We'd like to have a look if you could dig them out. Also, think you could ask the cops in the basic car if they've noticed the Rolls here the last few days?'

'Is this where I'm supposed to thank you for letting me have a part in the big bad investigation and ask you to put in a good word for me with the deputy chief of dicks?'

Bosch stared at him a few moments before answering.

'No, this is where I tell you to have the cards ready for us by nine tonight or I'll put in a word about that with the patrol skipper. And never mind the basic car people. We'll go ahead and talk to them ourselves. Don't want you to miss your ten-seven two shifts in a row, Powers.'

Bosch started back toward the crime scene, moving slowly again and checking the other side of the gravel road. Twice he had to step off the gravel and into the brush to let the official police garage truck pass and then the Scientific Investigation Division van.

By the time he got to the clearing, he again had come up with nothing during his search and was sure the victim had been murdered in the trunk while the Rolls was parked in the clearing. He saw Art Donovan, the SID tech, and Roland Quatro, the photographer who came with him, starting their work. Bosch walked up to Rider.

'Anything?' she asked.

'No. You?'

'Nothing. I think the Rolls must've been driven in with our guy in the trunk. Then the doer gets out, opens the lid and pops him twice. He closes the trunk and walks out.

Somebody picks him up out on Mulholland. Clean scene back here.'

Bosch nodded.

'Him?'

'Well, I'm going with the percentages for now.'

Bosch walked over to Donovan, who was bagging the wallet and airline ticket in a clear plastic evidence envelope.

'Art, we've got a problem.'

'You're telling me. I was just thinking I can rig some tarps over light tripods, but I don't think you'll be able to block the view for everybody in the Bowl. Some of them are going to get a show all right. I guess it will make up for canceling the fireworks. That is, unless you're just planning to sit tight with it until after the show.'

'Nah, we do that and some defense lawyer will tear us new assholes in court for delaying things. Every lawyer went to school on O.J., Art. You know that.'

'So then what do we do?'

'Just do what you've got to do here with some speed and then we'll take the whole thing to the print shed. You know if anybody's in there right now?'

'No, it should be free,' Donovan said slowly. 'You mean you're talking about the whole thing? The body, too?'

Bosch nodded.

'Besides, you can do a better job with it in the shed, right?'

'Absolutely. But what about the ME? They've got to sign off on something like this, Harry.'

'I'll deal with that. Before we put it on the flatbed, though, make sure you guys have got stills and video in case things shift during transit. Also, run a print card off the guy and give it to me.'

'You got it.'

While Donovan went to Quatro to explain the drill, Bosch huddled with Edgar and Rider.

'Okay, for now we're going to run with this one. If you had plans for the rest of the night, make your calls. It's going to be a long one. This is how I want to break it up.'

He pointed up to the homes on the crestline.

'First, Kiz, I want you to go up there and do a house-to-house. You know the routine. See if anybody remembers seeing the Rolls or knows how long it's been here. Maybe somebody heard the shots. They might've echoed up the side of the hill. We want to try to pin down the time this happened. After that, I – you got a phone?'

'No. I have a rover in the car.'

'No. I want to keep everything about this off the air.'

'I can use a phone in somebody's house.'

'Okay, call me when you're done or I'll page you when I'm done. Depending on how things shake out, you and I will either do next of kin or his office after that.''

She nodded. Bosch turned to Edgar.

'Jerry, you go in and work from the station. You've got the paper on this one.'

'She's the rookie.'

'Well, then, next time don't show up in a T-shirt. You can't go knocking on doors dressed like that.'

'I got a shirt in the car. I'll change.'

'Next time. You're on the paper on this one. But before you start, I want you to put Aliso through the box and see what you get on him. He's got a DL issued last year, so they've got his thumb print on file through DMV. See if you can get somebody from prints to compare it to the print card Art's getting for you right now. I want the ID confirmed as soon as possible.'

'There ain't going to be anybody in prints t'night. Art's the guy on call. He should do this.'

'Art's going to be tied up. See if you can shake somebody at home loose. We need the ID.'

'I'll try but I can't prom—'

'Good. After that, I want you to call everybody who works a basic car in this area and see if anyone's seen the Rolls. Powers – the guy up at the road – is going to pull shake cards on the kids who hang out here. I want you to start running them down, too. After that you can start the paper going.'

'Shit, with all this, I'll be lucky if I start typing before *next* Monday.'

Bosch ignored his whining and appraised both his partners.

'I'll stay with the body. If I get tied up, Kiz, you go on to check out the office address and I'll handle next of kin. Okay, everybody know what's what?'

Rider and Edgar nodded. Bosch could tell Edgar was still annoyed about something.

'Kiz, you head out now.'

She walked away and Bosch waited until she was out of earshot before speaking.

'Okay, Jerry, what's the problem?'

'I just want to know if that's how it's going to be on this team. Am I going to get the shit work while the princess skates?'

'No, Jerry, it's not going to be like that, and I think you know me well enough not to ask. What's the real problem?'

'I don't like your choices on this, Harry. We should be on the phone with Organized Crime right now. If anything looks like an OC case, this is it. I think you should call 'em, but I think 'cause you're fresh back on the table and been waiting for a case so long, you're not making the call. That's the problem.'

Edgar held his hands out as if to indicate how obvious this was.

'You know, you've got nothing to prove here, Harry. And there's never going to be a shortage of bodies to come along. This is Hollywood, remember? I think we should just turn this one over and wait for the next one.'

Bosch nodded.

'You may be right,' he said. 'You probably are. About all of it. But I'm the three. So we do it my way for now. I'm going to call Bullets and tell her what we've got, then I'm going to call OCID. But even if they roll out, we're going to keep a part of this. You know that. So let's do it good. Okay?'

Edgar nodded reluctantly.

'Look,' Bosch said, 'your objection is noted for the record, okay?'

'Sure, Harry.'

Bosch saw the blue ME's van pull into the clearing then. The tech behind the wheel was Richard Matthews. It was a break. Matthews wasn't as territorial as some of the others, and Bosch figured he could convince him to go along with the plan to move the whole package to the print shed. Matthews would understand that it was the only choice.

'Stay in touch,' Bosch said as Edgar walked off.

Edgar sullenly waved without looking back.

For the next few moments Bosch stood alone in the midst of the activities of the crime scene. He realized he truly reveled in his role. The start of a case always seemed to jazz him this way, and he knew how much he had missed it and craved it during the last year and a half.

Finally, he put his thoughts aside and walked toward the ME's van to talk to Matthews. There was a burst of applause from the Bowl as *Sheherazade* ended.

The print shed was a World War II Quonset hut that sat in the City Services equipment yard behind the police head-quarters at Parker Center. It had no windows and a double-wide garage door. The interior was painted black and every crack or crevice where light might come in was taped over. There were thick black curtains that could be pulled closed after the garage door was shut. When they were pulled, the interior was as black as a loan shark's heart. The techs who worked there even referred to the place as 'the cave'.

While the Rolls was being unloaded from the OPG truck, Bosch took his briefcase to a workbench inside the shed and got the phone out. The Organized Crime

Investigation Division was a secret society within the greater closed society of the department. Bosch knew very little about OCID and was acquainted with few detectives assigned to the unit. The OCID was a mysterious force, even to those within the department. Not many knew exactly what it did. And this, of course, bred suspicions and jealousies.

Most OCID detectives were known in Detective Services as big-footers. They swooped down to take investigations away from detectives like Bosch, but they didn't often make cases in return. Bosch had seen many investigations disappear under their door with not many prosecutions of OC wise guys resulting. They were the only division in the department with a black budget – approved in closed session by the chief and a police commission that largely followed his lead. From there, the money disappeared into the dark, to pay for informants, investigations and high-tech equipment. Many of their cases disappeared in that netherworld as well.

Bosch asked the communications operator to connect his call to the OCID supervisor on call for the weekend. As he waited for the patch through, he thought again about the body in the trunk. Anthony Aliso – if that was who it was – had seen it coming and closed his eyes. Bosch hoped it wouldn't be that way for himself. He didn't want to know.

'Hello,' a voice said.

'Yes, this is Harry Bosch. I'm the D-three on a homicide call out in Hollywood. Who am I speaking with?'

'Dom Carbone. I've got the weekend call out. You going to spoil it?'

'Maybe.' Bosch tried to think. The name was vaguely familiar but he could not place it. He was sure they had never worked together. 'That's why I'm calling. You might want to take a look at this.'

'Run it down for me.'

'Sure. White male found in the trunk of his Silver Cloud with two in the back of the head. Probably twenty-twos.'

'What else?'

'Car was on a fire road off Mulholland. Doesn't look like a straight robbery. At least, not a personal robbery. I got cards and cash in the wallet and a Presidential on his wrist. Diamonds at every hour on the hour.'

'You're not telling me who the stiff is. Who's the stiff?'

'Nothing confirmed yet but—'

'Just give it to me.'

Bosch had trouble not being able to put a face with the voice over the phone.

'It looks like the ID is going to be Anthony N. Aliso, forty-eight years old. Lives up in the hills. Looks like he has some kind of company with an office at one of the studios down on Melrose near Paramount. TNA Productions is the name of his outfit. I think it's over at Archway Studios. We'll know more in a little while.'

He only got silence in return.

'Mean anything?'

'Anthony Aliso.'

'Yeah, right.'

'Anthony Aliso.'

Carbone repeated the name slowly, as if it were a fine wine he was tasting before deciding whether to accept the bottle or spit it out. He was then quiet for another long moment.

'Nothing hits me right away, Bosch,' he finally said. 'I can make a couple calls. Where you going to be?'

'The print shed. He's here with us and I'll be here a while.'

'What do you mean, you got the guy's body there in the shed?'

'It's a long story. When do you think you can get back to me?'

'As soon as I make the calls. You been over to his office?'

'Not yet. We'll get there sometime tonight.'

Bosch gave him the number of his cellular phone, then closed it and put it in his coat pocket. For a moment he thought about Carbone's reaction to the victim's name. He finally decided he could not read anything into it.

After the Cloud was rolled into place in the shed and the doors shut, Donovan pulled the curtains closed. There was fluorescent lighting overhead which he left on while he got his equipment ready. Matthews, the coroner's tech, and his two assistants – the body movers – huddled over a workbench getting the tools they would need out of a case.

'Harry, I'm going to take my time with this, okay? First I'll laser the trunk with the guy in it. Then we take him out. Then we glue it and laser it again. Then we worry about the rest of it.'

'Your show, man. Whatever time you need.'

'I'll need your help with the wand when I shoot pictures. Roland had to go to shoot another scene.'

Bosch nodded and watched as the SID tech screwed an orange filter onto a Nikon camera. He put the camera strap over his head and turned on the laser. It was a box about the size of a VCR with a cable attachment that led to a foot-long wand with a hand grip on it. From the end of the wand a strong orange beam was emitted.

Donovan opened a cabinet and took out several pairs of orange-tinted safety glasses which he handed to Bosch and the others. He put the last pair on himself. He gave Bosch a pair of latex gloves to put on as well.

'I'll do a quick run around the outside of the trunk and then open her up,' Donovan said.

Just as Donovan moved to the switch box to cut off the overheads, the phone in Bosch's pocket buzzed. Donovan waited while Bosch answered. It was Carbone.

'Bosch, we're taking a pass.'

Harry didn't say anything for a moment and neither did Carbone. Donovan hit the light switch and the room plunged into complete blackness.

'You're saying you don't have this guy.' Bosch finally spoke into the dark.

'I checked around, made some calls. Nobody seems to know this guy. Nobody's working him . . . Clean, as far as we know . . . You said he was put in his trunk and capped twice, huh? . . . Bosch, you there?'

'Yeah, I'm here. Yeah, capped twice in the trunk.'

'Trunk music.'

'What?'

'It's a wise guy saying outta Chicago. You know, when they whack some poor slob they say, "Oh, Tony? Don't worry about Tony. He's trunk music now. You won't see him no more." But the thing is, Bosch, this doesn't seem to fit. We don't know this guy. People I talked to, they think maybe somebody's trying to make you think it's OC connected, know what I mean?'

Bosch watched as the laser beam cut through the blackness and bombarded the rear of the trunk with searing light. With the glasses on, the orange was filtered out and the light was a bright, intense white. Bosch was ten feet away from the Rolls, but he could see glowing patterns on the trunk lid and the bumper. This always reminded him of those National Geographic shows in which a submersible camera moved through the ocean's black depths, putting its light on sunken ships or aircraft. It was somehow eerie.

'Look, Carbone,' he said, 'you aren't even interested in coming out to take a look?'

'Not at this time. Of course, give me a call back if you come across anything, you know, that shows different than what I told you. And I'll do some more checking tomorrow. I got your number.'

Bosch was secretly pleased that he wasn't going to get bigfooted by the OCID, but he was also surprised at the brush-off. The quickness with which Carbone had dismissed the case seemed unusual.

'Any other details you want to give me, Bosch?'

'We're just starting. But let me ask you, you ever hear of a hitter takes the vic's shoes with him? Also, he unties the body afterward.'

'Takes his shoes . . . unties him. Uh, not offhand, no. Nobody specific. But like I said, I'll ask around in the morning and I'll put it on our box. Anything else cute about this one?'

Bosch didn't like what was happening. Carbone seemed too interested while saying he wasn't. He said Tony Aliso wasn't connected, yet he still wanted the details. Was he just trying to be helpful or was there something more to it?

'That's about all we got at the moment,' Bosch said, deciding not to give up anything else for free. 'Like I said, we're just getting going here.'

'Okay, then, give me the morning and I'll do some more checking. I'll call if I come up with anything, okay?'

'Right.'

'Check you later. But you know what I think you have there, Bosch? You've got a guy, he was probably making sandwiches with somebody's wife. Lotta times things look like pro hits that aren't, you know what I mean?'

'Yeah, I know what you mean. I'll talk to you later.'

Bosch walked to the rear of the Rolls. Up close he could see the pattern swirls he had noticed in the laser light before appeared to be swipe marks made with a cloth. It looked like the whole car had been wiped down.

But when Donovan moved the wand over the bumper, the laser picked up a partial shoe print on the chrome.

'Did anybody—'

'No,' Bosch said. 'Nobody put their foot there.'

'Okay, then. Hold the wand on the print.'

Bosch did so while Donovan bent over and took several photos, bracketing the exposure settings to make sure he had at least one clear shot. It was the forward half of the foot. There was a circle pattern at the ball of the foot with lines extending from it like the rays of a sun. There was a cross-cut pattern through the arch and then the print was cut off by the edge of the bumper.

'Tennis shoe,' Donovan said. 'Maybe a work shoe.'

After he photographed it, he moved the wand around the trunk again, but there was nothing but wipe marks.

'Okay,' Donovan said. 'Open it.'

Using a penlight to guide his way, Bosch made it to the driver's door and bent in to pull the trunk release. Shortly afterward, the smell of death flooded the shed.

It looked to Bosch as though the body had not shifted during the transport. But the victim took on a ghoulish look under the harsh examination of the laser, his face almost skeletal, like the monsters painted in Day-Glo in fun-house hallways. The blood seemed blacker and the bone chips in the jagged wound were luminescent in bright counterpoint.

On his clothes, small strands of hair and tiny threads glowed. Bosch moved in with a pair of tweezers and a plastic vial like the kind made to hold a stack of silver half dollars. He carefully picked these pieces of potential evidence off the clothing and collected them in the vial. It was painstaking work and there was nothing much there. He knew this kind of material could be found on anybody at anytime. It was common.

When he was done he said to Donovan, 'The tail of the jacket. I flipped it up to check for a wallet.'

'Okay, pull it back down.'

Bosch did so, and there on Aliso's hip was another footprint. It matched the footprint on the bumper but was more complete. On the heel was another circle pattern with off-shooting lines. In the lower arch was what looked like a brand name but it was unreadable.

Regardless of whether they could identify the shoe, Bosch knew it was a good find. It meant that a careful killer had made a mistake. At least one. If nothing else, it gave rise to the hope that there might be other mistakes, that they might eventually lead him to the killer.

'Take the wand.'

Bosch did so and Donovan did his thing with the camera again.

'I'm just shooting this to document it, but we'll take the jacket off before the body goes,' he said.

Next Donovan moved the laser up around the inside of the trunk lid. Here the laser illuminated numerous finger-prints, mostly thumbprints, where a hand would have been placed to prop the lid open while loading things in or out. Many of the prints overlapped each other, a sign that they were old, and Bosch knew right away they probably belonged to the victim himself.

'I'll shoot these, but don't count on anything,' Donovan said.

'I know.'

When he was done, Donovan put the wand and the camera on top of the laser box and said, 'Okay, why don't we take this fellow out of there, lay 'im out and scan 'im real quick before he's outta here?'

Without waiting for an answer, he flipped the fluores-cents back on and everybody put their hands to their eyes as the harsh light blinded them. A few moments later the body movers and Matthews went to the trunk and started transferring the corpse to a black plastic body bag they had unfolded on a gurney.

'This guy is loose,' Matthews said as they put the corpse down.

'Yeah,' Bosch said. 'What do you think?'

'Forty-two to forty-eight hours. But let me do some stuff and see what we've got.'

But first Donovan put out the lights again and moved the wand over the body, from the head down. The tear pools in the eye sockets glowed white in the light. There were a few hairs and fibers on the dead man's face and Bosch dutifully collected them. There was also a slight abrasion high on the right cheekbone, which had been hidden when the body was lying on its right side in the trunk.

'He could've been hit or it mighta been from being shoved into the trunk,' Donovan said.

As the beam moved down over the chest, Donovan got excited.

'Well lookee here.'

Glowing in the laser light were what looked like a complete handprint on the right shoulder of the leather jacket and two smudged thumbprints, one on each of the lapels. Donovan bent down very close to look.

'This is treated leather, it doesn't absorb the acids in the prints. We caught a major break here, Harry. This guy wears anything else and forget it. The hand is excellent. These thumbs didn't take . . . I think we can raise them up with some glue. Harry, bend one of the lapels over.'

Bosch reached for the left lapel and carefully turned the cloth over. There on the inside of the crease were four more fingerprints. He turned the right lapel and saw four more there. It appeared that someone had grabbed Tony Aliso by the lapels.

Donovan whistled.

'This looks like two different people. Look at the size of the thumbs on the lapel and the hand on the shoulder. I'd say the hand is smaller, Harry. Maybe a woman. I don't know. But the hands that grabbed this guy by the lapels were big.'

Donovan got scissors from a nearby toolbox and carefully cut the sport coat off the body. Bosch then held it as Donovan went over it with the laser wand. Nothing else came up besides the shoe print and the fingerprints they had already sighted. Bosch carefully hung the jacket over a chair at the counter and came back to the body. Donovan was moving the laser over the lower extremities.

'What else?' Donovan said to no one except maybe the body. 'Come on now, tell us a story.'

There were more fibers and some old stains on the pants. Nothing that stood out as possibly significant until they reached the cuffs. Bosch pulled open the cuff on the right leg and in the crease was a large buildup of dust and fibers. Also, five tiny pieces of gold glitter glowed in the laser beam. Bosch carefully tweezered these into a separate plastic vial. From the left cuff, he recovered two more similar pieces.

'What is it?' he asked.

'Got me. Looks like glitter or something.'

Donovan moved the wand over the bare feet. They were clean, which indicated to Bosch that the victim's shoes had probably been removed after he was forced into the trunk of the Rolls.

'Okay, that's it,' Donovan said.

The lights came back on and Matthews went to work with the corpse, rotating joints, opening the shirt to look at the lividity level of the blood, opening the eyes and swiveling the head. Donovan paced around, waiting for the coroner's tech to finish so he could continue the laser show. He walked over to Bosch.

'Harry, you want the swag on this?'

'Swag?'

'Scientific wild ass guess.'

'Yeah,' Bosch said, amused. 'Give me the swag.'

'Well, I think somebody gets the drop on this guy. Ties him up, dumps him in the trunk and drives him to that fire road. He's still alive, okay? Then our doer gets out, opens the trunk, puts his foot on the bumper ready to do the job but can't get all the way in there to put the muzzle against the bone, you know? That was important to him. To do the job right. So he sticks his big foot on this poor guy's hip, leans further in and bam, bam, out go the headlights. What do you think?'

Bosch nodded.

'I think you are on to something.'

He had already been thinking along the same lines but was past those deductions to the problem.

'Then how does he get back?' he asked.

'Back to where?'

'If this guy was in the trunk the whole time, then the doer drove the Rolls. If he drove there in the Rolls, then how'd he get back to wherever he intercepted Tony?'

'The other one,' Donovan said. 'We've got two different prints on the jacket. Somebody could've followed behind the Rolls. The woman. The one who put her hand on the vic's shoulder.'

Bosch nodded. He had already been puzzling with this but didn't like something about the scenario Donovan had woven. He wasn't sure what it was.

'Okay, Bosch,' Matthews interrupted. 'You want to hear this tonight or you want to wait for the report?'

'T'night,' Bosch said.

'Okay then, listen up. Lividity was fixed and unchanged. The body was never moved once the heart stopped pumping.' He referred to a clipboard. 'Let's see, what else. We've got ninety percent rigor mortis resolution, cornea clouding and we've got skin slippage. I think you take all of that and it's forty-eight hours, maybe a couple hours less. Let us know if you come up with any markers and we might do better.'

'Will do,' Bosch said.

By markers he knew Matthews meant that if he traced the victim's last day and found out what he had eaten last and when, the ME could get a better fix on time of death by studying the digestion of food in the stomach.

'He's all yours,' Bosch said to Matthews. 'Any idea on the post?'

'You caught the tail end of a holiday weekend. That's bad luck for you. Last I heard, we've run on twenty-seven homicides in the county so far. We probably won't cut this one until Wednesday, if you're lucky. Don't call us, we'll call you.'

'Yeah, I've heard that one before.'

But the delay didn't really bother Bosch this time. In

cases like this, the autopsy usually held few surprises. It was pretty clear how the victim died. The mystery was why and by whom.

Matthews and his assistants wheeled the corpse out, leaving Bosch and Donovan alone with the Rolls. Donovan stared at the car silently, contemplating it the way a matador looks at the bull he is going to fight.

'We're going to get her secrets, Harry.'

Bosch's phone buzzed then and he fumbled getting it out of his jacket and open. It was Edgar.

'We got the ID, Harry. It is Aliso.'

'You got this off the prints?'

'Yeah. Mossler's got a fax at home. I sent him everything and he eyeballed it.'

Mossler was one of the SID's latent-print men.

'This is with the DL thumbprint?'

'Right. Also, I pulled a full set of Tony's prints from an old pop for soliciting. Mossler had those to look at, too. It's Aliso.'

'Okay, good work. What else you got?'

'Like I said, I ran this guy. He's pretty clean. Just the soliciting arrest back in seventy-five. Few other things, though. His name comes up as a victim on a burglary up at his house in March. And on the civil indexes I've got a few civil actions against the guy. Breach-of-contract stuff, it looks like. A trail of broken promises and pissed-off people, Harry, good motive stuff.'

'What were the cases about?'

'That's all I've got for now, just the abstracts in the civil index. I'll have to pull the actual cases when I can get into the courthouse.'

'Okay. Did you check Missing Persons?'

'Yeah, I did. He was never reported. You got anything there?'

'Maybe. We might've gotten lucky. Looks like we are going to get some prints off the body. Two sets.'

'Off the body? That's very cool.'

'Off the leather jacket.'

Bosch could tell Edgar was excited. Both detectives knew that if the prints were not those of a suspect, then they would surely be fresh enough to belong to people who had seen the victim in the time shortly before his death.

'You call OCID?'

Bosch was waiting for him to ask.

'Yeah. They're taking a pass.'

'What?'

'That's what they said. At least for now. Until we find something they might be interested in.'

Bosch wondered if Edgar even believed he had made the call.

'That doesn't figure, Harry.'

'Yeah, well, all we can do is our job. You hear from Kiz?'

'Not yet. Who'd you talk to over at Organized Crime?'

'Guy named Carbone. He was on call.'

'Never heard of him.'

'Well, neither had I. I gotta go, Jerry. Let me know what you know.'

As soon as Bosch hung up, the door to the shed opened and in stepped Lieutenant Grace Billets. She quickly scanned the room and saw Donovan working in the car. She asked Bosch to step outside and that was when he knew she was unhappy.

She closed the door after he stepped out. She was in her forties and had as many years on the job as Bosch, give or take a couple, but they had never worked together before her assignment as his commanding officer. She was of medium build, with reddish-brown hair she kept short. She wore no makeup. She was dressed entirely in black – jeans, T-shirt and blazer. She also wore black cowboy boots. Her only concession to femininity was the pair of thin gold hoop earrings. Her manner was no concession to anything.

'What's going on, Harry? You moved the body *in* the car?'

'Had to. It was either that or dump it out of the car with

about ten thousand people watching us instead of the fireworks they were supposed to see.'

Bosch explained the situation in detail and Billets listened silently. When he was done, she nodded.

'I'm sorry,' she said. 'I didn't know the details. It looks like it was your only choice.'

Bosch liked that about her. She wasn't always right and she was willing to admit it.

'Thanks, Lieutenant.'

'So what do we have?'

When Bosch and Billets stepped back into the shed, Donovan was at one of the worktables working with the leather jacket. He had hung it on a wire inside an empty one-hundred-gallon aquarium and then dropped in a Hard Evidence packet. The packet, when broken open, emitted cyanoacrylate fumes which would attach to the amino acids and oils of fingerprints and crystallize, thereby raising the ridges and whorls and making them more visible and photo-ready.

'How's it look?' Bosch asked.

'Real good. We're going to get something off this. Howdy, Lieutenant.'

'Hello there,' Billets said.

Bosch could tell she didn't remember Donovan's name.

'Listen, Art,' he said, 'when you get those together, get them over to the print lab and then call me or Edgar and tell us. We'll get somebody over there to do them code three.'

Code three was a patrol response code meaning lights and siren authorized. Bosch needed the prints to be handled quickly. So far, they were the best lead.

'Will do, Harry.'

'What about the Rolls? Can I get in it yet?'

'Well, I'm not quite through with it. You can go in. Just be careful.'

Bosch began searching the interior of the car, checking the door and seat pockets first and finding nothing. He checked the ashtray and found it empty, not even an ash. He made a mental note that the victim apparently didn't smoke.

Billets stood nearby, watching but not helping. She had risen to detective bureau commander primarily on the success of her skills as an administrator, not as an investigator. She knew when to watch and not get in the way.

Bosch checked under the seats and found nothing of interest. He opened the glove compartment last and a small square piece of paper fell out. It was a receipt for an airport valet company. Holding it by the corner, Bosch walked it over to the workbench and told Donovan to check it for prints when he got the chance.

He went back to the glove compartment and found the lease agreement and registration of the car, its service records and a small tool kit with a flashlight. There was also a half-used tube of Preparation H, a hemorrhoid medication. It seemed like an odd place to keep it, but Bosch guessed that maybe Aliso kept the tube handy for long drives.

He bagged all of the items from the compartment separately and while doing so noticed an extra battery in the tool kit. It struck him as odd because the flashlight obviously took two batteries. Having one extra would not do much good.

He pressed the flashlight's on/off switch. It was dead. He unscrewed the cap and one battery slid out. Looking into the barrel, Bosch saw a plastic bag. He used a pen to reach in and pull the bag out. It contained about two dozen brown capsules.

Billets stepped closer.

'Poppers,' Bosch said. 'Amyl nitrate. Supposed to help you get it up and keep it there. You know, improve your orgasm.'

He suddenly felt the need to explain his knowledge was not based on personal experience.

'It's come up in other cases before.'

She nodded. Donovan walked over with the valet ticket in a clear plastic envelope.

'A couple smudges. Nothing we can work with.'

Bosch took it back. He then carried the various plastic evidence bags he had to the counter.

'Art, I'm taking the receipt, the poppers and the car's service records, okay?'

'You got it.'

'I'll leave you the plane ticket and the wallet. You are also going to put some speed on the prints from the jacket and what else? Oh yeah, those sparkles. What do you think?'

'Hopefully tomorrow. The rest of the fiber stuff I'll take a look at, but it's probably going to be exclusionary.'

That meant most of the material they had collected would sit in storage after a quick examination by Donovan, and come into play only if a suspect was identified. It would then be used either to tie that suspect to the crime scene or to exclude him.

Bosch took a large envelope off a shelf over the counter, put all the pieces of evidence he was taking into it, then put it in his briefcase and snapped it closed. He headed for the curtain with Billets.

'Good to see you again, Art,' she said.

'Likewise, Lieutenant.'

'You want me to call OPG to come get the car?' Bosch asked.

'Nah, I'm going to be here a while,' Donovan said. 'Gotta use the vac and I might think of something else to do. I'll take care of it, Harry.'

'Okay, man, later.'

Bosch and Billets stepped through the curtain and then through the door. Outside he lit a cigarette and looked up at the dark, starless sky. Billets lit one of her own.

'Where to?' she asked.

'Next of kin. You want to come? It's always a fun thing.'

She smiled at his sarcasm.

'No, I think I'll pass on that. But before you leave, what's your gut on this, Harry? I mean, OCID passing without taking a look, that kind of bothers me.'

'Me, too.' He took a long drag and exhaled. 'My gut is that this one's going to be tough. Unless something good comes out of those prints. That's our only real break so far.'

'Well, tell your people that I want everybody in at eight for a roundtable on what we've got so far.'

'Let's make it nine, Lieutenant. I think by then we should have something back from Donovan on the prints.'

'Okay, nine then. I'll see you then, Harry. And from now on, when we're talking like this, you know, informally, call me Grace.'

'Sure, Grace. Have a nice night.'

She expelled her smoke in a short burst that sounded like the start of a laugh.

'You mean, what's left of it.'

On the way up to Mulholland Drive and Hidden Highlands Bosch paged Rider and she called back from one of the houses she was visiting. She said it was the last of the houses overlooking the clearing where the Rolls was parked. She told him the best she could come up with was a resident who remembered seeing the white Rolls-Royce from the back deck of his home on Saturday morning about ten. The same resident also believed the car was not there on Friday evening when he was out on the deck to watch the sunset.

'That fits with the time frame the ME's looking at and the plane ticket. I think we're zeroing in on Friday night, sometime after he got in from Vegas. Probably on his way home from the airport. Nobody heard any shots?'

'Not that I've found. There's two houses where I got no answer. I was going to go back and try them now.'

'Maybe you can catch them tomorrow. I'm heading up to Hidden Highlands. I think you should go with me.'

They made arrangements to meet outside the entrance to

43

the development where Aliso had lived, and Bosch closed the phone. He wanted Kiz along when he told Aliso's next of kin he was dead because it would be good for her to learn the grim routine and because the percentages called for whoever that next of kin was to be considered a possible suspect. It was always good to have a witness with you when you first spoke to the person who later could become your quarry.

Bosch looked at his watch. It was nearly ten. Taking care of the notification meant they probably wouldn't be getting to the victim's office until midnight. He called the communications center and gave the operator the address on Melrose and had her look it up in the cross directory. It came back to Archway Pictures, as Bosch had guessed. He knew they had caught a bit of a break. Archway was a midsize studio that largely rented offices and production facilities to independent filmmakers. As far as Bosch knew, it hadn't made its own films since the 1960s. The break was that he knew someone in security over there. Chuckie Meachum was a former Robbery-Homicide bull who had retired a few years earlier and taken a job as assistant director of security at Archway. He would be useful in smoothing their way in. Bosch considered calling ahead and arranging for Chuckie Meachum to meet them at the studio but decided against it. He decided he didn't want anyone to know he was coming until he got there.

He got to Hidden Highlands fifteen minutes later. Rider's car was parked on the shoulder off Mulholland. Bosch pulled up and she got in his car. Then he pulled into the entrance lane next to the gatehouse. It was a small brick structure with a single guard inside. Hidden Highlands was maybe a little richer but not that different from many of the other small, wealthy and scared enclaves nestled in the hills and valleys around Los Angeles. Walls and gates, guardhouses and private security forces were the secret ingredients of the so-called melting pot of southern California.

A guard in a blue uniform stepped out of the gatehouse carrying a clipboard and Bosch had his badge wallet out and open. The guard was a tall, thin man with a worn, gray face. Bosch didn't recognize him, though he had heard in the station that most of the guards working here were off-duty uniforms from Hollywood Division. In the past he had seen postings for part-time jobs on the bulletin board outside the roll call room.

The guard gave Bosch a once-over in a laconic manner, avoiding a look at the badge on purpose.

'Kenahepyou?' he finally said.

'I need to go to the home of Anthony Aliso.'

He gave the address on Hillcrest that had been on the victim's driver's license.

'Your names?'

'Detective Harry Bosch, LAPD. Says it right here. This is Detective Kizmin Rider.'

He proffered the badge wallet, but it was still ignored. The guard was writing on his clipboard. Bosch saw his name tag said Nash. He also saw that the tin badge said CAPTAIN across it.

'They expecting you at the Aliso place?'

'I don't think so. It's police business.'

'Okay, but I've got to call ahead. It's the development's rules, you know.'

'I prefer you didn't do that, Captain Nash.'

Bosch hoped his use of the security guard's title would win him over. Nash thought a moment.

'Tell you what,' he said. 'You go on ahead and I'll come up with a reason for delaying making the call a few minutes. I'll just say I'm up here by myself t'night and I got kind of busy, if there's a complaint.'

He stepped back and reached in the open door of the gatehouse. He pressed a button on the inside wall and the crossguard went up.

'Thanks, Captain. You work out of Hollywood?'

Bosch knew he didn't. He could tell Nash wasn't even a

45

cop. He didn't have the cold eyes of a cop. But Bosch was playing to him, just in case he became a useful source of information later on.

'Nah,' Nash said. 'I'm full-time. That's why they made me captain of the watch. Everybody else is part-time out of Hollywood or West Hollywood sheriffs. I run the schedule.'

'Then how'd you get stuck on the night shift on Sunday night?'

'Everybody can use some OT now and then.'

Bosch nodded.

'You're right about that. Hillcrest, where's that?'

'Oh, yeah, forgot. Take your second left. That's Hillcrest. The Aliso place is about the sixth house on the right. Nice view of the city from the pool.'

'Did you know him?' Rider asked, leaning down so she could see Nash through Bosch's window.

'Aliso?' Nash said, bending further to look in at her. He thought a moment. 'Not really. Just like I know people when they come through here. I'm just the same to them as the pool man, I guess. I notice you asked *did* I know him. Am I not going to get the chance?'

'Smart man, Mr Nash,' Rider said.

She straightened up, finished with the conversation. Bosch nodded his thanks and drove through the gate to Hillcrest. As he passed the broad, manicured lawns surrounding houses the size of apartment buildings, he filled Rider in on what he had learned at the print shed and from Edgar. He also admired the properties they were passing. Many of them were surrounded by walls or tall hedges that looked as though they were trimmed into sharp edges every morning. Walls within walls, Bosch thought. He wondered what the owners did with all of their space besides fearfully guard it.

It took them five minutes to find the Aliso house on a cul-de-sac at the top of the hill. He passed through the open gates of an estate with a Tudor-style mansion set behind a

46

circular driveway made of gray paver stones. Bosch got out with his briefcase and looked up at the place. It was intimidating in its size, but its style was not much to speak of. He wouldn't want it, even if he had the money.

After getting to the door and pushing the doorbell button, he looked at Rider.

'You ever done this before?'

'No. But I grew up in South L.A. A lot of drive-bys. I was around when people got the news.'

Bosch nodded.

'Not to belittle that experience, but this is different. What is important is not what you hear said, it's what you observe.'

Bosch pushed the lighted button again. He could hear the bell sound from inside the house. He looked at Rider and could tell she was about to ask a question, when the door was opened by a woman.

'Mrs Aliso?' Bosch asked.

'Yes?'

'Mrs Aliso, I'm Detective Harry Bosch with the LAPD. This is my partner, Detective Kizmin Rider. We need to speak with you concerning your husband.'

He held out his badge wallet and she took it from his hand. Usually, they didn't do that. Usually, they recoiled from it or looked at it like it was some strange and fascinating object not to be touched.

'I don't under—'

She stopped when the sound of a phone ringing began somewhere behind her in the big house.

'Would you excuse me a moment. I have to—'

'That's probably Nash at the gate. He said he had to call ahead, but there was a lineup of cars behind us. I guess we beat him here. We need to come in to talk to you, ma'am.'

She stepped back in and opened the door wide for him. She looked about five to ten years younger than her husband had been. She was about forty, attractive, with dark straight hair and a trim build. She wore a lot of makeup on a

47

face Bosch guessed had been sculpted at times by the surgeon's knife. Still, through the makeup she looked tired, worn. He could see her face was flushed pink, as though she might have been drinking. She wore a light blue dress that showed off her legs. They were tan and the muscles still taut. Bosch could see she had been considered very beautiful at one time but was sliding into that stage when a woman believes her beauty may be leaving – even if it isn't. Maybe that was why she had all the makeup on, Bosch guessed. Or maybe it was because she was still expecting her husband to show up.

Bosch closed the door after they entered and they followed the woman into a large living room with an incongruous mix of modern prints on the walls and French antiques on the thick white carpet. The phone was still ringing. She told Bosch and Rider to sit down and then walked through the living room into another hallway, which she crossed to what looked like a den. He heard her answer the phone, tell Nash that the delay was all right and hang up.

She came back into the living room then and sat on a couch with a muted flower print. Bosch and Rider took nearby chairs with a matching pattern. Bosch took a quick look around and saw no photographs in frames. Only the artwork. It was always one of the first things he looked for when he had to quickly judge a relationship.

'I'm sorry,' he said. 'I didn't get your name.'

'Veronica Aliso. What about my husband, Detective? Is he hurt?'

Bosch leaned forward in his chair. No matter how many times he did this, he never got used to it and he was never sure he was doing it the right way.

'Mrs Aliso . . . I am very sorry, but your husband is dead. He was the victim of a homicide. I am sorry to have to tell you this.'

He watched her closely and she said nothing at first. She instinctively crossed her arms in front of her and brought her face down in a pained grimace. There were no tears. Not yet. In his experience, Bosch had seen them come either right away – as soon as they opened the door and saw him and knew – or much later, when it sank in that the nightmare was reality.

'I don't . . . How did this happen?' she asked, her eyes staring down at the floor.

'He was found in his car. He'd been shot.'

'In Las Vegas?'

'No. Here. Not far. It looks like he was coming home from the airport when . . . when he was somehow stopped by somebody. We're not sure yet. His car was found off Mulholland Drive. Down by the Bowl.'

He watched her a little more. She still had not looked up. Bosch felt a sense of guilt pass over him. Guilt because he was not watching this woman with sympathy. He had been in this place too many times for that. Instead, he watched her with an eye for false mannerisms. In these situations his suspicion outweighed his compassion. It had to.

'Can I get you anything, Mrs Aliso?' Rider asked. 'Water? Do you have coffee? Do you want something stronger?'

'No. I'm fine. Thank you. It's just a terrible shock.'

'Do you have any children in the house?' Rider asked.

'No, we . . . no children. Do you know what happened? Was he robbed?'

'That's what we're trying to find out,' Bosch said.

'Of course . . . Can you tell me, was there much pain?'

'No, there was no pain,' Bosch said.

He thought of the tears welled in Tony Aliso's eyes. He decided not to tell her about that.

'It must be hard, your job,' she said. 'Telling people this sort of thing.'

He nodded and looked away. For a moment he thought of the old squad room joke about the easiest way to do next-of-kin notification. When Mrs Brown opens the door, you say, 'Are you the widow Brown?'

He looked back at the widow Aliso.

'Why did you ask if it happened in Las Vegas?'

'Because that was where he was.'

'How long was he supposed to be there?'

'I don't know. He never scheduled it with a return. He always bought open-ended tickets so he could come back when he wanted to. He always said he'd be back when his luck changed. For the worse.'

'We have reason to believe he came back to Los Angeles on Friday night. His car wasn't found until this evening. That's two days, Mrs Aliso. Did you try to call him in Las Vegas during that time?'

'No. We usually didn't speak when he was over there.'

'And how often was it that he went?'

'Once or twice a month.'

'For how long each time?'

'Anywhere from two days to once he spent a week. Like I said, it all depended on how he was doing.'

'And you never called him there?' Rider asked.

'Rarely. Not at all this time.'

'Was it business or pleasure that took him there?' Bosch asked.

'He always told me it was both. He said he had investors to see. But it was an addiction. That's what I believed. He loved to gamble and could afford to do it. So he went.'

Bosch nodded but didn't know why.

'This last time, when did he go?'

'He went Thursday. After leaving the studio.'

'You saw him last then?'

'Thursday morning. Before he went to the studio. He left for the airport from there. It's closer.'

'And you had no idea when to expect him back.'

He said it as a statement. It was out there for her to challenge if she wanted to.

'To be honest, I was just beginning to wonder tonight. It usually doesn't take long for that place to separate a man from his money. I thought it was a little long, yes. But I didn't try to track him down. And then you came.'

'What did he like to play over there?'

'Everything. But poker the most. It was the only game where you weren't playing against the house. The house took a cut, but you were playing against the other players. That's how he explained it to me once. Only he called the other players schmucks from Iowa.'

'Was he always alone over there, Mrs Aliso?'

Bosch looked down at his notebook and acted as if he was writing something important and that her answer wasn't. He knew it was cowardly.

'I wouldn't know.'

'Did you ever go with him at all?'

'I don't like to gamble. I don't like that city. That city is a horrible place. They can dress it up all they want, it's still a city of vices and whores. Not just the sexual kind.'

Bosch studied the cool anger in her dark eyes.

'You didn't answer the question, Mrs Aliso,' Rider said.

'What question?'

'Did you ever go to Las Vegas with him?'

'At first, yes. But I found it boring. I haven't been in years.'

'Was your husband in any kind of serious debt?' Bosch asked.

'I don't know. If he was, he didn't tell me. You can call me Veronica.'

'You never asked if he was getting into trouble?' Rider asked.

'I just assumed that he would tell me if he was.'

She turned the hard dark eyes on Rider now, and Bosch felt a weight lift off him. Veronica Aliso was challenging them to disagree.

'I know this probably makes me some kind of a suspect, but I don't care,' she said. 'You have your job to do. It must be obvious to you that my husband and I . . . let's just say we coexisted here. So as to your questions about Nevada, I couldn't tell you whether he was a million up or a million down. Who knows, he could've beaten the odds. But I think he would have bragged about it if he had.'

Bosch nodded and thought about the body in the trunk. It didn't seem like that of a man who had beaten any odds.

'Where did he stay in Las Vegas, Mrs Aliso?'

'Always at the Mirage. I do know that. You see, not all of the casinos have poker tables. The Mirage has a classy one. He always said that if I needed to call, call there. Ask for the poker pit if there is no answer in the room.'

Bosch took a few moments to write this down. He found that often silence was the best way to get people to talk and reveal themselves. He hoped Rider realized that he was leaving holes of silence in the interview on purpose.

'You asked if he went there alone.'

'Yes?'

'Detectives, in the course of your investigation I believe you will undoubtedly learn that my husband was a philanderer. I ask only one thing of you, please do your best to keep that information from me. I simply don't want to know.'

Bosch nodded and was silent a moment while he composed his thoughts. What kind of woman wouldn't want to know, he wondered. Maybe one who already did. He looked back at her and their eyes connected again.

'Aside from gambling, was your husband in any other kind of trouble as far as you know?' he asked. 'Work-related, financial?'

'As far as I know he wasn't. But he kept the finances. I could not tell you what our situation is at the moment. When I needed money I asked him, and he always said cash a check and tell him the amount. I have a separate account for household expenses.'

Without looking up from the notebook, Bosch said, 'Just a few more and we'll leave you alone for now. Did your husband have any enemies that you know of? Anybody who would want to harm him?'

'He worked in Hollywood. Back stabbing is considered an art form there. Anthony was as skilled at it as anyone else who has been in the industry twenty-five years. Obviously that means there could always be people who were unhappy with him. But who would do this, I don't know.'

'The car . . . the Rolls-Royce is leased to a production company over at Archway Studios. How long had he worked there?'

'His office was there, but he didn't work for Archway per se. TNA Productions is his . . . was his own company. He simply rented an office and a parking spot on the Archway lot. But he had about as much to do with Archway as you do.'

'Tell us about his production company,' Rider said. 'Did he make films?'

'In a manner of speaking. You could say he started big and ended small. About twenty years ago he produced his first film. *The Art of the Cape*. If you saw it, you were one of the few. Bullfight movies are not popular. But it was critically acclaimed, played the film festival circuit and then the art houses and it was a good start for him.'

She said that Aliso had managed to make a couple more films for general release. But after that his production and moral values steadily declined, until he was producing a procession of exploitative dreck.

'These films, if you want to call them that, are notable only for the number of exposed breasts in them,' she said. 'In the business, it's called straight-to-video stock. In addition to that Tony was quite successful in literary arbitrage.'

'What is that?'

'He was a speculator. Mostly scripts, but he did manus-cripts, books on occasion.'

'And how would he speculate on them?'

'He'd buy them. Wrap up the rights. Then when they became valuable or the author became hot, he'd go to market with them. Do you know who Michael St John is?'

The name sounded familiar but Bosch could not place it. He shook his head. Rider did the same.

'He's one of the screenwriters of the moment. He'll be directing studio features within a year or so. He's the flavor-of-the-month, so to speak.'

'Okay.'

'Well, eight years ago when he was in the USC film school and was hungry and was trying to find an agent and trying to catch the attention of the studios, my husband was one of the vultures who circled overhead. You see, my husband's films were so low-budget that he'd get students to shoot them, direct them, write them. So he knew the schools and he knew talent. Michael St John was one he knew had talent. Once when he was desperate, he sold Anthony the rights to three of his student screenplays for two thousand dollars. Now, anything with St John's name on it goes for at least six figures.'

'What about these writers, how do they take this?'

'Not well. St John was trying to buy his scripts back.'

'You think he could have harmed your husband?'

'No. You asked me what he did and I told you. If you are asking who would kill him, I don't know.'

Bosch jotted a couple of notes down.

'You mentioned that he said that he saw investors when he went to Las Vegas,' Rider said.

'Yes.'

'Can you tell us who they were?'

'Schmucks from Iowa, I would assume. People he would meet and persuade to invest in a movie. You'd be surprised how many people jump at a chance to be part of a Hollywood movie. And Tony was a good salesman. He could make a two-million budget flick sound like the sequel to *Gone With the Wind*. He convinced me.'

'How so?'

'He talked me into being in one of his movies once. That's how I met him. Made it sound like I was going to be the new Jane Fonda. You know, sexy but smart. It was a studio picture. Only the director was a coke addict and the writer couldn't write and the movie was so bad it was never released. That was it for my career and Tony never made a studio picture again. He spent the rest of his life making video garbage.'

Looking around the tall-ceilinged room at the paintings and furniture, Bosch said, 'Doesn't look like he did too badly at it.'

'No, he didn't,' she responded. 'I guess we have those people from Iowa to thank for that.'

Her bitterness was stifling. Bosch looked down at his notebook just so he could avert his eyes from her.

'All this talk,' she said then. 'I need some water. Do either of you want something?'

'Water would be fine,' Bosch said. 'We're not going to be much longer.'

'Detective Rider?'

'I'm fine, thank you.'

'I'll be right back.'

While she was gone Bosch stood up and looked around the living room in a manner that suggested he wasn't really interested. He said nothing to Rider. He was standing near a side table looking at a carved glass figurine of a nude woman when Veronica Aliso came back in with two glasses of ice water.

'I just want to ask you a few more questions about this past week,' Bosch said.

'Fine.'

He sipped from his glass and remained standing.

'What would your husband have taken with him to Las Vegas as far as luggage went?'

'Just his overnighter.'

'What did it look like?'

'It was a hanging bag that, you know, folded over. It was

green with brown leather trim and straps. He had a name tag on it.'

'Did he take a briefcase or any work with him?'

'Yes, his briefcase. It was one of those aluminum shell kind. You know, they are lightweight but impossible to break into or something. Is the luggage missing?'

'We're not sure. Do you know where he kept the key to the briefcase?'

'On his key chain. With the car keys.'

There had been no car keys in the Rolls or on Aliso's body. Bosch realized that the reason they might have been taken was to open the briefcase. He put the glass down next to the figurine and looked at it again. He then began writing the descriptions of the briefcase and hanging bag in his notebook.

'Did your husband wear a wedding ring?'

'No. He did wear quite an expensive watch, though. It was a Rolex. I gave it to him.'

'The watch was not taken.'

'Oh.'

Bosch looked up from his notebook.

'Do you remember what your husband was wearing on Thursday morning? When you last saw him?'

'Um, just clothes . . . uh, he had on his white pants and a blue shirt and his sport coat.'

'His black leather sport coat?'

'Yes.'

'Mrs Aliso, do you remember if you hugged him or kissed him good-bye?'

This seemed to fluster her, and Bosch immediately regretted the way he had phrased the question.

'I'm sorry. What I meant was that we found some fingerprints on the jacket. On the shoulder. And if you might have touched him there on the day he left, it could explain this piece of evidence.'

She was quiet a moment and Bosch thought that she was finally going to begin to cry. But instead, she said, 'I might have but I don't remember . . . I don't think I did.'

Bosch opened his briefcase and looked for a print screen. He found one in one of the pockets. It looked like a photo slide but the center was a double-sided screen with ink between the screens. A thumb could be pressed on the A side and a fingerprint would be imprinted on a card held against the B side.

'I want to take your thumbprint so we can compare it to the print taken off the jacket. If you did not touch him there, then it might be a good lead for us.'

She stepped over to him and he pressed her right thumb down on the print screen. When he was done she looked at her thumb.

'No ink.'

'Yes, that's nice. No mess. We just started using these a few years ago.'

'The print on the jacket, did it belong to a woman?'

He looked at her and held her eyes for a moment.

'We won't know for sure until we get a match.'

As he put the card and the print screen back in the briefcase, he noticed the evidence bag containing the poppers. He took it out and held it up for her to look at.

'Do you know what these are?'

She narrowed her eyes and shook her head no.

'Amyl nitrate poppers. Some people use them to enhance sexual performance and satisfaction. Do you know if your husband ever used these?'

'You found them with him?'

'Mrs Aliso, I'd rather that you'd just answer my questions. I know this is difficult, but there are some things I can't tell you yet. I will when I can. I promise.'

'No, he didn't use them . . . with me.'

'I'm sorry that I have to be so personal, but we want to catch the person who did this. We both want that. Now, your husband was about ten or twelve years older than you.' He was being charitable here. 'Did he have problems performing sexually? Is there any chance he might have been using poppers without your knowledge?'

She turned to go back to her chair. When she was seated again she said, 'I wouldn't know.'

Now Bosch narrowed his eyes. What was she trying to say? His silence worked. She answered before he had to ask, but as she spoke she looked directly at Rider, the unspoken message being that as a woman Rider might sympathize.

'Detective, I haven't had . . . I guess, sexual relations is the way it is said in these matters. My husband and I . . . not in almost two years.'

Bosch nodded and looked down at his notebook. The page was blank but he couldn't bring himself to write this latest piece of information down with her watching them. He folded the notebook closed and put it away.

'You want to ask me why, don't you?'

He just looked at her and she answered with a measure of defiance in her face and voice.

'He had lost interest.'

'Are you sure?'

'He told me that to my face.'

Bosch nodded.

'Mrs Aliso, I'm sorry for the loss of your husband. I'm also sorry for the intrusion and the personal questions. I'm afraid, though, that there will be more as the investigation progresses.'

'I understand.'

'There is one other thing I'd like to cover.'

'Yes, what is it?'

'Did your husband have a home office?'

'Yes.'

'Could we take a quick look at it?'

She stood up and they followed her down the second hallway to the office. They both stepped into the room and Bosch looked around. It was a small room with a desk and two file cabinets. There was a TV on a cart in front of a wall of shelves. Half were filled with books and the rest stacked with scripts, the titles written with Magic Markers on the edges of the pages. There was a golf bag leaning in the corner.

Bosch walked over and studied the desk. It was spotless. He came around and saw that the desk contained two file drawers. He opened these and found one empty and one containing several files. He quickly looked through the file tabs and saw that they apparently were files containing personal finance records and tax documents. He closed the drawers, deciding that a search of the office could probably keep.

'It's late,' he said. 'This is not the time. I want you to understand, though, that investigations like this often shoot off into many directions. But we have to follow up on everything. We're going to need to come in here tomorrow and go through your husband's things. We'll probably take a lot with us. We'll have a warrant so everything will be perfectly legal.'

'Yes. Of course. But can't I just give you permission to take what you need?'

'You could, but it would be better this way. I'm talking about check books, savings account records, credit card statements, insurance, everything. We'll probably need the records on your household account, too.'

'I understand. What time?'

'I don't know yet. I'll call first. Or someone will. Do you know, did your husband leave a will?'

'Yes. Both of us made wills. They're with our attorney.'

'How long ago was that?'

'The will? Oh, a long time. Years.'

'In the morning, I'd like you to call the attorney and tell him we'll need a copy of it. Are you up to doing that?'

'Of course.'

'What about insurance?'

'Yes, we have policies. The attorney, Neil Denton in Century City, will have them also.'

'Okay, we'll worry about that tomorrow. I need to seal this room now.'

They stepped back into the hallway and Bosch closed the door. From his briefcase he took a sticker that said

CRIME SCENE
DO NOT ENTER PREMISES
CALL LAPD 213 485–4321

Bosch pressed the sticker across the door jamb. If anyone entered the room now, they would have to cut the sticker or peel it off. Bosch would know.

'Detective?' Veronica Aliso said quietly from behind him.

Bosch turned around.

'I am the suspect, aren't I?'

Bosch put the two papers he had peeled off the back of the sticker in his pocket.

'I suppose everyone and no one is a suspect at this point. We're looking at everything. But, yes, Mrs Aliso, we're going to be looking at you.'

'I guess I shouldn't have been so candid before, then.'

Rider said, 'If you've got nothing to hide, the truth shouldn't hurt you.'

Bosch knew from long experience never to say such a thing. He knew the words were false before they were out of her mouth. Judging by the small, thin smile on Veronica Aliso's face, she knew it as well.

'Are you new at this, Detective Rider?' she asked while looking at Bosch with that smile.

'No, ma'am, I've been a detective for six years.'

'Oh. And I guess I don't have to ask Detective Bosch.'

'Mrs Aliso?' Bosch asked.

'Veronica.'

'There is one last thing you could clear up for us tonight. We do not know yet exactly when your husband was killed. But it would help us concentrate on other matters if we could quickly eliminate routine avenues of—'

'You want to know if I have an alibi, is that it?'

'We just want to know where you were the last few days and nights. It's a routine question, nothing else.'

'Well, I hate to bore you with my life's details, because I'm afraid that's what they are, boring. But other than a trip to the mall and supermarket Saturday afternoon, I haven't left the house since I had dinner with my husband Wednesday night.'

'You've been here alone?'

'Yes . . . but I think you can verify this with Captain Nash at the gate. They keep records of who comes in as well as out of Hidden Highlands. Even the residents. Also, on Friday our pool man was here in the afternoon. I gave him his check. I can get you his name and number.'

'That won't be necessary right now. Thank you. And again, I'm sorry for your loss. Is there anything we can do for you right now?'

She seemed to be withdrawing into herself. He was not sure she had heard his question.

'I'm fine,' she finally said.

He picked up his briefcase and headed down the hallway with Rider. It ran behind the living room and took them directly to the front door. All the way along the hallway there were no photographs on the wall. It didn't seem right to him, but he guessed nothing had been right in this house for a while. Bosch studied dead people's rooms the way scholars studied dead people's paintings at the Getty. He looked for the hidden meanings, the secrets of lives and deaths.

At the door Rider went out first. Bosch then stepped out and looked back down the hall. Veronica Aliso was framed at the other end in the light. He hesitated for a beat. He nodded and walked out.

They drove in silence, digesting the conversation, until they got to the gatehouse and Nash came out.

'How'd it go?'

'It went.'

'He's dead, isn't he? Mr Aliso.'

'Yeah.'

Nash whistled quietly.

'Captain Nash, you keep records here of when cars come in and out?' Rider asked.

'Yes. But this is private property. You'd need a—'

'Search warrant,' Bosch said. 'Yes, we know. But before we go to all that trouble, tell me something. Say I come back with a warrant, are your gate records going to tell me when exactly Mrs Aliso came in and out of here the last few days?'

'Nope. It'll only tell you when her car did.'

'Gotcha.'

Bosch dropped off Rider at her car and they drove separately down out of the hills to the Hollywood Division station on Wilcox. On the way Bosch thought about Veronica Aliso and the fury she seemed to hold in her eyes for her dead husband. He didn't know how it fit or if it even fit at all. But he knew they would be coming back to her.

Rider and Bosch stopped briefly in the station to update Edgar and pick up cups of coffee. Bosch then called Archway and arranged for the security office to call in Chuckie Meachum from home. Bosch did not tell the duty officer who took the call what it was about or what office inside the studio they would be going to. He just told the officer to get Meachum there.

At midnight they went out the rear door of the station house, past the fenced windows of the drunk tank and to Bosch's car.

'So what did you think of her?' Bosch finally asked as he pulled out of the station lot.

'The embittered widow? I think there wasn't much to their marriage. At least at the end. Whether that makes her a killer or not, I don't know.'

'No pictures.'

'On the walls? Yeah, I noticed that.'

Bosch lit a cigarette and Rider didn't say anything about it, although it was a violation of department policy to smoke in the detective car.

'What do you think?' Rider asked.

'I'm not sure yet. There's what you said. The bitterness you could almost put in a glass if you ever ran out of ice. Couple other things I'm still thinking about.'

'Like what?'

'Like all the makeup she had on and the way she took my badge out of my hand. Nobody's ever done that before. It's like . . . I don't know, like maybe she was waiting for us.'

When they got to the entrance of Archway Pictures, Meachum was standing under the half-size replica of the Arc de Triomphe smoking a cigarette and waiting. He was wearing a sport coat over a golf shirt and had a bemused smile on his face when he recognized Bosch pulling up. Bosch had spent time with Meachum in the Robbery-Homicide Division ten years before. Never partnered, but they worked a few of the same task forces. Meachum had gotten out when the getting out was good. He pulled the pin a month after the Rodney King tape hit the news. He knew. He told everybody it was the beginning of the end. Archway hired him as the assistant director of security. Nice job, nice pay, plus he was pulling in the twenty-year pension of half pay. He was the one they talked about when they talked about smart moves. Now, with all the baggage the LAPD carried – the King beating, the riots, the Christopher Commission, O. J. Simpson and Mark Fuhrman – a retiring dick would be lucky if a place like Archway hired him to work the front gate.

'Harry Bosch,' Meachum said, leaning down to look in. 'What it is, what it is?'

The first thing Bosch had noticed was that Meachum had gotten his teeth capped since he'd last seen him.

'Chuckie. Long time. This is my partner, Kiz Rider.'

Rider nodded and Meachum nodded and studied her a moment. Black female detectives were a rarity in his day, even though he hadn't been off the job more than five years.

'So what's shaking, Detectives? Why'd you want to go and pull me out of the hot tub?'

He smiled, showing off the teeth. Bosch guessed he knew that they had been noticed.

'We got a case. We want to take a look at the vic's office.'

'It's here? Who's the stiff?'

'Anthony N. Aliso. TNA Productions.'

Meachum crinkled his eyes. He had the deep tan of a golfer who never misses his Saturday morning start and usually gets away for at least nine once or twice during the week.

'Doesn't do anything for me, Harry. You sure he—'

'Look it up, Chuck. He's here. Was.'

'All right, tell you what, park the car over in the main lot and we'll go back to my office, grab a cup and look this guy up.'

He pointed toward a lot directly through the gate and Bosch did as instructed. The lot was almost empty and was next to a huge soundstage with an outside wall painted powder blue with puffs of white clouds. It was used for shooting exteriors when the real sky was too brown with smog.

They followed Meachum on foot to the studio security offices. Entering the suite, they passed by a glass-walled office in which a man in a brown Archway Security outfit sat at a desk surrounded by banks of video monitors. He was reading the *Times* sports page, which he quickly dropped into a trash can next to the desk when he saw Meachum.

Bosch saw that Meachum didn't seem to notice because he had been holding the door open for them. When he turned, he casually saluted the man in the glass office and led Bosch and Rider back to his office.

Meachum slid in behind his desk and turned to his computer. The monitor screen depicted an intergalactic battle among assorted space ships. Meachum hit one key and the screen saver disappeared. He asked Bosch to spell Aliso's name and he punched it into the computer. He then tilted the monitor so Bosch and Rider couldn't see the screen. Bosch was annoyed by this but he didn't say anything. After a few moments, Meachum did.

'You're right. He was here. Tyrone Power Building. Had one of the little cubbyholes they rent to nonplayers. Three-office suite. Three losers. They share a secretary who comes with the rent.'

'How long's he been here? That say?'

'Yeah. Almost seven years.'

'What else you got there?'

Meachum looked at the screen.

'Not much. No record of problems. He complained once about somebody dinging his car in the parking lot. Says here he drove a Rolls-Royce. Probably the last guy in Hollywood who hadn't traded in his Rolls on a Range Rover. That's tacky, Bosch.'

'Let's go take a look.'

'Well, I'll tell you what, why don't you and Detective Riley go out there and grab a cup of joe while I make a call about that. I'm not sure what our procedure is for this.'

'First of all, Chuck, it's Rider, not Riley. And second, we're running a homicide investigation here. Whatever your procedures are, we are expecting you to allow us access.'

'You're on private property here, buddy. You've got to keep that in mind.'

'I will.' Bosch stood up. 'And when you make your call, the thing you should keep in mind is that so far the media haven't gotten wind of any of this. I didn't think it would be good to pull Archway into this sort of thing, especially since we don't know for sure what's involved here. You can tell whoever you're calling that I'll try to keep it that way.'

Meachum smirked and shook his head.

'Still the same old Bosch. Your way or the highway.'

'Something like that.'

While waiting, Bosch had time to gulp down a cup of lukewarm coffee from a pot that had been on a warmer in the outer office for the better part of the night. It was bitter, but he knew the cup he'd had at the station would not take him through the night. Rider passed on the coffee, instead drinking water from a dispenser in the hallway.

After nearly ten minutes Meachum came out of his office.

'Okay, you got it. But I'll tell you right now that me or one of my people gotta be in there the whole time as observers. That going to be a problem for you, Bosch?'

'No problem.'

'Okay, let's go. We'll take a cart.'

On the way out he opened the door to the glass room and stuck his head in.

'Peters, who's roving?'

'Uh, Serrurier and Fogel.'

'Okay, get on the air and tell Serrurier to meet us at Tyrone Power. He's got keys, right?'

'Right.'

'Okay, do it.' Meachum made a motion to close the door but stopped. 'And Peters? Leave the sports page in the trash can.'

They took a golf cart to Tyrone Power Building because it was on the other side of the lot from the security offices. Along the way Meachum waved to a man dressed entirely in black who was coming out of one of the buildings they passed.

'We've got a shoot on New York Street tonight, otherwise I'd take you through there. You'd swear you were in Brooklyn.'

'Never been,' Bosch said.

'Me neither,' Rider added.

'Then it doesn't matter, unless you wanted to see them shooting.'

'The Tyrone Power Building will be just fine.'

'Fine.'

When they got there, another uniformed man was waiting. Serrurier. At Meachum's instructions he first unlocked a door to a reception area that served the three separate offices of the suite, then the door to the office Aliso had used. Meachum then told him to go back out on roving patrol of the studio.

Meachum's calling it a closet was not too far off. Aliso's office was barely large enough for Bosch, Rider and Meachum to stand in together without having to smell each other's breath. It contained a desk with a chair behind it and two more close in front of it. Against the wall behind the desk was a four-drawer file cabinet. The left wall was hung with framed one-sheets advertising two classic films: *Chinatown* and *The Godfather*, both of which had been made down the street at Paramount. Aliso had countered these on the right wall with framed posters of his own efforts, *The Art of the Cape* and *Casualty of Desire*. There were also smaller frames of photos depicting Aliso with various celebrities, many of the shots taken in the same office with Aliso and the celebrity of the moment standing behind the desk smiling.

Bosch first studied the two posters. Each one carried the imprimatur along the top *Anthony Aliso Presents*. But it was the second poster, for *Casualty of Desire*, that caught his attention. The artwork beneath the title of the film showed a man in a white suit carrying a gun down at his side, a desperate look on his face. In larger scale, a woman with flowing dark hair that framed the image looked down on him with sultry eyes. The poster was a rip-off of the scene depicted in the *Chinatown* poster on the other wall. But there was something entrancing about it. The woman, of course, was Veronica Aliso, and Bosch knew that was one reason why.

'Nice-looking woman,' Meachum said from behind him.

'His wife.'

'I see that. Second billing. Only I never heard of her.'

Bosch nodded at the poster.

'I think this was her shot.'

'Well, like I said, nice-looking gal. I doubt she looks like that anymore.'

Bosch studied the eyes again and remembered the woman he had seen just an hour ago. The eyes were still as dark and gleaming, a little cross of light at the center of each.

Bosch looked away and began to study the framed photos. He immediately noticed that one of them was of Dan Lacey, the actor who had portrayed Bosch eight years earlier in a mini-series about the search for a serial killer. The studio that had produced it had paid Bosch and his then partner a lot of money to use their names and technical advice. His partner took the money and ran, retired to Mexico. Bosch bought a house in the hills. He couldn't run. He knew the job was his life.

He turned and took in the rest of the small office. There were shelves against the wall near the door and these were piled with scripts and videotapes, no books save for a couple of directories of actors and directors.

'Okay,' Bosch said. 'Chuckie, you stand back by the door and observe like you said. Kiz, why don't you start with the desk and I'll start with the files.'

The files were locked and it took Bosch ten minutes to open them with the picks he got out of his briefcase. It then took an hour just to make a cursory study of the files. The drawers were stocked with notes and financial records regarding the development of several films that Bosch had never heard of. This did not seem curious to him after what Veronica Aliso had said and because he knew little about the film business anyway. But it seemed from his understanding of the files he was quickly scanning that large sums of money had been paid to various film services companies during the production of the films. And what struck Bosch the most was that Aliso seemed to have financed a hell of a nice lifestyle from this little office.

After he was finished going through the fourth and bottom drawer, Bosch stood and straightened his back, his vertebrae popping like dominoes clicking together. He looked at Rider, who was still going through the drawers of the desk.

'Anything?'

'A few things of interest but no smoking gun, if that's what you mean. Aliso's got a flag here from the IRS. His corporation was going to be audited next month. Other than that, there is some correspondence between Tony Aliso and St John, the flavor-of-the-month Mrs Aliso mentioned. Heated words but nothing overtly threatening. I've still got one drawer to go.'

'There's a lot in the files. Financial stuff. We're going to have to go through it all. I'd like you to be the one. You going to be up for it?'

'No problem. What I'm seeing so far is a lot of routine, if not sloppy, business records. It just happens to be the movie business here.'

'I'm going outside to catch a smoke. When you're done there, why don't we switch and you take the files, I'll take the desk.'

'Sounds like a plan.'

Before going out he ran his eyes along the shelves by the door and read the titles of the videotapes. He stopped when he came to the one he was looking for. *Casualty of Desire*. He reached up and took it down. The cover carried the same artwork as the movie poster.

He stepped back and put it on the desk so it would be gathered with things they would be taking. Rider asked what it was.

'It's her movie,' he said. 'I want to watch it.'

'Oh, me too.'

Outside, Bosch stood in the small courtyard by a bronze statue of a man he guessed was Tyrone Power and lit a cigarette. It was a cool night and the smoke in his chest warmed him. The studio grounds were very quiet now.

He walked over to a trash can next to a bench in the courtyard and used it to tip his ashes. He noticed a broken coffee mug at the bottom of the can. There were several pens and pencils scattered in the can as well. He recognized the Archway insignia, the Arc de Triomphe with the sun rising in the middle of the arch, on one of the fragments. He was about to reach into the trash can to pick out what looked like a gold Cross pen when he heard Meachum's voice and turned around.

'She's going places, isn't she? I can tell.'

He was lighting his own cigarette.

'Yeah, that's what I hear. It's our first case together. I don't really know her, and from what I hear I shouldn't try. She's going to the Glass House as soon as the time is right.'

Meachum nodded and flicked his ashes onto the pavement. Bosch watched him glance up toward the roofline above the second floor and give another one of his casual salutes. Bosch looked up and saw the camera moored to the underside of the roof eave.

'Don't worry about it,' Bosch said. 'He can't see you. He's reading about the Dodgers last night.'

'S'pose you're right. Can't get good people these days, Harry. I get guys who like driving around in the carts all day, hoping they're going to be discovered like Clint Eastwood or something. Had a guy run into a wall the other day 'cause he was so intent on talking with a couple of creative execs walking by. There's one of them oxymorons for you. Creative executive . . .'

Bosch was silent. He didn't care about anything that Meachum had just said.

'You ought to come work here, Harry. You've gotta have your twenty in by now. You should pull the pin and then come work for me. Your lifestyle will rise a couple of notches. I guarantee it.'

'No thanks, Chuck. Somehow I just don't see myself tooling around in one of your golf carts.'

'Well, the offer's there. Anytime, buddy. Anytime.'

Bosch put his cigarette out on the side of the trash can and dropped the dead butt inside. He decided that he didn't want to go picking through the can with Meachum watching. He told Meachum he was heading back in.

'Bosch, I gotta tell you something.'

Bosch looked back at him and Meachum raised his hands. 'We're going to have a problem if you want to take anything out of that office without a warrant. I mean, I heard what you said about that tape and now she's in there stacking stuff on the desk to go. But I can't let you take anything.'

'Then you are going to be here all night, Chuck. There are a lot of files in there and a lot of work to do. It'd be a lot easier for us to haul it all back to the bureau now.'

'I know that. I've been there. But this is the position I've been instructed to take. We need the warrant.'

Bosch used the phone on the receptionist's desk to call Edgar, who was still in the detective bureau just beginning the paperwork the case would generate. Bosch told him to drop that work for the moment and start drawing up search warrants for all financial records in Aliso's home and the Archway offices and any being held by his attorney.

'You want me to call the duty judge tonight?' Edgar asked. 'It's almost two in the morning.'

'Do it,' Bosch said. 'When you have 'em signed, bring them out here to Archway. And bring some boxes.'

Edgar groaned. He was getting all the shit work. Nobody liked waking up a judge in the middle of the night.

'I know, I know, Jerry. But it's got to be done. Anything else going on?'

'No. I called the Mirage, talked to a guy in security. The room Aliso used was rebooked over the weekend. It's open now and he's got a hold on it, but it's spoiled.'

'Probably . . . Okay, man, next time you'll eat the bear. Get on those warrants.'

In Aliso's office, Rider was already looking through the files. Bosch told her Edgar was working on a warrant and that they would have to draw up an inventory for Meachum. He also told her to take a break if she wanted but she declined.

Bosch sat down behind the desk. It had the usual clutter. There was a phone with a speaker attachment, a Rolodex, a blotter, a magnetic block that held paper clips to it and a wood carving that said TNA Productions in script. There was also a tray stacked with paperwork.

Bosch looked at the phone and noticed the redial button. He lifted the handset and pushed the button. He could tell by the quick procession of tones that the last call made on the phone had been long distance. After two rings it was answered by a female voice. There was loud music in the background.

'Hello?' she said.

'Yes, hello, who's this?'

She giggled.

'I don't know, who's this?'

'I might have the wrong number. Is this Tony's?'

'No, it's Dolly's.'

'Oh, Dolly's. Okay, uh, then where are you located?'

She giggled again.

'On Madison, where do you think? How do you think we got the name?'

'Where's Madison?'

'We're in North Las Vegas. Where are you coming from?'

'The Mirage.'

'Okay, just follow the boulevard out front to the north. You go all the way past downtown and past a bunch of cruddy areas and into North Las Vegas. Madison is your third light after you go under the overpass. Take a left and we're a block down on your left. What's your name again?'

'It's Harry.'

'Well, Harry, I'm Rhonda. As in . . .'

Bosch said nothing.

'Come on, Harry, you're supposed to say, "Help me, Rhonda, help, help me, Rhonda."'

She sang the line from the old Beach Boys song.

'Actually, Rhonda, there *is* something you can help me with,' Bosch said. 'I'm looking for a buddy of mine. Tony Aliso. He been in there lately?'

'Haven't seen him this week. Haven't seen him since Thursday or Friday. I was wondering how you got the dressing room number.'

'Yeah, from Tony.'

'Well, Layla isn't here tonight, so Tony wouldn't be coming in anyway, I don't think. But you can come on out. He don't have to be here for you to have a good time.'

'Okay, Rhonda, I'll try to swing by.'

Bosch hung up. He took a notebook out of his pocket and wrote down the name of the business he had just called, the directions to it and the names Rhonda and Layla. He drew a line under the second name.

'What was that?' Rider asked.

'A lead in Vegas.'

He recounted the call and the inference made about the person named Layla. Rider agreed that it was something to pursue, then went back to the files. Bosch went back to the desk. He studied the things on top of it before going to the things in it.

'Hey, Chuckie?' he asked.

Meachum, leaning against the door with his arms folded in front of him, raised his eyebrows by way of response.

'He's got no phone tape. What about when the receptionist isn't out there? Do phone calls go to the operator or some kind of a phone service?'

'Uh, no, the whole lot's on voice mail now.'

'So Aliso had voice mail? How do I get into it?'

'Well, you've got to have his code. It's a three-digit code. You call the voice mail computer, punch in the code and you pick up your messages.'

'How do I get his code?'

73

'You don't. He programmed it himself.'

'There's no master code I can break in with?'

'Nope. It's not that sophisticated a system, Bosch. I mean, what do you want, it's phone messages.'

Bosch took out his notebook again and checked the notes for Aliso's birthday.

'What's the voice mail number?' he asked.

Meachum gave him the number and Bosch called the computer. After a beep he punched in 721 but the number was rejected. Bosch drummed his fingers on the desk, thinking. He tried 862, the numbers corresponding with TNA, and a computer voice told him he had four messages.

'Kiz, listen to this,' he said.

He put the phone on speaker and hung up. As the messages were played back Bosch took a few notes, but the first three messages were from men reporting on technical aspects of a planned film shoot, equipment rental and costs. Each call was followed by the electronic voice which reported when on Friday the call had come in.

The fourth message made Bosch lean forward and listen closely. The voice belonged to a young woman and it sounded like she was crying.

'Hey, Tone, it's me. Call me as soon as you get this. I almost feel like calling your house. I need you. That bastard Lucky says I'm fired. And for no reason. He just wants to get his dick into Modesty. I'm so . . . I don't want to have to work at the Palomino or any of those other places. The Garden. Forget it. I want to come out there to L.A. Be with you. Call me.'

The electronic voice said the call had come in at 4 a.m. on Sunday – long after Tony Aliso was dead. The caller had not given her name. It was therefore obviously someone Aliso would have known. Bosch wondered if it was the woman Rhonda had mentioned, Layla. He looked at Rider and she just shook her shoulders. They knew too little to judge the significance of the call.

Bosch sat in the desk chair contemplating things a few moments. He opened a drawer but didn't start through it. His eyes traveled up the wall to the right of the desk and roamed across the photos of the smiling Tony Aliso posed with celebrities. Some of them had written notes on the photos but they were hard to read. Bosch studied the photo of his celluloid alter ego, Dan Lacey, but couldn't read the small note scrawled across the bottom of the photo. Then he looked past the ink and realized what he was looking at. On Aliso's desk in the photo was an Archway mug crammed with pens and pencils.

Bosch took the photo off the wall and called Meachum's name. Meachum came over.

'Somebody was in here,' Bosch told him.

'What are you talking about?'

'When was the trash can emptied outside?'

'How the hell would I know? What are—'

'The surveillance camera out there on the roof, how long you keep the tapes?'

Meachum hesitated a second but then answered.

'We roll 'em over every week. We'd have seven days off that camera. It's all stop action, ten frames a minute.'

'Let's go take a look.'

Bosch didn't get home until four. That left him only three hours to sleep before an agreed-upon breakfast meeting with Edgar and Rider at seven-thirty, but he was too strung out on coffee and adrenaline to even think about shutting his eyes.

The house had the sour tang of a fresh-paint smell and he opened the sliders onto the back deck to let in the cool night air. He checked out the Cahuenga Pass below and watched the cars on the Hollywood Freeway cutting through. He was always amazed at how there were always cars on the freeway, no matter what the hour. In L.A. they never stopped.

He thought about putting on a CD, some saxophone music, but instead just sat down on the couch in the dark and lit a cigarette. He thought about the different currents running through the case. Going by the preliminary take on the victim, Anthony Aliso had been a financially successful man. That kind of success usually brought with it a thick insulation from violence and murder. The rich were seldom murdered. But something had gone wrong for Tony Aliso.

Bosch remembered the tape and went to his briefcase, which he had left on the dining room table. Inside it there were two video cassettes, the Archway surveillance tape and the copy of *Casualty of Desire*. He turned on the TV and put the movie in the video player. He began watching in the dark.

After viewing the tape it was obvious to Bosch that the movie deserved the fate it had received. It was badly lit and in some frames the end of a boom microphone hovered above the players. This was particularly jarring in scenes shot in the open desert where there should have been nothing above but blue sky. It was basic filmmaking gone wrong. And added to the amateurish look of the film were the poor performances of the players. The male lead, an actor Bosch had never seen before, was woodenly ineffective in portraying a man desperate to hold on to his young wife, who used sexual frustration and taunting to coerce him into committing crimes, eventually including murder, all for her morbid satisfaction. Veronica Aliso played the wife and was not much better an actor than the male lead.

When lighted well, she was stunningly beautiful. There were four scenes in which she appeared partially nude and Bosch watched these with a voyeuristic fascination. But overall it was not a good role for her, and Bosch also understood why her career, like her husband's, had not moved forward. She might blame her husband and harbor resentment toward him, but the bottom line was that she was like thousands of beautiful women who came to

Hollywood every year. Her looks could put a pause in your heart, but she could not act to save her life.

In the climactic scene of the film, in which the husband was apprehended and the wife cut him loose with the cops, she delivered her lines with the conviction and weight of a blank page of typing paper.

'It was him. He's crazy. I couldn't stop him until it was too late. Then I couldn't tell anyone because it . . . it would look like I was the one who wanted them all dead.'

Bosch watched all the way through the credits and then rewound the tape by using the remote. He never got off the couch. He then turned the TV off and put his feet up on the couch. Looking through the open sliders he could see the light of dawn etching the ridgeline across the Pass. He still wasn't tired. He kept thinking about the choices people make with their lives. He wondered what would have happened if the performances had been at least passable and the film had found a distributor. He wondered if that would have changed things now, if it would have kept Tony Aliso out of that trunk.

The meeting at the station with Billets didn't start until nine-thirty. Though the squad room was deserted because of the holiday, they all rolled chairs into the lieutenant's office and closed the door. Billets started things off by saying that members of the local media, apparently having picked up on the case by checking the coroner's over-night log, were already beginning to take a more than routine interest in the Aliso murder. Also, she said, the department weight all the way up the line was questioning whether the investigation should be turned over to the elite Robbery-Homicide Division. This, of course, grated on Bosch. Earlier in his career he had been assigned to RHD. But then a questionable on-duty shooting resulted in his demotion to Hollywood. And so it was particularly upsetting to him to think of turning over the case to the big shots downtown. If OCID had been interested, that would have been easier to accept. But Bosch told Billets that he could not accept turning the case over to RHD after his team had spent almost an entire night without sleep on it and had produced some viable leads. Rider jumped in and agreed with him. Edgar, still riding his sulk over being put on the paperwork, remained silent.

'Your point is well taken,' Billets said. 'But when we're done here, I have to call Captain LeValley at home and convince her we've got a handle on this. So let's go over what we have. You convince me, I'll convince her. She'll then let them know how we feel about it downtown.'

Bosch spent the next thirty minutes talking for the team and carefully recounting the night's investigation. The detective squad's only television/VCR was kept in the lieutenant's office because it wasn't safe to leave it unlocked, even in a police station. He put in the tape Meachum had dubbed off the Archway surveillance tape and queued up the part that included the intruder.

'The surveillance camera this was shot from turns a frame every six seconds, so it's pretty quick and jerky but we've got the guy on it,' Bosch said.

He hit the play button and the screen depicted a grainy black and white view of the courtyard and front of the Tyrone Power Building. The lighting made it appear to be late dusk. The time counter on the bottom of the screen showed the time and date to be eight-thirteen the evening before.

Bosch put the machine on slow motion, but still the sequence he wanted to show Billets was over very quickly. In six quick frames they showed a man go to the door of the building, hunch over the knob and then disappear inside.

'Actual time at the door was about thirty to thirty-five seconds,' Rider said. 'It may look from the tape like he had a key, but that's too long to open a door with a key. The lock was picked. Somebody good and fast.'

'Okay, here he comes back out,' Bosch said.

When the time counter hit eight-seventeen, the man was captured on the video emerging from the doorway. The video jumped and the man was in the courtyard heading toward the trash can, then it jumped and the man was walking away from the trash can. Then he was gone. Bosch backed the tape up and froze it on the last image of the man as he walked from the trash can. It was the best image. It was dark and the man's face was blurred but still possibly recognizable if they ever found someone to compare it to. He was white, with dark hair and a stocky, powerful build. He wore a golf shirt with short sleeves, and the watch on his right wrist, visible just above one of the black gloves he wore, had a chrome band that glinted with the reflection of the courtyard light. Above the wrist was the dark blur of a tattoo on the man's forearm. Bosch pointed these things out to Billets and added that he would be taking the tape to SID to see if this last frame, the best of those showing the intruder, could be sharpened in any way by computer enhancement.

'Good,' Billets said. 'Now, what do you think he was doing in there?'

'Retrieving something,' Bosch said. 'From the time he goes in until he comes out, we've got less than four minutes. Not a lot of time. Plus he had to pick the interior door to Aliso's office. Whatever he is doing in there, he knocks an Archway mug off the desk and it breaks on the floor. He does what he was there to do, then gathers up the broken mug and the pens and dumps them in the trash can on his way out. We found the broken mug and the pens in the can last night.'

'Any prints?' Billets asked.

'Once we figured there was a break-in, we backed out and had Donovan come on out when he was done with the Rolls. He got prints but nothing we can use. He got Aliso's and mine and Kiz's. As you can see on the video, the guy wore gloves.'

'Okay.'

Bosch involuntarily yawned and Edgar and Rider followed suit. He drank from the cup of stale coffee he had brought into the office with him. He had long had the caffeine jitters but knew if he stopped feeding the beast now he would quickly crash.

'And the theory on what this intruder was retrieving?' Billets asked.

'The broken mug puts him at the desk rather than the files,' Rider said. 'Nothing in the desk seemed disturbed. No empty files, nothing like that. We think it was a bug. Somebody put a bug in Aliso's phone and couldn't afford to let us find it. The phone was right next to the mug in the pictures on Aliso's walls. The intruder somehow knocked it over. Funny thing is, we never checked the phone for a bug. If whoever this guy was had left well enough alone, we probably would have never tumbled to it.'

'I've been to Archway,' Billets said. 'It's got a wall around it. It's got its own private security force. How's this guy get in? Or are you suggesting an inside job?'

'Two things,' Bosch said. 'There was a film shooting in progress at the studio on the New York Street set. That meant a lot of people in and out of the front gate. Maybe this guy was able to slip through with part of the shooting crew. The direction in which he walks off in the video is to the north. That's where New York Street is. The gate is to the south. Also, the north side of the studio butts up against the Hollywood Cemetery. You're right, there is a wall. But at night, after the cemetery is closed, it's dark and secluded. Our guy could've climbed the wall there. Whatever way he did it, he had practice.'

'What do you mean?'

'If he was taking a bug out of Tony Aliso's phone, it had to have been planted there in the first place.'

Billets nodded.

'Who do you think he was?' she asked quietly.

Bosch looked at Rider to see if she wanted to answer. When she didn't speak, he did.

'Hard to say. The timing is the catch. Aliso's probably been dead since Friday night, his body's not found till about six last night. Then this break-in comes at eight-thirteen. That's after Aliso's been found and after people start finding out about it.'

'But eight-thirteen, that's before you talked to the wife?'

'Right. So that kind of threw a wrench into it. I mean, I was all set to say let's go full speed on the wife and see what we get. Now, I'm not so sure. See, if she's involved, this break-in doesn't make sense.'

'Explain.'

'Well, first you've got to figure out why he was being bugged. And what's the most likely answer? The wife put a PI or somebody on Tony to see if he was screwing around. Okay?'

'Okay.'

'Now, saying that's the case, if the wife was involved in putting her husband down into that trunk, why would she or her PI or whoever wait until last night – this is after the body's been found – to pull the bug out of there? It doesn't make sense. It only makes sense if the two things were not related, if the killing and the bug are separate. Understand?'

'I think so.'

'And that's why I'm not ready to chuck everything and just look at the wife. Personally, I think she might be good for this. But there's too much we don't know right now. It doesn't feel right to me. There's something else running through all of this, and we don't know what yet.'

Billets nodded and looked at all the investigators.

'This is good. I know there isn't a lot that is solid yet, but it's still good work. Anything else? What about the prints Art Donovan pulled off the victim's jacket last night?'

'For now we've struck out. He put them on AFIS, NCIC, the whole works, and got blanked.'

'Damn.'

'They're still valuable. We come up with a suspect, the prints could be a clincher.'

'Anything else from the car?'

'No,' Bosch said.

'Yes,' Rider said.

Billets raised her eyebrows at the contradiction.

'One of the prints Donovan found on the inside lip of the trunk lid,' Rider said. 'It came back to Ray Powers. He's the P-3 who found the body. He overstepped when he popped the trunk. He obviously left his print when he opened it. We caught it and no harm, no foul, but it was sloppy work and he should have never opened the trunk in the first place. He should've called us.'

Billets glanced at Bosch and he guessed she was wondering why he hadn't brought this to her attention. He looked down at her desk.

'Okay, I'll take care of it,' Billets said. 'I know Powers. He's been around and he should certainly know procedure.'

Bosch could have defended Powers with the explanation the cop had given the day before but he let it go. Powers wasn't worth it. Billets went on.

'So where do we go from here?'

'Well, we've got a lot of ground to cover,' Bosch said. 'I once heard this story about a sculptor and somebody asked him how he turned a block of granite into a beautiful statue of a woman. And he said that he just chips away everything that isn't the woman. That's what we have to do now. We've got this big block of information and evidence. We've got to chip away everything that doesn't count, that doesn't fit.'

Billets smiled and Bosch suddenly felt embarrassed about the analogy, though he believed it was accurate.

'What about Las Vegas?' she asked. 'Is that part of the statue or the part we need to chip away?'

Now Rider and Edgar were smiling.

'Well, we've got to go there, for one thing,' Bosch said, hoping he didn't sound defensive. 'Right now all we know is that this victim went there and was dead pretty soon after he came back. We don't know what he did there, whether he won, lost, whether somebody tailed him back here from there. For all we know, he could've hit a jackpot there and was followed back here and ripped off. We've got a lot of questions about Las Vegas.'

'Plus, there's the woman,' Rider said.

'What woman?' Billets asked.

'Right,' Bosch said. 'The last call made on Tony Aliso's office line was to a club in North Las Vegas. I called it and got the name of a woman I think he was seeing over there. Layla. There was—'

'Layla? Like that song?'

'I guess. There also was a message from an unnamed woman on his office line. I think it might have been this Layla. We've got to talk to her.'

Billets nodded, made sure Bosch was done and then laid down the battle plan.

'All right,' Billets said. 'First off, all media inquiries are to be directed to me. The best way to control information on this is to have it come from one mouth. For the moment, we'll tell the reporters it is obviously under investigation and we are leaning toward a possible carjacking or robbery scenario. It's innocuous enough and will probably appease them. Everyone okay with that?'

The three detectives nodded.

'Okay, I'm going to make a case with the captain to keep the case here with us. It looks to me like we have three or four avenues which need to be pursued vigorously. Granite that we have to chip away at, as Harry would say.

'Anyway, it will also help me with the captain if we are already scrambling on these things. So, Harry, I want you to get on a plane as soon as possible and get to Vegas. I want you on that end of it. But if there's nothing there, I want you to get in and get out. We'll need you back here. Okay?'

Bosch nodded. It would have been his choice if he were the one making the decisions, but he felt a pang of discomfort that she was doing it.

'Kiz, you stick with the financial trail. I want to be in a position of knowing everything about this guy Anthony

Aliso by tomorrow morning. You're also going to have to go up to the house with the search warrant, so while you are there, take another shot at the wife, see what else you can get about the marriage when you're picking up the records. I don't know, if you get a chance, sit down with her, try to get a heart-to-heart.'

'I don't know,' Rider said. 'I think we're past the heart-to-heart. She's a smart woman, smart enough to already know we're taking a look at her. I almost think that to be safe we've got to advise her next time any of us talk to her. It was pretty close last night.'

'Use your judgment on that,' Billets said. 'But if you advise, she's probably going to call her lawyer.'

'I'll see what I can do.'

'And Jerry, you—'

'I know, I know, I've got the paper.'

It was the first time he had spoken in fifteen minutes. Bosch thought he was carrying his sulk to the limit.

'Yes, you have the paper. But I also want you on the civil cases and this screenwriter guy who was having the dispute with Aliso. It sounds to me to be the longest shot, but we've got to cover everything. Get that cleared up and it will help narrow our focus.'

Edgar mock-saluted her.

'Also,' she said, 'while Harry's putting together the trail in Vegas, I want you to put it together from the airport here. We've got his parking stub. I think you should start there. When I talk to the media I'll also give a detailed description of the car – can't be that many white Clouds around – and say we're looking for anyone who might've seen it Friday night. I'll say we're trying to re-create the victim's ride from the airport. Maybe we'll get lucky and get some help from the John Qs out there.'

'Maybe,' Edgar said.

'Okay then, let's do it,' Billets said.

The three of them stood up while Billets stayed seated. Bosch took his time taking the tape out of the VCR so that the other two were out of the office when he was done, and he was alone with Billets.

'I'd heard that you didn't have any actual time on a homicide table while you were coming up,' he said to her.

'That's true. My only job as an actual detective was working sexual crimes in Valley Bureau.'

'Well, for what it's worth, I would have assigned things just the way you just did.'

'But did it annoy you that I did it instead of you?'

Bosch thought a moment.

'I'll get over it.'

'Thank you.'

'No problem. Listen, that thing about Powers leaving his print, I probably would have told you about it, but I didn't think this meeting was the right time. I chewed him out for opening the car yesterday. He said if he hadn't opened it and waited for us to check it out, the car would probably still be sitting out there. He is an asshole but he makes a point.'

'I understand.'

'You pissed at me for not telling you?'

Billets thought a moment.

'I'll get over it.'

Bosch fell asleep a few minutes after belting himself into a window seat on the Southwest shuttle from Burbank to Las Vegas. It was a deep, dreamless sleep and he didn't wake until the clunk of the landing gear hitting the tarmac jolted him forward. As the plane taxied to its gate he came out of the fog and felt himself re- energized by the hour-long rest.

It was high noon and 104 degrees when he walked out of the terminal. As he headed toward the garage where his rental car was waiting, he felt his newfound energy being leached away by the heat. After finding his car in its assigned parking stall, he put the air-conditioning on high and headed toward the Mirage.

Bosch had never liked Las Vegas, though he came often on cases. It shared a kinship with Los Angeles; both were places desperate people ran to. Often, when they ran from Los Angeles, they came here. It was the only place left. Beneath the veneer of glitz and money and energy and sex beat a dark heart. No matter how much they tried to dress her up with neon and family entertainment, she was still a whore.

But if any place could sway him from that opinion it was the Mirage. It was the symbol of the new Las Vegas, clean, opulent, legit. The windows of its tower glinted gold in the sun. And inside no money had been spared in its rich casino design. As Bosch walked through the lobby he was first mesmerized by the white tigers in a huge glassed-in environment that any zookeeper in the world would salivate over. Next, as he waited in line to check in, he eyed the huge aquarium behind the front desk. Sharks lazily turned and moved back and forth behind the glass. Just like the white tigers.

When it was Bosch's turn to check in, the desk clerk noticed a flag on his reservation and called security. A day-shift supervisor named Hank Meyer appeared and introduced himself. He said that Bosch would have the complete cooperation of the hotel and casino.

'Tony Aliso was a good and valued customer,' he said. 'We want to do what we can to help. But it's highly unlikely that his death had anything to do with his stay here. We run the cleanest ship in the desert.'

'I know that, Hank,' Bosch said. 'And I know it is a reputation you don't want blemished. I'm not expecting to find anything inside the Mirage, but I need to go through the motions. So do you, right?'

'Right.'

'Did you know him?'

'No, I didn't. I've been on day shift the entire three years I've been here. From what I understand, Mr Aliso primarily gambled at night.'

Meyer was about thirty and had the clean-cut image that the Mirage, and now all of Las Vegas, wanted to present to the world. He went on to explain that the room Aliso had last stayed in at the hotel was sealed and was being held that way for Bosch's inspection. He gave Bosch the key and asked that he return it as soon as he was finished with the room. He also said the poker pit dealers and sports book clerks who worked the night shift would be made available for interviews. All of them knew Aliso because of his regular visits.

'You have an eye in the sky over the poker tables?'

'Uh, yes, we do.'

'You have video from Thursday going into Friday? I'd like to see it if you do.'

'That won't be a problem.'

Bosch made arrangements to meet Meyer at the second-floor security office at four. That was when the casino shifts changed and the dealers who knew Aliso would report for work. He could look at the surveillance tape from the poker pit's overhead camera then as well.

A few minutes later, alone in his room, Bosch sat on the bed and looked around. The room was smaller than he had expected but it was very nice, by far the most comfortably appointed room he had ever seen in Las Vegas. He pulled the phone off the side table onto his lap and called the Hollywood Division to check in. Edgar picked up the line.

'It's Bosch.'

'Well, the Michelangelo of murder, the Rodin of homicide.'

'Funny. So what's going on over there?'

'Well, for one thing, Bullets won the battle,' Edgar said. 'Nobody from RHD has come around to snatch the case.'

'That's good. What about you? You making any progress?'

'I almost have the murder book up to speed. I have to put it aside now, though. The screenwriter is coming in at one-thirty for a sit-down. Says he doesn't need a lawyer.'

'Okay, I'll leave you to it. Tell the lieutenant I checked in.'

'Yeah, and by the way, she wants another confab on how things are going at six. You should call in and we'll put you on the speaker.'

'Will do.'

Bosch sat on the bed a few moments wishing he could lie back on it and sleep. But he knew he couldn't. He had to drive the case forward.

He got up and unpacked his overnighter, hanging his two shirts and one pair of pants in the closet. He put his extra underwear and socks on the closet shelf, then left the room and took an elevator to the top floor. The room Aliso had used was at the end of the corridor. The card key Meyer had given him worked without a problem and he stepped into a room about twice the size of his own. It was a combination bedroom and sitting room and had an oval Jacuzzi next to the windows that looked out across the expanse of the desert and the smooth cocoa-colored mountain chain to the northwest of the city. Directly below was a view of the pool and the hotel's porpoise-habitat attraction. Looking down, he could see one of the gray fish moving beneath the shimmering water. It looked as out of place as Bosch felt in the suite he stood in.

'Dolphins in the desert,' he said out loud.

The room was plush by any standards in any city and obviously was kept for high rollers. Bosch stood by the bed for a few moments and just looked around. There was nothing that seemed out of place and the thick carpet had the uniformed waves left by a recent vacuuming. He guessed that if there had been anything of evidentiary value in the room it was gone now. But still he went through the motions. He looked under the bed and in the drawers. Behind the bureau he found a matchbook from a local Mexican restaurant called La Fuentes, but there was no telling how long it had been there.

The bathroom was tiled in pink marble floor to ceiling. The fixtures were polished brass. Bosch looked around for a moment but saw nothing of interest. He opened the glass door to the shower stall and looked in and also found nothing. But as he was closing the door his eyes caught on something on the drain. He reopened the door and looked down, then pressed his finger on the tiny speck of gold caught in the rubber sealant around the drain fitting. He raised his finger and found the tiny piece of glitter stuck to his finger. He guessed that it was a match to the pieces of glitter found in the cuffs of Tony Aliso's pants. Now all he needed was to figure out what they were and where they had come from.

*

The Metro Police Department was on Stewart Street in downtown. Bosch stopped at the front desk and explained he was an out-of-town investigator wanting to make a courtesy check-in with the homicide squad. He was directed to the third-floor detective bureau, where a desk man escorted him through a deserted squad room to the commander's office. Captain John Felton was a thick-necked, deeply tanned man of about fifty. Bosch figured he had probably given the welcome speech to at least a hundred cops from all over the country in the last month alone. Las Vegas was that kind of place. Felton asked Bosch to sit down and he gave him the standard spiel.

'Detective Bosch, welcome to Las Vegas. Lucky for you I decided to come in on the holiday to take care of some of this paperwork that haunts me. Otherwise, there'd be nobody here. Anyway, I hope you find your stay enjoyable and productive. If there is anything you need, don't hesitate to call. I can promise you nothing, but if you request something that is within my power to provide, I will be more than happy to provide it. So, that out of the way, why don't you tell me what brings you here?'

Bosch gave him a quick rundown on the case. Felton wrote down the name Tony Aliso and the last days he was known to have stayed in Las Vegas and where.

'I'm just trying to run down his activities on the days he was here.'

'You think he was followed from here and then taken off in L.A.?'

'I don't think anything at the moment. We don't have evidence of that.'

'And I hope you won't find any. That's not the kind of press we want to get in L.A. What else you got?'

Bosch pulled his briefcase onto his lap and opened it.

'I've got two sets of prints taken off the body. We—'

'The body?'

'He was wearing a treated leather jacket. We got the prints with the laser. Anyway, we ran them on AFIS,

93

NCIC, California DOJ, the works, but got nothing. I thought maybe you'd run them through your own computer, see what happens.'

While the Automated Fingerprint Identification System used by the LAPD was a computer network of dozens of fingerprint databases across the country, it didn't connect them all. And most big-city police departments had their own private databases. In Vegas they would be prints taken from people who applied for jobs for the city or the casinos. They were also prints taken from people on the sly, prints the department shouldn't legally have because their owners had simply fallen under the suspicion of the department but had never been arrested. It was against this database that Bosch was hopeful Felton would check the sets from the Aliso case.

'Well, let me see what you have,' Felton said. 'I can't promise anything. We've probably gotta few that the national nets don't, but it's a long shot.'

Bosch handed over print cards Art Donovan had prepared for him.

'So you are starting at the Mirage?' the captain asked after he put the cards to the side of his desk.

'Yeah. I'll show his picture around, go through the motions, see what I can come up with.'

'You're telling me everything you know, right?'

'Right,' Bosch lied.

'Okay.' Felton opened a desk drawer and took out a business card and handed it over to Bosch. 'That's got my office and pager on it. Call me if anything comes up. I've got the pager with me at all times. Meantime, I'll get back to you about the prints, one way or the other, by tomorrow morning.'

Bosch thanked him and left. In the lobby of the police station he called the SID office at LAPD and asked Donovan if he'd had time to check out the tiny pieces of glitter they had found in the cuffs of Tony Aliso's pants.

'Yeah, but you aren't going to like it,' Donovan said. 'It's just glitter. Tinted aluminum. You know, like they use in costuming and in celebrations. Your guy probably went to a party or something, they were throwing this stuff around, maybe popping it out of party favors or something, and some of it got on him. He could brush off what he could see, but he didn't see the particles that fell into the cuffs of his pants. They stayed.'

'Okay. Anything else?'

'Uh, no. Not on the evidence at least.'

'Then on what?'

'Well, Harry, you know the guy from OCID that you were talking on the phone with last night while we were in the shed?'

'Carbone?'

'Yeah, Dominic Carbone. Well, he dropped by the lab today. He was asking questions about what we found last night.'

Bosch's vision darkened. He said nothing and Donovan continued.

'He said he was here on something else and was just acting curious. But, Harry, I don't know. It seemed more than just a passing interest, if you know what I mean.'

'Yeah, I know what you mean. How much did you tell him?'

'Well, before I caught on and started wondering what was going on, I sort of let slip we pulled prints off the jacket. Sorry, Harry, but I was proud. It's rare that we pull righteous prints off a dead guy's jacket, and I guess I was sort of braggin' about it.'

'It's okay. You tell him we didn't get anything with them?'

'Yeah, I said they came back clean. But then . . . then he asked for a copy of the set, said he might be able to do something with them, whatever that means.'

'What did you do?'

'What do you think, I gave him a set.'

'You what?'

'Just kidding, Harry. I told him to call you if he wanted a set.'

'Good. What else you tell him?'

'That's it, Harry.'

'Okay, Art, it's cool. I'll check you later.'

'See you, Harry. Hey, where are you, anyway?'

'Vegas.'

'Really? Hey, put down a five for me on seven on the roulette wheel. Do it one time. I'll pay you when you get back. Unless I win. Then you pay me.'

Bosch got back to his room forty-five minutes before his appointment with Hank Meyer. He used the time to shower, shave and change into one of his fresh shirts. He felt refreshed, ready to go back into the desert heat.

Meyer had arranged to have the sports book clerks and dealers who worked the poker pit on the previous Thursday and Friday evening shifts to be interviewed one at a time in his office. There were six men and three women. Eight were dealers and one was the clerk Aliso always placed his sports bets with. During any shift, the poker dealers rotated around the casino's six poker tables every twenty minutes. This meant that all eight had dealt cards to Aliso during his last visit to Las Vegas, and by virtue of his regular trips to the casino, they readily recognized him and knew him.

With Meyer sitting by watching, Bosch quickly moved through the interviews with the poker dealers in an hour. He was able to establish that Aliso usually played the five-to-ten table. This meant each hand started with a five-dollar ante and each deal carried a minimum bet of five dollars and a maximum of ten. Three raises were allowed per deal. Since the game was seven card stud, that meant there were five deals per hand. Bosch quickly realized that if a table was full with eight players, each hand could easily result in several hundred dollars being at stake in the pot. Aliso was playing in a league far removed from the Friday night poker games Bosch had participated in with the dicks from the detective bureau.

According to the dealers, Aliso had played for about three hours on Thursday night and had come out about even. He played another two hours early Friday evening, and it was estimated that he left the tables a couple thousand short. None of them recalled Aliso ever being a big winner or loser during previous visits. He always came out a few thousand light or heavy. He seemed to know when to quit.

The dealers also noted that Aliso was quick with the gratuity. His standard tip was ten dollars in chips for every win, a twenty-five chip on particularly big pots. It was that practice more than anything else that endeared him to their memories. He always played alone, drank gin and tonic and small-talked with the other players. In recent months, the dealers said, Aliso had been in the company of a young blond woman, barely into her twenties. She never played but would work the slots nearby and come back to Tony when she needed more money. Tony never introduced her to anybody and none of the dealers ever overheard her name. In his notebook, where Bosch jotted this down, he wrote 'Layla?' after this entry.

After the dealers came Aliso's favorite sports book clerk. She was a mousy-looking bottle-blonde named Irma Chantry. She lit a cigarette as soon as she sat down and talked in a voice that indicated she had never gone long without a smoke. She said that on both of the last two nights Aliso had been in town he had bet on the Dodgers.

'He had a system,' she said. 'He always doubled up until he won.'

'How do you mean?'

'Well, that first night he put a grand down on the Dodgers to win. They lost. So the next day he comes in and puts down two big ones on them again. They won. So after you take out the casino vig, he was almost a grand up for the trip. Except he never picked it up.'

'He didn't collect?'

'Nope. But that's not unusual. His chit was good as long as he kept it. He could come in anytime and we'd stick it in the computer. It'd happened before. He'd win but he wouldn't collect until the next time he was in town.'

'How do you know he didn't take it to another clerk?'

'Tony wouldn't do that. He always cashed out with me, that way he could tip me. He always said I was his lucky charm.'

Bosch thought a moment. He knew the Dodgers had played at home Friday night and Aliso's plane left Las Vegas at ten. Therefore, it was a pretty safe bet that Aliso had to be at McCarran International or already on his plane heading back to L.A. before the game was over. But there was no betting receipt found in his wallet or on his person. Harry considered the missing briefcase again. Would it have been in there? Could a betting slip worth four thousand dollars minus the vig be motive for his murder? It seemed unlikely, but still, it was something to pursue. He looked at Irma, who was drawing so hard on her cigarette that he could see the outline of her teeth on her cheeks.

'What if somebody else cashed the bet? With another clerk. Is there any way to tell that?'

Irma hesitated and Meyer broke in.

'There's a good chance,' he said. 'Each receipt is coded with a clerk number and time the bet was placed.'

He looked at Irma.

'Irma, you remember taking very many two-thousand-dollar bets on the Dodgers on Friday?'

'Nope, not a one, other than Tony's.'

'We'll get on it,' Meyer said to Bosch. 'We'll start going through the cashed receipts going back to Friday night. If Mr Aliso's bet was cashed, then we'll know when it was cashed and we'll have video of who cashed it.'

Bosch looked at Irma again. She was the only one of the casino employees he had talked to who had referred to Aliso by his first name. He wanted to ask her if there was something more than a gambling relationship between them. But he knew that it was likely that employees were forbidden by the casino to date or fraternize with the guests. He couldn't ask her in front of Meyer and expect a straight reply. He made a mental note to track Irma down later and then excused her from the interview.

Bosch looked at his watch and saw he had forty minutes until the conference call with Billets and the others. He asked Meyer if he'd had a chance to get the surveillance tapes from the eye in the sky over the poker pit for Thursday and Friday.

'I just want to see the guy gambling,' he said. 'I want to get a feel for him in life.'

'I understand and, yes, the tapes are ready for viewing. I told you we wanted to cooperate completely.'

They left the office and walked down a corridor to a tech room. The room was dimly lit and very quiet except for the thrum of an air conditioner. There were six consoles arranged in two lines where men in gray blazers sat and watched banks of six video monitors per console. On the video screens Bosch could see various overhead views of gambling tables. Each console had an electronic control board that allowed the operator to change focus or magnification of a particular camera view.

'If they wanted to,' Meyer whispered, 'they could tell you what cards a player is holding at any black jack table in the house. It's amazing.'

Meyer led Bosch to a supervisor's office off the tech room. There was more video equipment as well as a bank of tape storage units. There was a small desk and another man in a gray blazer sat behind it. Meyer introduced him as Cal Smoltz, the supervisor.

'Cal, are we set up?'

'This screen here,' Smoltz said, pointing to one of the fifteen-inch monitors. 'We'll start with Thursday. I had one of the dealers come in and ID your guy. He shows up at eight-twenty on Thursday and plays until eleven.'

He started the tape. It was grainy black and white, similar

to the quality of the Archway surveillance tape, but this one was filmed in real time. No jerking movements. It began with the man Bosch recognized as Aliso being led to an open chair at a table by a pit boss. The pit boss carried a rack of chips which he put down on the table in front of Aliso's spot. Aliso nodded and exchanged smiles with the dealer, a woman Bosch had interviewed earlier, and began to play.

'How much in the rack?' Bosch asked.

'Five hundred,' Smoltz said. 'I've already gone through this on fast speed. He never buys another rack and at the end when he cashes out, he looks like he's just shy of a full rack. You want it on real time or fast speed?'

'Speed it up.'

Bosch watched closely as the tape sped through the hours. He saw Aliso take four gin and tonics, fold early on most of the deals, win five big pots and lose six others. It was pretty uneventful. Smoltz slowed the tape down when the time counter neared eleven, and Bosch watched as Aliso called for the pit boss, cashed out and left the frame of the camera.

'Okay,' Smoltz said. 'On Friday, we have two tapes.'

'How come?' Bosch asked.

'He played at two tables. When he first showed up, there wasn't a seat open at the five-and-dime table. We only have one because there aren't that many customers who want to play for those stakes. So he played on a one-to-five until something came open. This tape is the one-to-five, the cheaper table.'

Another video began and Bosch watched as Aliso went through the same motions as in the other tape. This time, Bosch noticed, Aliso was wearing the leather sports jacket. He also noticed that while Aliso exchanged the routine nod and smile with the dealer, he thought he saw Aliso nod at a player across the table. It was a woman and she nodded back. But the angle of the camera was bad and Bosch could not see her face. He told Smoltz to keep it on real-time play and he watched the tape for a few minutes, waiting to see if any other acknowledgment would pass between the two players.

It appeared that no further communication was occurring between the two. But five minutes into the tape a dealer rotation occurred, and when the new dealer sat down, also a woman Bosch had interviewed an hour earlier, she acknowledged both Aliso and the woman across the table from him.

'Can you freeze it there?' Bosch asked.

Without answering, Smoltz froze the image on the screen.

'Okay,' Bosch said. 'Which dealer is that?'

'That's Amy Rohrback. You talked to her.'

'Right. Hank, could you bring her back up here?'

'Uh, sure. Can I ask why?'

'This player,' Bosch said, pointing on the screen to the woman across from Aliso. 'She acknowledged Aliso when he sat down. Amy Rohrback just acknowledged her. She must be a regular. She knew Aliso and Rohrback. I might want to talk to her and your dealer might know her name.'

'Okay, I'll go get her, but if she's in the middle of a dealing rotation I'll have to wait.'

'That's fine.'

While Meyer went down to the casino, Bosch and Smoltz continued to review the tapes on fast speed. Aliso played for twenty-five minutes at the one-to-five table before the pit boss came around, picked up his rack of chips and moved him to the more expensive five-to-ten table. Smoltz put in the tape for that table and Aliso played there, losing miserably, for two more hours. Three times he bought five-hundred-dollar racks of chips and each time he quickly lost them. Finally, he put the few remaining chips he had left down as a tip for the dealer and got up and left the table.

The tape was finished and Meyer still hadn't returned with Rohrback. Smoltz said he would spool up the tape with the mystery woman on it so it would be ready. When it was, Bosch told him to fast-forward it to see if there was ever a moment when her face was visible. Smoltz did so and after five minutes of straining to watch the quick movements of the people on the tape, Bosch saw the mystery woman look up at the camera.

'There! Back it up and slow it down.'

Smoltz did so and Bosch watched the screen as the woman took out a cigarette, lit it and leaned her head back, her face toward the ceiling camera, and exhaled. The discharged smoke blurred her image. But before it had done so, Bosch thought he had recognized her. He was frozen to silence. Smoltz backed the tape up to the moment her face was most clearly visible and froze the image on the screen. Bosch just stared silently.

Smoltz was saying something about the image being the best they could hope for when the door opened and Meyer came back in. He was alone.

'Uh, Amy had just started a deal set, so it's going to be another ten minutes or so. I gave her the message to come back up.'

'You can call down there and tell her never mind,' Bosch said, his eyes still on the screen.

'Really? How come?'

'I know who she is.'

'Who is she?'

Bosch was silent a moment. He didn't know if it was seeing her light the cigarette or some pang of deeper anxiety, but he dearly wanted a cigarette.

'Just somebody. I knew her a long time ago.'

Bosch sat on the bed with the phone on his lap, waiting for the conference call. But his mind was far off. He was remembering a woman he had long believed was out of his life. What had it been now, four, five years? His mind was such a rush of thoughts and emotions, he couldn't remember for sure. It had been long enough, he realized. It should be no surprise that she was out of prison by now.

'Eleanor Wish,' he said out loud.

He thought of the jacaranda trees outside her townhouse in Santa Monica. He thought of them making love and the small crescent scar barely visible on her jawline. He remembered the question she had asked him so long ago, when they were making love. 'Do you believe you can be alone and not be lonely?'

The phone rang. Bosch jerked out of his reverie and answered. It was Billets.

'Okay, Harry, we're all here. Can you hear me all right?'

'It's not good but it probably won't get any better.'

'Right, city equipment. Okay, let's start by everybody kind of reporting on the day's events. Harry, you want to go first?'

'All right. There's not a lot to tell.'

He went over the details of what he had done so far, stressing the missing betting receipt as something to watch for. He told of his review of the surveillance tapes but left out mention of his recognizing Eleanor Wish. He had decided that there was no definitive sign of a connection between her and Aliso and that for the time being he would keep it to himself. He ended his summary by telling the others of his plans to check out Dolly's, the place Aliso had last called from his office line at Archway, and the woman named Layla who was mentioned when Bosch called there.

Next it was Edgar's turn. He announced the flavor-of-the-month screenwriter had been cleared through alibi and Edgar's own gut instinct that the young man might have rightfully hated Aliso but was not of the personality type that would act on that hate with a twenty-two.

Edgar said he had also interviewed the employees at the garage where Aliso had his car washed and waxed while he went to Las Vegas. Part of the service was airport pickup, and Edgar said the man who picked Aliso up said that Tony was alone, relaxed and in no hurry.

'It was a routine pickup,' Edgar said. 'Aliso took his car and went home. Gave the guy a twenty-buck tip. So whoever put him down, they intercepted him on the way home. My guess is it was somewhere up there on Mulholland. Lot of deserted curves. You could stop a guy if you did it quick. Probably two people.'

'What did the valet say about luggage?' Bosch asked.

'Oh, yeah,' Edgar said. 'He said that as near as he could remember, Tony had the two bags the wife described, a silver briefcase and one of those hanging bags. He hadn't checked either one for the flight.'

Bosch nodded, though he was alone.

'What about the media?' Bosch said. 'We put anything out yet?'

'It's being handled,' Billets said. 'Media relations is putting out a release first thing tomorrow. It will have a picture of the Rolls. They'll also make the car available at the OPG for video. And I'll be available for sound bites. I'm hoping the stations will pick it up. Anything else, Jerry?'

Edgar concluded by saying he had the murder book up to speed and that he was halfway through the list of plaintiffs from the various lawsuits against Aliso. He said he would be setting up interviews for the next day with others who had allegedly been wronged by Aliso. Lastly, he said he had called the coroner's office and the autopsy on Aliso had not yet been scheduled.

'Okay,' Billets said. 'Kiz, what do you have?'

Rider broke her report into two parts. The first was on her interview with Veronica Aliso, which she covered quickly, saying the woman had been extremely close-mouthed during their morning interview in comparison to the night before when Bosch and Rider brought her the news of her husband's death. The morning session consisted mostly of yes and no answers and a few added details. The couple had been married seventeen years. They had no children. Veronica Aliso had been in two of her husband's films and never worked again.

'You think she talked to a lawyer about talking to us?' Bosch asked.

'She didn't say so, but I think that's exactly what's going on,' Rider said. 'Just getting what I got was like pulling teeth.'

'Okay, what else?' Billets said, trying to keep the discussion moving.

Rider went on to the second part of her day's investigation, which was the focus on the financial records of Anthony Aliso. Even listening on the poor conference line connection, Bosch could tell Kiz was excited about what she had learned so far.

'Basically, this guy's financial portfolio shows an extremely comfortable standard of living. He's got high-five-figure sums in his personal bank accounts, zeroed-out credit cards, that house that has a seven-hundred-thousand mortgage against a value of a million one. That's it, though, as far as what I could find. The Rolls is leased, his wife's Lincoln is leased, and the office we know is leased.'

She paused a moment before going on.

'Incidentally, Harry, if you have the time, here's something you might want to check out over there. Both the cars are leased to his company, TNA Productions, through a dealership over there in Vegas. You might want to check it out if there's time. It's called Ridealong – one word – Incorporated. The address is two thousand and two Industrial Drive, suite three-thirty.'

Bosch's jacket, with his notebook inside it, was on a chair on the other side of the room. He wrote the name and address down on a little pad that was on the night table.

'Okay,' Rider said, 'so now we go on to his business, and this is where it gets pretty interesting. I'm really only halfway through the records we pulled out of his office, but so far it looks like this guy was into a class A scam. And I'm not talking about ripping off some schmuck's student screenplays. I think that was just his side hobby. I'm talking about him running a laundry. I think he was a front for somebody.'

She waited a beat before going on. Bosch moved to the edge of the bed, excitement tickling the back of his neck.

'We've got tax returns, production orders, equipment rentals, pays and owes from the making of several films – more than a dozen. All of it straight-to-video stuff. Like Veronica said, it's just this side of porno. I looked at some of the tapes he had in his office and it was all pretty awful stuff. Not much in the way of narrative unless you count the buildup of tension waiting for the female lead to get naked.

'The only problem is that the ledgers don't match what's on the film and most of the big checks paid by TNA Productions went to mail drops and companies that I'm finding out don't exist anywhere but on paper.'

'How do you mean?' Billets asked.

'I'm saying his business records show a million to a million five going into each of these so-called movies, and you look at the tapes and, I'm telling you, there can't be more than a hundred, maybe two hundred thousand involved. My brother works in the business as an editor, and I know enough to know that the kind of money Aliso's books show being spent on these movies is not being spent on these movies. I think that what he was doing was using these flicks to launder money, lots of money.'

'Run it down, Kiz,' Billets said. 'Just how would he do it?'

'Okay, start with his source. We'll call him Mr X for now. Mr X has a million bucks he shouldn't have. Whether it's from drugs or whatever, he needs to clean it up, legitimize it so he can put it in the bank and spend it without drawing attention. He gives it to Tony Aliso – invests it in Tony's production company. Aliso then makes a cheap movie with it, spending less than a tenth of it.

'But when it comes to keeping the books, he makes it look like he's used all of the money for production costs. He's got checks going out almost weekly to various production companies, prop companies, movie equipment companies. All the checks are in the eight- to nine-thousand range, just under the government reporting limit.'

Bosch listened carefully as she spoke. He had his eyes closed and concentrated. He admired Rider's ability to cull all of this out of the records.

'Okay, then at the end of production, Tony probably dubs a few thousand copies of the flick, sells them or tries to sell them to independent video stores and distributors – because the chains wouldn't touch this crap – and that's that, end of show. But what he has done is turned around and given back to Mr X, his original investor, about eighty cents on the dollar in the form of payments to these dummy companies. It's a shell game. Whoever is behind these companies is being paid with his own money for services *not* rendered. But now the money's legit. It's clean and he can walk into any bank in America and deposit it, pay taxes on it, then spend it. Meantime, Tony Aliso takes a nice production fee for his end of it and goes on to the next flick. It looks like he was handling two or three of these productions a year and clearing half a million in fees himself.'

They were all silent for a few moments before Rider spoke again.

'There's only one problem,' Rider said.

'He's got the IRS on him,' Bosch said.

'Riiiiight,' she responded, and he could visualize the smile on her face. 'It's a nice scam but it was about to go down the toilet. The IRS was going to take a look at Tony's books later this month, and there is a good chance that if I could come up with this in just one day, the feds would pick up on it in an hour.'

'That would make Tony a danger to Mr X,' Edgar said.

'Especially if he was going to cooperate with the audit,' Rider added.

Someone on the other end of the line whistled, but Bosch couldn't tell who it was. He guessed it was Edgar.

'So what's next, find Mr X?' Bosch asked.

'For starters,' Rider replied. 'I'm working up a request I'll fax to the state department of corporations tomorrow morning. It's got all the dummy companies on it. Maybe, whoever he is, he was foolish enough to put a real name or address on the incorporation forms. I'm also working on another search warrant. I have the canceled checks from Tony's company. I want the records of the accounts the checks were deposited to, maybe find out where the money went after Tony cleaned it up.'

'What about the IRS?' Bosch asked. 'Have you talked to them?'

'They're closed for the holiday. But according to the notice Aliso got in the mail, there is a criminal prefix on the audit number. That makes me think this wasn't a random audit. They were tipped somehow. There's an agent assigned to it and I'll be on the phone to him first thing in the morning.'

'You know,' Edgar said, 'this whole thing about OCID taking a pass is beginning to stink. Whether Tony was hooked up with the Eye-talians or not, this shit is as organized as organized crime can get. And I'd bet my last button that they'd heard somewhere along the line, whether it was from the IRS or not, about our guy here.'

'I think you're right,' Billets said.

'I forgot to mention something,' Bosch threw in. 'Today I was talking with Art Donovan. He said the guy I talked to at OCID last night, a supe named Carbone, well he just happens to show up over at SID today and starts asking Art about the case. Art says the guy's acting like he's not interested, but he's very interested, you know what I mean?'

Nobody said anything for a long moment.

'So what do we do?' Edgar asked.

Bosch closed his eyes again and waited. Whatever Billets said would determine the course of the case as well as affect his regard for her. Bosch knew what her predecessor would have done. He would have made sure the case was dumped on OCID.

'We don't do anything,' Billets finally said. 'It's our case, we work it. But be careful. If OCID is sniffing around after taking a pass, then there is something going on here we don't know about yet.'

Another silence passed and Bosch opened his eyes. He was liking Billets better all the time.

'Okay,' Billets said. 'I think we should be focusing on Tony's company as a priority. I want to shift most of our attention there. Harry, can you wrap up Vegas quickly and get back here?'

'Unless I find something, I should be out of here before lunch tomorrow. But remember this, last night Mrs Aliso told us that Tony always told her he came to Vegas to see investors. Maybe our Mr X is right here.'

'Could be,' Billets said. 'Okay then, again, people, it's been good work. Let's stay on it.'

They said their good-byes and Bosch put the phone back on the side table. He felt invigorated by the advances of the investigation. He just sat there a moment and reveled in the feeling of the adrenaline jazzing through his body. It had been a long time coming. He squeezed his hands into fists and banged them together.

Bosch stepped out of the elevator and began moving through the casino. It was quieter than most casinos he had been in – there wasn't any yelling or whooping from the craps table, no begging of the dice to come up seven. The people who gambled here were different, Bosch thought. They came with money and they'd leave with money no matter how much they lost. The smell of desperation wasn't here. This was the casino for the well-heeled and thick-walleted.

He passed by a crowded roulette wheel and remembered Donovan's bet. He squeezed between two smoking Asian women, put down a five and asked for a chip but was told it was a twenty-five-dollar-minimum table. One of the Asians pointed with her cigarette across the casino to another roulette table.

'They'll take your five over there,' she said with distaste.

Bosch thanked her and headed over to the cheap table. He put a five chip down on the seven and watched the wheel turn, the little metal ball bouncing over the numbers. It did nothing for him. He knew that true-blue gamblers said it wasn't the winning and losing, it was the anticipation. Whether it was the next card, the fall of the dice or the number the little ball stopped on, it was those few seconds of waiting and hoping and wishing that charged them, that addicted them. But it did nothing for Bosch.

The ball stopped on five and Donovan owed Bosch five. Bosch turned and started looking for the poker pit. He saw a sign and headed that way. It was early, not yet eight, and there were several chairs open at the tables. He checked the faces and did not see Eleanor Wish, though he wasn't really expecting to. Bosch recognized many of the dealers he had interviewed earlier, including Amy Rohrback. He was tempted to take one of the empty chairs at her table and ask how she had recognized Eleanor Wish but figured it wouldn't be cool to question her while she worked.

While he considered what to do, the pit boss stepped up to him and asked if he was waiting to play. Bosch recognized him as the one from the video who had led Tony Aliso to his place at the tables.

'No, I'm just watching,' Bosch said. 'You got a minute while it's slow?'

'A minute for what?'

'I'm the cop who's been interviewing your people.'

'Oh, yeah. Little Hank told me about that.'

He introduced himself as Frank King and Bosch shook his hand.

'Sorry, I couldn't come up. But I don't work on rotation. I had to be here. This is about Tony A, right?'

'Yeah, you knew him, right?'

'Sure, we all knew him. Good guy. Too bad about what happened.'

'How do you know what happened?'

Bosch had specifically not told any of the dealers about Aliso's demise during the interviews.

'Little Hank,' King said. 'He said he got shot up or something in L.A. What do you want, I mean you live in L.A. you take your chances.'

'I guess. How long have you known him?'

'We go back years, me and Tony. I used to be at the Flamingo before the Mirage opened. Tony stayed there back then. He's been coming out here a long time.'

'You ever socialize with him? Outside the casino?'

'Once or twice. But that was usually by accident. I'd be some place and Tony'd just happen to come in or something. We'd have a drink, be cordial, but that was about it. I mean, he was a guest of the hotel and I'm an employee. We weren't buddies, if you know what I mean.'

'I get it. What places did you run into him?'

'Oh, Jesus, I don't know. You're talking – hold on a sec.'

King cashed out a player who was leaving Amy Rohrback's table. Bosch had no idea how much the man had started with, but he was leaving with forty dollars and a frown. King sent him away with a better-luck-next-time salute and then came back to Bosch.

'Like I was saying, I saw him in a couple of bars. You're talking a long time ago. One was the round bar at the Stardust. One of my buddies was the barkeep and I used to drop by there after work time to time. I saw Tony there and he sent over a drink. This was probably three years ago, at least. I don't know what good it does you.'

'Was he alone?'

'No, he was with some broad. Young piece of fluff. Nobody I recognized.'

'All right, what about the other time, when was that?'

'That was maybe last year sometime. I was with a bachelor party – it was for Marty, who runs the craps here – and we all went to get straightened out at Dolly's. It's a strip club on the north side. And Tony was in there, too. He was by hisself and he came over and had a drink. In fact, he bought the whole table a drink. Must've been eight of us. He was a nice guy. That was it.'

Bosch nodded. So Aliso had been a regular at Dolly's going back at least a year. Bosch was planning to go there, to get a line on the woman named Layla. She was probably a dancer, Bosch guessed, and Layla was more than probably not her real name.

'You seen him more recently with anybody?'

'You mean a broad?'

'Yeah, some of the dealers said there was a blonde recently.'

'Yeah, I think I saw him a couple, three times with the blonde. He was giving her the dough to play the machines while he played cards. I don't know who it was, if that's what you mean.'

Bosch nodded.

'That it?' King asked.

'One more thing. Eleanor Wish, you know her? She was playing the cheap table on Friday night. Tony played for a while at the same table. It looked like they knew each other.'

'I know a player named Eleanor. I never knew her last name. She the looker, brown hair, brown eyes, still in nice shape despite, as they say, the encroachment of time?'

King smiled at his clever use of words. Bosch didn't.

'That sounds like her. She a regular?'

'Yeah, I see her in here maybe once a week, maybe less. She's a local, as far as I know. The local players run a circuit. Not all the casinos have live poker, see. It doesn't earn a lot for the house. We have it as a courtesy to our customers, but we hope they play a little poker and a lot of black jack. Anyway, the locals run a circuit so they don't play against the same faces all the time. So they maybe play here one night, over to Harrah's the next, then it's the Flamingo, then maybe they work the downtown casinos a few nights. You know, like that.'

'You mean she's a pro?'

'No, I mean she's a local and she plays a lot. Whether she's got a day job or lives off poker I don't know. I don't think I ever cashed her out for more than two bills. That's not a lot. The other thing is I heard she tips the dealers too well. The pros don't do that.'

Bosch asked King to list all the casinos in the city that he knew offered live poker, then thanked him.

'You know, I doubt you're going to find anything other than Tony knowin' her to say hello to, that's all.'

'Why's that?'

'Too old. She's a nice lookin' gal, but she was too old for Tony. He liked 'em young.'

Bosch nodded and let him go. He then wandered through the casino in a quandary. He didn't know what to do about Eleanor Wish. He was intrigued by what she was doing and King's explanation about her being a once-a-week regular seemed to make her recognition of Aliso innocent enough. But while she most likely had nothing to do with the case, Bosch felt the desire to talk to her. To tell her he was sorry for the ways things had turned out, for the way he had made them turn out.

He saw a bank of pay phones near the front desk and used one to call information. He asked for a listing for Eleanor Wish and got a recording saying the phone number was unlisted at the customer's request. Bosch thought a moment and then dug through the pocket of his jacket. He found the card that Felton, the Metro detectives captain, had given him and paged him. He waited with his hand on the phone so no one else could use it for four minutes before it rang.

'Felton?'

'Yeah, who's this?'

'Bosch. From earlier today?'

'Right. L.A. I still haven't gotten the prints back. I'm expecting to hear something first thing.'

'No, I'm not calling about that. I was wondering if you or any of your people have enough juice with the phone company to get me a listing, number and address.'

'It's unlisted?'

Bosch felt like telling him that he wouldn't be calling if the account was listed but let it go.

'Yeah, unlisted.'

'Who is it?'

'A local. Somebody who was playing poker with Tony Aliso on Friday night.'

'So?'

'So, Captain, they knew each other and I want to talk to her. If you can't help me, fine. I'll find her some other way. I was calling because you told me to call if I needed something. This is what I need. Can you do it or not?'

There was silence for a few moments before Felton came back.

'Okay, give it to me. I'll see what I can get. Where you going to be?'

'I'm mobile. Can I ring you back?'

Felton gave him his home number and told him to call back in a half hour.

Bosch used the time to walk across the Strip to Harrah's to check out the poker room. Eleanor Wish wasn't there. He then went back out onto the Strip and headed down to the Flamingo. He took his jacket off because it was still very warm out. It would be dark soon and he hoped it would cool off then.

In the Flamingo casino he found her. She was playing at a one-to-four table with five men. The seat on her left was open but Bosch didn't take it. Instead, he hung back with the crowd around a roulette table and watched her.

Eleanor Wish's face showed total concentration on the cards as she played. Bosch watched as the men she was playing against stole looks at her, and it gave Bosch a weird thrill to know they secretly coveted her. In the ten minutes he watched, she won one hand – he was too far away to see what she won with – and bailed out early on five others. It looked as though she was well ahead. She had a full rack in front of her and six stacks of chips on the blue felt.

After he watched her win a second hand – this time a massive pot – and the dealer began to push the pile of blue chips to her spot, Bosch looked around for a pay phone. He called Felton at home and got Wish's home phone and address. The captain told him that the address, on Sands Avenue, was not far off the strip in an area of apartment buildings mostly inhabited by casino employees. Bosch didn't tell him that he had already found her. Instead, he thanked him and hung up.

When Bosch got back to the poker room she was gone. The five men were still there, but there was a new dealer and no Eleanor Wish. Her chips were gone. She had cashed out and he had lost her. Bosch cursed to himself.

'You looking for someone?'

Bosch turned around. It was Eleanor. There was no smile on her face, just a slight look of irritation or maybe defiance. His eyes fell to the small white scar on her jawline.

'I, uh . . . Eleanor . . . yeah, I was looking for you.'

'You were always so obvious. I picked you out one minute after you were there. I would've gotten up then but I was bringing that guy from Kansas along. He thought he knew when I was bluffing. He didn't know shit. Just like you.'

Bosch was tongue-tied. This was not how he had envisioned this happening and he didn't know how to proceed.

'Look, Eleanor, I, uh, just wanted to see how you were doing. I don't know, I just . . .'

'Right. So you just flew out to Vegas to look me up? What's going on, Bosch?'

Bosch looked around. They were standing in a crowded section of the casino. Players passing on both sides of them, the cacophony of the slot machine din and whoops of success and failure created a blur of sight and sound around him.

'I'll tell you. Do you want to get a drink or something, maybe something to eat?'

'One drink.'

'You know a place that's quiet?'

'Not here. Follow me.'

They left through the front doors of the casino and walked out into the dry heat of the night. The sun was all the way down now and it was neon that lit the sky.

'There's a bar in Caesar's that's quiet. It doesn't have any machines.'

She led him across the street and onto the people mover that delivered them to the front door of Caesar's Palace. They walked past the front desk and into a circular bar where there were only three other customers. Eleanor had been right. It was an oasis with no poker or slot machines. Just the bar. He ordered a beer and she ordered scotch and water. She lit a cigarette.

'You didn't used to smoke before,' he said. 'In fact, I remember you were—'

'That was a long time ago. Why are you here?'

'I'm on a case.'

During the walk over he'd had time to compose himself and put his thoughts in order.

'What case and what does it have to do with me?'

'It's got nothing to do with you, but you knew the guy. You played poker with him on Friday at the Mirage.'

Curiosity and confusion creased her brow. Bosch remembered how she used to do that and remembered how attractive he'd found it. He wanted to reach over and touch her but he didn't. He had to remind himself that she was different now.

'Anthony Aliso,' he said.

He watched the surprise play on her face and believed instantly that it was real. He wasn't a poker player from Kansas who couldn't read a bluff. He had known this woman and believed from the look on her face she clearly did not know Aliso was dead until he told her.

'Tony A . . .,' she said and then let it trail off.

'Did you know him well or just to play against?'

She had a distant look in her dark eyes.

'Just when I'd see him there. At the Mirage. I've been playing there on Fridays. A lot of fresh money and faces come in. I'd see him there a couple times a month. For a while I thought he was a local, too.'

'How'd you find out he wasn't?'

'He told me. We had a drink together a couple months ago. There were no seats at the tables. We put our names in and told Frank, he's the night man, to come get us at the bar when there was an opening. So we had a drink and that's when he told me he was from L.A. He said he was in the movie business.'

'That's it, nothing else?'

'Well, yeah, he said other things. We talked. Nothing that stands out, though. We were passing the time until one of our names came up.'

'You didn't see him again outside of playing?'

'No, and what's it to you? Are you saying I'm a suspect because I had a drink with the guy?'

'No, I'm not saying that, Eleanor. Not at all.'

Bosch got out his own cigarettes and lit one. The waitress in a white-and-gold toga brought their drinks, and they settled into a silence for a long moment. Bosch had lost his momentum. He was back to not knowing what to say.

'Looked like you were doing pretty good tonight,' he tried.

'Better than most nights. I got my quota and I got out.'

'Quota?'

'Whenever I get two hundred up I cash out. I'm not greedy and I know luck doesn't last for long on any given night. I never lose more than a hundred, and if I'm lucky enough to get two hundred ahead, then I'm done for the night. I got there early tonight.'

'How'd you—'

He stopped himself. He knew the answer.

'How'd I learn to play poker well enough to live off it?

You spend three and a half years inside and you learn to smoke and play poker and other things.'

She looked directly at him as if daring him to say anything about it. After another long moment she broke away and got out another cigarette. Bosch lit it for her.

'So there's no day job? Just the poker?'

'That's right. I've been doing this almost a year now. Kind of hard to find a straight job, Bosch. You tell 'em you're a former FBI agent and their eyes light up. Then you tell them you just got out of federal prison and they go dead.'

'I'm sorry, Eleanor.'

'Don't be. I'm not complaining. I make more than enough to get by, every now and then I meet interesting people like your guy Tony A, and there's no state income tax here. What do I have to complain about, except maybe that it gets to be over a hundred degrees in the shade about ninety times a year too many?'

The bitterness was not lost on him.

'I mean I'm sorry about everything. I know it doesn't do you any good now, but I wish I had it to do all over again. I've learned things since then, and I would've played it all differently. That's all I wanted to tell you. I saw you on the surveillance tape playing with Tony Aliso and I wanted to find you to tell you that. That's all I wanted.'

She stubbed her half-finished smoke out in the glass ashtray and took a strong pull on her glass of scotch.

'I guess I should be going, then,' she said.

She stood up.

'Do you need a ride anywhere?'

'No, I actually have a car, thank you.'

She started out of the bar in the direction of the front doors but after a few yards stopped and came back to the table.

'You're right, you know.'

'About what?'

'About it not doing me any good now.'

With that she left. Bosch watched her push through the revolving doors and disappear into the night.

Following the directions he had written down when he spoke with Rhonda over the phone in Tony Aliso's office, Bosch found Dolly's on Madison in North Las Vegas. It was strictly an upper-crust club: twenty-dollar cover, two-drink minimum and you were escorted to your seat by a large man in a tuxedo with a starched collar that cut into his neck like a garrote. The dancers were upper-crust, too. Young and beautiful, they probably were just shy of having enough coordination and talent to work the big room shows on the Strip.

Bosch was led by the tuxedo to a table the size of a dinner plate about eight feet from the main stage, which was empty at the moment.

'A new dancer will be on stage in a couple of minutes,' the man in the tuxedo told Bosch. 'Enjoy the show.'

Bosch didn't know if he was supposed to tip the guy for seating him at such a close-up location as well as putting up with the tuxedo, but he let it go and the man didn't hang around with his hand out. Bosch had barely gotten his cigarettes out when a waitress in a red silk negligee, high heels and black fishnet stockings floated over and reminded him of the two-drink minimum. Bosch ordered beer.

While he waited for his two beers, Bosch took a look around. Business seemed slow, it being the Monday night tail-end of a holiday weekend. There were maybe twenty men in the place. Most of them were sitting by themselves and not looking at each other while they waited for the next nude woman to entertain them.

There were full-length mirrors on the side and rear walls. A bar ran along the left side of the room, and cut into the wall in the back was an arched entrance above which a red neon sign that glowed in the darkness announced PRIVATE DANCERS. The front wall was largely taken up by a shimmering curtain and the stage. A runway projected from the stage through the center of the room. The runway was the focus of several bright lights attached to a metal gridwork on the ceiling. Their brightness made the runway almost glow in contrast to the dark and smoky atmosphere of the seating area.

A disk jockey in a sound booth at the left side of the stage announced the next dancer would be Randy. An old Eddie Money song, 'Two Tickets to Paradise,' started blaring over the sound system as a tall brunette wearing blue jeans cut off to expose the lower half of her bottom and a neon pink bikini top charged through the shimmering curtain and started moving to the beat of the music.

Bosch was immediately mesmerized. The woman was beautiful and the first thought he had was to question why she was doing this. He had always believed that beauty helped women get away from many of the hardships of life. This woman, this girl, was beautiful and yet here she was. Maybe that was the real draw for these men, he thought. Not the glimpse of a naked woman, but the knowledge of submission, the thrill of knowing another one had been broken. Bosch began to think he had been wrong about beautiful women.

The waitress put down two beers on the little table and told Bosch he owed fifteen dollars. He almost asked her to repeat the price but then figured it came with the territory. He handed her a twenty, and when she started digging through the stack of bills on her tray for his change he waved it off.

She clutched at his shoulder and bent down to his ear, making sure that she was at an angle that afforded him a look at her full cleavage.

'Thank you, darlin'. I 'preciate that. Let me know if you need anything else.'

'There is one thing. Is Layla here tonight?'

'No, she's not here.'

Bosch nodded. And the waitress straightened up.

'How about Rhonda then?' Bosch asked.

'That's Randy up there.'

She pointed to the stage and Bosch shook his head and signaled her to come closer.

'No, Rhonda, like help, help me Rhonda. She working tonight? She was here last night.'

'Oh, that Rhonda. Yeah, she's around. You just missed her set. She's probably in the back changing.'

Bosch reached into his pocket for his money and put a five on her bar tray.

'Will you go back and tell her the friend of Tony's she talked to last night wants to buy her a drink?'

'Sure.'

She squeezed his shoulder again and went off. Bosch's attention was drawn to the stage, where Randy's first song had just ended. The next song was 'Lawyers, Guns and Money' by Warren Zevon. Bosch hadn't heard it in a while and he remembered how it had been an anthem among the uniforms back when he had worked patrol.

The dancer named Randy soon slipped out of her outfit and was nude except for a garter stretched tightly around her left thigh. Many of the men got up and met her as she danced her way slowly down the runway. They slid dollar bills under the garter. And when a man put a five under the strap, Randy bent down over him, using his shoulder to steady herself, and did an extra wiggle and kissed his ear.

Bosch watched this and was thinking that he now had a pretty good idea how Tony Aliso ended up with the small handprint on his shoulder, when a petite blond woman slid into the seat next to him.

'Hi. I'm Rhonda. You missed my show!'

'I heard that. I'm sorry.'

'Well, I go back on in a half hour and do it all over again. I hope you'll stay. Yvonne said you wanted to buy me a drink?'

As if on cue Bosch saw the waitress heading their way. Bosch leaned over to Rhonda.

'Listen, Rhonda, I'd rather take care of you than give my money to the bar. So do me a favor and don't go exorbitant on me.'

'Exorbitant . . .'

She crinkled her face up in a question.

'Don't go ordering champagne.'

'Oh, I gotcha.'

She ordered a martini and Yvonne floated back into the darkness.

'So, I didn't catch your name.'

'Harry.'

'And you're a friend of Tony's from L.A. You make movies, too?'

'No, not really.'

'How do you know Tony?'

'I just met him recently. Listen, I'm trying to find Layla to get a message to her. Yvonne tells me she's not on tonight. You know where I can find her?'

Bosch noticed her stiffen. She knew something wasn't right.

'First of all, Layla doesn't work here anymore. I didn't know that when I talked to you last night, but she's gone and won't be back. And secondly, if you're a friend of Tony's, then how come you're asking me how to find her?'

She wasn't as dumb as Bosch had thought. He decided to go direct.

'Because Tony got himself killed, so I can't ask him. I want to find Layla to tell her and maybe warn her.'

'*What?*' she shrieked.

Her voice cut through the loud music like a bullet through a slice of bread. Everybody in the place, including the naked Randy on the stage, looked in their direction. Bosch had no doubt that everyone in the place must think he had just propositioned her, offering an insulting fee for an equally insulting act.

'Keep it down, Randy,' he quickly said.

'It's Rhonda.'

'Rhonda then.'

'What happened to him? He was just here.'

'Somebody shot him in L.A. when he got back. Now, do you know where Layla is or not? You tell me and I'll take care of you.'

'Well, what are you? Are you really his friend or not?'

'In a way I'm his only friend right now. I'm a cop. My name's Harry Bosch and I'm trying to find out who did it.'

Her face took on a look that seemed even more horrified than when he told her Aliso was dead. Sometimes telling people you were a cop did that.

'Save your money,' she said. 'I can't talk to you.'

She got up then and moved quickly away toward the door next to the stage. Bosch threw her name out after her but it was crushed by the sound of the music. He casually took a look around and noticed behind him that the tuxedo man was eyeing him through the darkness. Bosch decided he wasn't going to stick around for Rhonda's second show. He took one more gulp of beer – he hadn't even touched his second glass – and got up.

As he neared the exit the tuxedo leaned back and knocked on the mirror behind him. It was then that Bosch realized there was a door cut into the glass. It opened and the tuxedo stepped to the side to block Bosch's exit.

'Sir, could you step into the office, please?'

'What for?'

'Just step in. The manager would like a word with you.'

Bosch hesitated but through the door he could see a lighted office where a man in a suit sat behind a desk. He stepped in and the tuxedo came in behind him and shut the door.

Bosch looked at the man behind the desk. Blond and beefy. Bosch wouldn't know whom to bet on if a fight broke out between the tuxedoed bouncer and the so-called manager. They were both brutes.

'I just got off the phone with Randy in the dressing room, she says you were asking about Tony Aliso.'

'It was Rhonda.'

'Rhonda, whatever, never-the-fuck-mind. She said you said he was dead.'

He spoke with a midwestern accent. Sounded like southside Chicago, Bosch guessed.

'Was and still is.'

The blond nodded to the tuxedo and his arm came up in a split second and hit Bosch with a backhand in the mouth. Bosch went back against the wall, banging the back of his head. Before his mind cleared, the tuxedo twirled him around until he was face-against-the-wall and leaned his weight against him. He felt the man's hands begin patting him down.

'Enough of the wiseass act,' the blond said. 'What are you doing talking to the girls about Tony?'

Before Bosch could say anything the hands running over his body found his gun.

'He's strapped,' the tuxedo said.

Bosch felt the gun being jerked out of his shoulder holster. He also tasted blood in his mouth and felt rage building in his throat. The hands then found his wallet and his cuffs. Tuxedo threw them on the desk in front of the blond and held Bosch pinned against the wall with one hand. By straining to turn his head Bosch could watch the blond open the wallet.

'He's a cop, let him go.'

The hand came off his neck and Bosch gruffly pulled away from the tuxedo.

'An L.A. cop,' the blond said. 'Hieronymus Bosch. Like that painter, huh? He did some weird stuff.'

Bosch just looked at him and he handed the gun and cuffs and wallet back.

'Why'd you have him hit me?'

'That was a mistake. See, most cops what come in here, they announce themselves, they tell us their business and we help 'em if we can. You were sneaking around, Anonymous Hieronymus. We have a business to protect here.'

He opened a drawer and pulled out a box of tissues and proffered it to Bosch.

'Your lip's bleeding.'

Bosch took the whole box.

'So this is true what she says you told her. Tony's dead.'

'That's what I said. How well did you know him?'

'See, that's good. You assume I knew him and put that assumption in your question. That's good.'

'So then answer it.'

'He was a regular in here. He was always trying to pick off girls. Told 'em he'd put 'em in the movies. Same old stuff. But, hell, they keep falling for it. Last two years he cost me three of my best girls. They're in L.A. now. He left 'em high and dry once he got them there and did what he wanted with 'em. They never learn.'

'Why'd you let him keep coming in if he was picking off your girls?'

'He spent a lot of bread in here. Besides, there's no shortage of quiff here in Vegas. No shortage at all.'

Bosch headed in another direction.

'What about Friday? Was he here?'

'No, I don't – yes, yes he was. He stopped by for a short while. I saw him out there.'

With his hand he indicated a panel of video monitors showing every angle of the club and front entrance. It was equally as impressive as the setup Hank Meyer had shown Bosch at the Mirage.

'You remember seeing him, Gussie?' the blond asked the tuxedo.

'Yeah, he was here.'

'There you go. He was here.'

'No problems? He just came and went?'

'Right, no problems.'

'Then why'd you fire Layla?'

The blond pinched his lips tight for a moment.

'Now I get it,' he said. 'You're one of those guys what likes to weave a web with words, get somebody caught in it.'

'Maybe.'

'Well, nobody's caught anywhere. Layla was Tony's latest fuck, that's true, but she's gone now. She won't be back.'

'Yeah, and what happened to her?'

'Like you heard, I fired her. Saturday night.'

'For what?'

'For any number of infractions of the rules. But it doesn't really matter because it's none of your business, now is it?'

'What did you say your name is?'

'I didn't.'

'Then how 'bout if I just call you asshole, how would that be?'

'People 'round here call me Lucky. Can we get on with this, please?'

'Sure, we can get on with it. Just tell me what happened to Layla.'

'Sure, sure. But I thought you were here to talk about Tony, least that's what Randy said.'

'Rhonda.'

'Rhonda, right.'

Bosch was losing his patience but managed to just stare at him and wait him out.

'Layla, right. Well, Saturday night she got into a beef with one of the other girls. It got a little nasty and I had to make a choice. Modesty is one of my best girls, best producers. She gave me an ultimatum: either Layla goes or she goes. I had to let Layla go. Modesty, man, she sells ten, twelve splits of champagne a night to those suckers out there. I had to back her over Layla. I mean, Layla's good and she's a looker but she ain't no Modesty. Modesty's our top girl.'

Bosch just nodded. So far his story jibed with the phone message Layla had left for Aliso. By drawing it out of the blond man, Bosch was getting a sense of how much he could be believed.

'What was the trouble between Layla and the other girl about?' he asked.

'I don't know and don't really care. Just your typical catfight. They didn't like each other since day one. See, Bosch, every club has its top girl. And here, it's Modesty. Layla was trying to move in on that and Modesty didn't want to be moved in on. But I have to say, Layla was trouble since she came here. None of the girls liked her act. She stole songs from the other girls, wouldn't stop with the pussy dust even when I told her, we just had a lot of trouble with her. I'm glad she's gone. I gotta business to run here. I can't be babysitting a bunch of spoiled cunts.'

'Pussy dust?'

'Yeah, you know, she put that sparkly stuff on her snatch, made it sparkle in the dark and twinkled in the lights. Only problem is those sparkles come off and get on the suckers. She does a lap dance on you and *you* end up with a crotch that glitters. Then you go home and the wife figures it out and raises holy hell. I lose customers. I can't have that shit, Bosch. If it hadn't been Modesty, it would have been something else. I got rid of Layla when I got the chance.'

Bosch thought about the story for a few moments.

'Okay,' he said. 'Just give me her address and I'll be on my way.'

'I would but I can't.'

'Don't start that shit now. I thought we were having a conversation. Let me see your payroll records. There's got to be an address.'

The man called Lucky smiled and shook his head.

'Payroll? We don't pay these broads a dime. They ought to pay us. Comin' in here, it's a license to make money.'

'You must have a phone number or an address. You want your man Gussie here to go down to Metro on an assaulting-a-police-officer clip?'

'We don't have her address, Bosch, what can I tell you? Or her phone number.'

He held his hands out, palms up.

'I mean, I don't have addresses on any of the girls. I set a schedule and they come in and dance. They don't show, they aren't allowed back. See, it's nice and simple, streamlined, that way. It's the way we do it. And as far as the assault thing goes with Gussie, if you want to do that dance we'll do it. But remember you're the guy what came in here by hisself, never said who you were or what you wanted to nobody, had four beers in less than an hour and insulted one of the dancers before we asked you to leave. We can have affidavits to that effect in an hour.'

He raised his arms again, this time in a hands-off manner as if to say it was Bosch's call. Bosch had no doubt that Yvonne and Rhonda would tell the story they were told to tell. He decided to cut his losses. He smiled glibly.

'Have a good night,' he said and turned to the door.

'You, too, Officer,' Lucky said to his back. 'Come back when you have time and can enjoy the show.'

The door opened by some unseen electronic means apparently controlled from the desk. Gussie allowed Bosch to leave first. He then followed behind as Bosch went through the main door to the valet stand. Bosch gave a Mexican man with a face like a crumpled paper lunch bag his parking stub. He and Gussie then waited in silence for the car to be brought up.

'No hard feelings, right?' Gussie finally said as the car was approaching. 'I didn't know you was a cop.'

Bosch turned to face him.

'No, you just thought I was a customer.'

'Yeah, right. And I had to do what the boss told me to do.'

He put his hand out. In his peripheral vision Bosch could see his car still coming. He took Gussie's hand and in a sharp move pulled the big man toward him at the same time he raised his knee and drove it into his groin. Gussie let out an *oomph* and doubled over. Bosch let go of his hand and quickly jerked the tail of the man's jacket up over his head, pinning his arms in the tangle. Finally, he brought his knee up into the jacket and felt it connect solidly with Gussie's face. The big man fell forward onto the hood of a black Corvette parked near the door just as the valet jumped out of Bosch's rental car and came scrambling around to defend his boss. The man was older and smaller than Bosch. This one wouldn't even be close and Bosch wasn't interested in any innocent bystanders. He held his finger up to stop the man.

'Don't,' he said.

The man considered his situation while Gussie groaned through his tuxedo jacket. Finally, the valet raised his hands and stepped back, allowing Bosch a path to the car door.

'At least somebody around here makes the right choices,' Bosch said as he slid in.

He looked through the windshield and saw Gussie's body slide down the slope of the Corvette's hood and fall to the pavement. The valet ran to his side.

As Bosch pulled out onto Madison, he checked the rearview mirror. The valet was pulling the jacket back over Gussie's head. Bosch could see blood on the bouncer's white shirt.

Bosch was too keyed up to go back to the hotel to sleep. He also had a bad mix of emotions weighing on him. Seeing the naked woman dancing still bothered him. He didn't even know her but thought he had invaded some private world of hers. He also felt angry at himself for lashing out at the brute, Gussie. But most of all, what bothered him was that he had played the whole scene wrong. He had gone to the strip club to try to get a line on Layla and he got nothing. At best, all he had come up with was the probable explanation for what the specks of glitter found in the cuffs of Tony Aliso's pants and the shower drain were and where they came from. It wasn't enough. He had to go back to L.A. in the morning and he had nothing.

When he got to a traffic light at the beginning of the Strip, he lit a cigarette, then took out his notebook and opened it to the page on which he had written down the address Felton had given him earlier in the night.

At Sands Boulevard he turned east and within a mile he came to the apartment complex where Eleanor Wish lived. It was a sprawling development with numbered buildings. It took him a while until he found hers and then figured out which unit was hers. He sat in his car and smoked and watched her lighted windows for a while. He wasn't sure what he was doing or what he wanted.

Five years earlier Eleanor Wish had done the worst and the best to him. She had betrayed him, put him in danger and she had also saved his life. She had made love to him. And then it all went bad. Still, he had often thought about her, the old what-might-have-been blues. She had a hold on him through time. She had been cold to him this night but he thought for sure the hold went both ways. She was his reflection, he had always been sure of that.

He got out of the car, dropped his dead cigarette and went to her door. She answered his knock quickly, almost as if she was expecting him. Or someone.

'How'd you find me? Did you follow me?'

'No. I made a call, that's all.'

'What happened to your lip?'

'It's nothing. Are you going to ask me in?'

She backed up to allow him to enter. It was a small place with spare furnishings. It looked as though she was adding things over time, as she could afford them. He first noticed the print of Hopper's *Nighthawks* on the wall over the couch. It was a painting that always struck a chord with him. He had once had the same print on his own wall. It had been a gift from her five years before. A good-bye gift.

He looked from the painting to her. Their eyes met and he knew everything she had said earlier had been a front. He stepped closer to her and touched her, put his hand on her neck and ran a thumb along her cheek. He looked closely at her face. It was resolute, determined.

'This time it's been a long time for me,' she whispered.

And he remembered that he had told her the same on the night they'd first made love. That was a lifetime ago, Bosch thought. What am I doing now? Can you pick up after so long and so many changes?

He pulled her close and they held each other and kissed for a long moment and then she wordlessly led him to the bedroom, where she quickly unbuttoned her blouse and dropped her jeans to the floor. She pressed herself to him again and they kissed while she worked her hands up his shirt, opening it and pressing her skin to his. Her hair smelled of smoke from the tables, but there was an underlying scent of perfume that reminded him of a night five years before. He remembered the jacaranda trees outside her window and how they put a violet snow on the ground.

They made love with an intensity that Bosch had forgotten that he had. It was a bruising, huffing physical act devoid of love, invigorated and driven solely, it seemed, by lust and maybe a memory. When he was done she pulled him toward her, into her, in rhythmic thrusts until she, too, reached her moment and subsided. Then, with the clarity of thought that always comes after, they became embarrassed about their nakedness, about how they had coupled with the ferocity of animals and now looked at each other as human beings.

'I forgot to ask,' she said. 'You're not married now, are you?'

She giggled. He reached to the floor to where his jacket had been thrown and pulled out the cigarettes.

'No,' he said. 'I'm alone.'

'I should've known. Harry Bosch, the loner. I should've known.'

She was smiling at him in the darkness. He saw it when

the match flared. He lit the cigarette and then offered it to her. She shook her head no.

'How many women have there been since me? Tell me.'

'I don't know, just a few. There was one, we were together about a year. That was the most serious one.'

'What happened to her?'

'She went to Italy.'

'For good?'

'Who knows?'

'Well, if you don't know, then she isn't coming back. At least to you.'

'Yeah. I know. That one's been over a while.'

He was silent for a moment and then she asked him who else there had been.

'There was a painter I met in Florida on a case. That didn't last long. After that, there's you again.'

'What happened to the painter?'

Bosch shook his head as if to dismiss the inquiry. He didn't really enjoy reviewing his ill-fated romantic record.

'Distance, I guess,' he said. 'It just didn't work. I couldn't leave L.A., she couldn't leave where she was.'

She moved closer to him and kissed him on the chin. He knew he needed a shave.

'What about you, Eleanor? Are you alone?'

'Yes . . . The last man to make love to me was a cop. He was gentle but very strong. I don't mean in a physical way. In a life way. It was a long time ago. At the time we both needed healing. We gave it to each other . . .'

They looked at each other in the darkness for a long moment and then she came closer. Just before their mouths met she whispered, 'A lot of time gone past.'

He thought about those words as she kissed him and then pushed him back on the pillows. She straddled him and started a gentle rocking motion with her hips. Her hair hung down around his face until he was in a perfect darkness. He ran his hands along her warm skin from her hips to her shoulders and then underneath to touch her breasts. He could feel her wetness on him but it was too soon for him.

'What's the matter, Harry?' she whispered. 'You want to rest a while?'

'I don't know.'

He kept thinking of those words. A lot of time gone past. Maybe too much time. She kept rocking.

'I don't know what I want,' he said. 'What do you want, Eleanor?'

'All I want is the moment. We've fucked everything else up, it's all we've got left.'

After a while he was ready and they made love again. She was very silent, her movements steady and gentle. She stayed on top of him, her face above him, breathing in short rhythmic clips. Near the end, when he was just trying to hang on, waiting for her, he felt a teardrop hit his cheek. He reached up and smeared the tears on her face with his thumbs.

'It's all right, Eleanor, it's all right.'

She put one of her hands on his face, feeling it in the dark as if she were a blind woman. In a short while they met at the moment when nothing in the world can intrude. Not words or even memories. It was just them together. They had the moment.

He slept on and off in her bed until nearly dawn. She slept soundly with her head on his shoulder but when he was lucky enough to doze off, it never lasted long. For the most part he lay there staring into the gray darkness, smelling their sweat and sex, wondering what road he was on now.

At six he extricated himself from her unconscious embrace and got dressed. When he was ready he kissed her awake and told her he must go.

'I go back to L.A. today but I want to come back to you as soon as I can.'

She nodded sleepily.

'Okay, Bosch, I'll be waiting.'

It was finally cool outside. He lit his first smoke of the day as he walked to his car. When he pulled onto Sands to head up to the Strip, he saw the sun was throwing a golden light on the mountains west of town.

The Strip was still lit by a million neon lights, though the crowds on the sidewalk had greatly decreased by this hour. Still, Bosch was awed by the spectacle of light. In every imaginable color and configuration, it was a megawatt funnel of enticement to greed that burned twenty-four hours a day. Bosch felt the same attraction that all the other grinders felt tug at them. Las Vegas was like one of the hookers on Sunset Boulevard in Hollywood. Even happily married men at least glanced their way, if only for a second, just to get an idea what was out there, maybe give them something to think about. Las Vegas was like that. There was a visceral attraction here. The bold promise of money and sex. But the first was a broken promise, a mirage, and the second was fraught with danger, expense, physical and mental risk. It was where the real gambling took place in this town.

When he got to his room, he noticed the message light was blinking. He called the operator and was told that someone named Captain Felton had called at one and then again at two and then someone named Layla at four. There were no messages or numbers left by either of the callers. Bosch put the phone down and frowned. He figured it was too early to call Felton. But it was the call from Layla that most interested him. If it had been the real Layla who had called, then how did she know where to reach him?

He decided that it had probably been through Rhonda. The night before when he had called from Tony Aliso's office in Hollywood, he had asked Rhonda for directions from the Mirage. She could have passed that on to Layla. He wondered why she had called. Maybe she hadn't heard about Tony until Rhonda had told her.

Still, he decided to put Layla on a back burner for the moment. With the financial probe Kizmin Rider had opened up in L.A., the focus of the case seemed to be shifting. It was important for them to talk to Layla but his priority was to get back to L.A. He picked the phone back up and called Southwest and booked a 10:30 flight to L.A. He figured that would give him time to check in with Felton, then check out the dealership where Rider said Tony Aliso had leased his cars and still make it back to the Hollywood Division by lunchtime.

Bosch stripped off his clothes and took a long hot shower, washing the sweat of the night away. When he was done he wrapped a towel around himself and used another to wipe the fog off the mirror so he could shave. He noticed that his lower lip had swollen on one side to the size of a marble and his mustache did little to hide it. His eyes were red-rimmed and bloodshot. He wondered as he got the bottle of Visine drops out of his shaving bag if Eleanor had found a single thing about him attractive.

When he stepped back into the room to get dressed, he was greeted by a man he had never seen before sitting in the chair by the window. He was holding a newspaper, which he put down when he noticed Bosch step into the room clad only in the towel.

'It's Bosch, right?'

Bosch looked to the bureau and saw his gun was still sitting there. It was closer to the man in the chair but Bosch thought he might be able to get to it first.

'Easy now,' the man said. 'We're in this together. I'm a cop. With Metro. Felton sent me.'

'What the fuck you doing in my room?'

'I came up, got no answer. I could hear the shower. I had a friend from downstairs slip me in. I didn't want to wait around in the hall. Go ahead, get dressed. Then I'll tell you what we got.'

'Let me see some ID.'

The man got up and approached Bosch, pulling a wallet

from his inside coat pocket and putting a bored look on his face. He opened the wallet, flashing the badge and ID card.

'Iverson. From Metro. Captain Felton sent me.'

'What's so important that Felton had to send somebody to break into my room?'

'Look, I didn't break in, okay? We've been calling all night and got no answer. We first of all wanted to make sure you were all right. And, secondly, the captain wants you to be in on the arrest, so he sent me over to try to find you. We gotta get going. Why don't you get dressed?'

'What arrest?'

'That's what I'm trying to tell you if you'd get dressed and we could get going. You hit the jackpot with those prints you flew in here with.'

Bosch looked at him for a moment and then went to the closet to grab a pair of pants and some underwear. He then went into the bathroom to put them on. When he came back out, he said one word to Iverson.

'Talk.'

Bosch quickly finished dressing as Iverson began.

'You know the name Joey Marks?'

Bosch thought a moment and then said it sounded familiar but he couldn't place it.

'Joseph Marconi. They call him Joey Marks. Used to, before he tried to put on legitimate airs. Now, it's Joseph Marconi. Anyway, he got the name Joey Marks 'cause that's what he did, he left marks on anybody who crossed him, got in his way.'

'Who is he?'

'He's the Outfit's guy in Vegas. You know what the Outfit is, right?'

'The Chicago Mafia family. They control or have the say, at least, on everything west of the Mississippi. That includes Vegas and L.A.'

'Hey, you took some geography, didn't you? I probably won't have to school you too much then on what's what out here. You already've got a score card.'

'You're saying the prints on my vic's jacket came from Joey Marks?'

'In your dreams. But they did come back to one of his top guys and, Bosch, that's like manna from heaven. We're taking this guy down today, pulling him right the fuck out of bed. We're going to turn him, Bosch, make him our boy and through him we'll finally get Joey Marks. He's been a thorn in our side going on near a decade now.'

'Aren't you forgetting something?'

'No, I don't think – oh, yeah, of course you and the LAPD have our undivided thanks for this.'

'No, you're forgetting it's my case. It's not your case. What the fuck you people think you're doing taking this guy down without even talking to me?'

'We tried to call. I told you that.'

Iverson sounded hurt.

'So? You don't get me and you just go ahead with the plan?'

Iverson didn't answer. Bosch finished tying his shoes and stood up ready to go.

'Let's go. Take me to Felton. I can't believe you guys.'

On the elevator down Iverson said that while Bosch's exception to the plan was noted, it was too late to stop anything. They were heading out to a command post in the desert and from there they would move in on the suspect's house, which was out near the mountains.

'Where's Felton?'

'He's out there at the CP.'

'Good.'

Iverson was silent during most of the ride out, which was good because it allowed Bosch to think about this latest development. He realized suddenly that Tony Aliso might have been washing money for Joey Marks. Marks was Rider's Mr X, he guessed. But something went wrong. The IRS audit was endangering the scheme and thereby endangering Joey Marks. Marks had responded by eliminating the washer.

137

The story felt good to Bosch, but there were still things that didn't jibe. The break-in at Aliso's office two days after he was dead. Why did whoever that was wait until then, and why didn't they take all the financial records? The records – if connections between the dummy corporations and Joey Marks could be made – might be just as dangerous to Marks as Aliso was. Bosch found himself wondering if the hitter and the B&E man were the same person. It didn't seem so.

'What's this guy's name, the one the prints matched?'

'Luke Goshen. We only had his prints on file because he had to give 'em to get the entertainment license for one of Joey's strip clubs. The license is in Goshen's name. It keeps Joey out of it. Nice and clean. Only not anymore. The prints tie Goshen to a murder and that means Joey isn't far behind.'

'Wait a minute, what's the name of the club?'

'Dolly's. It's in—'

'North Las Vegas. Son of a bitch.'

'What, I say something?'

'This Goshen guy, do they call him Lucky?'

'Probably not after today. His luck's about to run out. Sounds like you know of him.'

'I met the prick last night.'

'You're shitting me.'

'At Dolly's. The last phone call from Aliso's office in L.A. was to Dolly's. I found out he was coming out here and spending time with one of the dancers at that place. I went to check it out last night and fucked up. Goshen had one of his guys give me this.'

Bosch touched the bump on his lip.

'I was wondering where you got that. Which one give you that?'

'Gussie.'

'Fucking Big John Flanagan. We'll be bringing his lard ass in today, too.'

'John Flanagan? How they get Gussie out of that?'

'It's on account he's the best-dressed bouncer in the country. You know, the tuxedo. He gets all gussied up to go to work. That's how he got that one. I hope you didn't let him get away with puttin' that knot on your lip.'

'We had a little discussion in the parking lot before I left.' Iverson laughed.

'I like you, Bosch. You're a tough nut.'

'I'm not sure I like you yet, Iverson. I'm still not happy about you people trying to take over my case.'

'It'll work out for all of us. You're going to clear your case and we're going to take a couple of major douche bags out of the picture. City fathers are going to be smiling all around.'

'We'll see.'

'There's one other thing,' Iverson said. 'We were already working a tip on Lucky when you showed up.'

'What are you talking about?'

'We got a tip. It was anonymous. Came in Sunday to the bureau. Guy won't give his name but says he was in a strip club the night before and hears a couple of big guys talking about a hit. He heard one call the other Lucky.'

'What else?'

'Just something about the guy being put in the trunk and then getting capped.'

'Felton know this when I talked to him yesterday?'

'No, it hadn't filtered up to him. It came up last night after he found out the prints you brought matched Goshen. One of the guys in the bureau had taken the tip and was going to check it out. Put out a flier on it. It would've eventually gotten over there to L.A. and you woulda come calling. You're just here sooner rather than later.'

They had completely left the urban sprawl of the city and the chocolate-brown mountain chain rose in front of them. There were sporadic patches of neighborhoods. Homes that were built way out and were waiting for the city to catch up. Bosch had been out this way once before on an investigation, going to a retired cop's house. It had reminded him of no-man's-land then and it still did now.

'Tell me about Joey Marks,' Bosch said. 'You said he's trying to go legitimate?'

'No, I said he's trying to give the appearance of legitimacy. That's two different things. Guy like that, he'll never be legitimate. He can clean up his act, but he's always going to be a grease spot on the road.'

'What's he into? If you believe the media, the mob was run out of town to make way for all the All-American family.'

'Yeah, I know the tune. It's true, though. Vegas has changed in ten years. When I first made it to the bureau, you could practically take your pick of the casinos and go to work. They all had connections. If it wasn't the front office, then it was the supplies, the unions, whatever. Now it's cleaned up. It's gone from sin city to fuckin' Disneyland. We got more water slides than whorehouses now. I think I liked it the old way. Had more of an edge, know what I mean?'

'Yeah, I know what you mean.'

'Anyway, the important thing is we ninety-nine percent have the mob out of the casinos. That's the good thing. But there's still a lot of what we call ancillary action around. That's where Joey fits in. He runs a string of high-rent strip bars, mostly in North Vegas because nudity and alcohol are allowed there and the money is in alcohol. Very hard to watch, that money. We figure he's siphoning a couple mil a year off the top on the clubs alone. We've had the IRS go after his books but he does too good a job.

'Let's see, we think he also has a piece of some of the brothels up north. Then he's got the usual, your standard loan-sharking and fencing operations. He runs a book and has the street tax on almost anything that moves in town. You know, the escort services, peep shows, all of that. He's the king. He can't go in any of the casinos 'cause he's in the commission's black book but it doesn't matter. He's the king.'

'How does he have a betting book in a town where you

can walk into any casino and bet on any game, any race, anywhere?'

'You gotta have money to do that. Not with Joey. He'll take your bet. And if you are unlucky enough to lose, then you better come up with the money quick or you're one sorry motherfucker. Remember how he got his name. Well, suffice it to say his employees carry on the tradition. See, that's how he gets his hooks into people. He gets them to owe him and then they have to give him a piece of what they have, whether it's a company that makes paint in Dayton or something else.'

'Maybe a guy who makes cheap movies in L.A.'

'Yeah, like that. That's how it works. They open up to him or they get two broken knees or worse. People still disappear in Vegas, Bosch. It might look like it's all volcanoes and pyramids and pirate ships on the outside, but on the inside it's still dark enough for people to disappear in.'

Bosch reached over and turned the air up a notch. The sun was already all the way up and the desert was beginning to bake.

'This is nothing,' Iverson said. 'Wait till about noon. If we're out here then, forget about it. We'll be over one-ten easy.'

'What about Joey's air of legitimacy?'

'Yeah, well, like I said, he's got holdings all over the country. Pieces of the legitimate world he got through these various scams. He also reinvests. He cleans up all the cash he's pulling out of his various enterprises and then puts it into legit stuff, even charities. He's got car dealerships, a country club on the east side, a goddamn wing of a hospital named after one of his kids who died in a swimming pool. His picture gets in the paper at ribbon cuttings, Bosch. I tell you, we've either got to fucking take the guy down or give him the key to the city and I don't know which would be more appropriate.'

Iverson shook his head.

After a few minutes of silence they were there. Iverson pulled into a county fire station and drove around back, where there were several more detective cars and several men standing around them holding paper cups of coffee. One of them was Captain Felton.

Bosch had forgotten to take a bulletproof vest with him from Los Angeles and had to borrow one from Iverson. He was also given a plastic raid jacket that said LVPD in bright yellow letters across the chest when it was zipped closed.

They were standing around Felton's Taurus, going over the plan and waiting for the uniform backup. Execution of the warrant was going to be done by Vegas rules, the captain said. That meant at least one uniform team had to be there when they kicked the door.

By this time Bosch had already had his 'friendly' exchange with Felton. The two had gone into the fire station to get Bosch some coffee, and Bosch had given the police captain an earful for the way he had handled the discovery that the prints Bosch had brought with him belonged to Lucky Luke Goshen. Felton feigned contrition and told Bosch he'd be involved in calling the shots from that moment on. Bosch had to back down after that. He'd gotten what he wanted, at least in the captain's words. Now he just had to watch that Felton walked the talk.

Besides Felton and Bosch, there were four others standing around the car. They were all from Metro's Organized Crime Unit. It was Iverson and his partner, Cicarelli, and then another pair, Baxter and Parmelee. The OCU was part of Felton's domain in the department, but it was Baxter who was running the show. He was a black man who was balding, with gray hair lightly powdered around the sides of his head. He was heavily muscled and had a countenance that said I want no hassles. He seemed to Bosch to be a man accustomed to both the violent and violence. There was a difference.

Luke Goshen's home was known to them. From their banter Bosch figured that they had watched the place before. It was about a mile further west from the station, and Baxter had already made a drive-by and determined that Goshen's black Corvette was in the carport.

'What about a warrant?' Bosch asked.

He could just envision the whole thing getting kicked out of court because of a warrantless entry into the suspect's house.

'The prints were more than enough for a warrant to search the premises and arrest your man,' Felton said. 'We took it to a judge first thing this morning. We also had our own information, which I think Iverson told you about.'

'Look, his prints were on the guy but it doesn't mean he did it. It doesn't make a case. We're acting too quickly here. My guy was put down in L.A. I've got nothing putting Luke Goshen there. And your own information? That's a joke. You've got an anonymous call, that's it. It doesn't mean shit.'

They all looked at Bosch as if he had just belched at the debutante ball.

'Harry, let's get another cup,' Felton said.

'I'm fine.'

'Let's get one anyway.'

He put his arm on Bosch's shoulder and led him back toward the station. Inside at the kitchen counter, where there was a coffee urn, Felton poured himself another cup before speaking.

'Look, Harry, you gotta go with this. This is a major opportunity for us and for you.'

'I know that. I just don't want to blow it. Can't we hold off on this until we're sure of what we've got? It's my case, Captain, and you're still running the show.'

'I thought we had that all straightened out.'

'I thought we did, too, but I might as well be pissing in the wind.'

'Look, Detective, we're going to go up the road and take

this guy down, search his place and put him in a little room. I guarantee that if he isn't your man, he's going to give him to you. And he's going to give us Joey Marks along the way. Now, come on, get with the program and get happy.'

He cuffed Bosch on the shoulder and headed back out to the lot. Bosch followed in a few moments. He knew that he was whining over nothing. You find somebody's prints on a body, you bring him in. That's a given. You sweat the details later. But Bosch didn't like being a bystander. That was the real rub and he knew it. He wanted to run the show. Only out here in the desert, he was a fish out of water, flopping on the sand. He knew he should call Billets, but it was too late for her to do anything and he didn't like the idea of telling her he had let this one get away from him.

The patrol car with the two uniforms was there when Bosch stepped out of the fire station and back into the oven.

'All right,' Felton said. 'We're all here. Mount up and let's go get this fucker.'

They were there in five minutes. Goshen lived in a house that rose out of the scrubland on Desert View Avenue. It was a large house but not one that looked particularly ostentatious. The one thing that looked out of the ordinary was the concrete-block wall and gate that surrounded the half-acre property. The house was in the middle of nowhere but its owner needed to put a security wall around it.

They all stopped their cars on the shoulder of the road and got out. Baxter had come prepared. From the trunk of his Caprice he pulled out two stepladders that they would use to scale the wall next to the driveway gate. Iverson was the first to go over. When he got to the top of the wall, he put the other ladder in place on the other side but hesitated before climbing down into the front yard.

'Anybody see any dogs?'

'No dogs,' Baxter said. 'I checked this morning.'

Iverson went down and the others followed him over. While he waited for his turn, Bosch looked around and could just see the neon demarcation of the Strip several miles to the east. Above this the sun was a neon red ball. The air had gone from warm to hot and was as dry and rough as sandpaper. Bosch thought of the cherry-flavored Chap Stick in his pocket that he had bought at the hotel gift shop. But he didn't want to use it in front of the local boys.

After Bosch had scaled the wall and was approaching the house behind the others, he looked at his watch. It was now almost nine but the house seemed dead. No movement, no sound, no lights, nothing. Curtains were closed across every window.

'You sure he's here?' Bosch whispered to Baxter.

'He's here,' Baxter replied without lowering his voice. 'I jumped the wall about six and touched the hood of the Vette. It was warm. He hadn't been home long. He's in there asleep, I guarantee it. Nine o'clock to this guy is like four in the morning for normal people.'

Bosch looked over at the Corvette. He remembered it from the night before. As he looked around further, he realized the confines within the walls of the compound were carpeted in lush, green grass. It must have cost a fortune to plant and another one to keep it watered. The property sat in the desert like a towel on the beach. Bosch was drawn from his wonder by the sound of Iverson hitting the front door with his foot.

With weapons drawn, Bosch and the others followed Iverson into the dark opening to the house. They went in screaming the usual identifiers – *Police!* and *Don't Move!* – and quickly moved down a hallway to the left. Bosch followed the sharp slashes of light from their flashlights. Almost immediately he heard female screams and then a light came on in a room at the end of the hall.

By the time he got in there, he saw Iverson kneeling on a king-size bed, holding his Smith & Wesson short barrel six inches from the face of Luke Goshen. The big man Bosch had encountered the night before was wrapped in the bed's black silk sheets and looked as calm about the situation as Magic Johnson used to look while shooting free throws with the game on the line. He even took the time to glance up at the ceiling to view the reflection of the scene in the mirror.

It was the women who weren't calm. Two of them, both nude, stood on either side of the bed, oblivious to their nakedness but fully in the latter stages of fright. Finally, Baxter quieted them with a loud shout of 'Shut up!'

It took a few moments for the silence to sink in. Nobody moved. Bosch never took his eyes off Goshen. He was the only danger in the room. He sensed that the other cops, who had branched off to search the house, had now moved into the room behind him along with the two uniform cops.

'On your face, Luke,' Iverson finally ordered. 'You girls get some clothes on. Now!'

One of the women said, 'You can't just—'

'Shut up!' Iverson cut her off. 'Or you go in to town like that. Your choice.'

'I'm not go—'

'Randy!' Goshen boomed with a voice as deep as a barrel. 'Shut the fuck up and get dressed. They're not taking you anywhere. You, too, Harm.'

All the men but Goshen instinctively looked at the woman he had called Harm. She looked like she weighed about ninety pounds. She had soft blond hair, breasts she could hide in a child's tea cups and a gold hoop piercing one of the folds of her vagina. There was a look of fright etched on her face that had completely crowded out any hint of beauty.

'Harmony,' she whispered, understanding their dilemma.

'Well, get dressed, Harmony,' Felton said. 'Both of you. Turn to the wall and get dressed.'

'Just get 'em their clothes and get 'em out of here,' Iverson said.

Harmony was stepping into a pair of jeans when she stopped and looked at the men giving conflicting orders.

'Well, which is it?' Randy asked in an irritated voice. 'You people got your shit together or what?'

Bosch recognized her as the woman who had been dancing in Dolly's the night before.

'Get 'em out of here!' Iverson yelled. 'Now.'

The uniforms moved in to usher the naked women out.

'We're going,' Randy yelped. 'Don't touch me.'

Iverson yanked the sheets off Goshen and began cuffing his hands behind his back. Goshen's blond hair ran in a thin and tightly braided ponytail down his back. Bosch hadn't noticed that the night before.

'Whatsa matter, Iverson?' he said, his face against the mattress. 'You got a problem with a little poon hangin' around? You a little punk or something?'

'Goshen, do yourself a favor, shut your fuckin' hole.'

Goshen laughed off the threat. He was a deeply tanned man who seemed even larger than Bosch recalled from the night before. He was completely buffed, his arms the size of hams. For a short moment, Bosch thought he understood Goshen's desire to sleep with two women. And why they willingly went with him in twos.

Goshen faked a yawn to make sure everyone knew he wasn't the least bit threatened by what was happening. He wore only black bikini underwear that matched the sheets. There were tattoos on his back. A one percent sign on the left shoulder blade, a Harley Davidson insignia on the right. On the upper left arm there was another tattoo. The number eighty-eight.

'What's this, your IQ?' Iverson said as he sharply slapped the arm.

'Fuck you, Iverson, and the phony fuckin' warrant you rode in on.'

Bosch knew what the tattoo meant. He had seen it enough in L.A. The eighth letter of the alphabet was H. Eight-eight meant HH, short for Heil Hitler. It means Goshen had spent some time with white supremacists. But most of the assholes Bosch came across with similar tattoos had gotten them in prison. It was amazing to him that Goshen apparently had no criminal record and had spent no time in stir. If he had, his name would have come up when the prints from Tony Aliso's jacket had been run through the AFIS computer. He put thoughts of this contradiction aside when Goshen managed to turn his head so that he was looking at Bosch.

'You,' he said. 'You're the one they should be arresting. After what you did to Gussie.'

Bosch bent over the bed to reply.

'This ain't about last night. This is about Tony Aliso.'

Iverson roughly turned Goshen over on the bed.

'What the fuck are you talking about?' Goshen asked angrily. 'I'm clean on that, man. What are you—'

He tried to pull himself up into a sitting position but Iverson pushed him back down hard.

'Just sit tight,' Iverson said. 'We'll hear your sorry side of things. But we're going to have a look around first.'

He took the warrant out of his pocket and dropped it on Goshen's chest.

'There's your warrant.'

'I can't read it.'

'Not my fault you didn't stay in school.'

'Just hold it up for me.'

Iverson ignored him and looked at the others.

'Okay, let's split up and see what we've got here. Harry, you take this room, okay, keep our friend here company?'

'Right.'

Iverson then addressed the two uniforms.

'I want one of you guys in here. Just stand out of the way and keep your eyes on douche bag here.'

One of the uniforms nodded and the others left the room. Bosch and Goshen looked at each other.

'I can't read this thing,' Goshen said.

'I know,' Bosch said. 'You said that.'

'This is bullshit. It's just a roust. You couldn't possibly have anything on me because I didn't do it.'

'Then who'd you have do it? Gussie?'

'No, man, nobody. There's no way you'll be able to pin this on me. No fucking way. I want my lawyer.'

'As soon as you're booked.'

'Booked for what?'

'For murder, Lucky.'

Goshen continued his denials and demands for a lawyer while Bosch ignored him and started looking around the room, checking the drawers of the dresser. He glanced back at Goshen every few seconds. It was like walking around a lion's cage. He knew he was safe but that didn't stop him from checking. He could tell Goshen was watching him in the mirror over the bed. When the big man finally quieted, Bosch waited a few moments and then started asking questions. He did it casually while he continued the search, as if he didn't really care about the answers.

'So where were you Friday night?'

'Fuckin' your mother.'

'She's dead.'

'I know it. It wasn't all that good.'

Bosch stopped what he was doing and looked at him. Goshen wanted him to hit him. He wanted the violence. It was the playing field he understood.

'Where were you, Goshen? Friday night.'

'Talk to my lawyer.'

'We will. But you can talk, too.'

'I was working the club. I have a fucking job, you know.'

'Yeah, I know. When did you work till?'

'I don't know. Four. I go home after that.'

'Yeah, right.'

'It's the truth.'

'Where were you, in that office?'

'That's right.'

'Anybody see you? You ever come out before four?'

'I don't know. Talk to my lawyer.'

'Don't worry. We will.'

Bosch went back to the search and opened the closet door. It was a walk-in but it was only a third lined with clothes. Goshen lived light.

'Fuckin' A it's right,' Goshen called from the bed. 'You go check. Check it out.'

The first thing Bosch did was to turn over the two pairs of shoes and the Nikes that were lined on the floor. He studied the sole patterns and none of them appeared even remotely like the pattern found on the bumper of the Rolls and Tony Aliso's hip. He glanced back out at Goshen to make sure the big man wasn't moving. He wasn't. Bosch next reached to the shelf above the clothes rod. He took a box down and found it full of photos. They were eight by ten publicity shots of dancers. They weren't nudes. Each young woman was posed provocatively in a skimpy costume. Each one's name was printed in the white border below the photo, accompanied by the name and number of Models A Million, which Bosch guessed was a local agency that provided dancers to clubs. He looked through the box until he found a photo with the name Layla on it.

He studied the photo of the woman he had been looking for the previous night. She had long flowing brown hair with blond highlights, a full figure, dark eyes and bee sting lips. In the photo they were parted just enough to show a hint of white teeth. She was a beautiful woman and there was something familiar about her but he couldn't place it. He decided that maybe the familiarity was the sexual malice that all the women in the photos and those whom he had seen the night before in the club seemed to convey.

Bosch took the box out of the closet and dropped it on the bureau. He held the picture of Layla out of it.

'What's with the pictures, Lucky?'

'They're all the girls I've been with. How 'bout you, cop? You had that many? I bet the ugliest one in there is better than the best one you've ever had.'

'So what do you want to do, compare pricks, too? I'm glad you've had your fill of women, Lucky, 'cause there aren't going to be any more. I mean, sure, you'll be able to fuck or be fucked. It just won't be with women is all I'm saying.'

Goshen was quiet while he contemplated this. Bosch put the photo of Layla on the bureau next to the box.

'Look, Bosch, just tell me what you guys've got and I'll tell you what I know so we can get this straightened out. You're wrong on this. I didn't do anything, so let's get this over with, stop wasting each other's time.'

Bosch didn't answer. He went back into the closet and hiked up on his toes to see if there was anything else on the shelf. There was. A small cloth folded like a handkerchief. He took it down and unfolded it. It was soiled with oil. He smelled it and recognized it.

Bosch came out of the closet, tossed the rag so it hit Goshen in the face and fell onto the bed.

'What's this?'

'I don't know. What is it?'

'It's a rag with gun oil on it. Where's the gun?'

'I don't have a gun and that isn't mine, either. Never saw it before.'

'Okay.'

'What do you mean, okay? I never fuckin' saw it before.'

'I mean, okay, Goshen. That's all. Don't get nervous.'

'It's hard with you people sticking your nose up my ass.'

Bosch bent over the night table. He opened the top drawer, found an empty cigarette box, a set of pearl earrings and an unopened box of condoms. Bosch threw the box at Goshen. It bounced off his huge chest and fell to the floor.

'You know, Goshen, just buying them ain't safe sex. You gotta put 'em on.'

He opened the bottom drawer. It was empty.

'How long you lived here, Goshen?'

'Moved in right after I kicked your sister out on her ass. Put her on the street. Last I seen, she was selling it over on Fremont outside the Cortez.'

Bosch straightened up and looked at him. Goshen was smiling. He wanted to provoke something. He wanted to control things, even handcuffed on the bed. Even if it cost him some blood.

'My mother, now my sister, who's next, my wife?'

'Yeah, I got something planned for her. I'll—'

'Shut up, would you? It's not working, understand? You're not getting to me. You can't get to me. So save your strength.'

'Everybody can be gotten to, Bosch. Remember that.'

Bosch looked at him and then stepped into the master bathroom. It was a large room with a separate shower and tub, almost in the same configuration as the room Tony Aliso had used at the Mirage. The toilet was in a small closet-size room behind a door with a slatted grill. Bosch started there. He quickly lifted the top of the water tank and found nothing unusual. Before putting the porcelain top back in place he leaned over the toilet and looked down the wall behind the tank. What he saw made him immediately call for the uniform in the bedroom.

'Yes, sir?' the cop said.

He looked like he wasn't yet twenty-five. His black skin had almost a bluish tint to it. He kept his hands on his equipment belt in a relaxed mode, his right just a few inches from his gun. It was the standard pose. Bosch saw that the nameplate above his breast pocket said Fontenot.

'Fontenot, take a look down here behind the tank.'

The cop did as he was asked without even taking his hands off his belt.

'What is it?' he asked.

'I think it's a gun. Why don't you step back and let me pull it out.'

Bosch flattened his hand and reached it down into the two-inch space between the wall and the tank. His fingers closed on a plastic bag attached to the back of the tank with gray duct tape. He managed to pull it free and get the bag out. He held it up for Fontenot to see. The bag contained a blue metal pistol equipped with a three-inch screw-on silencer.

'A twenty-two?' Fontenot asked.

'Oh, yeah,' Bosch said. 'Go get Felton and Iverson, would you?'

'Right away.'

Bosch followed Fontenot out of the bathroom. He was holding the bag containing the gun the way a fisherman holds a fish by its tail. When he stepped into the bedroom he couldn't help but smile at Goshen, whose eyes noticeably widened.

'That ain't mine,' Goshen immediately protested. 'That's a plant, you fuck! I don't be – Get me my goddamned lawyer, you son of a bitch!'

Bosch let the words go by but studied the look. He saw something flash in Goshen's eyes. It was there for only a second and then he covered up. It wasn't fear. He didn't think that was something Goshen would let slip into his eyes. Bosch believed he had seen something else. But what? He looked at Goshen and waited a moment for the look to return. Was it confusion? Disappointment? Goshen's eyes showed nothing now. But Bosch believed he knew the look. What he had seen had been surprise.

Iverson, Baxter and Felton then filed into the room. They saw the gun and Iverson yelped in triumph.

'Sayonara, *bay-bee!*'

His glee showed on his face. Bosch explained how and where he had found the weapon.

'These fuckhead gangsters,' Iverson said, looking at Goshen. 'Think the cops never saw *The Godfather?* Who'd you put it there for, Goshen? Michael Corleone?'

'I said get me my fucking lawyer!' Goshen yelled.

'You'll get your lawyer,' Iverson said. 'Now get up, you piece of shit. You gotta get dressed for the ride in.'

Bosch held him at gunpoint while Iverson took one of the cuffs off. Then they both pointed guns at him while he got dressed in black jeans, boots and T-shirt – the shirt manufactured for a much smaller man.

'You guys are always tough in numbers,' Goshen said as

he went about putting the clothes on. 'You ever come up against me alone, then it's going to be wet ass time.'

'Come on, Goshen, we don't have all day,' Iverson said.

When he was done, they cuffed him and stuffed him into the back of Iverson's car. Iverson locked the gun in the trunk, then they went back inside the house. In a short meeting inside the front hallway it was decided that Baxter and two of the other detectives would stay behind to finish the search of the house.

'What about the women?' Bosch asked.

'The uniforms will watch them until these boys are done,' Iverson said.

'Yeah, but as soon as they leave they'll be on the phone. We'll have Goshen's lawyer down our throat before we even get started.'

'I'll take care of that. Goshen's got one car here, right? Where's the keys?'

'Kitchen counter,' one of the other detectives said.

'Okay,' Iverson said. 'We're out of here.'

Bosch followed him through the kitchen, watching him pocket the keys that were on the counter, and then out into the carport by the Corvette. There was a little workroom here with tools hanging on a peg board. Iverson selected a shovel and then stepped out of the carport and around to the back yard.

Bosch followed and watched as Iverson found the spot where the telephone line came in from a pole at the street and connected to the house. He swung the shovel up and with one strike disconnected the line.

'Amazing how strong the wind can get out here in the open desert,' he said.

He looked around behind the house.

'Those girls have no car and no phone,' he said. 'Nearest house is a half mile, city's about five. My guess is they'll stay put a while. That'll give us time. All we need.'

Iverson took a baseball swing with the shovel and launched it out over the property wall and into the scrub brush. He started walking toward the front of the house and his car.

'What do you think?' Bosch asked.

'I think the bigger they are, the harder they fall. Goshen's ours, Harry. Yours.'

'No. I mean about the gun.'

'What about it?'

'I don't know . . . It seems too easy.'

'Nobody said criminals gotta be smart. Goshen's not smart. He's just been lucky. But not anymore.'

Bosch nodded but he still didn't like it. It wasn't really a question of being smart or not. Criminals followed routines, instincts. This didn't make sense.

'I saw something in his eyes when he saw the gun. Like he was just as surprised to see it as we were.'

'Maybe. Maybe he's just a good actor. And maybe it's not even the right gun. You'll have to take it back with you to run tests. Find out if it's the gun, Harry, then worry about if it's too easy.'

Bosch nodded. He took out a cigarette and lit it.

'I don't know. I feel like I'm missing something.'

'Look, Harry, you want to make a case or not?'

'I want a case.'

'Then let's take him in and put him in a room, see what he has to say.'

They were at the car. Bosch realized he had left the photo of Layla inside. He told Iverson to start the car and he'd be right back. When he came back with the photo and got in, he checked Goshen in the back and saw a trickle of blood running down from the corner of his mouth. Bosch looked at Iverson, who was smiling.

'I don't know, he must've bumped his face getting in. Either that or he did it on purpose to make it look like I did it.'

Goshen said nothing and Bosch just turned around. Iverson pulled the car out onto the road and they headed back toward the city. The temperature was climbing rapidly and Bosch could already feel the sweat sticking his shirt to his back. The air conditioner labored to overcome the heat that had built up in the car while they were inside the house. The air was as dry as old bones. Bosch finally took out the Chap Stick and rolled it across his sore lips. He didn't care what Iverson or Goshen thought about it.

They took Goshen up to the detective bureau in a back elevator in which Goshen audibly farted. Then Bosch and Iverson walked him down a hallway off the squad room and into an interview room barely larger than a rest-room stall. They handcuffed him to a steel ring bolted to the center of the table and locked him in. Then they left him there. As Iverson closed the door, Goshen called after him that he wanted to make his phone call.

Bosch noticed that the squad room was almost deserted as they walked back toward Felton's office.

'Somebody die?' Bosch asked. 'Where is everybody?'

'They're out picking up the others.'

'What others?'

'The captain wanted to bring in your pal, Gussie, throw a scare at him. They're bringing in the girl, too.'

'Layla? They found her?'

'No, not her. The one you had us run last night. The one that played with your victim at the Mirage. Turns out she's got a jacket.'

Bosch reached over and yanked Iverson's arm to stop him.

'Eleanor Wish? You're bringing in Eleanor Wish?'

He didn't wait for Iverson's reply. He broke away from the man and charged into Felton's office. The captain was on the phone and Bosch paced anxiously in front of the desk waiting for him to hang up. Felton pointed at the door but Bosch shook his head. He could see Felton's eyes start to smolder as he told whoever was on the other end of the line he had to go.

'I can't talk right now,' he said. 'You don't have to worry, it's under control. I'll talk to you.'

He hung up and looked at Bosch.

'What is it now?'

'Call your people. Tell them to leave Eleanor Wish alone.'

'What are you talking about?'

'She had nothing to do with this. I checked her out last night.'

Felton leaned forward and clasped his hands together as he thought.

'When you say you checked her out, what does that mean?'

'I interviewed her. She had a passing acquaintance with the victim, that's it. She's clean.'

'Do you know who she is, Bosch? I mean, do you know her history?'

'She was an FBI agent assigned to the L.A. bank robbery squad. She went to prison five years ago on a conspiracy charge stemming from a series of burglaries involving bank safe deposit vaults. It doesn't matter, Captain, she's clean on this.'

'I think it might be good to sweat her a little bit and take another go at her with one of my guys. Just to be sure.'

'I'm already sure. Look, I—'

Bosch looked back at the office door and saw Iverson hanging around, trying to listen in. Bosch walked over and closed the door, then pulled a chair away from the wall and sat right in front of Felton's desk and leaned across to him.

'Look, Captain, I knew Eleanor Wish in L.A. I worked that case with the bank vaults. I . . . we were more than just partners on it. Then it all turned to shit and she went away. I hadn't seen her in five years until I saw her on the surveillance tape at the Mirage. That's why I called you last night. I wanted to talk to her but not because of the case. She's clean. She did her time and she's clean. Now call your people.'

Felton was quiet. Bosch could see the wheels turning.

'I've been up most of the night working on this. I called your room a half dozen times to bring you in on it but you weren't there. I don't suppose you want to tell me where you were?'

'No, I don't.'

Felton thought some more and then shook his head.

'I can't do it. I can't cut her loose yet.'

'Why not?'

'Because there is something about her you apparently don't know.'

Bosch closed his eyes for a moment like a boy expecting to get slapped by an angry mother but steadying himself to take it.

'What don't I know?'

'She might've only had a passing acquaintance with your victim, but she's got more than that with Joey Marks and his group.'

It was worse than he expected.

'What are you talking about?'

'I put her name up for discussion with some of my people last night after you called. We've got her in a file. On numerous occasions she has been seen in the company of a man named Terrence Quillen who works for Goshen who works for Marks. Numerous times, Detective Bosch. In fact, I've got a team out looking for Quillen now. See what he has to say.'

'In the company of, what does that mean?'

'Looked like strictly business, according to the reports.'

Bosch felt like he'd been punched. This was impossible. He had spent the night with the woman. The sense of betrayal was building in him but a deeper gut sense told him she was true, that this was all some huge mix-up.

There was a knock on the door and Iverson poked his head in.

'FYI, the others are back, boss. They're puttin' them in the interview rooms.'

'Okay.'

'You need anything?'

'No, we're fine. Close the door.'

After Iverson left, Bosch looked at the captain.

'Is she arrested?'

'No, we asked her to come in voluntarily.'

'Let me talk to her first.'

'I don't think that would be wise.'

'I don't care if it's wise. Let me go talk to her. If she'll tell anybody, she'll tell me.'

Felton thought a moment and then finally nodded his head.

'Okay, go ahead. You get fifteen minutes.'

Bosch should have thanked him but didn't. He just got up quickly and went to the door.

'Detective Bosch?' Felton said.

Harry looked back from the door.

'I'll do what I can for you on this. But this cuts us in in a big way, you understand that?'

Bosch stepped out without answering. Felton had no finesse. It was understood without being said that Bosch was now beholden to him. But Felton had to say it anyway.

In the hallway, Bosch passed the first interview room, where they had placed Goshen, and opened the door to the second. Sitting there handcuffed to the table was Gussie Flanagan. His nose was misshapen and looked like a new potato. He had cotton jammed into the nostrils. He looked at Bosch with bloodshot eyes and recognition showed on his face. Bosch backed out and closed the door without saying a word.

Eleanor Wish was behind door number three. She was disheveled, obviously dragged from sleep by the Metro cops. But her eyes had the alert and wild quality of a cornered animal and that cut Bosch to the bone.

'Harry! What are they doing?'

He closed the door and moved quickly into the tiny

room, touching her shoulder in a consoling manner and taking the seat across from her.

'Eleanor, I'm sorry.'

'What? What did you do?'

'Yesterday when I saw you on the tape at the Mirage I asked Felton, he's the captain here, to get me your number and address because you were unlisted. He did. But then without my knowledge he ran your name and pulled up your package. Then on his own he had his people get you this morning. It's all part of this Tony Aliso thing.'

'I told you. I didn't know him. I had one drink with him once. Just because I happened by chance to be at the same table with him they bring me in?'

She shook her head and looked away, the distress written on her face. This was the way it would always be, she now knew. The criminal record she carried would guarantee it.

'I've got to ask you something. I want to get this cleared up and get you out of here.'

'What?'

'Tell me about this man Terrence Quillen.'

He saw the shock in her eyes.

'Quillen? What does he – is he the suspect?'

'Eleanor, you know how this works. I can't tell you things. You tell me. Just answer the question. Do you know Terrence Quillen?'

'Yes.'

'How do you know him?'

'He came up to me about six months ago when I was leaving the Flamingo. I had been out here four or five months. I was settling in, playing six nights a week by then. He came up to me and in his words told me what's what. He somehow knew about me. Who I was, that I'd just gotten out. He said there was a street tax. He said I had to pay it, that all the locals paid it, and that if I didn't there'd be trouble. He said that if I did pay it, he'd watch out for me. Be there if I ever got in a jam. You know how it goes, extortion plain and simple.'

She broke then and started to cry. It took all of Bosch's will not to get up and try to hold her and comfort her in some way.

'I was alone,' she said. 'Scared. I paid. I pay him every week. What was I supposed to do. I had nothing and nowhere to go.'

'Fuck it,' Bosch said under his breath.

He got up and squeezed around the end of the table and grabbed hold of her. He pulled her to his chest and kissed the top of her head.

'Nothing's going to happen,' he whispered. 'I promise you that, Eleanor.'

He held her there in silence for a few moments, listening to her quiet crying, until the door opened and Iverson stood there. He had a toothpick in his mouth.

'Get the fuck out of here, Iverson.'

The detective slowly closed the door.

'I'm sorry,' Eleanor said. 'I'm getting you in trouble.'

'No, you're not. It's all on me. Everything is on me.'

A few minutes later he walked back into Felton's office. The captain looked up at him wordlessly.

'She was paying off Quillen to leave her alone. Two hundred a week. That was all it was. The street tax. She doesn't know anything about anything. She happened by chance to be at the same table as Aliso for about an hour Friday. She's clean. Now kick her loose. Tell your people.'

Felton leaned back and started tapping his lower lip with the end of a pen. He was showing Bosch his deep-thinking pose.

'I don't know,' he said.

'Okay, this is the deal. You let her go and I make a call to my people.'

'And what'll you tell 'em?'

'I'll tell them I've gotten excellent cooperation from Metro out here and that we ought to run this as a joint operation. I'll say we're going to put the squeeze on Goshen here and go for the two-for-one sale. We're going to go for

161

Goshen and Joey Marks because Marks was the one who would've ultimately pushed the button on Tony Aliso. I'll say it's highly recommended that Metro take the lead out here because they know the turf and they know Marks. Do we have a deal?'

Felton tapped out another code message on his lip, then reached over and turned the phone on his desk so Bosch could have access to it.

'Make the call now,' he said. 'After you talk to your CO, put me on the line. I want to talk to him.'

'It's a her.'

'Whatever.'

A half hour later Bosch was driving a borrowed unmarked Metro car with Eleanor Wish sitting crumpled in the passenger seat. The call to Lieutenant Billets had gone over well enough for Felton to keep his end of the deal. Eleanor was kicked loose, though the damage was pretty much done. She had been able to eke out a new start and a new existence, but the underpinnings of confidence and pride and security had all been kicked out from beneath her. It was all because of Bosch and he knew it. He drove in silence, unable to even fathom what to say or how to make it better. And it cut him deeply because he truly wanted to. Before the previous night he had not seen her in five years, but she had never been far from his deepest thoughts, even when he had been with other women. There had always been a voice back there that whispered to him that Eleanor Wish was the one. She was the match.

'They're always going to come for me,' she said in a small voice.

'What?'

'You remember that Bogart movie where the cop says, "Round up the usual suspects," and they go out and do it? Well, that's me now. They are going to mean me. I guess I never realized that until now. I'm one of the usual suspects.

I guess I should thank you for slapping me in the face with reality.'

Bosch said nothing. He didn't know how to respond because her words were true.

In a few minutes they were at her apartment and Bosch walked her in and sat her on the couch.

'You okay?'

'Fine.'

'When you get a chance, look around and make sure they didn't take anything.'

'I didn't have anything to take.'

Bosch looked at the *Nighthawks* print on the wall above her. It was a painting of a lonely coffee shop on a dark night. A man and a woman sitting together, another man by himself. Bosch used to think he was the man alone. Now he stared at the couple and wondered.

'Eleanor,' he said. 'I have to go back. I'll come back here as soon as I can.'

'Okay, Harry, thanks for getting me out.'

'You going to be okay?'

'Sure.'

'Promise?'

'Promise.'

Back at Metro, Iverson was waiting for Bosch before they took their first shot at Goshen. Felton had acceded to leaving Goshen for Bosch. It was still his case.

In the hallway outside the interview room, Iverson tapped Bosch on the arm to stop him before going in.

'Listen, Bosch, I just want to say I don't know what you got going on with that woman and I guess it's nobody's business anymore since the captain let her go, but since we're going to be working together on Lucky here, I thought I'd clear the air. I didn't appreciate the way you spoke to me, telling me to get the fuck out and all.'

Bosch looked at him a minute. The detective still had a

toothpick in his mouth and Bosch wondered if it was the same one from before.

'You know, Iverson, I don't even know your first name.'

'It's John, but people call me Ivy.'

'Well, Iverson, I didn't appreciate the way you were sneaking around the captain's office or the interview room. In L.A. we've got a name for cops who sneak around and eavesdrop and are assholes on general principle. We call 'em squints. And I don't really care if you're offended by me or not. You're a squint. And you make any trouble for me from here on out and I'll go right to Felton and make trouble for you. I'll tell him about finding you in my room today. And if that's not enough, I'll tell 'im that I won six hundred bucks on the wheel in the casino last night but the money disappeared off the bureau after you were there. Now, you want to do this interview or not?'

Iverson grabbed Bosch by the collar and shoved him against the wall.

'Don't you fuck with me, Bosch.'

'Don't you fuck with me, *Ivy*.'

A smile slowly cracked across Iverson's face and he released his grip and stepped back. Bosch straightened his tie and shirt.

'Then let's do it, cowboy,' Iverson said.

When they squeezed into the interview room, Goshen was waiting for them with his eyes closed, his legs up on the table and his hands laced behind his head. Bosch watched Iverson look down at the torn metal where the cuff ring had been attached to the table. Red flares of anger burst on his cheeks.

'Okay, asshole, get up,' Iverson ordered.

Goshen stood up and brought his cuffed hands up. Iverson got out his keys and took the cuff off one wrist.

'Let's try this again. Sit down.'

When Goshen was back down, Iverson cuffed his wrists behind his back, looping the chain through one of the steel slats of the chair back. Iverson then kicked out a chair and sat to the side of the gangster. Bosch sat across from him.

'Okay, Houdini, you also've got destroying public property on your list now,' Iverson said.

'Wow, that's bold, Iverson. Really bold. That's like the time you came into the club and took Cinda into the fantasy booth. I think you called it interrogation. She called it something else. What's this going to be?'

Iverson's face now glowed with anger. Goshen puffed his chest up proudly and smirked at the detective's embarrassment.

Bosch shoved the table into Goshen's midsection and the big man doubled over it as his breath burst out. Bosch was up quickly and around the table. As he went, he pulled his keychain from his pocket. Then, using his elbow to keep Goshen's chest down on the table, he flicked open the blade of his pocket knife and sawed off the big man's ponytail. He went back to his seat and when Goshen lifted up, threw the six-inch length of hair on the table in front of him.

'Ponytails went out of style at least three years ago, Goshen. You probably didn't hear about it.'

Iverson burst out in uproarious laughter. Goshen looked at Bosch with pale blue eyes that seemed as soulless as buttons on a machine. He didn't say a word. He was showing Bosch he could take it. He was stand-up. But Bosch knew even he couldn't stand up forever. Nobody can.

'You've got a problem, Lucky,' Iverson said. 'Big problems. You—'

'Wait a minute, wait a minute. I don't want to talk to you, Iverson. I don't want you to talk to me. You're a runt. I've got no respect for you. Understand? Anybody talks, let him talk.'

Goshen nodded to Bosch. There was a silence during which Bosch looked from him to Iverson and then back.

'Go get a cup,' Bosch said, without looking at Iverson. 'We'll be fine in here.'

'No, you—'

'Go get a cup.'

'You sure?'

Iverson looked as if he were being kicked out of the college fraternity because the boys didn't think he fit in.

'Yeah, I'm sure. You got a rights form on you?'

Iverson got up. He took a folded piece of paper out of his coat pocket and tossed it on the table.

'I'll be right outside the door.'

When Goshen and Bosch were alone they studied each other for a moment before Bosch spoke.

'You want a smoke?'

'Don't play the good guy with me. Just tell me what's what.'

Bosch shrugged off the rebuke and got up. He moved behind Goshen and took his keys out again. This time he unlocked one of the cuffs. Goshen brought his hands up and began rubbing the wrists to get circulation going. He noticed the length of hair on the table and slapped it onto the floor.

'Let me tell you something, Mr L.A. I've been to a place where it doesn't matter what they do to you, where nothing can hurt you. I've been there and back.'

'Everybody's been to Disneyland, so what?'

'I'm not talking about fuckin' Disneyland, asshole. I spent three years in the penta down in Chihuahua. They didn't break me then, you aren't going to do it now.'

'Let me tell you something then. In my life I've killed a lot of people. Just wanted you to know that up front. Time comes again, there won't be any hesitation. None. This isn't about good guy cops and bad guy cops, Goshen. That's the movies. The movies where the bad guys have ponytails, I guess. But this is real life. You are nothing to me but meat. And I'm gonna put you down. That's a given. It's just up to you how hard and how far you want to go down.'

Goshen thought a moment.

'All right, so now we know each other. Talk to me. And I'll take that smoke now.'

Bosch put his cigarettes and matches on the table. Goshen got one out and lit it. Bosch waited until he was done.

'I gotta advise you first. You know the routine.'

Bosch opened the piece of paper Iverson had left and read Goshen his rights. He then had the man sign his name on it.

'This is being taped, isn't it?'

'Not yet.'

'Okay then, what've you got?'

'Your fingerprints were on Tony Aliso's body. The gun we found behind the toilet will be going back to L.A. today. The prints are good to have, real good. But if the bullets they pick out of Tony's gourd match that gun, then it's all over. I don't care what kind of alibi you line up or what your explanation will be or if your lawyer's Johnny fucking Cochran, you won't just be meat, you'll be one hundred percent grade A dead meat.'

'That gun ain't mine. It's a plant, goddamn it. You know it and I know it. And it's not going to fly, Bosch.'

Bosch looked at him a moment and felt his face getting hot.

'You're saying I put that there?'

'I'm saying I watched the O.J. show. Cops out here are no different. I'm saying I don't know if it was you or Iverson or whoever, but that gun's a fuckin' plant, goddammit. That's what I'm saying.'

Bosch traced a finger along the top of the table, waiting for the anger to dissipate to the point where he could control his voice.

'You hang on to that bullshit story, Goshen, and you'll go far with it. You'll go about ten years and then they'll strap you down and stick a needle in your arm. At least it's not the gas chamber anymore. They make it easy on you guys now.'

Bosch leaned back but there wasn't a lot of room. The back of the chair hit the wall. He took out the Chap Stick and reapplied it.

'We own you now, Goshen. All you have left is one small

window of opportunity. Call it a little piece of destiny still in your grasp.'

'And what window's that?'

'You know what window, you know what I'm talking about. Guy like you doesn't move an inch without the okay. Give us the guy you worked the hit with and the guy who told you to put Tony in the trunk. You don't make a deal and there's no light at the end of the tunnel.'

Goshen let out his breath and shook his head.

'Look, I did not do this. I did not!'

Bosch didn't expect him to say anything different. It wasn't that easy. He had to wear him down. He leaned across the table conspiratorially.

'Listen, I'm going to tell you something so that you know that I'm not bullshitting you. Maybe save some time, so you can decide where to go from here.'

'Go ahead, but it's not going to change anything.'

'Anthony Aliso was wearing a black leather jacket Friday night. Remember that? One with the two-inch lapels. It—'

'You're wasting your—'

'You grabbed him there, Goshen. Just like this.'

Bosch reached across the table and demonstrated, using both hands to grab an imaginary set of lapels on a jacket Goshen wasn't wearing.

'Remember that? Tell me I'm wasting my time now. Remember, Goshen? You did it, you grabbed him like that. Now who is bullshitting who?'

Goshen shook his head but Bosch knew he had scored. The pale blues were looking inward at the memory.

'Kind've a freaky thing. Processed leather like that holds the amino acids from the prints. That's what the tech tells me. We got some nice ones. Enough to take to the DA or the grand jury. Enough for me to come out here. Enough for us to come right into your fucking house and hook you up.'

He hesitated a moment until Goshen was looking at him.

'And now this gun turns up in your house. I guess we'll just have to wait on the ballistics if you don't want to talk anymore. But I've got a hunch about it. I like my chances.'

Goshen slammed two open palms down on the steel table. It made a sound like a shot and echo.

'This is a setup. You people put—'

Iverson burst through the door, his gun out and aimed at Goshen. He jerked the weapon up like a TV cop.

'You okay?'

'Yeah,' Bosch said. 'Lucky here is just a little mad, is all. Give us a few more minutes.'

Iverson went back out without a word.

'Nice play, but that's all it was,' Goshen said. 'Where's my phone call?'

Bosch leaned back across the table.

'You can make the call now. But you make the call and it's over right here. Because that won't be your lawyer. That will be Joey's lawyer. He'll be here to represent you, but we both know the one he'll be watching out for is Joey Marks.'

Bosch stood up.

'I guess then we'll just have to settle for you. We'll go the distance on you.'

'Yeah, but you don't have me, you prick. Fingerprints? You need more than that. That gun's a plant and everybody's going to know it.'

'Yeah, you keep saying it. I'll know what I need to know from ballistics by tomorrow morning.'

It was hard for Bosch to tell if that had registered because Goshen didn't give it much time to.

'I've got a fuckin' alibi! You can't pin this on me, man!'

'Yeah? What's your fuckin' alibi? How do you even know when he got hit?'

'You asked me about Friday night, right? That's the night.'

'I didn't say that.'

Goshen sat silent and motionless for a half minute. Bosch

could see the eyes going to work. Goshen knew he had crossed one line with what he had said. Bosch guessed he was considering how far he should cross. Bosch pulled the chair out and sat back down.

'I got an alibi, so I'm in the clear.'

'You're not in the clear till we say you are. What's your story?'

'No. I'm gonna tell my lawyer what it is.'

'You're hurting yourself, Goshen. You've got nothing to lose telling me.'

'Except my freedom, right?'

'I could go out, verify your story. Maybe then I'd start listening to your story about the gun being planted.'

'Yeah, right, that's like puttin' the inmates in charge of the prison. Talk to my lawyer, Bosch. Now get me a fucking phone.'

Bosch stood up and signaled for him to put his arms behind his back. He did so and Bosch cuffed him again, then left the room.

After Bosch filled them in on how Goshen had won round one, Felton told Iverson to take a phone into the interview room and allow the suspect to call his lawyer.

'I guess we'll let him stew,' Felton said when he and Bosch were alone. 'See how he likes his first taste of incarceration.'

'He told me he did three years down in Mexico.'

'He tells that to a lot of people he's trying to impress. Like the tattoos. When we were backgrounding him after he showed up a couple years ago, we never found anything about a Mexican prison and as far as we know, he's never ridden a Harley, let alone with any motorcycle gang. I think a night in county might soften him up. Maybe by round two we'll have the ballistics back.'

Bosch said he had to use a phone to call his CO to check on what the plan was for the gun.

'Just pick an empty desk out there,' Felton said. 'Make yourself at home. Listen, I'll tell you how this most likely will go and you can tell your Lieutenant Billets. The lawyer he calls is most likely going to be Mickey Torrino. He's Joey Marks's top guy. He's going to object to extradition and meantime try to get bail. Any bail will do. All they want to do is get him out of our hands and into their hands and then they can make their decision.'

'What decision?'

'Whether or not to whack him. If Joey thinks Lucky might flip, he'll just take him out to the desert somewhere and we'll never see him again. Nobody will.'

Bosch nodded.

'So you go make your call and I'll call over to the prosecutor's office, see if we can't get an X hearing scheduled. I think the sooner the better. If you can get Lucky to L.A., he's going to be even more likely to start thinking about cutting a deal. That is, if we don't break him first.'

'It'd be nice to have the ballistics before the extradition hearing. If we get a ballistics match, it will seal it. But things don't move so quickly in L.A., if you know what I mean. I doubt there's even been an autopsy.'

'Well, make your call and then we'll reconnoiter.'

Bosch used an empty desk next to Iverson's to make his call. He got Billets at her desk and he could tell she was eating. He quickly updated her on his failed effort to scam Goshen into talking and the plans to have the prosecutor's office in Las Vegas handle the extradition hearing.

'What do you want to do about the gun?' he asked when he was done.

'I want it back here as soon as possible. Edgar talked somebody over at the coroner's office into doing the cut this afternoon. We should have the bullets by tonight. If we have the gun, we can take the whole thing over to ballistics tomorrow morning. Today's Tuesday. I doubt there'd be an extradition hearing before Thursday. We'd have an answer from ballistics by then.'

'Okay, I'll grab a plane.'

'Good.'

Bosch sensed something off about her tone. She was preoccupied by something other than ballistics and what she was eating.

'Lieutenant,' he said. 'What's up? Is there something I don't know about?'

She hesitated a moment and Bosch waited her out.

'Actually, something's come up.'

Bosch's face flashed warm. He guessed that Felton had screwed him and told Billets about the Eleanor Wish situation.

'What is it?'

'I've made an ID on the guy who was in Tony Aliso's office.'

'That's great,' Bosch said, relieved but confused by her somber tone. 'Who?'

'No, it's not great. It was Dominic Carbone from OCID.'

Bosch was stunned into silence for a long moment.

'Carbone? What the . . . ?'

'I don't know. I've got some feelers out. I'd like you back here until we figure out what to do with this. Goshen will keep until the extradition hearing. He's not going to be talking to anyone but his lawyer. If you can get back, I'd like us all to get together and hash this around. I haven't talked to Kiz and Jerry yet today. They're still working the financial trail.'

'How'd you make the ID on Carbone?'

'Pure luck. Things were kind of slow after I talked to you and the captain out there this morning. I took a drive downtown and stopped by Central. I've got a friend, she's a lieutenant, too, up in OC. Lucinda Barnes, you know her?'

'No.'

'Anyway, I went up to see her. I wanted to kind of feel around, maybe get an idea why they took the pass on this one. And, lo and behold, we're sitting there talking and this guy walks through the squad and I think I recognize him but I'm not sure from where. I ask who he is and she tells me that's Carbone. And that's when I remembered. He's the guy on the tape. He had his suit jacket off and his sleeves rolled up. I even saw the tattoo. It's him.'

'You tell all this to your friend?'

'Hell no. I just acted natural and got the hell out of there. I tell you, Harry, I don't like this inside stuff. I don't know what to do.'

'We'll figure something. Look, I'm going to go. I'll be there as soon as I can. What you might want to do in the meantime, Lieutenant, is try to use some juice with ballistics. Tell them we'll be coming in with a code three in the morning.'

Billets said she would do what she could on that.

After making arrangements to fly back to L.A., Bosch barely had time to take a cab back to the Mirage and check out and still make it by Eleanor's apartment to say good-bye. But his knock on her door went unanswered. He didn't know what kind of car she had, so it was impossible for him to check the lot to make sure she was gone. He went back to his rental and sat inside and waited as long as he could, until he was at risk of missing his flight. He then scribbled a message on a page from his notebook saying he would call her and went back to the door. He folded the page up tight and stuck it in the crack of the door jamb so that it would fall and be noticed the next time she opened the door.

He wanted to wait around longer and talk to her in person but he couldn't. Twenty minutes later he was leaving the security office of the airport. The gun from Goshen's house was wrapped in an evidence bag and safely in his briefcase. Five minutes later he was aboard a jet headed for the city of angels.

Billets had a weighted and worried look on her face when Bosch stepped into her office.

'Harry.'

'Lieutenant. I dropped the gun at ballistics. They're waiting on the bullets. Whoever it was you talked to over there, they snapped to.'

'Good.'

'Where is everybody?'

'They're both over at Archway. Kiz spent the morning at the IRS and then went over to help Jerry with the interviews with Aliso's associates. I also borrowed a couple of people from Major Fraud to help with the books. They're tracing down these dummy corporations. They're going to go after the bank accounts. Search and seizure. When we freeze the money, then maybe some real live people will come out of the woodwork and claim it. My theory is that this Joey Marks was not the only one Aliso was washing money for. There's too much involved – if Kiz's numbers are right. Aliso was probably working for every mob combine west of Chicago.'

Bosch nodded.

'Oh, by the way,' she continued, 'I told Jerry that you'd take the autopsy so he can stay at Archway. Then I want everybody back here at six to talk about what we have.'

'Okay, when's the autopsy?'

'Three-thirty. That going to be a problem?'

'No. Can I ask you something, why'd you call Major Fraud in instead of OCID?'

'For obvious reasons. I don't know what to do about Carbone and OCID. I don't know whether to bring in Internal Affairs, look the other way or what.'

'Well, we can't look the other way. They have something we need. And if you call in IAD, then forget it. That will freeze everything up down there and that will be that.'

'What do they have that we need?'

'It stands to reason that if Carbone was pulling a bug out of that office, then—'

'There's tapes. Jesus, I forgot about that.'

They dropped into silence for a few moments. Bosch pulled the chair out across from her desk and finally sat down.

'Let me take a run at Carbone, see if I can figure out what they were doing and get the tapes,' he said. 'We've got the leverage.'

'This may have something to do with the chief and Fitzgerald, you know.'

'Maybe.'

She was referring to the intradepartmental skirmish between Deputy Chief Leon Fitzgerald, commander of OCID for more than a decade, and the man who was supposed to be his boss, the chief of police. In the time Fitzgerald had run the OCID, he had taken on an aura akin to J. Edgar Hoover's at the FBI, a keeper of secrets who would use them to protect his position, his division and his budget. It was believed by many that Fitzgerald had his minions investigate and keep tabs on more honest citizens, cops and elected officials of the city than the mobsters his division was charged with rooting out. And it was no secret within the department that there was an ongoing power struggle between Fitzgerald and the police chief. The chief wanted to rein in OCID and its deputy chief but Fitzgerald didn't want to be reined in. In fact, he wanted his domain to broaden. He wanted to be police chief. The struggle was largely at a name-calling standstill. The chief could not fire Fitzgerald outright because of civil service protections; and he could not get backing to simply gut and overhaul OCID from the police commissions, mayor or city council members because it was believed that Fitzgerald had thick files on all of them, including the chief. These elected and appointed officials did not know what was in those files but they had to assume that the worst things they had ever done were duly recorded. And therefore they would not back the chief's move against Fitzgerald unless they and the chief were in a guaranteed no-lose position.

Most of this was department legend or rumor, but Bosch knew even legend and rumor usually have some basis in reality. He was reluctant to step behind this curtain and possibly into this fight, as Billets clearly was, but offered to do so because he saw no alternative. He had to know what OCID had been doing and what it was that Carbone was trying to protect by breaking into the Archway office.

'Okay,' Billets said after some long thought. 'But be careful.'

'Where's the video from Archway?'

She pointed to the safe on the floor behind her desk. It was used to secure evidence.

'It will be safe,' she said.

'It better be. It will probably be the only thing that keeps them off me.'

She nodded. She knew the score.

The OCID offices were on the third floor of Central Division in downtown. The division was located away from police headquarters at Parker Center because the work of the OCID involved many undercover operations and it would not be wise to have so many undercovers going in and out of a place as public as the so-called Glass House, Parker Center. But it was that separation that helped foster the deepening gulf between Leon Fitzgerald and the police chief.

On the drive over from Hollywood, Bosch thought about a plan and knew just how he was going to play it by the time he got to the guard shack and flipped his ID to the rookie assigned parking lot duty. He read the name off the tag above the cop's breast pocket and drove into the lot and over toward the back doors of the station, then put the car in park and got out his phone. He called the OCID's main number and a secretary answered.

'Yeah, this is Trindle down on the parking lot,' Bosch said. 'Is Carbone there?'

'Yes, he is. If you hold a—'

'Just tell him to come down. Somebody busted into his car.'

Bosch hung up and waited. In three minutes one of the doors at the rear of the station house opened and a man hurried out. Bosch recognized him from the Archway surveillance tape. Billets had been right on. Bosch put the car in drive and followed along behind the man. Eventually, he pulled up alongside him and lowered the window.

'Carbone.'

'Yeah, what?'

He kept walking, barely giving Bosch a glance.

'Slow down. Your car's all right.'

Carbone stopped and now looked closely at Bosch.

'What? What are you talking about?'

'I made the call. I just wanted to get you out here.'

'Who the fuck are you?'

'I'm Bosch. We talked the other night.'

'Oh, yeah. The Aliso caper.'

Then it dawned on him that Bosch could have just taken the elevator up to the third floor if he wanted to see him.

'What is this, Bosch? What's going on?'

'Why don't you get in? I want to take a little ride.'

'I don't know, man. I don't like the way you're doing this.'

'Get in, Carbone. I think you better.'

Bosch said it in a tone and with an accompanying stare that invited no choice but compliance. Carbone, who was about forty with a stocky build, hesitated a moment, then walked around the front of the car. He was wearing a nice dark blue suit like most mob cops liked to wear and he filled the car with the smell of a brisk cologne. Right away Bosch didn't like him.

They drove out of the parking lot and Bosch went north toward Broadway. There was a lot of traffic and pedestrians and they moved slowly. Bosch said nothing, waiting for Carbone.

'Okay, so what's so important you have to kidnap me away from the station?' he finally asked.

Bosch drove another block without answering. He wanted Carbone to sweat a little.

'You've got problems, Carbone,' he finally said. 'I just thought I should tell you. See, I want to be your friend, Carbone.'

Carbone looked at Bosch with caution.

'I know I got problems,' he said. 'I'm paying two different women child support, my house still has cracks in the walls from the earthquake and the union ain't going to get us a raise again this year. So fuckin' what?'

'Those aren't problems, man. Those are inconveniences. I'm talking about real problems. About the break-in you did the other night over at Archway.'

Carbone was silent for a long moment and Bosch wasn't sure but he thought the man was holding his breath.

'I don't know what you're talking about. Take me back.'

'No, Carbone, see, that's the wrong answer. I'm here to help you, not hurt you. I'm your friend. And that goes for your boss, Fitzgerald, too.'

'I still don't know what you're talking about.'

'Okay, then I'll tell you what I'm talking about. I called you Sunday night and asked you about my stiff named Aliso. You call me back and tell me not only is OCID taking a pass, but you never heard of the guy. But as soon as you hang up

181

the phone, you get over to Archway, break into the guy's office and pop the bug you people planted in his phone. That's what I'm talking about.'

Bosch looked over at him for the first time and he saw the face of a man whose mind is racing to find a way out. Bosch knew he had him now.

'Bullshit, that's what you're talking about.'

'Yeah, you dumb fuck? Next time you decide to do a little breaking and entering, look up. Check for cameras. Rodney King Rule Number One, don't get caught on tape.'

He waited a moment to let that sink in and then put the final nails in the coffin.

'You knocked the mug off the desk and broke it. You then dumped it outside hoping nobody would notice anything. And one last thing about the rules. If you're going to do a B&E in short sleeves, then you ought to get yourself a Band-Aid or somethin' and cover up that tattoo on your arm, know what I mean? That's a slam-bang identifier when you got it on tape. And, Carbone, you're on tape, lots of tape.'

Carbone wiped a hand across his face. Bosch turned on Third and they went into the tunnel that runs under Bunker Hill. In the darkness that shrouded the car, Carbone finally spoke.

'Who knows about this?'

'For the moment, just me. But don't get any ideas. Anything happens to me and the tape will get known by a lot of people. But for the moment, I can probably contain it.'

'What do you want?'

'I want to know what was going on and I want all the tapes you took off his phone.'

'Impossible. Can't do it. I don't have those tapes. It wasn't even my file. I just did what . . .'

'What Fitz told you to do. Yeah, I know. But I don't care about that. You go to Fitz or whoever's file it was and get it. I'll go with you if you want or I'll wait out in the car. But we're going back now to get them.'

'I can't do it.'

What Bosch knew he meant was that he couldn't get the tapes without going to Fitzgerald and telling him how he had so badly messed up the break-in.

'You're going to have to, Carbone. I don't give a shit about you. You lied to me and fucked with my case. You either get me the tapes and an explanation or this is what I do. I dub off three copies of the surveillance tape. One goes to the chief's office in the Glass House, one goes to Jim Newton at the *Times* and the last goes over to Stan Chambers at Channel 5. Stan's a good man, he'll know what to do with it. Do you know he's the one who got the Rodney King tape first?'

'Jesus, Bosch, you're killing me!'

'You've got your choice.'

The autopsy was being conducted by a deputy coroner named Salazar. He had already started by the time Bosch got to the coroner's office at County–USC Medical Center. They said their perfunctory hellos and Bosch, garbed in the protective paper body suit and plastic mask, leaned back against one of the stainless counters and just watched. He wasn't expecting much from the autopsy. He had really only come for the bullets and his hope was that one of them would be usable for comparison purposes. It was well known that one reason hitters preferred to use twenty-twos on the job was that the soft bullets often became so misshapen after bouncing around in the brain case that they were worthless for ballistic comparison.

Salazar kept his long black hair in a ponytail that he then wrapped in a larger paper cap. Because he was in a wheelchair, he worked at an autopsy table that was lowered to accommodate him. This gave Bosch an unusually clear vantage point in viewing what was happening to the body.

In years past, Bosch would have maintained an ongoing banter with Salazar while the autopsy proceeded. But since his motorcycle accident, his nine-month medical leave and his return in a wheelchair, Salazar was no longer a cheerful man and rarely engaged in small talk.

Bosch watched as Salazar used a dulled scalpel to scrape a sample of the whitish material from the corners of Aliso's eyes. He placed the material in a paper bindle and put it in a petri dish. He placed the dish on a tray that held a small stand containing the test tubes filled with blood, urine and other samples of body materials to be scanned and tested.

'Think it was tears?' Bosch asked.

'I don't think so. Too thick. He had something in his eyes or on his skin. We'll find out what.'

Bosch nodded and Salazar proceeded to open the skullcap and examine the brain.

'The bullets mushed this puppy,' he said.

After a few minutes he used a pair of long tweezers to pick out two bullet fragments and drop them in a dish. Bosch stepped over and looked at them and frowned. At least one of the bullets had fragmented upon impact. The pieces were probably worthless for comparison purposes.

Then Salazar pulled out a complete bullet and dropped it in the tray.

'You might be able to work with this one,' he said.

Bosch took a look. The bullet had mushroomed on impact but about half the shaft was still intact, and he could see the tiny scratches made when it was fired through the barrel of a gun. He felt a twinge of encouragement.

'This might work,' he said.

The autopsy wrapped up in about ten more minutes. Overall, Aliso had gotten fifty minutes of Salazar's time. It was more than most. Bosch checked a clipboard that was on the counter and saw that it was the eleventh autopsy of the day for Salazar.

Salazar cleaned the bullets and put them in an evidence envelope. As he handed it to Bosch, he told the detective that he would be informed of the results of the analysis of the samples retrieved from the body as soon as it was completed. The only other thing that he thought was worth mentioning was that the bruise on Aliso's cheek was antemortem by four or five hours. This Bosch found to be very curious. He didn't know how it fit in. It would mean that someone had roughed Aliso up while he was in Las Vegas, yet he had been killed here in L.A. He thanked Salazar, calling him Sally as many people did, and headed out. He was in the hallway before he remembered something and went back to the door of the autopsy suite. When he stuck his head in, he saw Salazar tying the sheet around the body, making sure the toe tag hung free and could be read.

'Hey, Sally, the guy had hemorrhoids, right?'

Salazar looked back at him with a quizzical look on his face.

'Hemorrhoids? No. Why do you ask?'

'I found a tube of Preparation H in his car. In the glove box. It was half used.'

'Hmmm . . . well, no hemorrhoids. Not on this one.'

Bosch wanted to ask him if he was sure but knew that would be insulting. He let it go for the moment and left.

Details fueled any investigation. They were important and not to be misplaced or forgotten. As he headed toward the glass exit doors of the coroner's office, Bosch found himself bothered by the detail of the tube of Preparation H found in the glove box of the Silver Cloud. If Tony Aliso hadn't suffered from hemorrhoids, then whom did the tube belong to and why was it in his car? He could dismiss it as probably being unimportant, but that wasn't his way. Everything had its place in an investigation, Bosch believed. Everything.

His deep concentration on this problem caused Bosch to go through the glass doors and down the stairs to the parking lot before he saw Carbone standing there smoking a cigarette and waiting. When Bosch had dropped him off earlier, the OCID detective had begged for a couple of hours to get the tapes together. Bosch had agreed but hadn't told him that he was heading to an autopsy. So he now assumed that Carbone had called the bureau in Hollywood and been told by Billets or someone else that he was at the coroner's office. Bosch wouldn't check this with Carbone because he didn't want to show any kind of concern that the OCID detective had so easily found him.

'Bosch.'

'Yeah.'

'Somebody wants to talk.'

'Who? When? I want the tapes, Carbone.'

'Cool your jets for a couple minutes. Over here in the car.'

He led Bosch to the second parking row, where there was a car with its engine running and its dark-tinted windows all the way up.

'Hop in the back,' Carbone said.

Bosch nonchalantly walked to the door, still showing no concern. He opened it and ducked in. Leon Fitzgerald was sitting in the back. He was a tall man – more than six and a half feet – and his knees were pressed hard against the back of the driver's seat. He wore a beautiful suit of blue silk and held the stub of a cigar between his fingers. He was almost sixty and his hair was a jet-black dye job. His eyes, behind steel-rimmed glasses, were pale gray. His skin was pasty white. He was a night man.

'Chief,' Bosch said, nodding.

He had never met Fitzgerald before but had seen him often enough at cop funerals and on television news reports. He was the embodiment of the OCID. No one else from the secretive division ever went on camera.

'Detective Bosch,' Fitzgerald said. 'I know of you. Know of your exploits. Over the years you have been suggested to me more than once as a candidate for our unit.'

'Why didn't you call?'

Carbone had come around and gotten in the driver's seat. He started moving the car slowly through the lot.

'Because like I said, I know of you,' Fitzgerald was saying. 'And I know you would not leave homicide. Homicide is your calling. Am I correct?'

'Pretty much.'

'Which brings us to the current homicide case you are pursuing. Dom?'

With one hand, Carbone passed a shoebox over the seat. Fitzgerald took it and put it on Bosch's lap. Bosch opened it and found it full of audiocassette tapes with dates written on tape stuck to the cases.

'From Aliso's phone?' he asked.

'Obviously.'

'How long were you on it?'

'We'd only been listening for nine days. It hadn't been productive, but the tapes are yours.'

'And what do you want in return, Chief?'

'What do I want?'

Fitzgerald looked out the window, down at the railroad switching yard in the valley below the parking lot.

'What do I want?' he asked again. 'I want the killer, of course. But I also want you to be careful. The department's been through a lot these past few years. No need to hang our dirty laundry in public once again.'

'You want me to bury Carbone's extracurricular activities.'

Neither Fitzgerald nor Carbone said anything but they didn't have to. Everybody in the car knew that Carbone did what he did on orders. Probably orders from Fitzgerald himself.

'Then you've got to answer some questions.'

'Of course.'

'Why was there a bug on Tony Aliso's phone?'

'Same reason there's a bug on anyone's phone. We heard things about the man and set about finding out if they were true.'

'What did you hear?'

'That he was dirty, that he was a scumbag, that he was a

187

launderer for the mob in three states. We opened a file. We had just begun when he was killed.'

'Then when I called, why did you pass on it?'

Fitzgerald took a long pull on his cigar and the car filled with its smell.

'There's a complicated answer to that question, Detective. Suffice it to say that we thought it best if we remained uninvolved.'

'The tap was illegal, wasn't it?'

'It is extremely difficult under state law to gather the required information needed for a wiretap. The feds, they can get it done on a whim. We can't and we don't want to work with the feds all the time.'

'It still doesn't explain why you passed. You could've taken the case from us and then controlled it, buried it, done whatever you wanted with it. No one would have known about illegal wiretaps or anything else.'

'Perhaps. Perhaps it was a wrong choice.'

Bosch realized they had underestimated himself and his crew. Fitzgerald had believed the break-in would go unnoticed and therefore his unit's involvement would not be discovered. Bosch understood the tremendous leverage he held over Fitzgerald. Word about the illegal wiretap would be all the police chief would need to rid himself of Fitzgerald.

'So what else do you have on Aliso?' he asked. 'I want everything. If I hear at any point you held something back, then your little-black-bag job is going to get known. You know what I mean? It will get known.'

Fitzgerald turned from the window and looked at him.

'I know exactly what you mean. But you are making a mistake if you are going to smugly sit there and believe you have all the high cards in this game.'

'Then put whatever cards you have on the table.'

'Detective, I am about to fully cooperate with you, but know this. If you seek to hurt me or anyone in my division with the information you get here, I will hurt you more. For example, there's this matter of your keeping company last night with a convicted felon.'

He let that hang in the air with his cigar smoke. Bosch was stunned and angry but managed to swallow down his urge to throttle Fitzgerald.

'There is a department prohibition against any officer knowingly associating with criminals. I'm sure you know that, Detective, and understand the need for such a safeguard. If this were to become known about you, then your job could be in jeopardy. Then where would you and your mission be?'

Bosch didn't answer. He looked straight ahead, over the seat and out the front window. Fitzgerald leaned over so that he was almost whispering in his ear.

'This is what we know about you in just one hour,' he said. 'What if we spend a day? A week? And it's not just you, my friend. You can tell your lieutenant that there is a glass ceiling in the department for lesbians, especially if something like that should get out. Now her girlfriend, she could go further, her being black. But the lieutenant, she'd have to get used to Hollywood, you ask me.'

He leaned back to his spot and returned his voice to normal modulation.

'Do we have an understanding here, Detective Bosch?'

Bosch turned and finally looked at him.

'We have an understanding.'

After dropping the bullets retrieved from Tony Aliso's head at the ballistics lab in Boyle Heights, Bosch made it back to the Hollywood Division just as the investigators were gathering in Billets's office for the six o'clock meeting. Bosch was introduced to Russell and Kuhlken, the two fraud investigators, and everybody sat down. Also sitting in was a deputy district attorney. Matthew Gregson was from Special Prosecutions, a unit that handled organized crime cases as well as the prosecution of police officers and other delicate matters. Bosch had never met him.

Bosch gave his report first and concisely brought the others up to date on the occurrences in Las Vegas as well as the autopsy and his swing by the department's gun shop. He said he'd been promised that the ballistics comparison would be done by ten the following morning. But Bosch made no mention of his meetings with Carbone and Fitzgerald. Not because of the threat Fitzgerald had made – or so Bosch told himself. But because the information he had gleaned from those meetings was best not discussed with such a large group in general and a prosecutor in particular. Apparently, feeling the same way, Billets asked him no questions in this regard.

When Bosch was finished, Rider went next. She said she had talked to the IRS auditor assigned to the TNA Productions case and gotten very little information.

'Basically, they have a whistle-blowing program,' she said. 'You blow the whistle on a tax scofflaw and you get a share of whatever taxes the IRS finds it's been cheated out of. That's how this started. Only problem is, according to Hirschfield, he's the IRS guy, this tip came in anonymously. Whoever blew the whistle didn't want a share. He said they got a three-page letter outlining Tony Aliso's money-washing scam. He would not show it to me because he claimed, anonymous or not, the guidelines of the program call for strict confidence and the specific language of the letter could lead to identification of the author. He—'

'That's bullshit,' Gregson said.

'Probably,' Rider said. 'But there was nothing I could do about it.'

'Afterwards, give me the guy's name and I'll see what I can do.'

'Sure. Anyway, they got this letter, did some preliminary looking at TNA's corporate filings over the years and decided the letter had merit. They sent the audit letter to Tony on August 1 and were going to do him at the end of this month. That was it with him – oh, the one thing he would tell me about the letter was that it was mailed from Las Vegas. It was on the postmark.'

Bosch almost nodded involuntarily because that last bit of information fit with something Fitzgerald had told him.

'Okay, now for Tony Aliso's associates. Jerry and I spent the better part of the day interviewing the core group of people he used when making this trash he called film. He basically raided the local film schools, low-rent acting schools and strip bars for the so-called artistic talent for these shoots, but there were five men that he repeatedly worked with to get them off the ground. We took them all one by one and it appears they were not privy to financing of the movies or the books Tony kept. We think they were in the dark. Jerry?'

'That's right,' Edgar said. 'I personally think Tony picked these guys because they were stupid and didn't ask questions about that sort of stuff. He just sent them out, you know, over to USC or UCLA to grab some kid who'd want to direct or write one of these things. They'd go over to the Star Strip on La Cienega and talk girls into taking the bimbo parts. On and on, you know how it goes. Our conclusion is that this little money washing scam was Tony's. Only he and his customers knew.'

'Which leads us to you guys,' Billets said, looking at Russell and Kuhlken. 'You got anything to tell us, yet?'

Kuhlken said they were still waist-deep in the financial records but they had so far traced money from TNA Productions to dummy corporations in California, Nevada and Arizona. The money went into the corporation bank accounts and was then invested in other, seemingly legitimate, corporations. He said when the trail was fully documented they would be in a position to use the IRS and federal statutes to seize the money as the illegal funds of a racketeering enterprise. Unfortunately, Russell said, the documentation period was long and difficult. It would be another week before they could move.

'Keep at it and take the time you need,' Billets said, then

she looked at Gregson. 'So then, how are we doing? What should we be doing?'

Gregson thought a moment.

'I think we are doing fine. First thing tomorrow I'll call Vegas and find out who's handling the extradition hearing. I'm thinking that I possibly should go out there to babysit that. I'm not that comfortable at the moment with all of us here and Goshen over there with them. If we are lucky enough to pull a match out of ballistics, I think you and I, Harry, should go over there and not leave until we have Goshen with us.'

Bosch nodded his agreement.

'After hearing all of these reports, I really have just one question,' Gregson continued. 'Why isn't there someone from OCID sitting in this room right now?'

Billets looked at Bosch and almost imperceptibly nodded. The question was being passed to him.

'Initially,' Bosch said, 'OCID was informed of the murder and the victim's ID and they passed. They said they didn't know Tony Aliso. As recently as two hours ago I had a conversation with Leon Fitzgerald and told him what it looked like we had. He offered whatever expertise his people had but felt we were too far along now to have fresh people come in. He wished us best of luck with it.'

Gregson stared at him a long moment and then nodded. The prosecutor was in his mid-forties with short-cropped hair already completely gray. Bosch had never worked with him but he'd heard the name. Gregson had been around – long enough to know there was more to what Bosch had said. But he had also been around long enough to let it go for the time being. Billets didn't give him a lot of time to make something of it anyway.

'Okay, so why don't we brainstorm a little bit before we call it a night?' she said. 'What do we think happened to this man? We're gathering a lot of information, a lot of evidence, but do we know what happened to him?'

She looked at the faces gathered in the room. Finally, Rider spoke up.

'My guess is that the IRS audit brought it all about,' she said. 'He got the notice in the mail and he made a fatal mistake. He told this guy in Vegas, Joey Marks, that the government was going to look at his books and his cheap movies and the scam was likely going to come out. Joey Marks responded the way you expect these guys to respond. He whacked him. He had his man Goshen follow Tony back home from Vegas so it would happen far away from him and Goshen puts him in the trunk.'

The others nodded their heads in agreement. This included Bosch. The information he'd received from Fitzgerald fit with this scenario as well.

'It was a good plan,' Edgar said. 'Only mistake was the fingerprints Artie Donovan got off the jacket. That was pure luck and if we didn't have that, we probably wouldn't have any of this. That was the only mistake.'

'Maybe not,' Bosch said. 'The prints on the jacket just hurried things along, but Metro in Vegas was already working a tip from an informant who overheard Lucky Goshen talking about hitting somebody and putting them in a trunk. It would've gotten back to us. Eventually.'

'Well, I'd rather be already on it than waiting for eventually,' Billets said. 'Any alternative theories we should also be chasing? Are we clear on the wife, the angry screenwriter, his other associates?'

'Nothing that sticks out,' Rider said. 'There definitely was no love lost between the victim and the wife but she seems clean so far. I pulled the gatehouse log up there with a warrant and her car never left Hidden Highlands on Friday night. She seems clean.'

'What about the letter to the IRS?' Gregson asked. 'Who sent it? Obviously, someone with pretty good knowledge of what this man was doing, but who would that be?'

'This could all be part of a power play within the Joey Marks group,' Bosch said. 'Like I said before, something about the look on Goshen's face when he saw that gun and his claims later that it was a plant . . . I don't know, maybe somebody tipped the IRS knowing it would get Tony whacked and that they could then possibly lay it off on Goshen. With Goshen gone, this person moves up.'

'You're saying Goshen didn't do it?' Gregson asked, his eyebrows arched.

'No. I think Goshen is probably good for it. But I don't think he was counting on that gun showing up behind the toilet. It doesn't make sense, anyway, to keep it around. So say he whacks out Tony Aliso on orders from Joey Marks. He gives the gun to somebody in his crew to get rid of. Only that person goes and plants it at the house – this is the same person who sent the letter to the IRS in the first place to get the whole thing going. Now we come along and wrap Goshen up in a bow. The guy who stashed the gun and sent the letter, he's in a position to move up.'

Bosch looked at their faces as they tried to follow the logic.

'Maybe Goshen isn't the intended target,' Rider said.

Everyone looked at her.

'Maybe there's one more play. Maybe it's someone who wants Goshen and Joey Marks out of the way so he can move in.'

'How will they get Marks now?' Edgar asked.

'Through Goshen,' she said.

'If those ballistics come back a match,' Bosch said, 'then you can stick a fork in Goshen because he'll be done. He'll be looking at the needle or life without possibility. Or a reduced sentence if he gives us something.'

'Joey Marks,' Gregson and Edgar said at the same time.

'So who is the letter writer?' Billets asked.

'Who knows?' Bosch answered. 'I don't know enough about the organization over there. But there's a lawyer who was mentioned by the cops there. A guy who handles everything for Marks. He'd know about Aliso's scam. He could pull this off. There's probably a handful of people close to Marks capable of doing it.'

They all were silent for a long moment, each one thinking the story through and seeing that it could work. It was a natural conclusion to the meeting and Billets stood up to end it.

'Let's keep up the good work,' she said. 'Matthew, thanks for coming out. You'll be the first one I call when we get the ballistics in the morning.'

Everyone else started standing up.

'Kiz and Jerry, flip a coin,' Billets said. 'One of you will have to go to Vegas to work the extradition escort with Harry. It's regulations. Oh, and Harry, could you wait a minute? There's something I need to discuss with you about another case.'

After the others left, Billets told Bosch to close the door. He did so and then sat down in one of the chairs in front of her desk.

'So what happened?' she asked. 'Did you really talk to Fitzgerald?'

'Well, I guess it was more that he talked to me, but, yeah, I met with him and Carbone.'

'What's the deal?'

'Basically, the deal is that they didn't know Tony Aliso from a hole in the ground until they, too, got a letter, probably the same one that went to the IRS. I've got a copy of it. It has details. It was from somebody with knowledge, just like Kiz said. The letter OCID got also was postmarked in Las Vegas and it was addressed specifically to Fitzgerald.'

'So their response was to bug his office phone.'

'Right, illegal bug. They had just started – I have nine days' worth of tapes to listen to – when I call up and say Tony got whacked. They panicked. You know his situation with the chief. If it came out that first of all they illegally put the bug on Tony and second of all might have somehow been the cause of his death because Joey Marks found out, then the chief would pretty much have all he'd need to move Fitzgerald out and reestablish controls on OCID.'

'So Fitzgerald sends Carbone in to get the bug and they play dumb about Tony.'

'Right. Carbone didn't see the camera or we wouldn't know any of this.'

'That prick. When this is over, the first thing I'm going to do is give it all to the chief.'

'Uh . . .'

Bosch wasn't sure how to say it.

'What is it?'

'Fitzgerald could see that coming. I cut a deal with him.'

'*What?*'

'I cut a deal. He gave me everything, the tapes, the letter. But their activities go no further than you and me. The chief never knows.'

'Harry, how could you? You had no—'

'He's got something on me, Lieutenant. He's got something on you, too . . . and Kiz.'

A long silence followed and Bosch watched the anger flush her cheeks.

'That arrogant bastard,' she said.

Bosch told her what it was Fitzgerald had come up with. Since Bosch now was privy to her secret, he thought it was only fair that he tell her about Eleanor. Billets just nodded. She was clearly thinking more about her own secret and the consequences of Fitzgerald having knowledge of it.

'Do you think he actually put people on me? A tail?'

'Who knows? He's the kind of guy who sees opportunities and acts on them. He keeps information like money in a bank. In case of a rainy day. This was a rainy day for him and he pulled it out. I made the deal. Let's forget about it and move on with the case.'

She was silent a moment and Bosch watched her for any sign of embarrassment. There was none. She looked directly at Bosch, her eyes searching him for any sign of judgment. There was none. She nodded.

'What else did they do after the letter came?'

'Not much. They put Aliso on a loose surveillance. I have the logs. But they weren't watching him Friday night. They knew he'd gone to Las Vegas, so they were planning to pick him up again after the holiday if he was back. They were really just getting started when it all went down.'

She nodded again. Her mind wasn't on the subject. Bosch stood up.

'I'll listen to the tapes tonight. There's about seven hours but Fitzgerald said it's mostly Aliso talking to his girlfriend in Vegas. Nothing much else. But I'll listen anyway. You need anything else, Lieutenant?'

'No. Let's talk in the morning. I want to know about the ballistics as soon as you know.'

'You got it.'

Bosch headed to the door but she stopped him.

'It's weird, isn't it, when sometimes you can't tell the good guys from the bad.'

He looked back at her.

'Yeah, it's weird.'

The house still smelled of fresh paint when Bosch finally got home. He looked at the wall he had started to paint three days before and it seemed long ago. He didn't know when he'd finish now. The house had been a ground-up rebuilding job after the earthquake. He'd only been back a few weeks after more than a year of living in a residence hotel near the station. The earthquake, too, seemed long ago. Things happened fast in this city. Everything but the moment seemed like ancient history.

He got out the number Felton had given him for Eleanor Wish and called it but there was no answer, not even a machine picking up. He hung up and wondered if she had gotten the note he left for her. His hope was that they would somehow be together after this case was over. But if it came to that, he realized, he wasn't sure how he'd deal with the department's prohibition against associating with a convicted felon.

His thoughts about this spun into the question of how Fitzgerald had found out about her and the night they had spent together in her apartment. It seemed to him it was likely that Fitzgerald would maintain contacts with Metro, and he guessed that maybe Felton or Iverson had informed the deputy chief about Eleanor Wish.

Bosch made two sandwiches of lunch meat from the refrigerator and then took them, two bottles of beer and the box of tapes Fitzgerald had given him over to the chair next to his stereo. As he ate, he arranged the tapes in chronological order and then started playing them. There was a photocopy of a log and pen register with entries showing what time of day Aliso either received or made the calls and what number he had called.

More than half the calls were between Aliso and Layla, either placed to the club – Bosch could tell because of the background music and noise – or a number he assumed was her apartment. She never identified herself on any of the calls, but on the occasions Tony called her at the club he asked for her by her stage name, Layla. Other than that, he never used her name. Most of their conversations were about the minutiae of daily life. He called her most often at home in the midafternoon. In one call to her home, Layla was angry at Aliso for waking her up. He complained that it was already noon and she reminded him that she had worked until four at the club. Like a chastened boy, he apologized and offered to call back. He did, at two.

In addition to the conversations with Layla there were calls to other women involving the timing of a scene that needed to be reshot for one of Tony's movies and various other film-related business calls. There were two calls placed by Aliso to his home but both of his conversations with his wife were quick and to the point. One time he said he was coming home and the other time he said he was going to be held up and wouldn't be home for dinner.

When Bosch was done it was after midnight and he had counted only one of the conversations as being of even marginal interest. It was a call placed to the dressing room at the club on the Tuesday before Aliso was murdered. In the midst of their rather boring, innocuous conversation, Layla asked him when he was coming out next.

'Comin' out Thursday, baby,' Aliso replied. 'Why, you miss me already?'

'No – I mean, yeah, sure, I miss you and all, Tone. But Lucky was asking if you were coming. That's why I asked.'

Layla had a soft, little-girl voice that seemed unpracticed or fake.

'Well, tell him I'll be in Thursday night. You working then?'

'Yeah, I'm working.'

Bosch turned off the stereo and thought about the one call that mattered. It meant Goshen knew, through Layla, that Aliso was coming out. It wasn't much, but it could probably be used by a prosecutor as part of an argument for premeditation. The problem was that it was tainted evidence. In legal terms, it did not exist.

He looked at his watch. It was late but he decided to call. He took the number off the log where Layla's number had been recorded by a pen register which read the tones that sounded when a number was punched into a phone. After four rings it was answered by a woman with a slow voice laced with practiced sexual intent.

'Layla?'

'No, this is Pandora.'

Bosch almost laughed but he was too tired.

'Where's Layla?'

'She isn't here.'

'This is a friend of hers. Harry. She tried to call me the other night. You know where she is or where I could reach her?'

'No. She hasn't been around for a couple days. I don't know where she is. Is this about Tony?'

'Yeah.'

'Well, she's pretty upset. I guess if she wants to talk to you, she'll call you again. You in town?'

'Not right now. Where d'you guys live?'

'Uh, I don't think I'm going to tell you that.'

'Pandora, is Layla scared of something?'

'Of course she is. Her old man gets killed. She thinks people might think she knows something, but she doesn't. She's just scared.'

Bosch gave Pandora his home number and told her to have Layla call if she checked in.

After he hung up he looked at his watch and took out the little phone book he kept in his jacket. He called Billets's number and a man answered. Her husband. Bosch apologized for the late call, asked for the lieutenant and wondered while he waited what the husband knew about his wife and Kizmin Rider. When Billets picked up, Bosch told her about his review of the tapes and how little value they had.

'The one call establishes Goshen's knowledge of Aliso's trip to Vegas, as well as his interest in it. But that's about it. I think it's kind of marginal and we'll be okay without it. When we find Layla, we should be able to get the same information from her. Legally.'

'Well, that makes me feel better.'

Bosch heard her exhale. Her unspoken worry had obviously been that if the tapes contained any vital information, they would have to have been brought forward to prosecutors, thereby alienating Fitzgerald and ending her own career.

'Sorry for the late call,' Bosch said, 'but I thought you might want to know as soon as I knew.'

'Thanks, Harry. I'll see you in the morning.'

After he hung up he tried Eleanor Wish's line once more and again there was no answer. Now the slight worry he'd had in his chest bloomed into a full-fledged concern. He wished he was still in Vegas so he could go to her apartment to see if she was there and just not answering or if it was something worse.

Bosch got himself another beer from the refrigerator and went out to the back deck. The new deck was larger than its predecessor and offered a deeper view into the Pass. It was dark and peaceful out. The usual hiss of the Hollywood Freeway far below was easily tuned out. He watched the spotlights from Universal Studios cut across the starless sky and finished his beer, wondering where she was.

On Wednesday morning, Bosch got to the station at eight and typed out reports detailing his moves and investigation in Las Vegas. He made copies and put them in the lieutenant's mailbox and then clipped the originals into the already inch-thick murder book that Edgar had started. He filed no report on his conversations with Carbone and Fitzgerald or his review of the tapes OCID had made off Aliso's office phone. His work was only interrupted by frequent walks to the watch office for coffee.

He had completed these chores by ten o'clock but waited another five minutes before calling the department's gun shop. He knew from experience that he should not call before the time the report on the bullet comparisons was to be finished. He threw in the extra five minutes just to make sure. It was a long five minutes.

As he called, Edgar and Rider gravitated toward his spot at the homicide table so that they could immediately get the comparison results. It was a make-or-break point in the investigation and they all knew it. Bosch asked for Lester Poole, the gun tech assigned the case. They had worked together before. Poole was a gnomish man whose whole life revolved around guns, though as a civilian employee of the department he did not carry one himself. But there was no one more expert at the gun shop than he. He was a curious man in that he would not acknowledge anyone who called him Les. He insisted on being called Lester or even just

Poole, never the diminutive of Lester. Once he confided to Bosch that this was because he feared that if he became known as Les Poole, it would only be a matter of time before some smartass cops started calling him Cess Poole. It was his intention never to let that happen.

'Lester, it's Harry,' Bosch said when the tech picked up. 'You're the man this morning. What have you got for me?'

'I've got good and bad news for you, Harry.'

'Give me the bad first.'

'Just finished with your case. Haven't written the report yet but this is what I can tell you. The gun has been wiped clean of prints and is not traceable. Your doer used acid on the serial and I couldn't bring it up with any of my magic tricks. So that's that.'

'And the good?'

'I *can* tell you that you've got yourself a match between the weapon and the bullets extracted from your victim. It's a definite match.'

Bosch looked up at Edgar and Rider and gave the thumbs-up. They exchanged a high five and then Bosch watched as Rider gave Lieutenant Billets the thumbs-up through the glass of her office. Bosch then saw Billets pick up her phone. Bosch presumed she was calling Gregson at the DA's office.

Poole told Bosch that the report would be finished by noon and shipped through intradepartmental courier. Bosch thanked him and hung up. He stood up smiling and then walked with Edgar and Rider into the lieutenant's office. Billets spent another minute on the phone and Bosch could tell she was talking to Gregson. She then hung up.

'That's a very happy man there,' she said.

'He should be,' Edgar said.

'All right, so now what?' Billets asked.

'We go over there and drag that desert dirtbag's ass back here,' Edgar said.

'Yes, that's what Gregson said. He's going to go over to babysit the hearing. It's tomorrow morning, right?'

'Supposed to be,' Bosch said. 'I'm thinking of heading over there today. There are a couple loose ends I want to square away, maybe take another shot at finding the girlfriend, and then I want to make the arrangements so we can get out of there with him as soon as the judge says go.'

'Fine,' Billets said. Then to Edgar and Rider, she asked, 'Did you two decide who is going with Harry?'

'Me,' Edgar said. 'Kiz is more plugged in on the financial stuff. I'll go with Harry to get this sucker.'

'Okay, fine. Anything else?'

Bosch told them about the gun being untraceable, but this didn't seem to dent the euphoria engendered by the ballistics match. The case was looking more and more like a slam dunk.

They left the office after a few more self-congratulatory statements and Bosch went back to his phone. He dialed Felton's office at Metro. The captain picked up right away.

'Felton, it's Bosch in L.A.'

'Bosch, what's up?'

'Thought you might want to know. The gun checks out. It fired the bullets that killed Tony Aliso.'

Felton whistled into the phone.

'Damn, that's nice and neat. Lucky ain't going to feel so lucky when he hears about that.'

'Well, I'm coming out in a little while to tell him.'

'Good. When you going to be here?'

'Haven't set it up yet. What about the extradition hearing? We still on for tomorrow morning?'

'Absolutely, as far as I know. I'll have somebody double-check to make sure. His lawyer might be trying to make waves but that won't work. This added piece of evidence will help, too.'

Bosch told him that Gregson would be coming out in the morning to aid the local prosecutor if needed.

'That's probably a wasted trip but he's welcome just the same.'

'I'll tell him. Listen, if you've got a spare body, there's still one loose end bugging me.'

'What?'

'Tony's girlfriend. She was a dancer at Dolly's till she got fired by Lucky on Saturday. I still want to talk to her. She goes by the name of Layla. That's all I have. That and her phone number.'

He gave Felton the number and the captain said he'd have somebody check into it.

'Anything else?'

'Yeah, one other thing. You know Deputy Chief Fitzgerald out here, don't you?'

'Sure do. We've worked cases together.'

'You talked to him lately?'

'Uh, no . . . no. Not in – it's been a while.'

Bosch thought he was lying but decided to let it go. He needed the man's cooperation for at least another twenty-four hours.

'Why do you ask, Bosch?'

'No reason. Just thought I'd ask. He's been advising us from this end, that's all.'

'Good to hear that. He's a very capable individual.'

'Capable. Yeah, that he is.'

Bosch hung up and then immediately set about making travel arrangements for himself and Edgar. He booked two rooms at the Mirage. They were above the department's maximum allowance for hotel rooms but he was sure Billets would approve the vouchers. Besides, Layla had called him once at the Mirage. She might try again.

Last, he reserved round-trip tickets for himself and Edgar out of Burbank. On the Thursday afternoon return he reserved one more seat for Goshen.

Their flight out left at three-thirty and got them into Las Vegas an hour later. He figured that would give them plenty of time to do what they had to do.

Nash was in the gatehouse and came out to greet Bosch with a smile. Harry introduced Edgar.

'Looks like you guys've got yourself a real whodunit, eh?'

'Looks that way,' Bosch said. 'You got any theories?'

'Not a one. I gave your girl the gate log, she tell you that?'

'She's not my girl, Nash. She's a detective. Pretty good one, too.'

'I know. I didn't mean nothing.'

'So, is Mrs Aliso home today?'

'Let's take a look.'

Nash slid the door of the gatehouse back open, went inside and picked up a clipboard. He scanned it quickly and flipped back to the prior page. After scanning it he put the clipboard down and came back out.

'She should be there,' he said. 'Hasn't been out in two days.'

Bosch nodded his thanks.

'I gotta call her, you know,' Nash said. 'Rules.'

'No problem.'

Nash raised the gate and Bosch drove through.

Veronica Aliso was waiting at the open door of her house when they got there. She was wearing tight gray leggings beneath a long loose T-shirt with a copy of a Matisse painting on it. She had on a lot of makeup again. Bosch introduced Edgar and she led them to the living room. They declined an offer for something to drink.

'Well, then, what can I do for you men?'

Bosch opened his notebook and tore out a page he had already written on. He handed her the page.

'That's the number of the coroner's office and the case number,' he said. 'The autopsy was completed yesterday and the body can be released to you now. If you are already working with a funeral home, just give that case number to them and they'll take care of it.'

She looked at the page for a long moment.

'Thank you,' she finally said. 'You came all the way up here to give me this?'

'No. We also have some news. We've arrested a man for your husband's murder.'

Her eyes widened.

'Who? Did he say why he did this?'

'His name is Luke Goshen. He's from Las Vegas. Have you ever heard of him?'

Confusion spread across her face.

'No, who is he?'

'He's a mobster, Mrs Aliso. And your husband knew him pretty well, I'm afraid. We're going to Las Vegas now to get him. If all goes well, we will be coming back with him tomorrow. Then the case will proceed through the courts. There will be a preliminary hearing in municipal court, and then if Goshen is bound over for trial as we assume he will be, there will be a trial in Los Angeles Superior Court. It is likely you will have to testify briefly during the trial. Testify for the prosecution.'

She nodded, her eyes far off.

'Why did he do it?'

'We're not sure yet. We're working on that. We do know that your husband was involved in business dealings with this man's, uh, employer. A man named Joseph Marconi. Do you recall if your husband ever mentioned Goshen or Joseph Marconi?'

'No.'

'What about the names Lucky or Joey Marks?'

She shook her head in the negative.

'What business dealings?' she asked.

'He was cleaning money for them. Washing it through his film business. You sure you did not know anything about this?'

'Of course not. Do I need my lawyer? You know he already told me not to talk to you people.'

Bosch gave an easy smile and held his hands up.

'No, Mrs Aliso, you don't need your lawyer. We're just trying to get to the facts of the case. If you knew something about your husband's business dealings, it might help us build a case against this man Goshen and possibly his employer. You see, right now we've got this Goshen character pretty well tied up for this. We're not sweating that. We've got ballistics, fingerprints, hard evidence. But he wouldn't have done what he did if Joey Marks didn't tell him to. Joey Marks is who we'd really like to get. And the more information I have about your husband and his business, the better the chance we have of getting to Joey Marks. So if there is anything you can help us with, now is the time to tell us.'

He was silent and waited. She looked down at the now folded piece of paper in her hand. She finally nodded to herself and looked at him.

'I know nothing about his business,' she said. 'But there was a call last week. It came here on Wednesday night. He took it in the office and closed the door but . . . I went to the door and listened. I could hear his side of it.'

'What did he say?'

'He called the caller Lucky. I know that. He did a lot of listening and then he said he'd be out there by the end of the week. He then said he'd see the caller at the club. And that was it.'

Bosch nodded.

'Why didn't you tell us this before?'

'I didn't think it was important. I . . . you see, I thought he was talking to a woman. The name Lucky, I thought it was a woman's name.'

'Was that why you were listening through the door?'

She averted her eyes and nodded her head.

'Mrs Aliso, have you ever hired a private investigator to follow your husband?'

'No. I thought about it but I didn't.'

'But you suspected he was having an affair?'

'Affairs, Detective. I not only suspected, I knew. A wife can tell.'

'Okay, Mrs Aliso. Do you remember anything else about the telephone conversation? Anything else that was said?'

'No. Just what I told you.'

'It might help us with the court case, as far as questions of premeditation go, if we could isolate this call. Are you sure it was Wednesday?'

'Yes, because he left the next day.'

'What time did the call come in?'

'It was late. We were watching the news on Channel 4. So it was after eleven and before eleven-thirty. I don't think I can narrow it down any further.'

'Okay, Mrs Aliso, that's good.'

Bosch looked over at Edgar and raised his eyebrows. Edgar just nodded. He was ready to go. They stood up and Veronica Aliso led them to the door.

'Oh,' Bosch said before he got to the door. 'There was a question that came up about your husband. Do you know, did he have a regular doctor that he went to?'

'Yes, on occasion. Why?'

'Well, I wanted to check to see if he suffered from hemorrhoids.'

She looked like she was about to laugh.

'Hemorrhoids? I don't think so. I think Tony would've complained loud and often if he did.'

'Really?'

Bosch was standing in the doorway now.

'Yes, really. Besides, you just told me that the autopsy was completed, wouldn't that doctor be able to tell you the answer to that question?'

Bosch nodded. She had him there.

'I guess so, Mrs Aliso. The only reason I ask is that we found a tube of Preparation H in his car. I was wondering why it was there if, you know, he didn't need it.'

She smiled this time.

'Oh, that's an old performer's trick.'

'A performer's trick?'

'You know, actresses, models, dancers. They use that stuff.'

Bosch looked at her, waiting for more. She didn't say anything.

208

'I don't get it,' he said. 'Why do they use it?'

'Under their eyes, Detective Bosch. You know, shrinks the swelling? Well, you put it under your eyes and the bags from all that hard living get shrunk, too. Probably half the people who buy that stuff in this town use it under their eyes, not what it's supposed to be used for. My husband . . . he was a vain man. If he was going to Las Vegas to be with some young girl, I think he would have done this. It was just like him.'

Bosch nodded. He thought of the unidentified substance under Tony Aliso's eyes. You learn something new every day, he thought. He would have to call Salazar.

'How do you think he would have known about that?' he asked.

She was about to answer but hesitated, then she just hiked her shoulders.

'It's a not-so-secret Hollywood secret,' she said. 'He could've learned it anywhere.'

Including from you, Bosch thought but didn't say. He just nodded and stepped through the door.

'Oh, one last thing,' he said before she closed it. 'This arrest is probably going to hit the media today or tomorrow. We'll try to contain it as much as possible. But in this town, nothing's ever sacred or secret for long. You should be prepared for that.'

'Thank you, Detective.'

'You might want to think about a small funeral. Something inside. Tell the director not to give information out over the phone. Funerals always make good video.'

She nodded and closed the door.

On the way out of Hidden Highlands, Bosch lit a cigarette and Edgar didn't object.

'She's a cold piece of work,' Edgar said.

'That she is,' Bosch answered. 'What do you think of the phone call from Lucky?'

'It's just one more piece. We got Lucky by the balls. As far as he's concerned, it's over.'

Bosch took Mulholland along the crest of the mountains until it wound down to the Hollywood Freeway. They passed without comment the fire road down which Tony Aliso had been found. At the freeway, Bosch turned south so he could pick up the 10 in downtown and head east.

'Harry, what's up?' Edgar asked. 'I thought we were leavin' outta Burbank.'

'We're not flying. We're driving.'

'What are you talking about?'

'I only reserved the flights in case somebody checked. When we get to Vegas, we let on that we flew in and that we're flying out right after the hearing with Goshen. Nobody has to know we're driving. You okay with that?'

'Yeah, sure, fine. I get it. Precautions, settin' a smoke screen in case somebody checks. I can dig it. You never know with the mobsters, do you?'

'Or with the cops.'

IV

VI

Averaging over ninety miles an hour, including a fifteen-minute stop at a McDonald's, they got to Las Vegas in four hours. They drove to McCarran International Airport, parked in the garage and took their briefcases and overnighters out of the trunk. While Edgar waited outside, Bosch went into the terminal and rented a car at the Hertz counter.

It was almost four-thirty by the time they got to the Metro building. As they walked through the detective bureau, Bosch saw Iverson sitting at his desk and talking to Baxter, who stood nearby. A thin smile played on Iverson's face but Bosch ignored it and went straight to Felton's office. The police captain was behind his desk doing paperwork. Bosch knocked on the open door and then entered.

'Bosch, where ya been?'

'Taking care of details.'

'This your prosecutor?'

'No, this is my partner, Jerry Edgar. The prosecutor isn't coming out until the morning.'

Edgar and Felton shook hands but Felton continued to look at Bosch.

'Well, you can call him and tell him not to bother.'

Bosch looked at him a moment. He knew now why Iverson had smiled. Something was going on.

'Captain, you're always full of surprises,' he said. 'What is it this time?'

Felton leaned back in his chair. He had an unlit cigar, one end soggy with saliva, on the edge of the desk. He picked it up and clenched it between two fingers. He was playing it out, obviously trying to get a rise out of Bosch. But Bosch didn't bite and the captain finally spoke.

'Your boy, Goshen, is packing his bags.'

'He's waiving extradition?'

'Yeah, he got smart.'

Bosch took the chair in front of the desk and Edgar took one to the right. Felton continued.

'Fired that mouthpiece Mickey Torrino and got his own guy. Not that much of an improvement, but at least the new guy's got Lucky's best interest in mind.'

'And how did he get smart?' Bosch asked. 'You tell him about the ballistics?'

'Sure, I told him. Brought him over, told him the score. I also told him how we broke his alibi down to shit.'

Bosch looked at him but didn't ask the question.

'Yeah, that's right, Bosch. We haven't been exactly sitting over here on our asses. We went to work on this guy and we're helping to pound him into the ground for you. He said he never left his office Friday night until it was time to go home at four. Well, we went over and checked that office out. There's a back door. He could've come in and gone out. Nobody saw him from the time Tony Aliso left until four, when he came out to close the club. That gave him plenty of time to go out there, take down Tony and hop the last flight back. And here's the kicker. Girl that works over there goes by the name of Modesty. She got into it with another dancer and went to the office to complain to Lucky. She said nobody answered when she knocked. So she tells Gussie she wants to see the boss and he tells her the boss ain't in. That was about midnight.'

Felton nodded and winked.

'Yeah, and what did Gussie say about that?'

'He isn't saying shit. We don't expect him to. But if he wants to get on the stand and back up Lucky's alibi, you can tear him apart easy. He's got a record goin' back to the seventh grade.'

'All right, never mind him. What about Goshen?'

'Like I said, we brought him over this morning and told him what we got and that he was running out of time right quick. He had to make a decision and he made it. He switched lawyers. That's about as clear a sign as you're going to get. He's ready to deal, you ask me. That means you'll get him and Joey Marks, a few of the other douche bags in town. We'll take the biggest bite out of the outfit in ten years. Everybody's happy.'

Bosch stood up. Edgar followed suit.

'This is the second time you've done this to me,' Bosch said, his voice measured and controlled. 'You're not going to get a third. Where is he?'

'Hey, cool down, Bosch. We're all working for the same thing.'

'Is he here or not?'

'He's in interview room three. Last I checked, Weiss was in there with him, too. Alan Weiss, he's the new lawyer.'

'Has Goshen given you any statement?'

'No, of course not. Weiss gave us the particulars. No negotiating until you get him to L.A. In other words, he'll waive and you take him home. Your people will have to work out the deal over there. We're out of it after today. Excepting when you come back to pick up Joey Marks. We'll help with that. I've been waiting for that day for a long time.'

Bosch left the office without further word. He walked through the squad room without looking at Iverson and made his way to the rear hallway that led to the interview rooms. He lifted the flap that covered the door's small window and saw Goshen in blue jail overalls sitting at the small table, a much smaller man in a suit across from him. Bosch knocked on the glass, waited a beat and opened the door.

'Counselor? Could we speak for a moment outside?'

'Are you from L.A.? It's about time.'

'Let's talk outside.'

As the lawyer got up, Bosch looked past him at Goshen. The big man was handcuffed to the table. It was barely thirty hours since Bosch had seen him last but Luke Goshen was a different man. His shoulders seemed slumped, as if he was closing in on himself. His eyes had a hollow look, the kind of stare that comes from a night of looking at the future. He didn't look at Bosch. After Weiss stepped out, Bosch closed the door.

Weiss was about Bosch's age. He was trim and deeply tanned. Bosch wasn't sure but thought he wore a hairpiece. He wore glasses with thin gold frames. In the few seconds he had to size the lawyer up, Bosch decided that Goshen had probably done well for himself.

After introductions Weiss immediately got down to business.

'My client is willing to waive any challenge to extradition. But, Detectives, you need to act quickly. Mr Goshen does not feel comfortable or safe in Las Vegas, even in Metro lockup. My hope was that we would have been able to go before a judge today but it's too late now. But at nine a.m. tomorrow, I'll be in court. It's already arranged with Mr Lipson, the local prosecutor. You'll be able to take him to the airport by ten.'

'Slow down a second, Counselor,' Edgar said. 'What's the hurry all of a sudden? Is it 'cause Luke in there heard about the ballistics we got or because maybe Joey Marks has heard, too, and figures he better cut his losses?'

'I guess maybe it's easier for Joey to put the hit out on him in Metro than all the way over in L.A., right?' Bosch added.

Weiss looked at them as if they were some form of life he had not previously encountered.

'Mr Goshen doesn't know anything about a hit and I hope that statement is just part of the usual intimidation tactics you employ. What he does know is he is being set up to take the fall for a crime he did not commit. And he feels the best way to handle this is to cooperate fully in a new environment. Someplace away from Las Vegas. Los Angeles is his only choice.'

'Can we talk to him now?'

Weiss shook his head.

'Mr Goshen won't be saying a word until he's in Los Angeles. My brother will take the case from there. He has a practice there. Saul Weiss, you may have heard of him.'

Bosch had but shook his head in the negative.

'I believe he has already contacted your Mr Gregson. So, you see, Detective, you're just a courier here. Your job is to get Mr Goshen on a plane tomorrow morning and get him safely to Los Angeles. It will most likely be out of your hands after that.'

'Most likely not,' Bosch said.

He stepped around the lawyer and opened the door to the interview room. Goshen looked up. Bosch stepped in and moved to the table. He leaned over it and put his hands flat on the table. Before he could speak, Weiss had moved into the room and was talking.

'Luke, don't say a word to this man. Don't say a word.'

Bosch ignored Weiss and looked only at Goshen.

'All I want, Lucky, is a show of faith. You want me to take you to L.A., get you there safe, then give me something. Just answer one question. Where—'

'He has to take you anyway, Luke. Don't fall for this. I can't represent you if you don't listen to me.'

'Where's Layla?' Bosch asked. 'I'm not leaving Vegas until I talk to her. If you want to get out of here in the morning, I've got to talk to her tonight. She's not at her place. I talked to her roommate, Pandora, last night and she says Layla's been gone a couple of days. Where is she?'

Goshen looked from Bosch to Weiss.

'Don't say a word,' Weiss said. 'Detective, if you step out, I'd like to confer with my client. I think, actually, that might be something I won't have a problem with him answering.'

'Hope not.'

Bosch went back into the hallway with Edgar. He put a cigarette in his mouth but didn't light it.

'Why's Layla so important?' Edgar asked.

'I don't like loose ends. I want to know how she fits.'

Bosch didn't tell him that he knew from the illegal tapes that Layla had called Aliso and asked, at Goshen's request, when he'd be coming out to Vegas. If they found her, he would have to draw it out of her during the interview without giving away that he already knew it.

'It's also a test,' he did tell Edgar. 'To see how far we can get Goshen to go with us.'

The lawyer stepped out then and closed the door behind him.

'If you try that again, talking to him when I specifically said he would not respond, then we will have no relationship whatsoever.'

Bosch felt like asking what relationship they already had but let it go.

'Is he going to tell us?'

'No. I am. He said that when this person Layla first came to work at the club, he gave her a ride home a few nights. On one of those nights she asked him to drop her at a different place because she was trying to avoid somebody she was dating at the time and she thought he might be waiting at her apartment. Anyway, it was a house in North Las Vegas. She told him it was where she grew up. He doesn't have the exact address but said the place was at the corner of Donna Street and Lillis. The northeast corner. Try there. That's all he had.'

Bosch had his notebook out and wrote the street names down.

'Thank you, Counselor.'

'While you have the notebook out, write down court-room ten. That's where we will be tomorrow at nine. I trust you will make secure arrangements for my client's safe delivery?'

'That's what a courier is for, right?'

'I'm sorry, Detective. Things are said in the heat of the moment. No offense.'

'None taken.'

Bosch went out to the squad room and used the phone at an empty desk to call Southwest and change the reservations on the return flight from three in the afternoon to a ten-thirty morning flight. Bosch didn't look at Iverson but could tell the detective was watching him from a desk fifteen feet away.

When he was done Bosch stuck his head in Felton's office. The captain was on the phone. Bosch just mock-saluted him and was gone.

Back in the rental car, Edgar and Bosch decided to go over to the jail and make arrangements for the custody transfer before trying to find Layla.

The jail was next to the courthouse. A discharge sergeant named Hackett gave the detectives a rudimentary rundown on how and where Goshen would be delivered to them. Since it was after five and the shifts had changed, Bosch and Edgar would be dealing with a different sergeant in the morning. Still, it made Bosch feel more comfortable seeing the routine ahead of time. They would be able to put Goshen into their car in an enclosed and safe loading-dock area. He felt reasonably sure that there wouldn't be trouble. At least not there.

With directions from Hackett, they drove into a middle-class neighborhood in North Las Vegas and found the house where Goshen had once dropped Layla off. It was a small bungalow-style house with an aluminum awning over each window. There was a Mazda RX7 parked in the carport.

An older woman answered the door. She was mid-sixties and well preserved. Bosch thought he could see some of the photo of Layla in her face. Bosch held his badge up so she could see it.

'Ma'am, my name is Harry Bosch and this is Jerry Edgar. We're over from Los Angeles and we are looking for a young woman we need to talk to. She's a dancer and goes by the name Layla. Is she here?'

'She doesn't live here. I don't know what you're talking about.'

'I think you do, ma'am, and I'd appreciate it if you'd help us out.'

'I told you, she's not here.'

'Well, we heard she's staying here with you. Is that right? Are you her mother? She's tried to contact me. There's no reason for her to be afraid or to not want to talk to us.'

'I'll tell her that if I see her.'

'Can we come in?'

Bosch put his hand on the door and firmly but slowly started to push it open before she could reply.

'You can't just . . .'

She didn't finish. She knew what she was going to say would be meaningless. In a perfect world the cops couldn't just push their way in. She knew it wasn't a perfect world.

Bosch looked around after he entered. The furnishings were old, having to last a few more years than they were intended to and she probably thought they would have to when she bought them. It was the standard couch and matching chair setup. There were patterned throws on each, probably to cover the wear. There was an old TV, the kind with a dial to change the channels. There were gossip magazines spread on a coffee table.

'You live here alone?' he asked.

'Yes, I do,' she said indignantly, as if his question was an insult.

'When was the last time you saw Layla?'

'Her name's not Layla.'

'That was my next question. What is her name?'

'Her name's Gretchen Alexander.'

'And you are?'

'Dorothy Alexander.'

'Where is she, Dorothy?'

'I don't know and I didn't ask.'

'When'd she leave?'

'Yesterday morning.'

Bosch nodded to Edgar and he took a step back, turned and headed down a hallway leading to the rear of the house.

'Where's he going?' the woman asked.

'He's just going to take a look around, that's all,' Bosch said. 'Sit down here and talk to me, Dorothy. Faster we get this over with, the faster we're out of here.'

He pointed to the chair and remained standing until she finally sat. He then moved around the coffee table and sat on the couch. Its springs were shot. He sank so low in it that he had to lean forward and even then it felt like his knees were halfway up to his chest. He got out his notebook.

'I don't like him messing around in my things,' Dorothy said, looking back over her shoulder toward the hallway.

'He'll be careful.' Bosch took out his notebook. 'You seemed to know we were coming. How'd you know that?'

'I know what she told me, is all. She said the police might come. She didn't say anything about them coming all the way from Los Angeles.'

She said *Angeles* with a hard G.

'And you know why we're here?'

'Because of Tony. She said he went and got himself killed over there.'

'Where did Gretchen go, Dorothy?'

'She did not tell me. You can ask me all the times you like but my answer's always going to be the same. I don't know.'

'Is that her sports car in the carport?'

'Sure is. She bought it with her own money.'

'Stripping?'

'I always said money was the same whether it was made one way or the next.'

Edgar came in then and looked at Bosch. Harry nodded for him to report.

'Looks like she was here. There's a second bedroom. Ashtray on the nightstand's full. There's a space on the rod in the closet where it looks like somebody had hung up some clothes. They're gone now. She left this.'

He held his hand out and cradled in his palm was a small oval picture frame with a photograph of Tony Aliso and Gretchen Alexander. They had their arms around each other and were smiling at the camera. Bosch nodded and looked back at Dorothy Alexander.

'If she left, why'd she leave her car here?'

'Don't know. A taxi came for her.'

'Did she fly?'

'How could I know that if I don't know where she was going?'

Bosch pointed a finger at her like a gun.

'Good point. Did she say when she'd be back?'

'No.'

'How old is Gretchen?'

'She'll be twenty-three.'

'How'd she take the news about Tony?'

'Not well. She was in love and now her heart's broken. I'm worried about her.'

'You think she might do something to hurt herself?'

'I don't know what she might do.'

'Did she tell you she was in love, or did you just think that?'

'I just didn't think it up, she told me. She confided in me and it was the truth. She said they were going to get married.'

'Did she know Tony Aliso was already married?'

'Yes, she knew. But he told her, he said that it was over and it was just a matter of time.'

Bosch nodded. He wondered if it was the truth. Not the truth that Gretchen might have believed, but the truth that Tony Aliso believed. He looked down at the blank page of his notebook.

'I'm trying to think if there is anything else,' he said. 'Jerry?'

Edgar shook his head, then spoke.

'I guess I'd just like to know why a mother would let her daughter do that for a living. Taking her clothes off like that.'

'Jerry, I—'

'She has a talent, mister. Men came from all over the country and when they see her they keep coming back. Because of her. And I'm not her mother. I might as well have been, her own went and left her with me a long time ago. But she has a talent and I'm not talking to you two anymore. Get out of my house.'

She stood up, as if ready to physically enforce her edict if she needed to. Bosch decided to let her have her say and stood up, putting his notebook away.

'I'm sorry for the intrusion,' he said as he dug a business card out of his wallet. 'If you hear from her, would you give her this number? And tonight she can get me at the Mirage again.'

'I'll tell her if I hear from her.'

She took the card and followed them to the door. On the front step Bosch looked back at her and nodded.

'Thanks, Mrs Alexander.'

'For what?'

They were quiet for a while driving back to the Strip. Eventually, Bosch asked Edgar what he thought of the interview.

'She's a crusty old bitch. I had to ask that question. Just to see how she'd react. Other than that, I think this Layla or Gretchen is just a dead end. Just some stupid girl Tony was leading on. You know, it's usually the strippers that are working the angles. But this time I think it was Tony.'

'Maybe.'

Bosch lit a cigarette and dropped back into silence. He

was no longer thinking of the interview. As far as he was concerned, the work for the day was over and he was now thinking about Eleanor Wish.

When he got to the Mirage, Bosch swung the car into the circle in front and pulled to a stop near the front doors.

'Harry, man, what are you doing?' Edgar said. 'Bullets might pop for the Mirage, but she isn't going to dig into the company wallet for valet parking.'

'I'm just dropping you off. I'm going to go switch the cars tonight. I don't want to go anywhere near that airport tomorrow.'

'That's cool, but I'll go with you, man. Nothin' to do here but lose money on the machines.'

Bosch reached over and opened the glove box and pushed the trunk-release button.

'No, Jed, I'm going on my own. I want to think about some things. Grab your stuff outta the trunk.'

Edgar looked at him a long moment. Bosch had not called him Jed in a long time. Edgar was about to say something but apparently thought better of it. He opened the door.

'Okay, Harry. You want to grab dinner or something later?'

'Yeah, maybe. I'll call you in your room.'

'You're the man.'

After Edgar slammed the trunk, Bosch drove back out onto Las Vegas Boulevard and then north to Sands. It was dusk and the day's dying light was being replaced with the neon glow of the city. In ten minutes he pulled into a parking space in front of Eleanor Wish's apartment building. He took a deep breath and got out of the car. He had to know. Why had she not answered his calls? Why had she not responded to his message?

When he got to the door, he felt his guts seize as if gripped in a huge fist. The note he had carefully folded and squeezed into the doorjamb two nights before was still there. Bosch looked down at the worn doormat and then squeezed his eyes shut. He felt a tremendous wave of the guilt he had worked so hard to bury come forth from inside. He had once made a phone call that got an innocent man killed. It had been a mistake, something he could not possibly have seen coming, but it happened just the same and he had worked hard to put it not behind him but, at least, in a place where he could live with it. But now Eleanor. Bosch knew what he would find behind the door. Asking Felton for her number and address had sent things into motion, a terrible motion that ended with her being hauled into Metro and her fragile dignity and belief that bad things were behind her being crushed.

Bosch kicked over the doormat on the off chance she had left a key. There was none. His lock picks were in the glove compartment of the car parked at the airport. He hesitated a moment, focused on a spot over the doorknob, then stepped back, raised his left leg and drove his heel into the door. It splintered along the jamb and flew open. Bosch slowly stepped into the apartment.

He noticed nothing amiss in the living room. He moved quickly into the hallway and then down into the bedroom. The bed was unmade and empty. Bosch stood there for a moment, taking it all in. He realized he hadn't taken a breath since he had kicked in the door. He slowly exhaled and began breathing normally. She was alive. Somewhere. At least he thought so. He sat down on the bed, took out a cigarette and lit it. His feeling of relief was quickly crowded by other doubts and nagging questions. Why hadn't she called? Hadn't there been something real about what they had shared?

'Hello?'

A man's voice came from the front of the apartment. Bosch assumed it was someone who had heard him pop the door. He stood up and headed out of the bedroom.

'Yeah,' he said. 'I'm back here. I'm with the police.'

He stepped into the living room and saw a man

impeccably dressed in a black suit with a white shirt and black tie. It wasn't what Bosch expected.

'Detective Bosch?'

Bosch tensed and didn't answer.

'There's someone outside who would like to talk to you.'

'Who?'

'He'll tell you who he is and what his business is.'

The man walked out the front door, leaving it up to Bosch whether to follow. He hesitated a moment and did.

There was a stretch limousine in the parking lot, its engine running. The man in the black suit walked around and got into the driver's seat. Bosch watched this for a moment and then walked toward the limo. He brought his arm up instinctively and brushed it against his coat until he felt the reassuring shape of his gun beneath it. As he did this, the rear door closest to him opened and a man with a rough, dark face beckoned to him. Bosch showed no hesitation. It was too late now.

Bosch ducked into the big car and took a seat facing the rear. There were two men sitting on the plushly padded backseat. One was the rough-faced man, who was casually dressed and slouching in his luxurious spot, and the other an older man in an expensive three-piece suit, the tie pulled tight to his neck. Sitting between the two men on a padded armrest was a small black box with a green light glowing on it. Bosch had seen such a box before. It detected electronic radio waves emitted by eavesdropping devices. As long as that green light glowed they could talk and be reasonably assured they wouldn't be overheard and recorded.

'Detective Bosch,' the rough-faced man said.

'Joey Marks, I presume.'

'My name is Joseph Marconi.'

'What can I do for you, Mr Marconi?'

'I thought we'd have a little conversation, that's all. You, me and my attorney here.'

'Mr Torrino?'

The other man nodded.

'Heard you lost a client today.'

'That's what we want to talk to you about,' Marconi said. 'We've got a problem here. We—'

'How did you know where I was?'

'I've had some fellows watching it for me. We kind of figured you'd be back. Once you left that note, especially.'

They had obviously followed him and he wondered when that had started. His mind then jumped to another conclusion and he suddenly knew what the meeting was all about.

'Where's Eleanor Wish?'

'Eleanor Wish?' Marconi looked at Torrino and then back at Harry. 'I don't know her. But I suppose she'll turn up.'

'What do you want, Marconi?'

'I just wanted this chance to talk, that's all. Just a little calm conversation. We've got a problem here and maybe we can work it out. I want to work with you, Detective Bosch. Do you want to work with me?'

'Like I said, what do you want?'

'What I want is to straighten this out before it gets too far out of hand. You are going down the wrong road here, Detective. You are a good man. I had you checked out. You've got ethics and I appreciate that. Whatever you do in life, you need a code of ethics. You have that. But you are on the wrong road here. Tony Aliso, I had nothing to do with that.'

Bosch smirked and shook his head.

'Look, Marconi, I don't want your alibi. I'm sure it's airtight but I couldn't care less. You can still pull a trigger from three hundred fifty miles away. It's been done from farther away, know what I mean?'

'Detective Bosch, there is something wrong here. Whatever that rat bastard is telling you, it's a lie. I'm clean on Tony A., my people are clean on Tony A., and I'm simply giving you this opportunity to make it right.'

'Yeah, and how do I do that? Just kick Lucky loose so you

can pick him up outside the jail in your limo here, take him for a ride out into the desert? Think we'll ever see Lucky again?'

'You think you'll ever see that lady ex-FBI agent again?'

Bosch stared at him a moment, letting his anger build up until he felt a slight tremor tick in his neck. Then, in one quick move, he pulled his gun and leaned across the space between the seats. He grabbed the thick gold braided chain around Marconi's neck and jerked him forward. He pressed the barrel deep into Marconi's cheek.

'Excuse me?'

'Easy now, Detective Bosch,' Torrino said then. 'You don't want to do something rash.'

He put a hand on Bosch's arm.

'Take your hand off me, you asshole.'

Torrino removed his hand and raised it along with his other one in a surrendering gesture.

'I just want to calm things down a little here, that's all.'

Bosch leaned back into his seat but kept his gun in his hand. The muzzle had left a ring of skin indentation and gun oil on Marconi's cheek. He wiped it away with his hand.

'Where is she, Marconi?'

'I just heard she wanted to get away for a few days, Bosch. No need to overreact like that. We're friends here. She'll be back. In fact, now that I know you're so, uh, attached to her, I'll personally guarantee she'll be back.'

'In exchange for what?'

Hackett was still on duty at the Metro jail. Bosch told him he had to talk to Goshen for a couple of minutes in regard to a security issue. Hackett hemmed and hawed about it being against regulations to set up an after-hours visit but Bosch knew it was done on occasion for the locals, against the rules or not. Eventually Hackett gave way and took Bosch to a room lawyers used to interview clients and told him to wait. Ten minutes later, Hackett waltzed Goshen into the room and cuffed one wrist to the chair he was placed in. Hackett then folded his arms and stood behind the suspect.

'Sergeant, I need to talk to him alone.'

'Can't do it. It's a security issue.'

'We're not going to talk anyway,' Goshen interjected.

'Sergeant,' Bosch said. 'What I tell this man, whether he chooses to talk to me or not, could put you in danger if it becomes known you have this knowledge. Know what I mean? Why add that potential danger to your list? Five minutes. It's all I want.'

Hackett thought a moment and without a word left them alone.

'Pretty smooth, Bosch, but I'm not talking to you. Weiss said you might try a backdoor run. He said you'd want to try to get into the candy jar before it's time. I'm not playing with you. Get me to L.A., sit me in front of the people who can deal, and then we'll deal. Everybody will get what they want then.'

'Shut up and listen, you stupid fuck. I don't give a shit about any deal anymore. The only deal I'm worried about now is whether to keep you alive or not.'

Bosch saw he had his attention now. He waited a few moments to turn the squeeze up and then began.

'Goshen, let me explain something to you. In all of Las Vegas there is exactly one person I care about. One. You take her out of the picture and the whole place could dry up and blow away and I really wouldn't worry about it. But there's that one person I care about. And out of all the people in this place, she's the one that your employer decides to grab and hold against me.'

Goshen's eyes narrowed in concern. Bosch was talking about his people. Goshen knew exactly what was coming.

'So the deal I'm talking about is this,' Bosch said. 'You for her. Joey Marks said if you never get to L.A., then my friend comes back. And vice versa. You understand what I'm telling you?'

Goshen looked down at the table and slowly nodded.

'Do you?'

Bosch pulled his gun and pointed it three inches from the big man's face. Goshen went cross-eyed looking at the barrel's black hole.

'I could blow your shit away right here. Hackett would come in here and I'd tell him you made a move for my gun. He'd go along. He set the meeting up here. It's against the rules. He'd have to go along.'

Bosch withdrew the gun.

'Or tomorrow. This is how it goes tomorrow. At the airport we're waiting for our flight. There's a commotion over at the machines. Somebody's won a big fucking jackpot and my partner and I make the mistake of looking over there. Meantime, somebody – maybe it's your pal Gussie – puts a six-inch stiletto in your neck. End of you, my friend comes home.'

'What do you want, Bosch?'

Bosch leaned across to him.

'I want you to give me the reason not to do it. I don't give a shit about you, Goshen, dead or alive. But I'm not going to let any harm befall her. I've made mistakes in my life, man. I once got somebody killed that shouldn't have been killed. You understand that? It's not going to happen again. This is redemption, Goshen. And if I have to give a piece of shit like you up to get it, I'll do it. There's only one alternative. You know Joey Marks, where would he have her?'

'Oh, Jesus, I don't know.'

Goshen rubbed a hand over his scalp.

'Think, Goshen. He's done this kind of thing before. It's routine for you people. Where would he hold somebody he doesn't want anyone to find?'

'There was . . . there's a couple of safe houses he uses. He'd, uh, . . . I think for this he'd use the Samoans.'

'Who are they?'

'These two big fuckers he uses. Samoans. They're brothers. Their names are too hard to say. We call them Tom and Jerry. They've got one of the safe houses. Joey would use their place for this. The other place is mostly for counting cash, putting up people from Chicago.'

'Where is the house with the Samoans?'

'It's in North Vegas, not too far from Dolly's, actually.'

On a piece of notebook paper Bosch gave him, Goshen drew a crude map with directions to the house.

'You've been there, Goshen?'

'A few times.'

Bosch turned the piece of paper over on the table.

'Draw the layout of the house.'

Bosch pulled the dusty detective car he had picked up at the airport into the valet circle at the Mirage and jumped out. A valet approached but Bosch walked past him.

'Sir, your keys?'

'I'll only be a minute.'

The valet was protesting that he couldn't just leave the car there when Bosch disappeared through the revolving door. As he crossed through the casino toward the lobby, Bosch scanned the players for Edgar, his eyes stopping on every tall black man, of whom there were few. He didn't see Edgar.

On a house phone in the lobby he asked for Edgar's room and then breathed an almost audible sigh of relief when his partner picked up the phone.

'Jerry, it's Bosch. I need your help.'

'What's up?'

'Meet me out front at the valet.'

'Now? I just got room service. When you didn't call I—'

'Right now, Jerry. And did you bring your vest from L.A.?'

'My vest? Yeah. What's—'

'Bring your vest with you.'

Bosch hung up before Edgar could ask any questions.

As he turned to head back to the car, he came face to face with someone he knew. At first, because the man was well dressed, Bosch thought it was one of Joey Marks's men, but then he placed him. Hank Meyer, Mirage security.

'Detective Bosch, I didn't expect to see you here.'

'Just got in tonight. Came to pick somebody up.'

'You got your man then?'

'We think so.'

'Congratulations.'

'Listen, Hank, I gotta go. I've got a car blocking traffic in the front circle.'

'Oh, that's your car. I just heard that on the security radio. Yes, please move it.'

'I'll talk to you later.'

Bosch made a move to pass him.

'Oh, Detective? Just wanted you to know we still haven't had that betting slip come in.'

Bosch stopped.

'What?'

'You asked if we'd check to see if anyone cashed the bet your victim put down Friday night. On the Dodgers?'

'Oh, yeah, right.'

'Well, we went through the computer tapes and located the sequence number. I then checked the number on the computer. No one has collected on it yet.'

'Okay, thanks.'

'I called your office today to let you know but you weren't there. I didn't know you were coming here. We'll keep an eye out for it.'

'Thanks, Hank. I gotta go.'

Bosch started walking away but Meyer kept talking.

'No problem. Thank *you*. We look forward to opportunities to cooperate with and hopefully help our law enforcement brethren.'

Meyer smiled broadly. Bosch looked back at him and felt like he had a weight tied to his leg. He couldn't get away from him. Bosch just nodded and kept going, trying to remember the last time he had heard the phrase *law enforcement brethren*. He was almost across the lobby when he glanced back and saw that Meyer was still behind him.

'One more thing, Detective Bosch.'

Bosch stopped but lost his patience.

'Hank, what? I've got to get out of here.'

'It will just take a second. A favor. I assume your department will go to the press with this arrest. I'd appreciate it if you kept any mention of the Mirage out of it. Even our help, if you don't mind.'

'No problem. I won't say a word. Talk to you later, Hank.'

Bosch turned and walked away. It was unlikely the Mirage would have been mentioned in any press release anyway, but he understood the concern. Guilt by association. Meyer was mixing public relations with casino security. Or maybe they were the same thing.

Bosch got to the car just as Edgar came out, carrying his bullet-proof vest in his hand. The valet looked at Bosch balefully. Bosch took out a five and handed it to him. It didn't do much to change his disposition. Then Bosch and Edgar jumped in the car and took off.

The safe house Goshen told Bosch about looked deserted when they drove by. Bosch pulled the car to a stop a half block away.

'I still don't know about this, Harry,' Edgar said. 'We should be calling in Metro.'

'I told you. We can't. Marks has to have somebody inside Metro. Or else he wouldn't have known to snatch her in the first place. So we call Metro, he finds out and she's dead or moved somewhere else before Metro even makes a move. So we go in and we call Metro afterward.'

'If there is an afterward. Just what the hell are we going to do? Go in blasting? This is cowboy shit, Harry.'

'No, all you're going to do is get behind the wheel, turn the car around and be ready to drive. We might have to leave in a hurry.'

Bosch had hoped to use Edgar as a backup but after he'd told him the situation on the way over, it was clear that Edgar wasn't going to be solid. Bosch went to plan B, where Edgar was simply a wheel man.

Bosch opened his door and looked back at Edgar before getting out.

'You're going to be here, right?'

'I'll be here. Just don't get killed. I don't want to have to explain it.'

'Yeah, I'll do my best. Let me borrow your cuffs and pop the trunk.'

Bosch put Edgar's cuffs into his coat pocket and went to the trunk. At the trunk, he took out his vest and put it on over his shirt and then put his coat back on to hide his holster. He pulled up the trunk liner and lifted up the spare tire. Below it was a Glock 17 pistol wrapped in an oily rag. Bosch popped the clip on it, checked the top bullet for corrosion and then put the weapon back together. He put it in his belt. If there was going to be any shooting on this mission, he wasn't going to use his service gun.

He came up alongside the driver's window, saluted Edgar and headed down the street.

The safe house was a small concrete-block-and-plaster affair that blended in with the neighborhood. After jumping a three-foot fence Bosch took the gun from his belt and held it at his side as he walked along the side of the house. He saw no light emitted from any of the front or side windows. But he could hear the muffled sound of television. She was here. He could feel it. He knew Goshen had told the truth.

When he got to the rear corner, he saw there was a pool in the backyard as well as a covered porch. There was a concrete slab with a satellite dish anchored to it. The modern Mafia crash pad, Bosch thought. You never knew how long you'd have to hole up, so it was good to have five hundred channels.

The backyard was empty but as Bosch turned the corner he saw a lighted window. He crept down the back of the house until he was close. The blinds were drawn on the window, but by getting close and looking between the cracks he could see them in there. Two huge men he immediately assumed were the Samoans. And Eleanor. The Samoans sat on a couch in front of a television. Eleanor sat on a kitchen chair next to the couch. One wrist and one ankle were handcuffed to the chair. Because the shade of a floor lamp was in the way, he could not see her face. But he recognized her clothes as those she had worn on the day they had dragged her into Metro. The three of them were sitting there watching a rerun of a Mary Tyler Moore show. Bosch felt the anger building in his throat.

Bosch crouched down and tried to think of a way to get her out of there. He leaned his back against the wall and looked across the yard and the shimmering pool. He got an idea.

After taking one more glimpse through the blind and seeing that no one had moved, Bosch went back to the corner of the house to the slab where the satellite dish sat. He put his gun back in his belt, studied the equipment for a few moments and then simply used two hands to turn the dish out of alignment and point its focus toward the ground.

It took about five minutes. Bosch figured most of this must have been spent with one or the other of the Samoans fiddling with the TV and trying to get the picture back. Finally, an outdoor floodlight came on, the back door opened and one of them stepped out onto the porch. He wore a Hawaiian shirt as big as a tent and had long dark hair that flowed over his shoulders.

When the big man got to the dish, he clearly wasn't sure how to proceed. He looked at it for a long moment, then came around to the other side to see if this afforded him a better angle. He now had his back to Bosch.

Bosch stepped away from the corner of the house and came up behind the man. He placed the muzzle of the

Glock against the small of the man's back, though even the small of his back wasn't small.

'Don't move, big man,' he said in a low, calm voice. 'Don't say a word, 'less you want to spend the rest of your life in a wheelchair with your piss sloshing around in a bag.'

Bosch waited. The man did not move and said nothing.

'Which are you, Tom or Jerry?'

'I'm Jerry.'

'Okay, Jerry, we're going to walk over to the porch. Let's go.'

They moved to one of two steel supporter beams that held up the porch roof. Bosch kept the gun pressed against the man's shirt the whole time. He then reached into his pocket and pulled out Edgar's cuffs. He handed them around the girth of the man and held them up.

'Okay, take 'em. Cuff yourself around the beam.'

He waited until he heard both cuffs click, then came around and checked them, clicking them tightly around the man's thick wrists.

'Okay, that's good, Jerry. Now, do you want me to kill your brother? I mean I could just walk in there and waste him and get the girl. That's the easy way. You want me to do it that way?'

'No.'

'Then do exactly what I tell you. If you fuck up, he dies. Then you die 'cause I can't afford to leave a witness. Got it?'

'Yes.'

'Okay, without saying his name, because I don't trust you, just call to him and ask if the picture's back on the TV. When he says no, tell him to come out here and help. Tell him she'll be fine, she's handcuffed. Do it right, Jerry, and everybody lives. Do it wrong and some people aren't going to make it.'

'What do I call him?'

'How 'bout "Hey, Bro?" That oughta work.'

Jerry did as he was told and did it right. After some back-and-forth banter, the brother stepped out onto the porch, where he saw Jerry with his back to him. Just as he realized something wasn't right, Bosch came from the blind spot to his right rear and put the gun on him. Using his own cuffs this time, he locked the second brother, who he guessed was slightly larger than the first and had on a louder shirt, to the porch's other support beam.

'Okay, take five, boys. I'll be back in a minute. Oh, who has the key to the cuffs on the woman?'

They both said, 'He does.'

'That's not smart, guys. I don't want to hurt anybody. Now who has the cuff key?'

'I do.'

The voice came from behind him, from the porch door. Bosch froze.

'Slowly, Bosch. Toss the gun into the pool and turn around real slow like.'

Bosch did what he was told and turned around. It was Gussie. And Bosch could see the delight and hate in his eyes, even in the dark. He stepped onto the porch and Bosch could see the shape of a gun in his right hand. Bosch immediately became angry with himself for not casing the house further or even asking Jerry if there was anyone other than his brother and Eleanor in the house. Gussie raised the gun and pressed its barrel against Bosch's left cheek, just below the eye.

'See how it feels?'

'Been talking to the boss, huh?'

'That's right. And we're not stupid, man, you're stupid. We knew you might try something like this. Now we gotta call him and see what he wants to do. But first off, what you're gonna do is unhook Tom and Jerry. Right the fuck now.'

'Sure, Gussie.'

Bosch was contemplating reaching into his coat and going for his other gun but knew it was suicide as long as

Gussie held his gun at point-blank range. He started slowly reaching into his pocket for his keys when he saw the movement to his left and heard the shout.

'Freeze it up, asshole!'

It was Edgar. Gussie didn't move an inch. After a few moments of this stand-off, Bosch reached into his coat, pulled his own gun and pushed the muzzle up into Gussie's neck. They stood there staring at each other for a long moment.

'What do you think?' Bosch finally said. 'You want to try it? See if we both get one off?'

Gussie said nothing and Edgar moved in. He put the muzzle of his gun against Gussie's temple. A smile broke across Bosch's face and he reached up and took Gussie's gun from him and threw it into the pool.

'I didn't think so.'

He looked over at Edgar and nodded his thanks.

'You got him? I'll go get her.'

'I got him, Harry. And I'm hoping he does something stupid, the big fat fuck.'

Bosch checked Gussie for another weapon and found none.

'Where's the cuff key?' he asked.

'Fuck you.'

'Remember the other night, Gussie? You want a repeat performance? Tell me where the fucking key is.'

Bosch figured his own cuff key would fit but he wanted to make sure he got one away from Gussie. The big man finally blew out his breath and told Bosch the key was on the kitchen counter.

Bosch went inside the house, his gun out, his eyes scanning for more surprises. There was nobody. He grabbed the cuff key off the kitchen counter and went into the back den where Eleanor was. When he stepped into the room and her eyes rose to his, he saw something that he knew he would always cherish. It wasn't something he believed he could ever put into words. The giving way of fear, the knowledge of safety. Maybe thanks. Maybe that was how people looked at heroes, he thought. He rushed to her and knelt in front of her chair so that he could unlock the cuffs.

'You okay, Eleanor?'

'Yes, yes. I'm fine. I knew, Harry. I knew you would come.'

He had the cuffs off and he just looked up at her face. He nodded and pulled her into a quick hug.

'We gotta go.'

They went out the back, where the scene did not look as if it had changed at all.

'Jerry, you got him? I'm going to find a phone and call Felton.'

'I got—'

'No,' Eleanor said. 'Don't call them. I don't want that.'

Bosch looked at her.

'Eleanor, what are you talking about? These guys, they abducted you. If we hadn't come here, there's a good chance they would've taken you out into the desert tomorrow and planted you.'

'I don't want the cops. I don't want to go through all of that. I just want this to end.'

Bosch looked at her a long moment.

'Jerry, you got him?' he asked.

'I got him.'

Bosch went to Eleanor and grabbed her arm and led her back into the house. When they were in the alcove by the kitchen and far enough away that the men outside could not hear them, he stopped and looked at her.

'Eleanor, what's going on?'

'Nothing. I just don't want—'

'Did they hurt you?'

'No, I'm—'

'Did they rape you? Tell me the truth.'

'No, Harry. It is nothing like that. I just want this to end here.'

'Listen to me, we can take down Marks, his lawyer and those three assholes out on the porch. That's why I'm here. Marks told me he had you.'

'Don't kid yourself, Harry. You can't touch Marks on this. What did he really tell you? And who's your witness going to be? Me? Look at me. I'm a convicted felon, Harry. Not only that, I used to be one of the good guys. Just think what a mob lawyer can do with that.'

Bosch didn't say anything. He knew she was right.

'Well, I'm not going to put myself through that,' she said. 'I got a dose of reality when they jerked me out of my home and took me down to Metro. I'm not going to go to bat for them on this. Now can you get me out of here?'

'As long as you are sure. You can't change your mind once we're out of here.'

'I'm as sure as I'll ever be.'

Bosch nodded and let her out to the porch.

'It's your lucky day, boys,' he said to the three thugs. Then to Edgar he said, 'We're pulling out of here. We'll talk about it later.'

Edgar just nodded. Bosch went one by one to the Samoans and put their own cuffs on their wrists and then took off the others. When he was done, he held the key up in front of the smaller of the two giants and then tossed it into the pool. He went over to the fence that ran behind the pool and took down a long pole with a net attached to the end of it. He fished his gun off the bottom and handed it to Eleanor to hold. He then returned to Gussie, who was dressed completely in black. Edgar was still standing to his right, holding the gun against his temple.

'Almost didn't recognize you without the tux, Gussie. Will you give Joey Marks a message?'

'Yeah. What?'

'Fuck you. Just tell him that.'

'He's not going to like that.'

'I don't really care. He's lucky I don't leave him three bodies here as a message.'

Bosch looked over at Eleanor.

'Anything you want to say or do?'

She shook her head.

'Then we're outta here. Only thing is, Gussie, we're one set of cuffs short. That's too bad for you.'

'There's rope in the—'

Bosch hit him on the bridge of the nose with the butt end of his gun, crushing whatever bone had not been broken in their earlier scuffle. Gussie dropped heavily to his knees, then pitched forward, his face making a thud on the porch tile.

'Harry! Jesus!'

It was Edgar. He looked shocked by the sudden violence.

Bosch just looked at him a moment and said, 'Let's go.'

When they got to Eleanor's apartment, Bosch backed the car up nearly to the door and popped the trunk.

'We don't have a lot of time,' he said. 'Jerry, you stay out here, watch for anybody coming. Eleanor, you can fill the trunk with whatever you can fit in there. That's about all you can take.'

She nodded. She understood. Las Vegas was over for her. She could no longer stay, not with what had happened. Bosch wondered if she also understood that it was all because of him. Her life would still be as it had been if he had not wanted to reach out to her.

They all got out of the car and Bosch followed Eleanor into the apartment. She studied the broken door for a moment until he told her he had done it.

'Why?'

'Because when I didn't hear from you I thought . . . I thought something else.'

She nodded again. She understood that, too.

'There's not a lot,' she said, looking around the place. 'Most of this stuff I don't care about. I probably won't even need the whole trunk.'

She went into the bedroom, took an old suitcase out of the closet and started filling it with clothes. When it was full, Bosch took it out and put it in the trunk. When he came back in, she was filling a box from the closet with her remaining clothes and other personal belongings. He saw her put a photo album in the box and then she went to the bathroom to clear the medicine cabinet.

In the kitchen all she took was a wine bottle opener and a coffee mug with a picture of the Mirage hotel on it.

'Bought this the night I won four hundred sixty-three dollars there,' she said. 'I was playing the big table and I was way in over my head but I won. I want to remember that.'

She put that in the top of the full box and said, 'That's it. That's all I have to show for my life.'

Bosch studied her a moment and then took the box out to the car. He struggled a bit, getting it to fit in next to the suitcase. When he was done, he turned around to call to Eleanor that they must go and she was already standing there, holding the framed print of *The Nighthawks*, the Edward Hopper painting. She was holding it in front of her like a shield.

'Will this fit?'

'Sure. We'll make it fit.'

At the Mirage, Bosch pulled into the valet circle again and saw the chief valet frown as he recognized the car. Bosch got out, showed the man his badge quickly so that he might not notice it wasn't a Metro badge, and gave him twenty dollars.

'Police business. I'll be twenty-thirty minutes tops. I need the car here because when we leave we're going to have to really book.'

The man looked at the twenty in his hand as if it were human feces. Bosch reached into his pocket, pulled out another twenty and gave it to him.

'Okay?'

'Okay. Leave me the keys.'

'No. No keys. Nobody touches the car.'

Bosch had to take the picture out of the trunk to get to Eleanor's suitcase and a gun kit he kept there. He then repacked the trunk and lugged the suitcase inside, waving off an offer of help from a doorman. In the lobby, he put the case down and looked at Edgar.

'Jerry, thanks a lot,' he said. 'You were there, man. Eleanor's going to change and then I'm going to shoot her out to the airport. I probably won't be back until late. So let's just meet here at eight o'clock tomorrow and we'll go to court.'

'Sure you don't need me for the airport run?'

'No, I think we're fine. Marks won't try anything now. And if we're lucky, Gussie won't be waking up for another hour or so anyway. I'm going to go check in.'

He left Eleanor there with him and went to the desk. There was no wait. It was late. After giving the clerk his credit card, he looked back at Eleanor saying her good-bye to Edgar. He put out his hand and she shook it but then she pulled him into an embrace. Edgar disappeared into the crowd of the casino.

Eleanor waited until they were in his room before she spoke.

'Why am I going to the airport tonight? You said you doubted they would do anything.'

'Because I want to make sure you're safe. And tomorrow I won't be able to worry about it. I've got court in the morning and then I'm driving Goshen to L.A. I have to know you're safe.'

'Where am I going to go?'

'You could go to a hotel but I think my place would be better, safer. You remember where it is?'

'Yes. Up off Mulholland?'

'Yeah. Woodrow Wilson Drive. I'll give you the key. Take a cab from the airport and I'll be there by tomorrow night.'

'Then what?'

'I don't know. We'll figure it out.'

She sat down on the edge of the bed and Bosch came around and sat next to her. He put his arms around her shoulders.

'I don't know if I could live in L.A. again.'

'We'll figure it out.'

He leaned in and kissed her on the cheek.

'Don't kiss me. I need to take a shower.'

He kissed her again and then pulled her back onto the bed. They made love differently this time. They were more tender, slower. They found each other's rhythm.

After, Bosch took the first shower and then while Eleanor bathed he used oil and a rag from his gun kit to clean the Glock that had been thrown into the pool. He worked the action and trigger several times to make sure the weapon was working properly. Then he filled the clip with fresh ammunition. He went to the closet and took a plastic laundry bag off the shelf, put the gun inside it and shoved it beneath a stack of clothes in Eleanor's suitcase.

After her shower Eleanor dressed in a yellow cotton summer dress and twined her hair into a French braid. Bosch liked watching her do it with such skill. When she was ready, he closed the suitcase and they left the room. The head valet came up to Bosch as he was putting the suitcase into the trunk.

'Next time, thirty minutes is thirty minutes. Not an hour.'

'Sorry 'bout that.'

'Sorry doesn't cut it. I could've lost my job, man.'

Bosch ignored him and got in the car. On the way to the airport he tried to compose his thoughts into articulate sentences that he could recite to her but it wasn't working. His emotions were too much of a jumble.

'Eleanor,' he finally said. 'Everything that's happened, it's my fault. And I want to try to make it up to you.'

She reached over and put her hand on his thigh. He put his hand on top of hers. She didn't say anything.

At the airport, Bosch parked in front of the Southwest terminal and got her suitcase out of the trunk. He locked his own gun and badge in the trunk so he could go through the airport's metal detector without a problem.

There was one last flight to L.A., leaving in twenty minutes. Bosch bought her a ticket and checked her bag. The gun would cause no problem as long as the bag was checked. He then escorted her to the terminal, where there was already a line of people making their way down the jetway.

Bosch took the key to his house off his keychain, gave it to her and told her the exact address.

'It's not the same as you might remember it,' he said. 'The old place got wrecked in the earthquake. It's been rebuilt and it's not all the way done. But it will be all right. The sheets, uh, I probably should've washed them a few days ago but didn't have time. There's fresh ones in the hallway closet.'

She smiled.

'Don't worry, I'll figure everything out.'

'Uh, listen, like I said before, I don't think that you've got anything to worry about anymore but just in case, you've got the Glock in your suitcase. That's why I checked it.'

'You cleaned it while I was in the shower, didn't you? I thought I smelled the oil when I came out.'

He nodded.

'Thanks but I don't think I'll need it anyway.'

'Probably not.'

She looked over at the line. The last people were boarding. She had to go.

'You're being very good to me, Harry. Thank you.'

He frowned.

'Not good enough. Not enough to make up for everything.'

She went up on her toes and kissed him on the cheek.

'Good-bye, Harry.'

'Good-bye, Eleanor.'

He watched her hand in her ticket and go through the door to the jetway. She didn't look back and there was a whisper in the back of his mind telling him he might never see her again. But he shut it off and walked back through the nearly deserted airport. Most of the slot machines stood mute and ignored. Bosch felt a deep sense of loneliness engulf him.

The only hitch in Thursday morning's court proceedings occurred before they started, when Weiss came out of lockup after conferring with his client and quickly went into the hall to find Bosch and Edgar conferring with Lipson, the local prosecutor who would handle the extradition hearing. Gregson had not made the trip from the L.A. County DA's office. Weiss and Lipson had given him their assurances that Luke Goshen was going to waive any objection to being brought back to California.

'Detective Bosch?' Weiss said. 'I was just in with my client and he asked me to get him some information before the hearing. He said he wanted an answer before he gave any waiver. I don't know what it's about, but I hope you haven't been in contact with my client.'

Bosch put a concerned yet puzzled look on his face.

'What's he want to know?'

'He just wanted to know how last night worked out, whatever that means. I'd like to know what is going on here.'

'Just tell him everything is fine.'

'What is fine, Detective?'

'If your client wants to tell you, he can tell you. Just deliver the message.'

Weiss stalked away, heading back toward the lockup door.

Bosch looked at his watch. It was five till nine and he figured the judge wouldn't come out to the bench at the crack of nine. None of them ever did. He reached into his pocket for his cigarettes.

'I'm going outside to have a smoke,' he told Edgar.

Bosch took the elevator down and went out to the front of the courthouse to have his cigarette. It was warm out and he thought the day would probably be another scorcher. With Las Vegas in September it was pretty much guaranteed. He was glad he'd be leaving soon. But he knew the ride through the desert during the heat of the day would be rough.

He didn't notice Mickey Torrino until the lawyer was a few feet away from him. He, too, was smoking a cigarette before going in to handle the day's business of mob-related legal work. Bosch nodded his greeting as did Torrino.

'I guess you heard by now. No deal.'

Torrino looked around to see if they were being watched.

'I don't know what you're talking about, Detective.'

'Yeah, I know. You guys never know anything.'

'I do know one thing and that's that you are making a mistake on this one. In case you care about things like that.'

'I don't think so. At least not in the big picture. We might not have the real shooter but we have the guy who set it up. And we're going to get the guy who ordered it. Who knows, maybe we'll get the whole crew. Who you going to work for then, Counselor? That is, if we don't get you, too.'

Torrino smirked and shook his head as if he were dealing with a foolish child.

'You don't know what you're dealing with here. It's not going to play. You'll be lucky if you get to keep Goshen. At best you've got only him. That's all.'

'You know, Lucky keeps making noises about being set up. He, of course, thinks it's us putting him in the frame and I know that's bullshit. But I keep thinking, "What if there is a frame?" I mean, I have to admit that him keeping that gun is hard to figure, though I've seen even dumber moves in my time. But if there is a frame and we didn't do it, who did? Why would Joey Marks frame his own guy when that guy's just going to roll over and put the finger back on Joey? Doesn't make sense. At least, from Joey's point of view. But then I started thinking, What if you were Joey's righthand man, say his lawyer, and you wanted to be the big shot, the one who makes the calls? See what I'm talking about here? This'd be a nice little way of getting rid of your nearest competitor and Joey at the same time. How would that play, Counselor?'

'If you ever repeat that bullshit story to anyone, you will be very, very sorry.'

Bosch took a step toward him so that their faces were only a foot apart.

'If you ever threaten me again, *you* will be very, very sorry. If anything ever happens to Eleanor Wish again, I will hold you personally responsible, asshole, and sorry is not the right word for how you will be then.'

Torrino stepped back, loser in the staring contest. Without another word he walked away from Bosch and toward the courthouse doors. As he opened the heavy glass door, he looked back at Bosch, then disappeared inside.

When Bosch got back to the third floor, he met Edgar as he was coming quickly out of the courtroom, followed by Weiss and Lipson. Bosch looked at the hallway clock. It was five after nine.

'Harry, whereya been, smokin' a whole pack?' Edgar asked.

'What happened?'

'It's over. He waived. We've got to bring the car around and get over to the release desk. We'll have him in fifteen minutes.'

'Detectives?' Weiss said. 'I want to know every detail of how my client will be moved and what security measures you're taking.'

Bosch put his arm on Weiss's shoulders and leaned into him in a confidential manner. They had stopped at the bank of elevators.

'The very first security measure we are taking is that we aren't telling anyone how or when we're getting back to L.A. That includes you, Mr Weiss. All you need to know is that he'll be in L.A. Municipal Court for arraignment tomorrow morning.'

'Wait a minute. You can't—'

'Yes, we can, Mr Weiss,' Edgar said as an elevator opened. 'Your client waived his opposition to extradition and in fifteen minutes he'll be in our custody. And we're not going to divulge any information about security, here or there or on the way there. Now, if you'll excuse us.'

They left him there and loaded onto the elevator. As the doors closed, Weiss shouted something about them not being allowed to talk to his client until his Los Angeles counsel had met with him.

A half hour later the Strip was in the rearview mirror and they were driving into the open desert.

'Say good-bye, Lucky,' Bosch said. 'You won't be back.'

When Goshen didn't say anything, Bosch checked him in the mirror. The big man was sitting sullenly in the back with his arms cuffed to a heavy chain that went around his waist. He returned Bosch's stare and for a brief moment Bosch thought he saw the same look he had let loose for a moment in his bedroom before he managed to drag it back inside like a naughty child.

'Just drive,' he said after he had recovered his demeanor. 'We're not having a conversation here.'

Bosch looked back at the road ahead and smiled.

'Maybe not now, but we will. We'll be talking.'

As Bosch and Edgar were leaving the Men's Central Jail in downtown Los Angeles, Bosch's pager sounded and he checked the number. He didn't recognize it but the 485 exchange told him the person paging him was in Parker Center. He took the phone out of his briefcase and returned the call. Lieutenant Billets answered.

'Detective, where are you?'

Her use of his rank instead of his name told him she probably wasn't alone. The fact that she was calling from Parker Center rather than the bureau in Hollywood told him that something had gone wrong.

'At Men's Central. What's up?'

'Do you have Luke Goshen with you?'

'No, we just dropped him off. Why, what is it?'

'Give me the booking number.'

Bosch hesitated a moment but then held the phone under his chin while he reopened his briefcase and got the number from the booking receipt. He gave Billets the number and once again asked what was going on. She once again ignored the question.

'Detective,' she said, 'I want you to come over to Parker right away. The sixth-floor conference room.'

The sixth floor was administration level. It was also where the Internal Affairs offices were. Bosch hesitated again before finally answering.

'Sure, Grace. You want Jerry, too?'

'Tell Detective Edgar to go back to Hollywood Division. I'll contact him there.'

'We've only got the one car.'

'Then tell him to take a cab and put it on his expense account. Hurry it up, Detective. We are waiting for you here.'

'We? Who's waiting?'

She hung up then and Bosch just stared at the phone for a moment.

'What is it?' Edgar asked.

'I don't know.'

Bosch stepped off the elevator into the deserted sixth-floor hallway and proceeded toward the conference room he knew was behind the last door before the entrance to the police chief's office at the end of the hall. The yellowed linoleum had been recently polished. As he walked toward his destiny with his head down, he saw his own dark reflection moving just in front of his steps.

The door to the conference room was open and as Bosch stepped in all eyes in the room were on him. He looked back at Lieutenant Billets and Captain Le Valley from the Hollywood Division and the recognizable faces of Deputy Chief Irvin Irving and an IAD squint named Chastain. But the four remaining men gathered in chairs around the long conference table were strangers to Bosch. Nevertheless, he guessed from their conservative gray suits that they were feds.

'Detective Bosch, have a seat,' Irving said.

Irving stood up, ramrod straight in a tight uniform. The dome of his shaven head shone under the ceiling fluorescents. He motioned to the empty seat at the head of the table. Bosch pulled the chair out and sat down slowly as his mind raced. He knew that this kind of showing of brass and feds was too big to have been caused by his affair with Eleanor Wish. There was something else going on and it involved only him. Otherwise, Billets would have told him to bring Edgar along.

'Who died?' Bosch asked.

Irving ignored the question. When Bosch's eyes traveled across the table to his left and up to Billets's face, the lieutenant glanced away.

'Detective, we need to ask you some questions pertaining to your investigation of the Aliso case,' Irving said.

'What are the charges?' Bosch responded.

'There are no charges,' Irving replied calmly. 'We need to clear some things up.'

'Who are these people?'

Irving introduced the four strangers. Bosch had been right, they were feds: John Samuels, an assistant U.S. Attorney assigned to the organized crime strike force, and three FBI agents from three different field offices. They were John O'Grady from L.A., Dan Ekeblad from Las Vegas and Wendell Werris from Chicago.

Nobody offered to shake Bosch's hand, nobody even nodded. They just stared at Bosch with looks that transmitted their contempt for him. Since they were feds, their dislike of the LAPD was standard issue. Bosch still couldn't figure out what was going on here.

'Okay,' Irving said. 'We're going to get some things cleared up first. I'm going to let Mr Samuels take it from here.'

Samuels wiped a hand down his thick black mustache and leaned forward. He was in the chair at the opposite end of the table from Bosch. He had a yellow legal tablet on the table in front of him but it was too far away for Bosch to be able to read what was on it. He held a pen in his left hand and used it to hold his place in his notes. Looking down at the notes, he began.

'Let's start with your search of Luke Goshen's home in Las Vegas,' Samuels said. 'Exactly who was it who found the firearm later identified as the weapon used in the killing of Anthony Aliso?'

Bosch narrowed his eyes. He tried looking at Billets again, but her eyes were focused on the table in front of her. As he scanned the other faces, he caught the smirk on Chastain's face. No surprise there. Bosch had hooked up with Chastain before. He was known as Sustained Chastain by many in the department. When departmental charges are brought against an officer, an Internal Affairs investigation and Board of Rights hearing result in one of two findings: the allegations are either sustained or ruled unfounded. Chastain had a high ratio of sustained to unfounded cases – thus the departmental moniker which he wore like a medal.

'If this is the subject of a department investigation, I think I'm entitled to representation,' Bosch said. 'I don't know what this is about but I don't have to tell you people anything.'

'Detective,' Irving said. He slid a sheet of paper across the table to Bosch. 'That is a signed order from the chief of police telling you to cooperate with these gentlemen. If you choose not to, you will be suspended without pay forthwith. And you'll be assigned your union rep then.'

Bosch looked down at the letter. It was a form letter and he had received them before. It was all part of the department's way of backing you into the corner, to the point that you had to talk to them or you didn't eat.

'I found the gun,' Bosch said without looking up from the order. 'It was in the master bathroom, wrapped in plastic and secreted between the toilet tank and the wall. Somebody said the mobsters in *The Godfather* did that. The movie. But I don't remember.'

'Were you alone when you supposedly found the weapon there?'

'Supposedly? Are you saying it wasn't there?'

'Just answer the question, please.'

Bosch shook his head in disgust. He didn't know what was going on but it was looking worse than he had imagined.

'I wasn't alone. The house was full of cops.'

'Were they in the master bathroom with you?' O'Grady asked.

Bosch just looked at O'Grady. He was at least ten years younger than Bosch, with the clean-cut looks the bureau prized.

'I thought Mr Samuels was going to handle the questioning,' Irving said.

'I am,' Samuels said. 'Were any of these cops in that bathroom with you when you located this weapon?'

'I was by myself. As soon as I saw it, I called the uniform in the bedroom in to take a look before I even touched it. If this is about Goshen's lawyer making some beef to you people about me planting the gun, it's bullshit. The gun was there, and besides, we've got enough on him without the gun. We've got motive, prints . . . why would I plant a gun?'

'To make it a slam dunk,' O'Grady said.

Bosch blew out his breath in disgust.

'It's typical of the bureau to drop everything and come after an L.A. cop just because some sleazeball gangster drops a dime. What, are they givin' annual bonuses now if you guys nail a cop? Double if it's an L.A. cop? Fuck you, O'Grady. Okay?'

'Yeah, fuck me. Just answer the questions.'

'Then ask them.'

Samuels nodded as if Bosch had scored a point and moved his pen a half inch down his pad.

'Do you know,' he asked, 'did any other police officer enter that bathroom before you entered to search it and subsequently found the gun?'

Bosch tried to remember, picturing the movements of the Metro cops in the room. He was sure no one had gone into the bathroom other than to take a quick look to make sure no one was in there hiding.

'I don't know for sure about that,' he said. 'But I doubt it. If somebody did go in, there wasn't enough time to plant the gun. The gun was already there.'

Samuels nodded again, consulted his legal pad and then looked at Irving.

'Chief Irving, I think that's as far as we want to take it for the moment. We certainly appreciate your cooperation in this matter and I expect we'll be talking again soon.'

Samuels made a move to stand up.

'Wait a minute,' Bosch said. 'That's it? You're just going to get up and leave? What the fuck is going on here? I deserve an explanation. Who made the complaint, Goshen's lawyer? Because I'm going to make a complaint right back at him.'

'Your deputy chief can discuss this with you, if he chooses to.'

'No, Samuels. You tell me. You're asking the questions, now you answer a few.'

Samuels drummed his pen on his pad for a moment and looked at Irving. Irving opened his hands to show it was his choice. Samuels then leaned forward and looked balefully at Bosch.

'If you insist on an explanation, I'll give you one,' he said. 'I'm limited, of course, in what I can say.'

'Jesus, would you just tell me what the hell is going on?'

Samuels cleared his throat before going on.

'About four years ago, in a joint operation involving the FBI offices in Chicago, Las Vegas and Los Angeles, the strike force instituted what we called Operation Telegraph. Personnel-wise it was a small operation but it had a large goal. Our goal was Joseph Marconi and the remaining tentacles of the mob's influence in Las Vegas. It took us more than eighteen months but we managed to get someone inside. An agent on the inside. And in the two years since that was accomplished, that agent was able to rise to a level of prominence in Joseph Marconi's organization, one in which he had the intended target's complete confidence. Conservatively, we were four to five months from closing the operation and going to a grand jury to seek indictments for more than a dozen high-ranking members of the Cosa Nostra in three cities, not to mention an assortment of burglars, casino cheats, bust-out artists, cops, judges, lawyers and even a few Hollywood fringe players such as Anthony N. Aliso. This is not to mention that, largely through the efforts of this undercover agent and the wiretaps authorized with probable cause gathered through him, we now have a greater understanding of the sophistication and reach of organized crime entities such as Marconi's.'

Samuels was talking as if he were addressing a press conference. He let a moment pass as he caught his breath. But he never took his eyes off Bosch.

'That undercover agent's name is Roy Lindell. Remember it, because he's going to be famous. No other agent was underground for so long and with such important results. You notice that I said *was*. He's no longer under, Detective Bosch. And for that we can thank you. The name Roy used undercover was Luke Goshen. Lucky Luke Goshen. So I want to thank you for fucking up the end of a wonderful and important case. Oh, we'll still get Marconi and all the others with what Roy's good work got us, but now it's all been marred by a . . . by you.'

Bosch felt anger backing up in his throat but tried to remain calm and he managed to speak in an even voice.

'Your suggestion then is – no, your accusation is – that I planted that gun. Well, you are wrong about that. Dead wrong. I should be angry and offended, but given the situation I understand how you made the mistake. But instead of pointing at me, maybe you folks ought to take a look at your man Goshen or whatever the hell his name is. Maybe you should question whether you left him under too long. Because that gun wasn't planted. You—'

'Don't you dare!' O'Grady blurted out. 'Don't you dare say a word about him. You, you're nothing but a fucking rogue cop! We know about you, Bosch, all your baggage. This time you went too far. You planted evidence on the wrong man this time.'

'I take it back,' Bosch said, still calm. 'I am offended. I am angry. So fuck you, O'Grady. You say I planted the gun, prove it. But first I guess you gotta prove that I was the one who put Tony Aliso in his trunk. Because how the hell else would I have the gun to plant?'

'Easy. You could've found it there in the bushes off the goddamned fire road. We already know you searched it by yourself. We—'

'Gentlemen,' Irving interjected.

'—will put you down for this, Bosch.'

'Gentlemen!'

O'Grady closed his mouth and everyone looked at Irving.

'This is getting out of hand. I'm ending this meeting. Suffice it to say, an internal investigation will be conducted and—'

'We are doing our own investigation,' Samuels said. 'Meantime, we have to figure out how to salvage our operation.'

Bosch looked at him incredulously.

'Don't you understand?' he said. 'There is no operation. Your star witness is a murderer. You left him in too long, Samuels. He turned, became one of them. He killed Tony Aliso for Joey Marks. His prints were on the body. The gun was found in his house. Not only that, he's got no alibi. Nothing. He told me he spent all night in the office, but I know he wasn't there. He left and he had time to get over here, do the job and get back.'

Bosch shook his head sadly and finished in a low voice.

'I agree with you, Samuels. Your operation is tainted now. But not because of me. It was you who left the guy in the oven too long. He got cooked. You were his handler. You fucked up.'

This time Samuels shook his head and smiled sadly. That was when Bosch realized the other shoe hadn't dropped. There was something else. Samuels angrily flipped up the top page of his pad and read a notation.

'The autopsy concludes time of death was between eleven p.m. Friday and two a.m. Saturday. Is that correct, Detective Bosch?'

'I don't know how you got the report, since I haven't seen it myself yet.'

'Was the death between eleven and two?'

'Yes.'

'Do you have those documents, Dan?' Samuels asked Ekeblad.

Ekeblad took several pages folded lengthwise from the inside of his jacket and handed them to Samuels. Samuels opened the packet and glanced at its contents and then tossed it across the table to Bosch. Bosch picked it up but didn't look at it. He kept his eyes on Samuels.

'What you have there are copies of a page from an investigative log as well as an interview report prepared Tuesday morning by Agent Ekeblad here. There are also two sworn affidavits from agents Ekeblad and Phil Colbert, who will be with us here shortly. What you'll find if you look at those is that on Friday night at midnight, Agent Ekeblad was sitting behind the wheel of his bureau car in the back parking lot at Caesar's, just off Industrial Road. His partner Colbert was there next to him and in the back seat, Agent Roy Lindell.'

He waited a beat and Bosch looked down at the papers in his hands.

'It was Roy's monthly meeting. He was being debriefed. He told Ekeblad and Colbert that just that night he had put four hundred and eighty thousand dollars cash from Marconi's various enterprises into Anthony Aliso's briefcase and sent him back to L.A. to have it put in the wash. He also, by the way, mentioned that Tony had been in the club drinking and got a little out of line with one of the girls. In his role as enforcer for Joey Marks and manager of the club, he had to get tough with Tony. He cuffed him once and jerked him around by his collar. This, I think, you might agree, would account for the fingerprints recovered from the deceased's jacket and the antemortem facial bruising noted in the autopsy.'

Bosch still refused to look up from the documents.

'Other than that, there was a lot to talk about, Detective Bosch. Roy stayed for ninety minutes. And there is no fucking way in the world he could have gotten to Los Angeles to kill Tony Aliso before two a.m., let alone three a.m. And just so you don't leave here thinking all three of these agents were involved in the murder, you should know that the meeting was monitored by four additional agents in a chase car also parked in the lot for security reasons.'

Samuels waited a beat before delivering his closing argument.

'You don't have a case. The prints can be explained and the guy you said did it was sitting with two FBI agents three hundred and fifty miles away when the shooting went down. You've got nothing. No, actually, that's wrong. You do have one thing. A planted gun, that's what you've got.'

As if on cue the door behind Bosch opened and he heard footsteps. Keeping his eyes on the documents in front of him, Bosch didn't turn around to see who it was until he felt a hand grip his shoulder and squeeze. He looked up into the face of Special Agent Roy Lindell. He was smiling, standing next to another agent who Bosch assumed was Ekeblad's partner, Colbert.

'Bosch,' Lindell said, 'I owe you a haircut.'

Bosch was dumbfounded to see the man he had just locked up standing there but quickly assimilated what had happened. Irving and Billets had already been told about the meeting in the parking lot behind Caesar's, had read the affidavits and believed the alibi. They had authorized Lindell's release. That was why Billets had asked for the booking number when Bosch had returned her page.

Bosch looked away from Lindell to Irving and Billets.

'You believe this, don't you? You think I found the gun out there in the weeds and planted it just to make the case a slam.'

There was a hesitation while each one left space for the other to answer. Finally, it was Irving.

'The only thing we know for sure is that it wasn't Agent Lindell. His story is solid. I'm reserving judgment on everything else.'

Bosch looked at Lindell, who was still standing.

'Then why didn't you tell me you were federal when we were in that room together at Metro?'

'Why do you think? For all I knew, you had already put a gun in my bathroom. You think I'm just going to tell you I'm an agent and everything would be cool after that? Yeah, right.'

'We had to play along, Bosch, to see what moves you'd make and to make sure Roy got out of the Metro jail in one piece,' O'Grady said. 'After that, we were two thousand feet above you and two thousand behind you all the way across the desert. We were waiting. Half of us were betting you made a deal with Joey Marks. You know, in for a pinch, in for a pound?'

They were taunting him now. Bosch shook his head. It seemed to be the only thing he could do.

'Don't you people see what is happening?' he said. 'You're the ones who made a deal with Joey Marks. Only you don't know it. He is playing you like a symphony. Jesus! I can't believe I'm sitting here and this is actually happening.'

'How is he playing us?' Billets asked, the first indication that she might not have gone all the way across to the other side on him.

Bosch answered, looking at Lindell.

'Don't you see? They found out about you. They knew you were an agent. So they set this all up.'

Ekeblad snorted in derision.

'They don't set things up, Bosch,' Samuels said. 'If they thought Roy was an informant, they'd just take him out to the desert and put him under three feet of sand. End of threat.'

'No, because we're not talking about an informant. I'm talking about them knowing specifically he was an agent and knowing that because of that they couldn't just take him out to the desert. Not an FBI agent. If they did that, they'd have more heat on them than the Branch Davidians ever felt. No, so what they did was make a plan. They know he's been around a couple years and knows more than enough to take them all down hard. But they can't just kill him. Not an agent. So they've got to neutralize him, taint him. Make him look like he crossed, like he's just as bad as they are. So when he testifies, they can take him apart with Tony Aliso's hit. Make a jury think that he'd carry out a hit to maintain his cover. They sell a jury that and they could all walk away.'

Bosch thought he had planted the seeds of a pretty convincing story, even having pulled it together on the fly. The others in the room looked at him in silence for a few moments, but then Lindell spoke up.

'You give them too much credit, Bosch,' he said. 'Joey's not that smart. I know him. He's not that smart.'

'What about Torrino? You going to tell me he couldn't come up with this? I just thought of it sitting here. Who knows how long he had to come up with something. Answer one question, Lindell. Did Joey Marks know that Tony Aliso had the IRS on his back, that an audit was coming?'

Lindell hesitated and looked to Samuels to see if he could answer. Bosch felt the sweat of desperation breaking on his neck and back. He knew he had to convince them or he wouldn't walk out of the room with his badge. Samuels nodded to Lindell.

'If he knew, he didn't tell me,' Lindell said.

'Well maybe that's it,' Bosch said. 'Maybe he knew but he didn't tell you. Joey knew he had a problem with Aliso and somehow he knew he had a bigger problem with you. And he and Torrino put their heads together and came up with this whole thing so they could kill two birds with the one stone.'

There was another pause, but Samuels shook his head.

'It doesn't work, Bosch. You're stretching. Besides we've got seven hundred hours of tapes. There's enough on them to put Joey away without Roy even testifying one word.'

'First of all, they might not have known there were tapes,' Billets said. 'And secondly, even if they did, it's fruit of the poison tree. You wouldn't have the tapes without Agent Lindell. You want to introduce them in court, you have to introduce him. They destroy him, they destroy the tapes.'

Billets had clearly shifted to Bosch's side of the equation and that gave him hope. It also made Samuels see that the meeting was over. He gathered up his pad and stood up.

'Well,' he said, 'I can see we aren't going any further with this. Lieutenant, you're listening to a desperate man. We don't have to. Chief Irving, I don't envy you. You have a problem and you have to do something about it. If on Monday I find out that Bosch is still carrying his badge, then I'm going to go to the sitting grand jury and get an indictment against him for evidence tampering and violating the civil rights of Roy Lindell. I will also ask our civil rights unit to look into every arrest this man has made in the last five years. A bad cop never plants evidence once, Chief. It's a habit.'

Samuels made his way around the table toward the door. The others got up and were following. Bosch wanted to jump up and throttle him but he remained outwardly calm. His dark eyes followed Samuels as the federal attorney moved to the door. He never looked back at Bosch. But before stepping out, he took one last shot at Irving.

'The last thing I want to have to do is air your dirty laundry, Chief. But if you don't take care of this, you'll leave me no choice.'

With that, the federals filed out and those remaining sat in silence for a long moment, listening to the sound of the steps tracking down the polished linoleum in the hallway. Bosch looked at Billets and nodded.

'Thanks, Lieutenant.'

'For what?'

'Sticking up for me at the end there.'

'I just don't believe you'd do it, is all.'

'I wouldn't plant evidence on my worst enemy. If I did that I'd be lost.'

Chastain shifted in his seat while a small smile played on his face, but not small enough to pass Bosch's notice.

'Chastain, you and I have hooked up a couple times before and you missed me both times,' Bosch said. 'You don't want to strike out, do you? You better sit this one out.'

'Look, Bosch, the chief asked me to sit in on this and I did that. It's his call, but I think you and that story you just wove out of thin air are full of shit. I agree with the feds on this one. If it was my choice, I wouldn't let you out of this room with a badge.'

'But it's not your choice, is it?' Irving said.

When Bosch got to his house, he carried a bag of groceries to the door and knocked but there was no answer. He kicked over the straw mat and found the key he had given Eleanor there. A feeling of sadness came over him as he bent to pick it up. She was not there.

Upon entering he was greeted by the strong smell of fresh paint, which he thought was odd because it had now been four days since he had painted. He went directly into the kitchen and put away the groceries. When he was finished, he took a bottle of beer from the refrigerator and leaned against the counter drinking it slowly, making it last. The smell of paint reminded him that now he would have plenty of time to finish all the work the house needed. He was strictly a nine-to-fiver at the moment.

He thought of Eleanor again and decided to look to see if there was a note from her or whether her suitcase might be in the bedroom. But he went no further than the living room, where he stopped and looked at the wall he had left half-painted after getting the call to the crime scene on Sunday. The wall was now completely painted. Bosch stood there a long moment, appraising the work as though it were a masterpiece in a museum. Finally he stepped to the wall and lightly touched it. It was fresh but dry. Painted just a few hours before, he guessed. Though no one was there to see it, a broad smile broke across his face. He felt a jolt of happiness break through the gray aura surrounding him. He didn't need to look for her suitcase in the bedroom. He took the painted wall as a sign, as her note. She'd be back.

An hour later, he had unpacked his overnighter and the rest of her belongings from the car and was standing in the darkness on the rear deck. He held another bottle of beer and watched the ribbon of lights moving along the Hollywood Freeway at the bottom of the hill. He had no idea how long she had stood in the frame of the sliding door to the deck and watched him. When he turned around, she was just there.

'Eleanor.'

'Harry . . . I thought you wouldn't be back until later.'

'Neither did I. But I'm here.'

He smiled. He wanted to go to her and touch her, but a cautious voice told him to move slowly.

'Thanks for finishing.'

He gestured toward the living room with his bottle.

'No problem. I like to paint. It relaxes me.'

'Yeah. Me, too.'

They looked at each other a moment.

'I saw the print,' she said. 'It looks good there.'

Bosch had taken her print of Hopper's *Nighthawks* out of the trunk and hung it on the freshly painted wall. He knew that how she reacted to seeing it there would tell him a lot about where they were and where they might be headed.

'Good,' he said, nodding and trying not to smile.

'What happened to the one I sent you?'

That had been a long time ago.

'Earthquake,' he said.

She nodded.

'Where'd you just come from?'

'Oh, I went and rented a car. You know, until I can figure out what I'm going to do. I left my car in Vegas.'

'I guess we could go over and get it, drive it back. You know, get in and out, not hang around.'

She nodded.

'Oh, I got a bottle of red wine, too. You want something? Or another beer?'

'I'll have what you're having.'

'I'm going to have a glass of wine. You sure you want that?'

'I'm sure. I'll open it.'

He followed her into the kitchen and opened the wine and took down two glasses from a cabinet and rinsed them. He hadn't had anyone who liked wine over in a long time. She poured and they touched glasses before drinking.

'So how's the case going?' she asked.

'I don't have a case anymore.'

She creased her brow and frowned.

'What happened? I thought you were bringing your suspect back.'

'I did. But it's no longer my case. Not since my suspect turned out to be a bureau agent with an alibi.'

'Oh, Harry.' She looked down. 'Are you in trouble?'

Bosch put his glass on the counter and folded his arms.

'I'm on a desk for the time being. I've got the squints investigating me. They think – along with the bureau – that I planted evidence against the agent. The gun. I didn't. But I guess somebody did. When I figure out who, then I'll be okay.'

'Harry, how did this—'

He shook his head, and moved toward her and put his mouth on hers. He gently took the glass out of her hand and put it on the counter behind her.

After they made love, Bosch went into the kitchen to open a bottle of beer and make dinner. He peeled an onion and chopped it up along with a green pepper. He then cleared the cutting board into a frying pan and sautéed the mixture with butter, powdered garlic and other seasonings. He added two chicken breasts and cooked them until the meat was easy to shred and pull away from the bone with a fork. He added a can of Italian tomato sauce, a can of crushed tomatoes and more seasonings. He finished by pouring a shot of red wine from Eleanor's bottle in. While it all simmered, he put a pot of water on to boil for rice.

It was the best dinner he knew how to cook in a kitchen. He would have preferred grilling something on the deck, but the grill had been hauled away when the original house was demolished after the earthquake. While he had re-placed the house, he had not yet gotten around to getting a new grill. He decided as he mixed rice into the boiling water that if Eleanor chose to stay for a while, he would get the grill.

'Smells good.'

He turned and she was standing in the doorway. She was dressed in blue jeans and a denim shirt. Her hair was damp from the shower. Bosch looked at her and felt the desire to make love to her again.

'I hope it tastes good,' he said. 'This is a new kitchen, but I don't really know how to use it yet. Never did much cooking.'

She smiled.

'I can tell already it will be good.'

'Tell you what, will you stir this every few minutes while I take a shower?'

'Sure. I'll set the table.'

'Okay. I was thinking we'd eat out on the deck. It doesn't smell like paint out there.'

'Sorry.'

'No, I mean it will be nice out there. I'm not complaining about the paint. In fact, that was all a ruse, you know, to leave the wall half painted like that. I knew you wouldn't be able to resist.'

She smiled.

'A regular Tom Sawyer, detective third grade.'

'Maybe not for long.'

His comment ruined the moment and she stopped smiling. He silently chastised himself on the way back to the bedroom.

After his shower, Bosch put the last part of his recipe into the frying pan. He took a handful of frozen peas and mixed them into the simmering chicken-and-tomato stew. As he brought the food and wine out to the picnic table on the deck, he told Eleanor, who was standing at the railing, to have a seat.

'Sorry,' he said as they settled in. 'I forgot about a salad.'

'This is all I need.'

They started the meal in silence. He waited.

'I like it a lot,' she finally said. 'What do you call this?'

'I don't know. My mother just called it Chicken Special. I think that's what it was called in a restaurant where she first had it.'

'A family recipe.'

'The only one.'

They ate quietly for a few minutes during which Bosch surreptitiously tried to watch her to see if she really enjoyed the food. He was pretty sure she did.

'Harry,' Eleanor said after a while, 'who are the agents involved in this?'

'They're from all over; Chicago, Vegas, L.A.'

'Who from L.A.?'

'Guy named John O'Grady? You know him?'

It had been more than five years since she had worked in the bureau's L.A. field office. FBI agents moved around a lot. He doubted she would know O'Grady and she said she didn't.

'What about John Samuels? He's the AUSA on it. He's from the OC strike force.'

'Samuels I know. Or knew. He was an agent for a while. Not a particularly good one. Had the law degree and when he figured out he wasn't much of an investigator, he decided he wanted to prosecute.'

She started laughing and shook her head.

'What?'

'Nothing. Just something they used to say about him. It's kind of gross.'

'What?'

'Does he still have his mustache?'

'Yeah.'

'Well, they used to say that he could sure put a case together for prosecution, but as far as investigating it out on the street went, he couldn't find shit if it was in his own mustache.'

She laughed again – a little too hard, Bosch thought. He smiled back.

'Maybe that's why he became a prosecutor,' she added.

Something occurred to Bosch then and he quickly withdrew into his thoughts. Eventually he heard Eleanor's voice.

'What?'

'You disappeared. I asked what you were thinking. I didn't think it was that bad a joke.'

'No, I was just thinking about what a bottomless hole I'm in. About how it doesn't really matter whether Samuels actually believes I'm dirty on this. He needs me to be dirty.'

'How so?'

'They've got cases to make with their undercover guy against Joey Marks and his crew. And they've got to be ready and able to explain how a murder weapon got to be in their guy's house. Because if they can't explain it, then Joey's lawyers are going to shove it down their throats, make it look like their guy is tainted, is a killer worse than the people he was after. That gun has reasonable doubt written all over it. So the best way to explain away the gun is

271

to blame it on the LAPD. On me. A bad cop from a bad department who found the gun in the weeds and planted it on the guy he thought did it. The jury will go along. They'll make me out to be this year's Mark Fuhrman.'

He saw the humor was long gone from her face now. There was obvious concern in her eyes but he thought there was also sadness. Maybe she understood, too, how well he was boxed in.

'The alternative is to prove that Joey Marks or one of his people planted the gun because they somehow knew Luke Goshen was an agent and needed to discredit him. Though that's the likely truth, it's a harder road to follow. It's easier for Samuels just to throw the mud on me.'

He looked down at his half-finished dinner and put his knife and fork on the plate. He couldn't eat anymore. He took a long drink of wine and then kept the glass in his hand, ready.

'I think I'm in big trouble, Eleanor.'

The gravity of his situation was finally beginning to weigh on him. He'd been operating on his faith that the truth would win out and now clearly saw how little truth would have to do with the outcome. He looked up at her. Their eyes connected and he saw that she was about to cry. He tried to smile.

'Hey, I'll think of something,' he said. 'I might be riding a desk for the time being, but I'm not taking both oars out of the water. I'm going to figure this out.'

She nodded but her face still looked distraught.

'Harry, remember when you found me in the casino that first night and we went to the bar at Caesar's and you tried to talk to me? Remember what you said about doing things differently if you had the chance to go back?'

'Yes, I remember.'

She wiped her eyes with her palms, before any tears could show.

'I have to tell you something.'

'You can tell me anything, Eleanor.'

'What I told you about me paying Quillen and the street tax and all of that . . . there's more to it.'

She looked at him with intensity now, trying to read his reaction before going further. But Bosch sat stone still and waited.

'When I first went to Vegas after getting out of Frontera, I didn't have a place or a car and I didn't know anyone. I just thought I'd give it a shot. You know, playing cards. And there was a girl I knew from Frontera. Her name was Patsy Quillen. She told me to look up her uncle – that was Terry Quillen – and that he'd probably stake me after he checked me out and saw me play. Patsy wrote him and gave me an introduction.'

Bosch sat silently, listening. He now had an idea where this was going but couldn't figure out why she was telling him.

'So he staked me. I got the apartment and some money to play with. He never said anything about Joey Marks, though I should have known the money came from somewhere. It always does. Anyway, later, when he finally told me who had really staked me, he said I shouldn't worry because the organization he worked for didn't want me to pay the nut back. What they wanted was just the interest. Two hundred a week. The tax. I didn't think I had a choice. I'd already taken the money. So I started paying. In the beginning it was tough. I didn't have it a couple times and it was double the next week plus that week's regular tax. You get behind and there's no way out.'

She looked down at her hands and clasped them on the table.

'What did they make you do?' Bosch asked quietly, also averting his eyes.

'It's not what you're thinking,' she said. 'I was lucky . . . they knew about me. I mean, that I had been an agent. They figured they could use my skills, as dormant as they were. So they had me just watch people. Mostly in casinos. But there were a few times I followed them outside. Most of the time I didn't even know exactly who they were or why they wanted the information, but I just watched, sometimes played at the same tables, and reported to Terry what the guy was winning or losing, who he was talking to, any nuances of his game . . . you know, things like that.'

She was just rambling now, putting off the meat of what she had to tell him, but Bosch didn't say anything. He let her go on.

'A couple days I watched Tony Aliso for them. They wanted to know how much he was dropping at the tables and where he was going, the usual stuff. But as it turned out, he wasn't losing. He actually was quite good at cards.'

'Where did you watch him go?'

'Oh, he'd go out to dinner, to the strip club. He'd run errands, things like that.'

'You ever see him with a girl?'

'One time. I followed him on foot from the Mirage into Caesar's and then into the shopping arcade. He went to Spago for a late lunch. He was alone and then the girl showed up. She was young. I thought at first it was like an escort thing, but then I could tell, he knew her. After lunch they went back to his hotel room for a while and when they came out, they took his rental and he took her to get a manicure and to buy cigarettes and to a bank while she opened an account. Just errands. Then they went to the strip club in North Vegas. When he left, he was alone. I figured then she was a dancer.'

Bosch nodded.

'Were you watching Tony last Friday night?' Bosch asked.

'No. That was just coincidence that we ended up at the same table. It was because he was waiting to go to the high-stakes table. I actually hadn't done anything for them in a month or so, other than pay the weekly tax, until . . . Terry . . .'

Her voice trailed off. They were finally at the point of no return.

'Until Terry what, Eleanor?'

She looked toward the fading horizon. The lights across the Valley were coming on and the sky was pink neon mixed with gray paint. Bosch kept his eyes on her. She spoke while still watching the end of the day.

'Quillen came to my apartment after you took me home from Metro. He took me to the house where you found me. They wouldn't tell me why and they told me not to leave. They said nobody would get hurt if I just did what I was told. I sat around that place for two days. They only put the handcuffs on me that last night. It was like they knew you'd be coming then.'

She let a beat of silence follow. It was there if Bosch wanted to use it but he didn't say a word.

'I guess what I'm trying to tell you is that the whole thing was something less than an abduction.'

She looked back down at her hands now.

'And that's obviously why you didn't want us to call out Metro,' Bosch said quietly.

She nodded.

'I don't know why I didn't tell you everything before. I'm really sorry, Harry. I . . .'

Now Bosch felt his own words sticking in his throat. Her story was understandable and believable. He even felt for her and understood that she was in her own bottomless pit. He saw how she had believed she had no choices. What he couldn't see, and what hurt him, was why she couldn't tell him everything from the start.

'Why couldn't you tell me, Eleanor?' he managed to get out. 'I mean right away. Why didn't you tell me that night?'

'I don't know,' she said. 'I wanted . . . I guess I hoped it would just go away and you would never have to know.'

'Then why are you telling me now?'

She looked right at him.

'Because I hated not telling you everything . . . and because while I was there at that house I heard something that you need to know now.'

Bosch closed his eyes.

'I'm sorry, Harry. Very sorry.'

He nodded. He was, too. He washed his hands over his face. He didn't want to hear this but knew he had to. His mind raced, jumping between feelings of betrayal and confusion and sympathy. One moment his thoughts were of Eleanor and the next they were on the case. They knew. Someone had told Joey Marks about Eleanor and him. He thought of Felton and Iverson, then Baxter and every cop he had seen at Metro. Someone had fed Marks the information and they used Eleanor as bait for him. But why? Why the whole charade? He opened his eyes and looked at Eleanor with a blank stare.

'What was it that you heard and that I need to know?'

'It was the first night. I was kept in that back room, where the TV was, where you came and got me. I was kept in there and the Samoans were there, in and out. But from time to time there were people in other parts of the house. I heard them talking.'

'Gussie and Quillen?'

'No, Quillen left. I know his voice and it wasn't him. And I don't think it was Gussie. I think it was Joey Marks and someone else, probably the lawyer, Torrino. Whoever it was, I heard the one man call the other Joe at one point. That's how come I think it was Marks.'

'Okay. Go on, what did they say?'

'I couldn't hear all of it. But one man was telling the other, the one he called Joe, what he had learned about the police investigation. About the Metro side of things, I think. And I heard the one called Joe get very angry when he was told the gun had been found at Luke Goshen's house. And I remember his words. Very clearly. He was yelling. He said, "How the hell did they find the gun there when we didn't do the goddamned hit?" And then he said some more things about the cops planting the gun and he said, "You tell our guy that if this is some kind of shakedown, then he can fuck off, he can forget it." I didn't hear much after that. They lowered their voices and the first guy was just trying to calm the other guy down.'

Bosch stared at her for a few moments, trying to analyze what she had overheard.

'Do you think it was a show?' he asked. 'You know, put on for your benefit because they figured you'd turn around and tell me what you heard?'

'I did at first, and that's another reason I didn't tell you this right away,' she said. 'But now I'm not so sure. When they first took me, when Quillen was driving me out there and I was asking a lot of questions, he wouldn't answer them. But he did say one thing. All he would tell me was that they needed me for a day or two to run a test on somebody. He would explain no further. A test, that's all he said.'

'A test?'

Bosch looked confused.

'Listen to me, Harry. I've done nothing but think about this since you got me out of there.'

She held up a finger.

'Let's start with what I overheard. Let's say it was Joey Marks and his lawyer, and let's say it wasn't a show but what they said was true. They didn't put the hit on Tony Aliso, okay?'

'Okay.'

'Look at it from their perspective. They had nothing to do with this, but one of their in-close guys gets picked up for it. And from what they hear from their source in Metro, it's looking like a slam-bang case. I mean, the cops have fingerprints and the murder weapon found right there in Goshen's bathroom. Joey Marks has to be thinking either it's all been planted by the cops or maybe Goshen went and did this on his own for some unknown reason. Either way, what do you think his immediate concern would be?'

'Damage control.'

'Right. He has to figure out what is going on with Goshen and what's the damage. But he can't because Goshen has gone and gotten himself his own attorney. Torrino has no access to him. So what Joey does instead is he and Torrino set up a test to see if the reason Goshen's gotten his own attorney is because he's going to talk.'

'Make a deal.'

'Right. Now, let's say that from their source in Metro they know that the lead cop on the case has a relationship with someone they know of and have their hooks in. Me.'

'So they just take you to the safe house and wait. Because they know that if I find out where the safe house is and show up to get you, or if I call up Metro and say I know where you are, then they know Goshen is the only one who could have told me. It means he's talking. That was the test Quillen was talking about. If I don't show, they're cool. It means Goshen is standing up. If I *do* show up, then they know they've got to get to Goshen in Metro right quick and put a hit on him.'

'Right, before he can talk. That's how I figured it, too.'

'So that would mean that Aliso wasn't really a hit – at least by Marks and his people – and that they had no idea Goshen was an agent.'

She nodded. Bosch felt the surge of energy that comes with making a huge step through the murky darkness of an investigation.

'There was no trunk music,' he said.

'What?'

'The whole Las Vegas angle, Joey Marks, all of that, it was all a diversion. We went completely down the wrong path. It had to be engineered by someone very close to Tony. Close enough to know what he was doing, to know about the money washing, and to know how to make his killing look mob connected. To pin it on Goshen.'

She nodded.

'And that's why I had to tell you everything. Even if it meant we . . .'

Bosch looked at her. She didn't finish the line and neither did he.

Bosch took a cigarette out of his pocket and put it in his

mouth but didn't light it. He leaned across the table and picked up her plate and his own. He spoke to her as he slid off the bench.

'I don't have any dessert, either.'

'That's okay.'

He took the plates into the kitchen and rinsed them and put them into the dishwasher. He had never used the new appliance before and spent some time leaning over it and trying to figure out how to operate it. Once he got it going, he started cleaning the frying pan and the pot in the sink. The simple work began to relax him. Eleanor came into the kitchen with her wineglass and watched him for a few moments before speaking.

'I'm sorry, Harry.'

'It's okay. You were in a bad situation and you did what you had to do, Eleanor. Nobody can be blamed for that. I probably would have done everything you did.'

It was a few moments before she spoke again.

'Do you want me to go?'

Bosch turned off the water and looked into the sink. He could make out his dark image reflected in the new stainless steel.

'No,' he said. 'I don't think so.'

Bosch arrived at the station at seven Friday morning with a box of glazed doughnuts from the Fairfax Farmers Market. He was the first one in. He opened the box and put it on the counter near the coffee machine. He took one of the doughnuts and put it on a napkin and left it at his spot on the homicide table while he went up to the watch office to get coffee from the urn. It was much better than what came out of the detective bureau's machine.

Once he had his coffee, he took his doughnut and moved to the desk that was behind the bureau's front counter. His assignment to desk duty meant that he would handle most of the walk-ins as well as the sorting and distribution of overnight reports. The phones he wouldn't have to worry about. They were answered by an old man from the neighborhood who donated his time to the department.

Bosch was alone in the squad room for at least fifteen minutes before the other detectives started to trickle in. Six different times he was asked by a new arrival why he was at the front desk, and each time he told the detective who asked that it was too complicated to get into but that the word would be out soon enough. Nothing remained a secret for long in a police station.

At eight-thirty the lieutenant from the a.m. watch brought the morning reports in before going off shift and smiled when he saw Bosch. His name was Klein and he and Bosch had known each other in a surface way for years.

'Who'd you beat up this time, Bosch?' he kidded.

It was well known that the detective who sat at the desk where Bosch now sat was either there by fate of the bureau rotation or on a desk duty assignment while the subject of an internal investigation. More often than not it was the latter. But Klein's sarcasm revealed that he had not yet heard that Bosch actually was under investigation. Bosch played off the question with a smile but didn't answer. He took the two-inch-thick stack of reports from Klein and gave him a mock salute back.

The stack Klein had given him constituted nearly all crime reports filed by Hollywood Division patrol officers in the last twenty-four hours. There would be a second, smaller delivery of stragglers later in the morning, but the stack in his hands constituted the bulk of the day's work in the bureau.

Keeping his head down and ignoring the buzz of conversations around him, it took Bosch a half hour to sort all the reports into piles according to crimes. Next he had to scan them all, using his experienced eye to possibly make connections between robberies and burglaries or assaults and so on, and then deliver the individual piles to the detective tables assigned to that particular classification of crime.

When he looked up from his work, he saw that Lieutenant Billets was in her office on the phone. He hadn't noticed that she had come in. Part of his desk job would be to give her a morning briefing on the reports, informing her of any significant or unusual crimes or anything else she should be aware of as the detective bureau commander.

He went back to work and weeded through the auto-theft reports first because they made up the largest pile he had culled from the stack of reports. There had been thirty-three cars reported stolen in Hollywood in the last twenty-four hours. Bosch knew that this was probably a below-average tally. After reading the summaries in the reports and checking for other similarities, he found nothing of significance and took the pile to the detective in charge of the auto-theft table. As he was heading back to the front of the squad room, he noticed that Edgar and Rider were standing at the homicide table putting things into a cardboard box. As he approached, he realized they were packing up the murder book and the ancillary files and evidence bags relating to the Aliso case. It was all being sent to the feds.

'Morning, guys,' Bosch said, unsure of how to start.

'Harry,' Edgar said.

'How are you doing, Harry?' Rider said, genuine concern in her voice.

'I'm hangin' in . . . Uh, listen, I just . . . I just want to say that I'm sorry you guys have been pulled into this, but I wanted you to know there is no way I—'

'Forget it, Harry,' Edgar said. 'You don't have to say one damn thing to us. We both know the whole thing is bullshit. In all my years on the job you are the most righteous cop I know, man. All the rest is bullshit.'

Bosch nodded, touched by Edgar's words. He didn't expect such sentiments from Rider because it had been their first case together. But she spoke anyway.

'I haven't worked with you long, Harry, but from what I do know I agree with what Jerry says. You watch, this will blow over and we'll be back at it again.'

'Thanks.'

Bosch was about to head back to his new desk when he looked down into the box they were packing. He reached in and pulled out the two-inch-thick murder book that Edgar had been charged with preparing and keeping up to date on the Aliso case.

'Are the feds coming here or you just sending it out?'

'S'posed to have somebody come pick it up at ten,' Edgar said.

Bosch looked up at the clock on the wall. It was only nine.

'Mind if I copy this? Just so we have something in case the whole thing drops into that black hole they keep over there at the bureau.'

'Be my guest,' Edgar said.

'Did Salazar ever send over a protocol?' Bosch asked.

'The autopsy?' Rider asked. 'No, not yet. Unless it's in dispatch.'

Bosch didn't tell them that if it was in transit, then the feds had somehow intercepted it. He took the murder book to the copy machine, unhooked the three rings and removed the stack of reports. He set the machine to copy both sides of the original documents and put the stack into the automatic feed tray. Before starting he checked to make sure the paper tray was filled with three-hole paper. It was. He pressed the start button and stood back to watch. There was a copying franchise chain in town that had donated the machine and regularly serviced it. It was the one thing in the bureau that was modern and could be counted on to work most of the time. Bosch finished the job in ten minutes. He put the original binder back together and returned it to the box on Edgar's desk. He then took a fresh binder from the supply closet, put his copies of the reports on the rings and dropped it into a file cabinet drawer that had his business card taped to it. He then told his two partners where it was if they needed it.

'Harry,' Rider said in a low voice, 'you're thinking of doing a little freelancing on it, aren't you?'

He looked at her a moment, unsure of how to answer. He thought about her relationship with Billets. He had to be careful.

'If you are,' she said, perhaps sensing his indecision, 'I'd like to be in on it. You know the bureau isn't going to work it with any due diligence. They're going to let it drop.'

'Count me in, too,' Edgar added.

Bosch hesitated again, looked from one to the other and then nodded.

'How 'bout we meet at Musso's at twelve-thirty?' he said. 'I'm buying.'

'We'll be there,' Edgar said.

When he got back to the front of the bureau, he saw through the glass window of her office that Billets was off the phone and looking at some paperwork. Her door was open and Bosch stepped in, knocking on the doorjamb as he entered.

'Good morning, Harry.' There was a wistfulness to her voice and demeanor, as if maybe she was embarrassed that he was her front-desk man. 'Anything happening I should know about right away?'

'I don't think so. It looks pretty tame. Uh, there's a hot prowler working the strip hotels again, though. At least it looks like one guy. Did one at the Chateau and another at the Hyatt last night. People never woke up. Looks like the same MO on both.'

'Were the vics anybody we should know and care about?'

'I don't think so but I don't read *People* magazine. I might not recognize a celebrity if they came up and bit me.'

She smiled.

'How much were the losses?'

'I don't know. I'm not done with that pile yet. That's not

why I came in. I just wanted to say thanks again for sticking up for me like you did yesterday.'

'That was hardly sticking up for you.'

'Yes it was. In those kinds of circumstances what you said and did was sticking your neck way out. I appreciate it.'

'Well, like I said, I did it because I don't believe it. And the sooner IAD and the bureau get on with it, the sooner they won't believe it. When's your appointment, by the way?'

'Two.'

'Who is your defense rep going to be?'

'Guy I know from RHD. Name's Dennis Zane. He's a good guy and he'll know what to do for me. You know him?'

'No. But listen, let me know if there is anything else I can do.'

'Thanks, Lieutenant.'

'Grace.'

'Right. Grace.'

When Bosch went back to his desk he thought about his appointment with Chastain. In accordance with department procedures, Bosch would be represented by a union defense rep who was actually a fellow detective. He would act almost as an attorney would, counseling Bosch on what to say and how to say it. It was the first formal step of the internal investigation and disciplinary process.

When he looked up, he saw a woman standing at the counter with a young girl. The girl had red-rimmed eyes and a marble-sized swelling on her lower lip that looked like it might have been the result of a bite. She was disheveled and stared at the wall behind Bosch with a distance in her eyes that suggested that a window was there. But there wasn't.

Bosch could have asked how he could help them without moving from his desk, but it didn't take a detective to guess why they were there. He got up, came around the desk and approached the counter so they could speak confidentially. Rape victims were the people who evoked the most sadness in Bosch. He knew he wouldn't be able to last a month on a rape squad. Every victim he had ever seen had that stare. It was a sign that all things in their lives were different now and forever. They would never get back to what they had had before.

After speaking briefly to the mother and daughter, Bosch asked if the girl needed immediate medical attention and the mother said she didn't. He opened the half door in the counter and ushered them both back to one of the three interview rooms off the hallway to the rear of the bureau. He then went to the sex crimes table and approached Mary Cantu, a detective who had been handling for years what Bosch knew he couldn't handle for a month.

'Mary, you've got a walk-in back in room three,' Bosch said. 'She's fifteen. Happened last night. She got too curious about the pusher who works the nearby corner. He grabbed her and sold her and a rock to his next customer. She's with her mother.'

'Thanks, Bosch. Just what I needed on a Friday. I'll go right back. You ask if she needed medical?'

'She said no, but I think the answer is yes.'

'Okay, I'll handle it. Thanks.'

Back at the front desk, it took Bosch a few minutes to clear his thoughts about the girl from his mind and another forty-five to finish reading through the reports and deliver them to the appropriate detective squads.

When he was done, he checked on Billets through the window and saw she was on the phone with a pile of paperwork in front of her. Bosch got up and went to his file cabinet and took out the copy of the murder book he had put there earlier. He lugged the thick binder back to his desk at the front counter. He had decided that in his free time between his duties at the front desk he would begin reviewing the murder book. The case had taken off so quickly earlier in the week that he had not had the time he usually liked to spend reviewing the paperwork. He knew from experience that command of the details and the nuances of an investigation was often the key to closing it out. He had just started turning through the pages in a cursory review when a vaguely familiar voice addressed him from the counter.

'Is that what I think it is?'

Bosch looked up. It was O'Grady, the FBI agent. Bosch felt his face burn with embarrassment that he'd been caught red-handed with the file and with his growing dislike for the agent.

'Yeah, it's what you think it is, O'Grady. You were supposed to be here a half hour ago to pick it up.'

'Yeah, well, I don't run on your time. I had things to do.'

'Like what, get your buddy Roy a new ponytail?'

'Just give me the binder, Bosch. And all the rest.'

Bosch still had not gotten up and made no move to now.

'What do you want it for, O'Grady? We all know you're going to let the thing drop. You people don't care who killed Tony Aliso and you don't want to know.'

'That's bullshit. Give me the file.'

O'Grady reached over the counter and was reaching around blindly for the release button on the half door.

'Hold your fucking horses, man,' Bosch said as he stood up. 'Just wait there. I'll get it all.'

Carrying the binder, Bosch walked back to the homicide table and, using his back to shield O'Grady's view, placed the binder on the table and picked up the box containing the original binder and the ancillary reports and evidence bags that Edgar and Rider had put in with it. He carried it back and dropped it on the counter in front of O'Grady.

'You gotta sign for it,' he said. 'We're extra careful about how we handle evidence and who gets to handle it.'

'Yeah, right. The whole world knows that from the O.J. case, don't they?'

Bosch grabbed O'Grady's tie and jerked his upper body down over the counter. The agent could not find a purchase with his hands that would give him the leverage to pull back. Bosch bent down so that he was talking directly into his ear.

'Excuse me?'

'Bosch you—'

'Harry!'

Bosch looked up. Billets was standing in the door of her office. Bosch let go of the tie and O'Grady's body sprang backward as he straightened up. His face was crimson with embarrassment and anger. As he jerked his tie loose from around his neck he yelled, 'You're certifiable, you know that? You're a fucking asshole!'

'I didn't know you agents used that kind of language,' Bosch said.

'Harry, just sit down,' Billets commanded. 'I'll take care of this.'

She had come up to the counter now.

'He's got to sign the receipt.'

'I don't care! I'll handle it!'

Bosch went back to his desk and sat down. He stared dead-eyed at O'Grady while Billets dug through the box until she found the inventory list and receipt Edgar had prepared. She showed O'Grady where to sign and then told him to go.

'You better watch him,' he said to Billets as he picked the box up off the counter.

'You better watch yourself, Agent O'Grady. If I hear anything else about this little disagreement here, I'll file a complaint against you for inciting it.'

'He's the one who—'

'I don't care. Understand? I don't care. Now leave.'

'I'm leaving. But you watch your boy there. Keep him away from this.'

O'Grady pointed to the contents of the box. Billets didn't answer. O'Grady picked the box up and made a move to step away from the counter but stopped and looked once more at Bosch.

'Hey, Bosch, by the way, I got a message from Roy.'

'Agent O'Grady, would you please leave!' Billets said angrily.

'What is it?' Bosch said.

'He just wanted to ask, who's the meat now?'

With that he turned around and headed down the hall to the exit. Billets watched him until he was gone and then turned around and looked at Bosch with anger in her eyes.

'You just don't know how to help yourself, do you?' she said. 'Why don't you grow up and quit these little pissing wars?'

She didn't wait for his reply because he didn't have one. She walked quickly back into her office and shut the door. She then closed the blinds over the interior window. Bosch leaned back with his hands laced behind his neck, looked up at the ceiling and exhaled loudly.

After the O'Grady incident Bosch almost immediately became busy with a walk-in case involving an armed robbery. At the time, the entire robbery crew was out on a carjacking that had involved a high-speed chase, and that meant Bosch, as the desk man, had to interview the walk-in victim and type up a report. The victim was a young Mexican boy whose job it was to stand on the corner of Hollywood Boulevard at Sierra Bonita and sell maps to the homes of movie stars up in the hills. At ten that morning, shortly after he had set up his plywood sign and begun waving down cars, an old American-made sedan had pulled up with a man driving and a woman in the passenger seat. After asking how much the maps cost and whether he had sold very many of them, the woman had pointed a gun at the boy and robbed him of thirty-eight dollars. He had come in to report the crime with his mother. As it turned out, he had sold only one map that day before the robbery, and nearly all of the money taken from him was his own – he had brought it with him to make change. His loss was about what he made for a whole day of standing on the corner and waving his arm like a windmill.

Because of the small take and sloppy method used by the robbers, Bosch immediately thought the suspects were a couple of hypes looking for a quick score to buy their next balloon of heroin. They had not even bothered to hide the car's license plate, which the boy had spotted and memorized as they drove away.

After he was finished with the boy and his mother, he went to the teletype machine and put out a wanted on the car with a description of the suspects. He found when he did this that there was already a wanted out on the vehicle for its use in two prior robberies in the last week. A lot of good that did the kid who lost a day's pay, Bosch thought. The robbers should have been picked up before they got to the boy. But this was the big city, not a perfect world. Disappointments like that didn't stay long with Bosch.

By this time the squad room had pretty much cleared out for lunch. Bosch saw only Mary Cantu at the sex crimes table, probably working on the paper from that morning's walk-in job.

Edgar and Rider were gone, apparently having decided it would be better to go separately to Musso's. As Bosch got up to leave, he noticed that the blinds were still drawn over the window to the lieutenant's office. Billets was still in there, he knew. He went to the homicide table and put the copy of the murder book into his briefcase and then went and knocked on her door. Before she could answer, he opened the door and stuck his head in.

'I'm going to go catch some lunch and then go downtown for the IAD thing. You won't have anybody out on the counter.'

'Okay,' she said. 'I'll put Edgar or Rider up there after lunch. They're just waiting around for a case, anyway.'

'Okay then, I'll see you.'

'Uh, Harry?'

'Yes?'

'I'm sorry for what happened earlier. Not for what I said. I meant what I said, but I should have taken you in here and spoken to you. Doing it out there in front of the others was wrong. I apologize.'

'Don't worry about it. Have a nice weekend.'

'You, too.'

'I'll try, Lieutenant.'

'Grace.'

'Grace.'

Bosch got to Musso and Frank's Restaurant on Hollywood Boulevard at exactly twelve-thirty and parked in the back. The restaurant was a Hollywood landmark, having been on the Boulevard since 1924. In its heyday it had been a popular destination for Hollywood's elite. Fitzgerald and Faulkner held forth. Chaplin and Fairbanks once raced each other down Hollywood Boulevard on horseback, the loser having to pick up the dinner tab. The restaurant now subsisted mostly on its past glory and faded charm. Its red leather padded booths still filled every day for lunch and some of the waiters looked and moved as if they had been there long enough to have served Chaplin. The menu hadn't changed in all the years Bosch had been eating there – this in a town where the hookers out on the Boulevard lasted longer than most restaurants.

Edgar and Rider were waiting in one of the prized round booths, and Bosch slid in after they were pointed out by the maître d' – he was apparently too old and tired to walk Bosch over himself. They were both drinking iced tea and Bosch decided to go along with that, though privately he lamented that they were in the place that made the best martini in the city. Only Rider was looking at the menu. She was new in the division and hadn't been to Musso's enough times to know what the best thing was to order for lunch.

'So what are we doing?' Edgar asked while she looked.

'We've got to start over,' Bosch said. 'The Vegas stuff was all misdirection.'

Rider glanced over the top of the menu at Bosch.

'Kiz, put that down,' he said. 'If you don't get the chicken pot pie you're making a mistake.'

She hesitated, nodded and put the menu aside.

'What do you mean, misdirection?' she asked.

'I mean whoever killed Tony wanted us to go that way. And they planted the gun out there to make sure we stayed out there. But they screwed up. They didn't know the guy they planted the gun on was a fed who would have a bunch of other feds as an alibi. That was the screwup. Now, once I learned that our suspect was an agent, I thought Joey Marks and his people must have figured out he was a fed and set the whole thing up to taint him.'

'I still think that sounds good,' Edgar said.

'It does, or it did until last night,' Bosch said as an ancient waiter in a red coat came to the table.

'Three chicken pot pies,' Bosch said.

'Do you want something to drink?' the waiter asked.

Hell with it, Bosch decided.

'Yeah, I'll have a martini, three olives. You can bring them some more iced tea. That's it.'

The waiter nodded and slowly glided away without writing anything on his pad.

'Last night,' Bosch continued, 'I learned from a source that Joey Marks did not know the man he thought was named Luke Goshen was a plant. He had no idea he was an informant, let alone an agent. In fact, once we picked Goshen up, Joey was engaged in a plan to try to find out whether Goshen was going to stand up or talk. This was because he had to decide whether to put a contract on him in the Metro jail.'

He waited a moment to let them think about this.

'So, you can see with that information in the mix now, the second theory no longer works.'

'Well, who's the source?' Edgar asked.

'I can't tell you that, guys. But it's solid. It's the truth.'

He watched their eyes float down to the table. He knew they trusted him, but they also knew how informants were often the most skilled liars in the game. It was a tough call to base everything from here on out on an informant.

'Okay, then you know who she is. She overheard all of what I told you while they had her in that house. Before we got there, both Joey and the lawyer, Torrino, were there. She overheard them and from what she heard, they didn't know about Goshen. See, that whole abduction was part of the test. They knew the only way I could find out where the safe house was would be to get it from Goshen. That was the test, to see if he was talking or not.'

They sat in silence for a few minutes while Edgar and Rider digested this.

'Okay,' Edgar finally said. 'I see what you're saying. But if Vegas was one big fucking red herring, how does the gun get over there in the agent's house?'

'That's what we have to figure out. What if there was someone outside of Tony's mob connections but close enough to him to know he was washing money and the reason why he made all the trips to Vegas? Someone who either had personal knowledge or maybe followed Tony to Vegas and watched how he worked, how he picked up the money from Goshen, everything? Someone who knew exactly how he did it, who knew Goshen could be set up to take the fall, and that Tony'd be coming back on Friday with a lot of money in his briefcase?'

'They would be able to set the whole thing up, as long as they could get into the agent's house to plant the gun,' Edgar answered.

'Right. And getting into the house would be no problem. It's out in the middle of nowhere. He was away at the club for long stretches at a time. Anybody could get in, plant the gun, and get out. The question is who?'

'You're talking about either his wife or his girlfriend,' Edgar said. 'Both could have had that kind of access.'

Bosch nodded.

'So which one do we set up on? The three of us can't do both, not on a freelance like this.'

'We don't need to,' Bosch said. 'I think the choice is obvious.'

'Which?' Edgar said. 'The girlfriend?'

Bosch looked at Rider, giving her the chance to answer. She saw his look and then her eyes narrowed as she went to work.

'It . . . it can't be the girlfriend because . . . because she called Tony on Sunday morning. On the voice mail. Why would she call the guy if she knew he was dead?'

Bosch nodded. She was good.

'Could have been part of a setup,' Edgar said. 'Another mis-direction.'

'Could be but I doubt it,' Bosch said. 'Plus, we know she worked Friday night. That would make it kind of tough for her to be over here whacking Tony.'

'So then it's the wife,' Edgar said. 'Veronica.'

'Right,' Bosch said. 'I think she was lying to us, acting like she didn't know anything about her husband's business when she knew everything. I think this whole thing was her plan. She wrote the letters to the IRS and to the OCID. She wanted to get something going against Tony, then when he ended up dead it would point toward a mob hit. Trunk music. Planting the gun on Goshen was just icing. If we found it, fine. If we didn't, then we'd be sniffing around Vegas until we shelved the case.'

'You're saying she did this all on her own?' Edgar asked.

'No,' Bosch said. 'I'm just saying I think this was her plan. But she had to have had help. An accomplice. It took two to do the actual hit and she sure didn't take the gun to Vegas. After the kill, she stays at the house and waits while the accomplice goes to Vegas and plants the gun while Luke Goshen's at the club.'

'But wait a minute,' Rider said. 'We're forgetting something. Veronica Aliso had it very cushy in her existing life. Tony was raking in the bread with his washing machine. They had the big house in the hills, the cars . . . why would she want to kill the cash cow? How much was in that briefcase?'

'According to the feds, four hundred and eighty thousand,' Bosch said.

Edgar whistled softly. Rider shook her head.

'I still don't see it,' she said. 'That's a hell of a lot of money, but Tony was making at least that much a year. In business terms, killing him was a short-term gain/long-term loss for her. Doesn't make sense.'

'Then there is something else running through all of this that we don't know about yet,' Bosch said. 'Maybe he was about to dump her. Maybe that old lady in Vegas who said Tony was going to go away with Layla was telling the truth. Or maybe there's money somewhere we don't know about. But for now I can't see anybody else fitting into this picture but her.'

'But what about the gatehouse?' Rider said. 'The log shows she never left Friday, the whole night. And she had no visitors.'

'Well, we've got to work on that,' Bosch said. 'There had to have been a way for her to get in and out.'

'What else?' Edgar asked.

'We start over,' Bosch said. 'I want to know everything about her. Where'd she come from, who are her friends, what does she do in that house all day long and what did she do and who did she do it with all those times Tony was away?'

Rider and Edgar nodded.

'There's got to be an accomplice. And my guess is that it's a man. And I'll bet we'll find him through her.'

The waiter came up with a tray and put it down on a folding cart. They watched silently as he prepared the meal. There were three separate chicken pot pies on the tray. The waiter used a fork and spoon to take the top crust off each and put it on a plate. Next he scooped the contents of each pie out and put it on the crust, served the three cops their dishes and put down fresh glasses of iced tea for Edgar and Rider. He then poured Bosch's martini from a small glass carafe and floated away without a word.

'Obviously,' Bosch said, 'we have to do this quietly.'

'Yeah,' Edgar said, 'and Bullets also put us on the top of

the rotation. Next call comes in, me and Kiz get it. And we hafta work it without you. That's going to take us away from this.'

'Well, do what you can. If you get a body you get a body, nothing we can do about that. Meantime, this is what I propose. You two work on Veronica's background, see what you can find. You got any sources at the *Times* or the trades?'

'I know a couple at the *Times*,' Rider said. 'And there's a woman I once had a case with – she was a vic – who's a receptionist or something at *Variety*.'

'You trust 'em?'

'I think I can.'

'See if they'll pull a search on Veronica for you. She had a brief flash of fame a while back. Her fifteen minutes. Maybe there were some stories about her, stories that would have names of people we could talk to.'

'What about talking to her again?' Edgar asked.

'I don't think we should do it yet. I want to have something to talk to her about.'

'What about neighbors?'

'You can do that. Maybe she'll look out the window and see you, give her something to think about. If you go up there, see if you can take another look at the gate log. Talk to Nash. I'm sure you can turn him without needing another search warrant. I'd like to take a look at the whole year, know who has been going in to see her, especially while Tony was out of town. We have Tony's credit records and can construct his travel history. You'll be able to know when she was in that house alone.'

Bosch raised his fork. He hadn't had a bite of food yet, but his mind was too full of the case and what needed to be done.

'The other thing is we need as much of the case file as we can get. All we've got is the copy of the murder book. I'm going down to Parker Center for my little chat with the IAD. I'll swing by USC and get a copy of the autopsy. The feds already have it. I'll also go talk to Donovan in SID and see if he came up with anything we pulled out of the car. Also, he's got the shoe prints. I'll get copies, hopefully before the feds come in and take everything. Anything else I'm missing?'

The other two shook their heads.

'You want to see what we get and then put our heads together after work?'

They nodded.

'Cat and Fiddle, about six?'

They nodded again. They were too busy eating to talk. Bosch took his first bite of food, which was already getting cold. He joined them in their silence, thinking about the case.

'It's in the details,' he said after a few moments.

'What?' Rider asked.

'The case. When you get one like this, the answer is always in the details. You watch, when we break it, the answer will have been sitting in the files, in the book. It always happens.'

The interview with Chastain at Internal Affairs began as Bosch expected it would. He sat with Zane, his defense rep, at a gray government table in one of the IAD interview rooms. An old Sony cassette player was turned on and everything said in the room was recorded. In police parlance, Chastain was locking up Bosch's story. Getting his words and explanation in as much detail as possible down on tape. Chastain really wouldn't begin his investigation until after Bosch's story was locked in. He would then hunt for flaws in it. All he had to do was catch Bosch in a single lie and he could take him to a Board of Rights hearing. Depending on the size and import of the lie, he could seek a penalty ranging from suspension to dismissal.

In a dull and laborious drone, Chastain read prepared questions from a legal pad and Bosch slowly and carefully answered them with as few words as possible. It was a game. Bosch had played it before. In the fifteen minutes they had before reporting to IAD, Zane had counseled Bosch on how it would go and how they should proceed. Like a good criminal defense lawyer, he never directly asked Harry if he had planted the gun. Zane didn't really care. He simply looked at IAD as the enemy, as a group of bad cops with the sole purpose of going after good cops. Zane was part of the old school who thought all cops were inherently good and though sometimes the job turned them bad, they should not be persecuted by their own.

Everything was routine for a half hour. But then Chastain threw an unexpected pitch at them.

'Detective Bosch, do you know a woman named Eleanor Wish?'

Zane reached out a hand in front of Bosch to stop him from answering.

'What is this shit, Chastain?'

'Who have you been talking to, Chastain?' Bosch added.

'Wait a minute, Harry,' Zane said. 'Don't say anything. Where's this going, Chastain?'

'It's very clear from the orders from the chief. I'm investigating Bosch's conduct during this investigation. As far as who I have been talking to or where I get my information, you are not privy to that at this point in the process.'

'This is supposed to be about a supposedly planted gun that we all know is bullshit. That's what we are here to answer.'

'Do you wish to read the order from the chief again? It's quite clear.'

Zane looked at him a moment.

'Give us five minutes so we can talk about this. Why don't you go get the points of your teeth filed?'

Chastain stood up and reached over and turned the tape recorder off. As he stepped to the door, he looked back at them with a smile.

297

'This time I got you both. You won't get out from under this one, Bosch. And Zane, well, I guess you can't win them all, can you?'

'You ought to know that better than me, you sanctimonious asshole. Get out of here and leave us alone.'

After Chastain was gone, Zane bent over the tape recorder to make sure it was off. He then got up and checked the thermostat on the wall to make sure it wasn't a secret listening device. After he was satisfied their conversation was private, he sat back down and asked Bosch about Eleanor Wish. Bosch told him about his encounters with Eleanor over the past few days but left out mention of the abduction and her subsequent confession.

'One of those cops over there in Metro must've told him you shacked up with her,' Zane said. 'That's all he's got. He's going for an associating beef. If you admit it here, then he's got you. But if that's all he gets, then it's a slap on the wrist at best. As long as he gets nothing else. But if you lie about it and say you weren't with her when you were, and he can prove you were, then you've got a problem. So my advice is that you tell him, yeah, you know her and you've been with her. Fuck it, it's nothing. Tell him it's over, and if that's all he's got, then he's a chickenshit asshole.'

'I don't know if it is or it isn't.'

'What?'

'Over.'

'Well, don't tell him nothin' about that unless he asks for it. Then use your best judgment. Ready?'

Bosch nodded and Zane opened the door. Chastain was sitting outside at a desk.

'Where ya been, Chastain?' Zane complained. 'We're waiting in here.'

Chastain didn't answer. He came in, turned the recorder back on and continued the Q and A.

'Yes, I know Eleanor Wish,' Bosch said. 'Yes, I've spent time with her over the last few days.'

'How much time?'

'I don't know exactly. A couple of nights.'

'While you were conducting the investigation?'

'Not *while* I was conducting it. At night, when I was done for the day. We all don't work around the clock like you, Chastain.'

Bosch smiled at him without humor.

'Was she a witness in this case?' Chastain asked with a tone that denoted that he was shocked that Bosch would cross that line.

'Initially, I thought she might be a witness. After I located her and talked to her, I learned pretty quickly that she was not an evidentiary witness of any kind.'

'But you did initially encounter her while you were in your capacity as an investigator on this case.'

'That's correct.'

Chastain consulted his pad for a long moment before asking the next question.

'Is this woman, that's the convicted felon Eleanor Wish I am still talking about, is she living in your home at this time?'

Bosch felt the bile rising in his throat. The personal invasion and Chastain's tone were getting to him. He struggled to remain calm.

'I don't know the answer to that,' he said.

'You don't *know* if someone is *living* in your house or not?'

'Look, Chastain, she was there last night, okay? Is that what you want to hear? She was there. But whether she'll be there tonight I don't know. She's got her own place in Vegas. She may have gone back today, I don't know. I didn't check. You want me to call and ask her if she is officially *living* in my home at this time, I will.'

'I don't think that's necessary. I think I have everything I need for the time being.'

He then went directly into the standard IAD end-of-interview spiel.

'Detective Bosch, you will be informed of the results of

299

the ongoing investigation into your conduct. If departmental charges are filed, you will be informed of the scheduling of a Board of Rights hearing in which three captains will hear evidence. You will be allowed to choose one of those captains, I will select a second and the third will be chosen at random. Any questions?'

'Just one. How can you call yourself a cop when all you do is sit up here and conduct these bullshit investigations into bullshit?'

Zane reached over and put a hand on Bosch's forearm to quiet him.

'No, that's okay,' Chastain said, waving off Zane's effort to calm things. 'I don't mind answering. In fact, I get that question a lot, Bosch. Funny, but it always seems I get it from the cops I happen to be investigating. Anyway, the answer is that I take pride in what I do because I represent the public, and if there is no one to police the police then there is no one to keep the abuse of their wide powers in check. I serve a valuable purpose in this society, Detective Bosch. I'm proud of what I do. Can you say the same?'

'Yeah, yeah, yeah,' Bosch said. 'I'm sure that sounds great on tape for whoever listens to it. I get the feeling you probably sit alone at night and listen to it yourself. Over and over again. After a while, you believe it. But let me ask you this, Chastain. Who polices the police who police the police?'

Bosch stood up and Zane followed. The interview was over.

After leaving IAD and thanking Zane for his help, Bosch went down to the SID lab on the third floor to see Art Donovan. The criminologist had just come back from a crime scene and was sorting through evidence bags and checking the material against an evidence list. He looked up as Bosch was approaching.

'How'd you get in here, Harry?'

'I know the combination.'

Most detectives who worked RHD knew the door-lock combo. Bosch hadn't worked RHD in five years and they still hadn't changed it.

'See,' Donovan said. 'That's how the trouble starts.'

'What trouble?'

'You coming in here while I'm handling evidence. Next thing you know some wiseass defense lawyer says it got tainted and I look like an asshole on national TV.'

'You're paranoid, Artie. Besides, we're not due for another trial of the century for at least a few years.'

'Funny. What do you want, Harry?'

'You're the second guy who said I was funny today. What happened with my shoe prints and all the rest of the stuff?'

'The Aliso case?'

'No, the Lindbergh case. What do you think?'

'Well, I heard that Aliso wasn't yours anymore. I'm supposed to have everything ready for the FBI to pick up.'

'When is that?'

Donovan looked up from what he was doing for the first time.

'They just said they'd send somebody by five.'

'Then it's still my case until they show up. What about the shoe prints you pulled?'

'There's nothing about them. I sent copies to the bureau's crime lab in DC to see if they could ID the make and model.'

'And?'

'And nothing. I haven't heard back. Bosch, every department in the country sends shit to them. You know that. And last I heard, they don't drop everything they're doing when a package from the LAPD comes in. It will probably be next week sometime before I hear back. If I'm lucky.'

'Shit.'

'It's too late to call the East Coast now, anyway. Maybe Monday. I didn't know they suddenly became so important to you. Communication, Harry, that's the secret. You ought to try it sometime.'

'Never mind that, do you still have a set of copies?'

'Yup.'

'Can I get a set?'

'Sure can, but you're going to have to wait about twenty minutes or so till I'm done with this.'

'Come on, Artie, it's probably just sitting in a file cabinet or something. It'll take you thirty seconds.'

'Would you leave me alone?' Donovan said with exasperation. 'I'm serious, Harry. Yes, it's sitting in a file and it would only take me half a minute to get it for you. But if I leave what I'm doing here, I could get crucified when I testify in *this* case. I can see it now, some shyster all righteous and angry and saying, "You are telling this jury that while in the middle of handling evidence from this case you got up and handled evidence from *another*?" And you don't have to be F. Lee Bailey anymore to make it sound good to a jury. Now leave me alone. Come back in a half hour.'

'Fine, Artie, I'll leave you alone.'

'And buzz me when you come back. Don't just come in. We gotta get that combination changed.'

The last line he said more to himself than to Bosch.

Bosch left the way he had come in and took the elevator down to go outside and have a smoke. He had to walk out to the curb and light up because it was now against departmental rules to stand outside the front door of Parker Center and smoke. So many cops working there were addicted to cigarettes that there had often been a crowd outside the building's main doors and a permanent haze of blue smoke had begun to hang over the entrance. The chief thought this was unsightly and instituted the rule that if you left the building to smoke, you had to leave the property as well. Now the front sidewalk along Los Angeles Street often looked like the scene of a labor action, with cops, some even in uniform, pacing back and forth in front of the building. The only thing missing from the scene was picket signs. The word was that the police chief had consulted with the city attorney to see if he could outlaw smoking on the sidewalk as well, but he was told that the sidewalk was beyond the bounds of his control.

As Bosch was lighting a second cigarette off the first, he saw the huge figure of FBI agent Roy Lindell waltzing leisurely out of the glass doors of the police headquarters. When he got to the sidewalk, he turned right and headed toward the federal courthouse. He was coming directly toward Bosch. Lindell didn't see Bosch until he was a few feet away. It startled him.

'What is this? Are you waiting for me?'

'No, I'm having a cigarette, Lindell. What are you doing?'

'None of your business.'

He made a move to pass but Bosch stopped him with the next line.

'Have a nice chat with Chastain?'

'Look, Bosch, I was asked to come over and give a statement and I obliged. I told the truth. Let the chips fall.'

'Trouble is you don't know the truth.'

'I know you found that gun and I didn't put it there. That's the truth.'

'Part of it, at least.'

'Well, it's the only part I know, and that's what I told him. So have a good day.'

He passed by Bosch and Harry turned around to watch him go. Once again he stopped him.

'You people might be satisfied with only part of the truth. But I'm not.'

Lindell turned around and stepped back to Bosch.

'What's that supposed to mean?'

'Figure it out.'

'No, you tell me.'

'We were all used, Lindell. I'm going to find out by who. When I do, I'll be sure to let you know.'

'Look, Bosch, you don't have the case anymore. We're working it and you better stay the fuck away from it.'

'Yeah, you guys are working the case, all right,' Bosch said sarcastically. 'I'm sure you're pounding the pavement on this one. Let me know when you figure it out.'

'Bosch, it's not like that. We care about it.'

'Give me one answer, Lindell.'

'What?'

'In the time you were under, did Tony Aliso ever bring his wife over there to make a pickup?'

Lindell was quiet a moment while he decided whether to answer. He finally shook his head.

'Not once,' he said. 'Tony always said she hated the place. Too many bad memories, I guess.'

Bosch tried to remain cool.

'Memories of Vegas?'

Lindell smiled.

'For somebody who supposedly has all the answers, you don't know much, do you, Bosch? Tony met her in the club something like twenty years ago. Long before my time. She was a dancer and Tony was going to make her a movie star. Same story he was using on 'em to the end. Only, after her I guess he got wise and learned not to marry every one of them.'

'Did she know Joey Marks?'

'Your one question is now up to three, Bosch.'

'Did she?'

'I don't know.'

'What was her name back then?'

'That's another one I don't know. I'll see you around, Bosch.'

He turned and walked away. Bosch threw his cigarette into the street and walked back toward the Glass House. A few minutes later, after being properly buzzed through the door into the SID offices, Bosch found Donovan at his desk again. The criminalist lifted a thin file from the desk and handed it to Harry.

'You got copies in there,' he said. 'Same thing I sent the bureau. What I did was shoot a copy of the negative and then shot the new negative and printed it in black-and-white contrast for comparison purposes. I also blew it up to actual size.'

Bosch didn't understand what Donovan had just said except for the last part. He opened the file. There were two pages of copy paper with the shoe prints in black. Both were partial prints of the same right shoe. But between the two partials almost all of the shoe was there. Donovan got up and looked at the open file. He pointed to a tread ridge on one of the copies. It was a curving line on the heel. But the line was broken.

'Now, if you find the shooter and he still has the shoes, this is where you'll get him. See how that line is broken there? That does not appear to be a manufacturer's design. This guy stepped on glass or something at some point and it cut the tread there. It's either that or a flaw in manufacturing. But if you find the shoe, we'll be able to make an ID match that should send the boy away.'

'Okay,' Bosch said, still looking at the copies. 'Now, did you get anything even preliminary from the bureau on this?'

'Not really. I've got a guy I go to pretty regularly with this kind of stuff. I know him, seen him at a couple of the SID conventions. Anyway, he called just to let me know he got the package and he'd get on it as soon as he could. He said that off the top of his head he thought it was one of those lightweight boots that are popular now. You know, they're like work boots but they're comfortable and wear like a pair of Nikes.'

'Okay, Artie, thanks.'

Bosch drove over to the County-USC Medical Center and around to the parking lot by the railroad yard. The coroner's office was located at the far end of the medical center property, and Bosch went in through the back door after showing his badge to a security guard.

He checked Dr Salazar's office first but it was empty. He then went down to the autopsy floor and looked in the first suite, where the lowered table that Salazar always used was located. Salazar was there, working on another body. Bosch stepped in and Salazar looked up from the open chest cavity of what looked like the remains of a young black man.

'Harry, what are you doing here? This is a South Bureau case.'

'I wanted to ask about the Aliso case.'

'Kind of got my hands full at the moment. And you shouldn't be in here without a mask and gown.'

'I know. You think you could have your assistant dub off a copy of the protocol for me?'

'No problem. I heard the FBI took an interest in the case, Harry. Is that true?'

'That's what I hear.'

'Funny thing, those agents didn't bother talking to me. They just came in and got a copy of the protocol. The protocol only has conclusions, none of the ruminating we doctors like to do.'

'So what would you have ruminated about with them if they had talked to you?'

'I would have told them my hunch, Harry.'

'Which is?'

Salazar looked up from the body but kept his rubber-gloved and bloody hands over the open chest so they wouldn't drip on anything else.

'My hunch is that you're looking for a woman.'

'Why's that?'

'The material in and below the eyes.'

'Preparation H?'

'What?'

'Nothing, never mind. What did you find?'

'The substance was analyzed and it came back oleo

capsicum. Found it on the nasal swabs, too. Know what oleo capsicum is better known as, Harry?'

'Pepper spray.'

'Shit, Harry, you ruin my fun.'

'Sorry. So somebody sprayed him with pepper spray?'

'Right again. That's why I think it's a woman. Someone who was either having problems controlling him or afraid of problems. That makes me think it's a woman. Besides, all these women around here, they all carry that stuff in their purses.'

Bosch wondered if Veronica Aliso was one of those women.

'That's good, Sally. Anything else?'

'No surprises. Tests came back clean.'

'No amyl nitrate?'

'Nope, but that has a short retention. We don't find it that often. Did you get anywhere with the slugs?'

'Yeah, we did all right. Can you call your guy?'

'Take me to the intercom.'

While Salazar held his hands up in front of himself so they wouldn't touch anything, Bosch pushed his wheelchair to the nearby counter, where there was a phone with an intercom attachment. Salazar told Bosch which button to push and then ordered someone to make a copy of the protocol immediately for Bosch.

'Thanks,' Bosch said.

'No problem. Hope it helps. Remember, look for a woman who carried pepper spray in her purse. Not mace. Pepper spray.'

'Right.'

The end-of-the-week traffic was intense and it took Bosch nearly an hour to get out of downtown and back to Hollywood. When he got to the Cat & Fiddle pub on Sunset it was after six, and as he walked through the gate he saw Edgar and Rider already sitting at a table in the open-air courtyard. There was a pitcher of beer on their table. And they weren't alone. Sitting at the table with them was Grace Billets.

The Cat & Fiddle was a popular drinking spot with the Hollywood cops because it was only a few blocks from the station on Wilcox. So Bosch didn't know as he approached the table whether Billets happened to be there by coincidence or because she knew of their freelance operation.

'Howdy, folks,' Bosch said as he sat down.

There was one empty glass on the table and he filled it from the pitcher. He then held the glass up to the others and toasted to the end of another week.

'Harry,' Rider said, 'the lieutenant knows what we've been doing. She's here to help.'

Bosch nodded and slowly looked at Billets.

'I'm disappointed that you didn't come to me first,' she said. 'But I understand what you are doing. I agree that it might be in the bureau's best interest to let this lie and not endanger their case. But a man was murdered. If they're not going to look for the killer, I don't see why we shouldn't.'

Bosch nodded. He was almost speechless. He'd never had a boss who wasn't a rigid by-the-book man. Grace Billets was a major change.

'Of course,' she said, 'we have to be very careful. We screw this up and we'll have more than just the FBI mad at us.'

The unspoken message was that their careers were at stake here.

'Well, my position's already pretty much shot,' Bosch said. 'So if anything goes wrong, I want you all to lay it on me.'

'That's bullshit,' Rider said.

'No, it's not. You all are going places. I'm not going anywhere. Hollywood is it for me and all of us here know it. So if this thing hits the fan, back out. I'll take the heat. If you can't agree to that, I want you to back out now.'

There was silence for a few moments, and then one by one the other three nodded.

'Okay, then,' he said, 'you may have told the lieutenant what you've been doing, but I'd like to hear it myself.'

'We've come up with a few things, not a lot,' Rider said. 'Jerry went up the hill to see Nash while I worked the computer and talked to a friend at the *Times*. First off, I ran Tony Aliso's TRW credit report and got Veronica's Social Security computer to try and get a work history and found out that Veronica is not her real name. The Social comes back to Jennifer Gilroy, born forty-one years ago in Las Vegas, Nevada. No wonder she said she hated Vegas. She grew up there.'

'Any work history?'

'Nothing until she came out here and worked for TNA Productions.'

'What else?'

Before she could answer, there was a loud commotion near the glass door to the interior bar. The door opened and a large man in a bartender's jacket pushed a smaller man through. The smaller man was disheveled and drunk and yelling something about the lack of respect he was getting. The bartender roughly walked him to the court-yard gate and pushed him through. As soon as the bartender turned to go back to the bar, the drunk spun around and started back in. The bartender turned around and pushed him so hard he fell backward onto the seat of his pants. Now embarrassed, he threatened to come back and get the bartender. A few people at some of the outside tables snickered. The drunk got up and staggered out to the street.

'They start early around here,' Billets said. 'Go ahead, Kiz.'

'Anyway, I did an NCIC run. Jennifer Gilroy got picked up twice in Vegas for soliciting. This is going back more than twenty years. I called over there and had them ship us the mugs and reports. It's all on fiche and they have to dig it out, so we won't get it till next week. There probably won't be much there, anyway. According to the computer, neither case went to court. She pleaded out and paid a fine each time.'

Bosch nodded. It sounded like a routine disposal of routine cases.

'That's all I've got on that. As far as the *Times* goes, there was nothing on the search. And my friend at *Variety* didn't do much better. Veronica Aliso was barely mentioned in the review of *Casualty of Desire*. Both she and the movie were panned, but I'd like to see it anyway. Do you still have the tape, Harry?'

'On my desk.'

'Does she get naked in it?' Edgar asked. 'If she does, I'd like to see it, too.'

He was ignored.

'Okay, what else?' Rider said. 'Uh, Veronica also got a couple mentions in stories about movie premieres and who attended. It wasn't a lot. When you said she had fifteen minutes, I think you confused minutes with seconds. Anyway, that's it from me. Jerry?'

Edgar cleared his throat and explained that he had gone up to the gatehouse at Hidden Highlands and run into a problem when Nash insisted on a new search warrant to look at the complete gate log. Edgar said he then spent the afternoon typing up the search warrant and hunting for a judge who hadn't left early for the weekend. He eventually was successful and had a signed warrant which he planned to deliver the next morning.

'Kiz and I are goin' up there in the morning. We'll get a look at the gate log and then we're probably going to hit some of the neighbors, do some interviews. Like you said, we're hopin' the widow will look out her window and catch our act, maybe get a little spooked. Maybe panic, make a mistake.'

It was then Bosch's turn, and he recounted his afternoon efforts, including his run-in with Roy Lindell and the agent's recollection that Veronica Aliso had started her show business career as a stripper in Vegas. He also discussed Salazar's finding that Tony Aliso had been hit in the face with a blast of pepper spray shortly before his death and shared the deputy coroner's hunch that it might have been a woman who sprayed him.

'Does he think she could have pulled this off by herself after hitting him with the pepper spray?' Billets asked.

'It doesn't matter, because she wasn't alone,' Bosch answered.

He pulled his briefcase onto his lap and took out the copies of the shoe prints Donovan had recovered from the body and the bumper of the Rolls. He slid the pages to the middle of the table so the three others could look.

'That's a size eleven shoe. It belongs to a man, Artie says. A big man. So the woman, if she was there, could have sprayed him with the pepper, but this guy finished the job.'

Bosch pointed to the shoe prints.

'He put his foot right on the victim so he could lean in close and do the job point-blank. Very cool and very efficient. Probably a pro. Maybe someone she knew since her Vegas days.'

'Probably the one who planted the gun in Vegas?' Billets asked.

'That's my guess.'

Bosch had been keeping his eye on the front gate of the courtyard, just in case the drunk who had been tossed out decided to come back and make his point. But when he glanced over now, he didn't see the drunk. He saw Officer Ray Powers, wearing mirrored glasses despite the lateness of the day, entering the courtyard and being met halfway across by the bartender. Waving his arms in an animated fashion, the bartender told the big cop about the drunk and the threats. Powers glanced around at the tables and saw Bosch and the others. When he had disengaged from the bartender he sauntered over.

'So, the detective bureau brain trust takes five,' he said.

'That's right, Powers,' Edgar said. 'I think the guy you're looking for is out there pissing in the bushes.'

'Yes, suh, I'll jus' go out there 'n' fetch him, boss.'

Powers looked around the table at the others with a satisfied smirk on his face. He saw the copies of the shoe prints on the table and pointed at them with his chin.

'Is this what you dicks call an investigative strategy session? Well, I'll give you a tip. Those there are what they call shoe prints.'

He smiled at his remark, proud of it.

'We're off duty, Powers,' Billets said. 'Why don't you go do your job and we'll worry about ours.'

Powers saluted her.

'Somebody's got to do the job, don't they?'

He walked away and out through the gate without waiting for a reply.

'He's got one hell of a bug up his ass,' Rider said.

'He's just mad because I told his lieutenant about the fingerprint he left on our car,' Billets said. 'I think he got his ass chewed. Anyway, back to business. What do you think, Harry? Do we have enough to take a hard run at Veronica?'

'I think we almost do. I'm going to go up there with these guys tomorrow, see what's on the gate log. Maybe we'll pay her a visit. I just wish we had something concrete to talk to her about.'

Billets nodded.

'I want to be kept informed tomorrow. Call me by noon.'

'Will do.'

'The more time that goes by on this, the harder it will be to keep this investigation among just us. I think by Monday we're going to have to take stock and decide whether to turn what we have over to the bureau.'

'I don't see that,' Bosch said, shaking his head. 'Whatever we give them, they're just going to sit on. If you want to clear this, you've got to let us alone, keep the bureau off us.'

'I will try, Harry, but there will come a point where that will be impossible. We're running a full-scale investigation off the books here. Word's going to get out. It has to. And all I'm saying is that it will be better if that word comes from me and can be controlled.'

Bosch nodded reluctantly. He knew she was right but he had to fight her suggestion. The case belonged to them. It was his. And all that had happened to him in the last week made it all the more personal. He didn't want to give it up.

He gathered up the copies of the shoe prints and put them back in his briefcase. He finished the last of his glass of beer and asked who and what he owed for it.

'It's on me,' Billets said. 'The next one, after we clear this, is on you.'

'It's a deal.'

When Bosch got to his house he found the door locked, but the key he had given Eleanor Wish was under the front mat. The first thing he checked when he got inside was the Hopper print. It was still there on the wall. But she was gone. He made a quick scan of the rooms and found no note. He checked the closet and her clothes were gone. So was her suitcase.

He sat on the bed and thought about her leaving. That morning they had left things open. He had risen early and, while she was still in bed, watching him get ready for the day, he'd asked her what she was going to do during the day. She had told him she didn't know.

Now she was gone. He rubbed a hand over his face. He was already beginning to feel the loss of her and he replayed in his mind their conversations of the night before. He had played it wrong, he decided. It had cost her something to tell him of her complicity. And he had only evaluated it in terms of what it meant to him and to his case. Not to her. Not to them.

Bosch leaned back until he was lying across the bed. He spread his arms and stared up at the ceiling. He could feel the beer working inside him, making him tired.

'Okay,' he said out loud.

He wondered if she would call or if another five years would go by before he saw her again by happenstance. He thought about how much had happened to him in the past five years and how long a wait that had been. His body ached. He closed his eyes.

'Okay.'

He fell asleep and dreamed about being alone in a desert with no roads and miles of open, desolate country ahead of him in every direction he looked.

VI

IV

Bosch picked up two containers of coffee and two glazed doughnuts from Bob's in the farmers market at seven Saturday morning, then drove to the clearing where Tony Aliso's body had been found in the trunk of his car. As he ate and drank, he looked out on the marine layer shrouding the quiet city below. The sun rising behind the towers of downtown cast them as opaque monoliths in the haze. It was beautiful but Bosch felt as though he were the only one in the world seeing it.

When he had finished eating, he used a napkin he had wet in the water fountain at the farmers market to clean the sticky residue of sugar off his fingers. He then stuffed all the papers and the first empty coffee cup back into the doughnut bag and started the car.

Bosch had fallen asleep early Friday evening and awakened in his clothes before sunrise. He felt the need to get out of the house and do something. He had always believed that you could make things happen in an investigation by staying busy and with hard work. He decided that he would use the morning to try to find the spot where Tony Aliso's Rolls-Royce was intercepted and pulled over by his killers.

He concluded for a couple of reasons that the abduction had to have taken place on Mulholland Drive near the entrance to Hidden Highlands. First, the clearing where the car had been found was off Mulholland. If the abduction had taken place near the airport, it was likely the car would have been dumped near the airport, not fifteen miles away. And second, the abduction could be done more easily and quietly up on Mulholland in the dark. The airport and the surrounding area were always congested with traffic and people and would have presented too much of a risk.

The next question was whether Aliso had been followed from the airport or his killers simply waited for him at the abduction spot on Mulholland. Bosch decided on the latter, figuring that it was a small operation – two people, tops – and a tail and vehicle stop would be too iffy a proposition, particularly in Los Angeles, where every owner of a Rolls-Royce would be acutely aware of the danger of carjackings. He thought that they had waited on Mulholland and somehow created a trap or scene that made Aliso stop his car, even though he was carrying $480,000 in cash in his briefcase. And Bosch guessed that the only way Aliso would make such a stop was if that scenario involved his wife. In his mind Bosch saw the headlights of the Rolls-Royce sweeping around a curve and illuminating a frantically waving Veronica Aliso. Tony would stop for that.

Bosch knew that the waiting spot had to be on a place on Mulholland they were sure Tony would pass. There were only two logical routes from the airport to Mulholland Drive and then to the gatehouse at Hidden Highlands. One way would be to go north on the 405 freeway and simply take the Mulholland Drive exit. The other way would have been to take La Cienega Boulevard from the airport north to Laurel Canyon and up the hill to Mulholland.

The two routes had only a one-mile stretch of Mulholland in common. And since there was no way of knowing for sure which route Aliso would take home that night, it seemed obvious to Bosch that the car stop and abduction would have been somewhere along that one mile of road. It was here that Bosch came, and for nearly an hour he drove back and forth along the stretch, finally settling on the spot he would have chosen for the abduction if it had been his plan. The location was at the bend in a hairpin curve a half mile from the Hidden Highlands gatehouse. It was in an area with few homes and those that were there were built on the south side on a promontory well above the road. On the north side, the undeveloped land dropped steeply away from the road into a heavily wooded arroyo where eucalyptus and acacia trees crowded one another. It was the perfect spot. Secluded, out of sight.

Once again Bosch envisioned Tony Aliso coming around the curve and the lights of his Rolls coming upon his own wife in the road. Aliso stops, confused – what is she doing there? He gets out and from the north side of the road her accomplice goes to the Rolls and pops the trunk. Aliso's hands are clawing at his eyes when he is roughly thrown into the trunk and his hands tied behind him. All they had to worry about was a car coming around the curve and throwing its lights on them. But at that late hour on Mulholland, it didn't seem likely. The whole thing could have been done in fifteen seconds. That's why the spray was used. Not because it was a woman, but because it would make it fast.

Bosch pulled off the road, got out and looked around. The spot had the right feel to him. It was as quiet as death. He decided that he would come back that night to see it in darkness, to further confirm what he felt in his gut to be true.

He crossed the street and looked down into the arroyo where her accomplice would have hidden and waited. Looking down he tried to find a spot just off the road where a man could have ducked down and been concealed. He noticed a dirt trail going into the woods and stepped down to it, looking for shoe prints. There were many prints and he squatted down to study them. The ground here was dusty and some of the prints were fully recognizable. He found prints from two distinctly different sets of shoes, an old pair of shoes with worn heels and a much newer pair with heels that left sharp lines in the dirt. Neither pair was what he was looking for, the work-shoe pattern with the cut in the sole that Donovan had noticed.

Bosch's eyes looked up from the ground and followed the trail into the brush and trees. He decided to take a few more steps in, lifted a branch of an acacia and ducked under it. After his eyes adjusted to the darkness under the canopy of foliage, they were drawn to a blue object he could see but not identify about twenty yards further into the dense growth. He would have to leave the trail to get to it, but he decided to investigate.

After slowly moving ten feet into the brush, he could see that the blue object was part of a plastic tarp, the kind you saw on roofs all over the city after an earthquake knocked down chimneys and opened up the seams of buildings. Bosch stepped closer and saw that two corners of the tarp were tied to trees and it was hung over the branch of a third, creating a small shelter on a level portion of the hillside. He watched for a few moments but saw no movement.

It was impossible to come up on the shelter quietly. The ground was covered with a thick layer of dead and dried leaves and twigs that crackled under Bosch's feet. When he was ten feet from the canvas tarp, a man's hoarse voice stopped him.

'I've got a gun, you fuckers!'

Bosch stood stock-still and stared at the tarp. Because it was draped over the long branch of an acacia tree, he was in a blind spot. He could not see whoever it was who had yelled. And the man who yelled probably couldn't see him. Bosch decided to take a chance.

'I've got one, too,' he called back. 'And a badge.'

'Police? I didn't call the police!'

There was a hysterical tinge to the voice now, and Bosch suspected he was dealing with one of the homeless wanderers who were dumped out of mental institutions during the massive cutbacks in public assistance in the 1980s. The city was teeming with them. They stood at almost every major intersection holding their signs and shaking their change cups, they slept under overpasses or burrowed like termites into the woods on the hillsides, living in makeshift camps just yards from million-dollar mansions.

'I'm just passing through,' Bosch yelled. 'You put down yours, I'll put down mine.'

Bosch guessed that the man behind the scared voice didn't even have a gun.

'Okay. It's a deal.'

Bosch unsnapped the holster under his arm but left his gun in place. He walked the final few steps and came slowly around the trunk of the acacia. A man with long gray hair and beard flowing over a blue silk Hawaiian shirt sat cross-legged on a blanket under the tarp. There was a wild look in his eyes. Bosch quickly scanned the man's hands and the surroundings within his immediate reach and saw no weapon. He eased up a bit and nodded at the man.

'Hello,' he said.

'I didn't do nothin'.'

'I understand.'

Bosch looked around. There were folded clothes and towels under the shelter of the tarp. There was a small folding card table with a frying pan on it along with some candles and Sterno cans, two forks and a spoon, but no knife. Bosch figured the man had the knife under his shirt or maybe hidden in the blanket. There was also a bottle of cologne on the table, and Bosch could tell that it had been liberally sprinkled about the shelter. Also under the tarp were an old tar bucket filled with crushed aluminum cans, a stack of newspapers and a dog-eared paperback copy of *Stranger in a Strange Land*.

He stepped to the edge of the man's clearing and squatted like a baseball catcher so they could face each other on the same level. He took a look around the outer edge of the clearing and saw that this was where the man discarded what he didn't need. There were bags of trash and remnants of clothing. By the base of another acacia there was a brown-and-green suit bag. It was unzipped and lying open like a gutted fish. Bosch looked back at the man. He could see he wore two other Hawaiian shirts beneath the blue one on top, which had a pattern of hula girls on surfboards. His pants were dirty but had a sharper crease in them than a homeless man's pants would usually have. His shoes were too well polished for a man of the woods. Bosch guessed that the pair he wore had made some of the prints up on the trail, the ones with the sharp-edged heels.

'That's a nice shirt,' Bosch said.

'It's mine.'

'I know. I just said it was nice. What's your name?'

'Name's George.'

'George what?'

'George whatever the hell you want it to be.'

'Okay, George whatever the hell you want it to be, why don't you tell me about that suit bag over there and those clothes you're wearing? The new shoes. Where did it all come from?'

'It was delivered. It's mine now.'

'What do you mean by delivered?'

'Delivered. That's what I mean. Delivered. They gave it all to me.'

Bosch took out his cigarettes, took one and offered the pack to the man. He waved them away.

'Can't afford it. Take me half a day to find enough cans to buy a pack of smokes. I quit.'

Bosch nodded.

'How long you been livin' up here, George?'

'All my life.'

'When did they kick you out of Camarillo?'

'Who told you that?'

It had been an educated guess, Camarillo being the nearest state institution.

'They did. How long ago was that?'

'If they told you about me, then they would've told you that. I'm not stupid, you know.'

'You got me there, George. About the bag and the clothes, when was it all delivered?'

'I don't know.'

Bosch got up and went over to the suit bag. There was an identification tag attached to the handle. He turned it over and read Anthony Aliso's name and address. He noticed the bag was lying on top of a cardboard box that was damaged from a tumble down the hill. Bosch tipped the box with his foot and read the markings on the side.

Scotch standard HS/T-90 VHS 96-count

He left the box and the suit bag there and went back to the man and squatted again.

'How's last Friday night sound for the delivery?'

'Whatever you say is good.'

'It's not what I say, George. Now if you want me to leave you alone and you want to stay here, you've got to help me. If you go into your nut bag, you're not helping me. When was it delivered?'

George tucked his chin down on his chest like a boy who'd been chastised by a teacher. He brought a thumb and forefinger up and pressed them against his eyes. His voice came out as if it were being strangled with piano wire.

'I don't know. They just came and dropped it off for me. That's all I know.'

'Who dropped it off?'

George looked up, his eyes bright, and pointed upward with one of his dirty fingers. Bosch looked up and saw a patch of blue sky through the upper limbs of the trees. He blew out his breath in exasperation. This wasn't going anywhere.

'So little green men dropped it down from their spaceship, is that right, George? Is that your story?'

'I didn't say that. I don't know if they were green. I didn't see them.'

'But you saw the spaceship?'

'Nope. I didn't say that, neither. I didn't see their craft. Only the landing lights.'

Bosch looked at him a moment.

'Perfect size,' George said. 'They got an invisible beam that measures you from up there, you don't even know it, then they send down the clothes.'

'That's great.'

Bosch's knees were beginning to ache. He stood up and they painfully cracked.

'I'm getting too old for this shit, George.'

'That's a policeman's line. I watched "Kojak" when I had the house.'

'I know. Tell you what, I'm going to take this suit bag with me, if you don't mind. And the box of videotapes.'

'Help yourself. I'm not going anywhere. And I don't have no video machine, either.'

Bosch walked toward the box and bag, wondering why they had been discarded and not just left in the Rolls. After a moment he decided they must have been in the trunk. And in order to make room for Aliso in there, the killers had yanked them out and thrown them down the hill out of sight. They were in a hurry. It was the kind of decision made in haste. A mistake.

He picked up the suit bag by a corner, careful not to touch the handle, though he doubted there would be any prints on it other than George's. The box was light but bulky. He would have to make a second trip for it. He turned and looked at the homeless man. He decided not to ruin his day yet.

'George, you can keep the clothes for now.'

'Okay, thanks.'

'You're welcome.'

As he climbed back up the hill to the road, Bosch was thinking about how he should declare the area a crime scene and call out SID to process everything. But he couldn't do that. Not without announcing he had been continuing an investigation he had been ordered away from.

It didn't bother him, however, because by the time he got up to the road, he knew he had a new direction. A plan was coming together. Quickly. Bosch was jazzed. When he stepped onto level ground he punched his fist in the air and walked quickly to his car.

Bosch worked out the details in his head while he was driving to Hidden Highlands. The Plan. He had been like a cork floating in a great wide ocean that was the case. Bouncing with the currents, not in control of anything. But now he had an idea, a plan that would hopefully draw Veronica Aliso into the box.

Nash was in the gatehouse when Bosch pulled up. He stepped out and leaned down on Bosch's door.

'Morning, Detective Bosch.'

'Howzit going, Captain Nash?'

'It's going. I gotta say your people are creating a bit of a stir already this morning.'

'Yeah, well, that can happen. Whaddaya gonna do?'

'Go with the flow, I guess. You going in to catch up with them or you heading to Mrs Aliso's?'

'I'm going to see the lady.'

'Good. Maybe that'll get her off my back. I gotta call, you know.'

'Why's she on your back?'

'She's just been calling up wondering why you people have been talkin' to the neighbors all morning.'

'What did you tell her?'

'I told her they got a job to do and a murder investigation requires them to talk to a lot of people.'

'That's good. I'll see you.'

Nash waved him off and opened the gate. Bosch drove to the Aliso house, but before he got there he saw Edgar walking from the front door of the home next door to his car. Bosch stopped and waved him over.

'Harry.'

'Jerry. Get anything yet?'

'Nah, not really. Thing about these rich neighborhoods, it's like working a shooting in South Central. Nobody ever wants to talk, nobody saw nothing. I get tired of these people.'

'Where's Kiz?'

'She's working the other side of the street. We met at the station and took one car. She's on foot down there somewhere. Hey, Harry, what do you think about her?'

'Kiz? I think she's good.'

'No, I don't mean as a cop. You know . . . what do you think?'

Bosch looked at him.

'You mean like you and her? What do I think?'

'Yeah. Me and her.'

Bosch knew Edgar was six months divorced and starting to pull his head out of the sand again. But he also knew something about Kiz that he didn't have the right to tell him.

'I don't know, Jerry. Partners shouldn't get involved.'

'I suppose. So you going to see the widow now?'

'Yeah.'

'Maybe I better go with you. You never know, if she figures out we think she's it, then she's liable to wig out, maybe try to take you out.'

'I doubt it. She's too cool for that. But let's go find Kiz. I think both of you should come. I've got a plan now.'

Veronica Aliso was waiting for them at her door.

'I've been waiting for you people to come by to explain just what is going on.'

'Sorry, Mrs Aliso,' Bosch said. 'We've been kind of busy.'

She ushered them in.

'Can I get you something?' she asked over her shoulder as she led them in.

'I think we're fine.'

Part of the plan was for Bosch to do all the talking, if possible. Rider and Edgar were to intimidate her with their silence and their cold-eyed stares.

Bosch and Rider sat where they had sat before and so did Veronica Aliso. Edgar remained standing on the periphery of the seating section of the living room. He put his hand on the mantel of the fireplace and the look on his face said he would rather be anywhere else on the planet on this Saturday morning.

Veronica Aliso was wearing blue jeans, a light blue Oxford shirt and dirty work boots. Her hair was pulled back and pinned up in the back. She was still very attractive though obviously dressing down. Through her open collar Bosch could see a scattering of freckles that he knew from her video went all the way down her chest.

'Are we interrupting something?' Bosch asked. 'Were you about to go out?'

'I wanted to go to the Burbank stables sometime today if I could. I keep a horse there. My husband's body was cremated and I want to take his ashes up the trail into the hills. He loved the hills . . .'

Bosch somberly nodded.

'Well, this won't take too long. First off, you've seen us in the neighborhood this morning. We're just conducting a routine canvass. You never know, maybe someone saw something, maybe somebody watching the house or a car here that shouldn't have been here. You never know.'

'Well, I think I'd be the one who would know about any car that shouldn't be here.'

'Well, I mean if you weren't here. If you were out and someone was here, you probably wouldn't know.'

'How could they get in past the gate?'

'It's a long shot, we know, Mrs Aliso. It's all we've got right now.'

She frowned.

'There's nothing else? What about what you told me the other day? About this man in Las Vegas?'

'Well, Mrs Aliso, I hate to tell you this, but we went down the wrong path on that. We gathered a lot of information about your husband and initially it looked like that was the way to go. But it didn't work out. We do think we're moving in the right direction now, and we're going to make up for the lost time.'

She seemed genuinely stunned.

'I don't understand. The wrong path?'

'Yes, well, I can explain it to you, if you want to hear it. But it involves your husband and some unsavory things.'

'Detective, I've prepared myself over the last few days for anything. Tell me.'

'Mrs Aliso, as I think I indicated to you on our last visit, your husband was involved with some very dangerous people in Las Vegas. I think I mentioned them, Joey Marks and Luke Goshen?'

'I don't recall.'

She kept the look of bewilderment on her face. She was good. Bosch had to give that to her. She might not have made it in the film business but she could act when she needed to.

'To put it bluntly, they're mobsters,' Bosch said. 'Organized crime. And it looks like your husband had been working for them for a long time. He took mob money from Vegas and put it into his films. Laundered it through. Then he gave it back to them, after taking out a fee. It was a lot of money and that's where we went down the wrong path. Your husband was about to get audited by the IRS. Did you know that?'

'Audited? No. He didn't tell me anything about an audit.'

'Well, we found out about the audit, which likely would have revealed his illegal activities, and we thought maybe these people he did business with became aware of it, too, and had him killed so he wouldn't be able to talk about their business. Only we don't think that anymore.'

'I don't understand. Are you sure of this? It seems obvious to me that these people had some involvement.'

She faltered a little bit there. Her voice was a little too urgent.

'Well, like I said, we thought that, too. We haven't fully dropped it, but so far it doesn't check out. The man we arrested over there in Vegas, this Goshen fellow I mentioned, he looked pretty good for it, I have to say. But then his alibi turned out to be a rock we couldn't break. It couldn't have been him, Mrs Aliso. It looks as though somebody went to great lengths to make it look like it was him, even planted a gun in his house, but we know it wasn't.'

She looked at him with dull eyes for a moment and then shook her head. Then she made her first real mistake. She should have said that if it wasn't Goshen, then it was probably the other one Bosch had mentioned or some other mobster associate. But she said nothing and that instinctively told Bosch that she knew of the setup on Goshen. She now knew the plan hadn't worked and her mind was probably scrambling.

'So then what will you do?' she finally asked.

'Oh, we already had to let him go.'

'No, I mean about the investigation. What's next?'

'Well, we're sort of starting from scratch. Looking at it like maybe it was a planned robbery.'

'You said his watch wasn't taken.'

'Right. It wasn't. But the Las Vegas angle wasn't a total waste. We found out that your husband was carrying a lot of money with him when he landed here that night. He was taking it back here to run through his company. To clean it up. It was a lot of money. Nearly a million dollars. He was carrying it for—'

'A *million* dollars?'

That was her second mistake. To Bosch, her emphasis on *million* and her shock betrayed her knowledge that there had been far less than that in Tony Aliso's briefcase. Bosch watched as her eyes stared blankly and all her movement was interior. He guessed – and hoped – she was now wondering where the rest of the money was.

'Yes,' he said. 'See, the man who gave your husband the money, the one we first thought was a suspect, is an FBI agent who infiltrated the organization your husband worked for. That is why his alibi is so solid. Anyway, he told us that your husband was carrying a million dollars. It was all in cash and there was so much that he couldn't fit it all into his briefcase. He had to put about half of it in his suit bag.'

He paused for a few moments. He could tell the story was playing in her internal theater. Her eyes had that faraway look in them. He remembered that look from her movie. But this time it was for real. He hadn't even finished the interview, but she was already making plans. He could see it.

'Was the money marked by the FBI?' she asked. 'I mean, could they trace it that way?'

'No, unfortunately their agent did not have it long enough to do that. There was too much of it, frankly. But the transaction did take place in an office with a hidden video camera. There is no doubt, Tony left there with a million dollars. Uh . . .'

Bosch paused to open his briefcase and quickly consult a page from a file.

'. . . actually, it was a million, seventy-six thousand. All in cash.'

Veronica's eyes went down to the floor as she nodded. Bosch studied her but his concentration was interrupted when he thought he heard a sound from somewhere in the house. It suddenly occurred to him that maybe there was someone else there. They had never asked.

'Did you hear that?' Bosch asked.
'What?'
'I thought I heard something. Are you alone in the house?'
'Yes.'
'I thought I heard a bump or something.'
'You want me to look around?' Edgar offered.

'Oh, no,' Veronica said quickly, ' . . . uh, it probably was just the cat.'

Bosch didn't remember seeing any sign of a cat when he had been in the house before. He glanced at Kiz and saw her almost imperceptibly turn her head to signal she didn't remember a cat either. He decided to let it go for the time being.

'Anyway,' he said, 'that's why we're canvassing and that's why we're here. We need to ask you some questions. They might go over some of the same ground we've covered before but, like I said, we're kind of starting over. It won't take too much longer. Then you'll be able to go to the stables.'

'Fine. Go ahead.'

'Would you mind if I have a drink of water first?'

'No, of course not. I'm sorry, I should have asked. Anybody else want something?'

'I'll pass,' Edgar said.

'I'm fine,' Rider said.

Veronica Aliso stood up and headed toward the hallway. Bosch gave her a head start and then stood up and followed.

'You did ask,' he said to her back. 'But I turned it down. I didn't think I'd get thirsty.'

He followed her into the kitchen, where she opened a cabinet and took down a glass. Bosch looked around. It was a large kitchen with stainless-steel appliances and black granite countertops. There was a center island with a sink in it.

'Tap water'd be fine for me,' he said, taking the glass from her and filling it at the island.

He turned and leaned against the counter and drank from it. He then poured the rest out and put the glass on the counter.

'That's all you want?'

'Yes. Just needed something to wash the dust down, I guess.'

He smiled and she didn't.

'Well then, should we go back to the living room?' she asked.

'That'd be fine.'

He followed her out of the kitchen. Just before he entered the hallway, he turned back and his eyes swept across the gray-tiled floor. He didn't see what he thought should be there.

Bosch spent the next fifteen minutes asking mostly questions that had been asked six days earlier and that had little bearing on the case now. He was going through the motions, the finishing touches. The trap was baited and this was his way of quietly stepping back from it. Finally, when he thought he had said and asked enough, Bosch closed the notebook in which he had been scribbling notes he'd never look at again and stood up. He thanked her for her time and Veronica Aliso walked the three detectives to the door. Bosch was the last one out, and as he stepped over the threshold she spoke to him. He somehow knew that she would. There were parts to her act that had to be played as well.

'Keep me informed, Detective Bosch. Please keep me informed.'

Bosch turned and looked back at her.

'Oh, I will. If anything happens, you'll be the first to know.'

Bosch drove Edgar and Rider back to their car. He didn't speak about the interview until he pulled in behind it.

'So what do you think?' he asked as he got out his cigarettes.

'I think we sunk the hook but good,' Edgar said.

'Yeah,' Rider said. 'It's going to be interesting.'

Bosch lit a cigarette.

'What about the cat?' he asked.

'What?' Edgar asked.

'The noise in the house. She said it was the cat. But in the kitchen there were no food bowls on the floor.'

'Maybe they were outside,' Edgar offered.

Bosch shook his head.

'I think people who keep cats inside feed them inside,' he said. 'In the hills you're supposed to keep 'em in. Coyotes. Anyway, I don't like cats. I get allergic to them. I can usually tell when somebody has a cat. I don't think she has a cat. Kiz, you didn't see a cat in there, did you?'

'I spent all Monday morning in there and I never saw a cat.'

'You think maybe it was the guy then?' Edgar asked. 'Whoever she worked this with?'

'Maybe. I think somebody was in there. Maybe her lawyer.'

'Nah, lawyers don't hide like that. They come out and confront.'

'True.'

'Should we watch the place, see who comes out?' Edgar asked.

Bosch thought a moment.

'No,' Bosch said. 'They spot us and they'll know the money thing is just bait. Better we let it go. Better just to get out of here, go get set up. We gotta get ready.'

VII

During his time in Vietnam, Bosch's primary assignment had been to fight the war in the tunnel networks that ranged beneath the villages in the Cu Chi province, to go into the darkness they called the black echo and to come back alive. But the tunnel work was done quickly, and between those missions he spent days in the bush, fighting and waiting under the jungle canopy. One time he and a handful of others got cut off from their unit and Bosch spent a night sitting in the elephant grass, his back pressed against the back of an Alabama boy named Donnel Fredrick, listening as a company of VC fighters moved through. They sat there and waited for Charlie to stumble onto them. There was nothing else they could do and there were too many to fight. So they waited and the minutes went by like hours. They all made it through, though Donnel was later killed in a foxhole by a direct mortar hit – friendly fire. Bosch always thought that night in the elephant grass was the closest he'd ever come to experiencing a miracle.

Bosch remembered that night sometimes when he was alone on a stakeout or in a tight spot. He thought about it now as he sat cross-legged against the base of a eucalyptus tree ten yards from the tarp the homeless man, George, had erected. Over his clothes, he wore a green plastic poncho he always kept in the trunk of his work car. The candy bars he had with him were Hershey's chocolate with almonds, the same kind he had taken with him into the bush so long ago. And like that night in the tall grass, he had not moved for what seemed like hours. It was dark, with only a glimmer of moonlight making it down through the overhead canopy, and he was waiting. He wanted a cigarette but couldn't afford to open a flame in the blackness. Every now and then he thought he could hear Edgar make a move or readjust himself twenty yards to his right, but he couldn't be sure that it was his partner and not a deer or maybe a coyote passing through.

George had told him there were coyotes. When he had put the old man into the back of Kiz's car for the ride to the hotel they were putting him up in, he had warned Bosch. But Bosch wasn't afraid of coyotes.

The old man had not gone easily. He was sure they were there to take him back to Camarillo. And the truth was, he should have been going back there but the institution wouldn't have him, not without a government-punched ticket. Instead he was going to be treated to a couple of nights at the Mark Twain Hotel in Hollywood. It wasn't a bad place. Bosch had lived there for more than a year while his house was being rebuilt. The worst room there beat a tarp in the woods hands down. But Bosch knew George might not see it that way.

By eleven-thirty the traffic up on Mulholland had thinned down to a car every five minutes or so. Bosch couldn't see them because of the incline and the thickness of the brush, but he could hear them and see the lights wash through the foliage above him as the cars made the curve. He was alert now because a car had slowly gone by twice in the last fifteen minutes, once each way. Bosch had sensed that it was the same car because the engine was over-throttled to compensate for the skip in the engine stroke.

And now it was back for a third time. Bosch listened intently as he heard the familiar engine, and this time there was the added sound of tires turning on gravel. The car was pulling off the road. In a few moments the engine stopped and the following silence was punctuated only by the sound of a car door being opened and then closed. Bosch slowly got up on his haunches, as painful as it was on his knees, and got ready. He looked into the darkness to his right, toward Edgar's position, and saw nothing. He then looked up the incline, toward the edge, and waited.

In a few moments he could see the beam of a flashlight cut through the brush. The light was pointed downward and was moving in a back-and-forth sweeping pattern as its holder slowly descended the hill toward the tarp. Under his poncho Bosch held his gun in one hand and a flashlight in the other, his thumb paused on the switch and ready to turn it on.

The movement of the light stopped. Bosch guessed that its holder had found the spot where the suit bag should have been. After a moment of seeming hesitation the beam was lifted and it swept through the woods, flicking across Bosch for a fraction of a second. But it didn't come back to him. Instead, it held on the blue tarp as Bosch guessed it probably would. The light began advancing, its holder stumbling once as he or she went toward George's home. A few moments later, Bosch saw the beam moving behind the blue plastic. He felt another charge of adrenaline begin to course through his body. Again, his mind flashed on Vietnam. This time it was the tunnels that he thought of. Coming upon an enemy in the darkness. The fear and thrill of it. It was only after he had left that place safely that he acknowledged to himself there had been a thrill to it. And in looking to replace that thrill, he had joined the cops.

Bosch slowly raised himself, hoping his knees wouldn't crack, as he watched the light. They had placed the suit bag in underneath the shelter after stuffing it first with crumpled newspaper. Bosch began to move as quietly as he could in behind the tarp. He was coming from the left. According to the plan, Edgar would be coming from the right, but it was still too dark for Bosch to see him.

Bosch was ten feet away now and could hear the excited breathing of the person under the tarp. Then there was the sound of a zipper being pulled open followed by the sharp cut-off of breath.

'Shit!'

Bosch moved in after hearing the curse. He realized he recognized the man's voice just as he came around the open side of the tarp and raised both his weapon and his flashlight from beneath his poncho.

'*Freeze! Police!*' Bosch yelled at the same moment he put on his light. 'All right, come out of there, Powers.'

Almost immediately Edgar's light came on from Bosch's right.

'What the . . .?' Edgar started to say.

Crouched there in the crossing beams of light was Officer Ray Powers. In full uniform, the big patrol cop held a flashlight in one hand and a gun in the other. A look of utter surprise played across his face. His mouth dropped open.

'Bosch,' he said. 'What the fuck are you doing here?'

'That's our line, Powers,' Edgar said angrily. 'Don't you know what the fuck you just did? You walked right into a – what are *you* doing here, man?'

Powers lowered his gun and slid it back into his holster.

'I was – there was a report. Somebody must've seen you guys sneaking in here. They said they saw two men sneaking around.'

Bosch stepped back from the tarp, keeping his gun raised.

'Come out of there, Powers,' he said.

Powers did as he was commanded. Bosch put the beam from his light right in the man's face.

'What about this report? Who called it in?'

'Just some guy driving by up on the road. Must've seen you going in here. Can you get the light out of my face?'

Bosch didn't move the focus of the light an inch.

'Then what?' he asked. 'Who'd he call?'

Bosch knew that after Rider had dropped them off, her job was to park on a nearby street and keep her scanner on. If there had been such a radio call, she would have heard it and called off the patrol response, telling the dispatcher it was a surveillance operation.

'He didn't call it in. I was cruising by and he waved me down.'

'You mean he claimed he just saw two guys going into the woods?'

'Uh, no. No, he waved me down earlier. I just didn't get a chance to check it out until now.'

Bosch and Edgar had gone into the woods at two-thirty. It was full daylight then and Powers hadn't even been on duty yet. And the only car that had been in the area at the time was Rider's. Bosch knew Powers was lying, and it was all beginning to fall into place. His finding the body, his fingerprint on the trunk, the pepper spray on the victim, the reason the bindings were taken off the wrists. It was already there, in the details.

'How much earlier?' Bosch asked.

'Uh, it was right after I came on duty. I can't remember the time.'

'Daylight?'

'Yeah, daylight. Can you put the fuckin' light down?'

Bosch ignored him again.

'What was the citizen's name?'

'I didn't get it. Just some guy in a Jag, he waved me down at Laurel Canyon and Mulholland. Told me what he saw and I said I'd check it when I got the chance. So I was checking it out and saw the bag here. I figured it belonged to the guy in the trunk. I saw the bulletin you people put out about the car and the luggage, so I knew you were looking for it. Sorry I blew it, but you people should've let the watch commander know what you were doing. Jesus, Bosch I'm going blind here.'

'Yeah, it's blown all right,' Bosch said, finally lowering the light. He lowered his gun to his side also but didn't put it away. He kept it ready there, under the poncho. 'Might as well pack it in now. Powers, go on up the hill to your car. Jerry, grab the bag.'

Bosch climbed up the hill behind Powers, careful to keep the light up and back on the patrol cop. He knew that if they had cuffed Powers down by the tarp, they'd never get him up the hill because of the steep terrain and because Powers might fight them. So he had to scam him. He let him think he was clear.

At the top of the hill, Bosch waited until Edgar came up behind them before making a move.

'Know what I don't get, Powers?' he said.

'What, Bosch?'

'I don't get why you waited until dark to check out a complaint you got during the day. You're told that two suspicious-looking characters went into the woods and you decide to wait until it's late and it's dark to check it out by yourself.'

'I told you. Didn't have the time.'

'You're full of shit, Powers,' Edgar said.

He had either just caught on or had played along with Bosch perfectly.

Bosch saw Powers's eyes go dead as he went inside to try to figure out what to do. In that instant Bosch raised his gun again and aimed it at a spot between those two vacant portals.

'Don't think so much, Powers,' he said. 'It's over. Now stand still. Jerry?'

Edgar moved in behind the big cop and yanked his gun out of its holster. He dropped it on the ground and jerked one of Powers's hands behind his back. He cuffed the hand and then he did the other. When he was done, he picked up the gun. It seemed to Bosch that Powers was still inside, still staring blankly at nothing. Then he came back.

'You people, you have just fucked up big time,' he said, controlled rage in his voice.

'We'll see about that. Jerry, you got him? I want to call Kiz.'

'Go ahead. I got his ass. I hope he does make a move. Go ahead, Powers, do something stupid for me.'

'Fuck you, Edgar! You don't know what you've just done. You're goin' down, bro. You're going *down!*'

Edgar remained silent. Bosch took the Motorola two-way out of his pocket, turned it on and keyed the mike.

'Kiz, you there?'

'Here. I'm here.'

'Come on over. Hurry.'

'On my way.'

Bosch put the two-way back and they stood there in silence for a minute until they saw the flashing blue light lead Rider's car around the bend. When it pulled up, the lights swept repeatedly through the tops of the trees on the incline. Bosch realized that from below, down in George's shelter, the lights on the trees might look as if they were coming from the sky. It all came to Bosch then. George's spacecraft had been Powers's patrol car. The abduction had been a traffic stop. The perfect way to get a man carrying nearly a half million in cash to stop. Powers had simply waited for Aliso's white Rolls, probably at Mulholland and Laurel Canyon, then followed and put the lights on when they approached the secluded curve. Tony probably thought he had been speeding. He pulled over.

Rider pulled off the road behind the patrol car. Bosch came over and opened the back door and looked in at her.

'Harry, what is it?' she asked.

'Powers. Powers is it.'

'Oh my God.'

'Yeah. I want you and Jerry to take him in. I'll follow with his car.'

He walked back over to Edgar and Powers.

'Okay, let's go.'

'You people have all lost your jobs,' Powers said. 'You fucked yourselves up.'

'You can tell us about it at the station.'

Bosch jerked him by the arm, feeling its thickness and strength. He and Edgar then hustled him into the back of Rider's car. Edgar went around and got in the other side next to him.

Looking in through the open rear door, Bosch went over what would be the procedure.

'Take all his shit away and lock him in one of the interview rooms,' he said. 'Make sure you get his cuff key. I'll be right behind you.'

Bosch slammed the door and knocked twice on the roof. He then went to the patrol car, put the suit bag in the back seat and got in. Rider pulled out and Bosch followed. They sped west toward Laurel Canyon.

It took Billets less than an hour to come in. When she got there, the three of them were sitting at the homicide table. Bosch was going through the murder book with Rider while she took notes on a legal pad. Edgar was at the typewriter. Billets walked in with a force and look on her face that clearly showed the situation. Bosch hadn't talked to her yet. It had been Rider who had called her in from home.

'What are you doing to me?' Billets asked, her piercing eyes clearly fixed on Bosch.

What she was really saying to him was that he was the team leader and the responsibility for this potential fuckup rested squarely on him. That was okay with Bosch, because not only was that right and fair, but in the half hour he'd had to go through the murder book and the other evidence, his confidence had grown.

'What am I doing to you? I'm bringing in your killer.'

'I told you to conduct a quiet and careful investigation,' Billets responded. 'I didn't tell you to conduct some kind of half-assed sting operation and then drag a cop in here! I can't believe this.'

Billets was now pacing behind Rider's back without looking at them. The squad room was deserted except for the three of them and the angry lieutenant.

'It's Powers, Lieutenant,' Bosch said. 'If you'd calm down, we—'

'Oh, it's him, is it? You have the evidence of that? Great! I'll call a DA in here right now and we'll write up the charges then. Because you really had me worried there for a minute that you three jerked this guy off the street with just enough probable cause to charge him with jaywalking.'

Now she was looking at Bosch with the angry eyes again. She had even stopped her pacing to level them at him. He responded as calmly as he could.

'First of all, it was my decision to take him off the street. And you're right, we don't have enough to call out a DA yet. But we'll get it. There's no doubt in my mind he's the man. It's him and the widow.'

'Well, I'm glad there's no doubt in *your* mind but you're not the DA or the goddamned jury.'

He didn't respond. It was no use. He had to wait for her anger to ebb and then they could talk sensibly.

'Where is he?' Billets asked.

'Room three,' Bosch said.

'What did you tell the watch commander?'

'Nothing. It happened at the end of shift. Powers was going to grab the suit bag and then go punch out. We were able to bring him in while most everybody else was still up in roll call. I parked his car and dropped the key at the watch office. I told the watch lieutenant we were using Powers for a little while on a warrant, that we wanted a uniform with us when we knocked on a door. He said fine and then I expect he went off shift. As far as I know, nobody knows we have him back there.'

Billets thought for a moment. When she spoke, she was calmer and more like the person who normally sat behind the desk in the glass office.

'Okay, I'm going to go back there and get some coffee, see if I get asked about him. When I come back, we'll go over all of this in detail and see what we have.'

She walked slowly to the hallway at the rear of the squad room that led to the watch office. Bosch watched her go and then picked up the phone and dialed the number of the security office of the Mirage hotel and casino. He told the officer who answered who he was and that he needed to speak with Hank Meyer immediately. When the officer mentioned that it was after midnight, Bosch told him it was an emergency and that he was sure that if Meyer was informed who needed to speak with him, he would return the call. Bosch gave him all the numbers he could be reached at, beginning with his number at the homicide table, and hung up. He went back to his work with the murder book.

'Did you say he's in three?'

Bosch looked up. Billets was back, a cup of steaming coffee in her hand. He nodded.

'I want to have a look,' she said.

Bosch got up and walked with her down the hallway to the four doors leading to the interview rooms. Doors marked one and two were on the left, three and four on the right. But there was no fourth interview room. The room marked four was actually a small cubicle with a one-way glass window that allowed for observation of room three. In three, the other side of the glass was a mirror. Billets entered four and looked through the glass at Powers. He sat ramrod straight at a table in a chair directly opposite the mirror. His hands were cuffed behind his back. He still wore his uniform but his equipment belt had been removed. He stared straight ahead at his own reflection in the mirror. This created an eerie effect in the fourth room because it appeared that he was looking right at them, as if there were no mirror or glass between them.

Billets said nothing. She just looked back at the man staring at her.

'There is a lot hanging in the balance tonight, Harry,' she said quietly.

'I know,' he said.

They stood there silently for a few moments until Edgar opened the door and told Bosch that Hank Meyer was on the phone. Bosch headed back, picked up the phone and told Meyer what he needed. Meyer said he was at home and that he'd have to go into the hotel, but he would call back as soon as possible. Bosch thanked him and hung up. Billets had now taken one of the empty seats at the homicide table.

'Okay,' she said, 'one of you tell me exactly how this went down tonight.'

Bosch remained in the lead and took the next fifteen minutes to recount how he found Tony Aliso's suit bag, set up the sting through Veronica Aliso and then waited in the woods off Mulholland until Powers showed up. He explained how the story Powers had offered for his being there did not make sense.

'What else did he say?' Billets asked at the end.

'Nothing. Jerry and Kiz put him in the room and that's where he's been ever since.'

'What else have you got?'

'For starters, we have his print on the inside of the trunk lid. We also have a record of association with the widow.'

Billets raised her eyebrows.

'That's what we were working on when you came in. On Sunday night when Jerry ran the victim's name through the computer, we got a hit on a burglary report from back in March. Somebody hit the Aliso house. Jerry pulled the report but it looked unconnected. Just a routine burglary. And it was, except the officer who took the initial report from Mrs Aliso was Powers. We think the relationship started with the burglary. That's when they met. After that, we have the gate records. Police patrols of Hidden Highlands are recorded on the gate logs by the car's roof number. The logs show the car assigned to Powers – the

Zebra car – has been going in there two, three nights a week on patrol, always on the nights we know from credit card records that Tony was out of town. I think he was poppin' over there to see Veronica.'

'What else?' the lieutenant asked. 'So far all you've got is a bunch of coincidences strung together.'

'There are no coincidences,' Bosch said. 'Not like this.'

'Then what else have you got?'

'Like I said, his story about why he came down into the woods doesn't check out. He came down looking for the suit bag and the only way he would have known that it was worth coming back for was through Veronica. It's him, Lieutenant. It's him.'

Billets thought about this. Bosch believed the facts he was giving her were beginning to have a cumulative effect in convincing her. He had one thing left with which to nail her down.

'There's one other thing. Remember our problem with Veronica? If she was involved in this, how did she get out of Hidden Highlands and not have it noted on the gate log?'

'Right.'

'Well, the gate log shows that on the night of the murder, the Zebra car cruised through on patrol. Twice. He was in and out both times. First time he was logged in at ten and out at ten-ten. Then back in at eleven-forty-eight and out four minutes later. It was noted as just routine patrol.'

'Okay, so?'

'So on the first time, he cruises in and picks her up. She gets down on the floor in the back. It's dark out, the gate guy only sees Powers heading back out. They go and wait for Tony, do the deed and then Powers takes her back home – the second set of entries on the log.'

'It works,' Billets said, nodding her approval. 'The actual abduction, how do you see it?'

'We've figured all along it took two people to do this job. First off, Veronica had to know from Tony what flight he was taking. So that set the time frame. Powers picks her up that night and they go to Laurel Canyon and Mulholland and wait for the white Rolls to go by. We figure that happens about eleven or so. Powers follows until Tony is close to the curve through the woods. He puts on the lights and pulls him over, like a routine traffic stop. Only he tells Tony to step out and go to the back of the car. Maybe he makes him open the trunk, maybe he does that himself after he cuffs him. Either way, the trunk is opened and Powers has a problem. Tony's suit bag and a box of videos are in the trunk and that doesn't leave much room for him. Powers doesn't have much time. A car could come around the bend any moment and light up the whole thing. So he takes the suit bag and the box out and throws them down the hill into the woods. He then tells Tony to get in the trunk. Tony says no or maybe he struggles a bit. Either way, Powers takes out his pepper spray and gives him a shot in the face. Tony is then real manageable, easy to throw into the trunk. Maybe Powers pulled his shoes off then to stop him from kicking around in there, making noise.'

'That's when Veronica pops out,' Rider said, picking up the story. 'She drives the Rolls while Powers follows in the squad car. They knew where they were going. They needed a spot where the car wouldn't be found for a couple days, giving Powers time to get over to Vegas on Saturday, plant the gun and lay down a few more clues like the anonymous call to Metro. That call was what was supposed to put the finger on Luke Goshen. Not the fingerprints. That was just luck for them. Anyway, that's getting ahead of the story. Veronica drives the Rolls and Powers follows. To the clearing over the Bowl. She pops the trunk and Powers leans in and does the job. Or maybe he puts one cap in Tony and he makes Veronica do the second. That way they're partners for good, partners in blood.'

Billets nodded, a serious look on her face.

'It seems kind of risky. What if he had to take a radio call? The whole plan would go down the drain.'

'We thought of that and Jerry checked with the watch office. Gomez was the CO Friday night. He says he remembers that Powers had such a busy shift he didn't take a dinner break until ten. He doesn't recall hearing from him until just before end of the watch.'

Billets nodded again.

'What about the shoe prints recovered? Are they his?'

'Powers got lucky there,' Edgar said. 'He's wearing brand-new boots in there. Looks like he maybe just bought 'em today.'

'Shit!'

'Yeah,' Bosch said. 'We figure he saw the shoe prints on the table last night at the Cat and Fiddle. He went out and got new ones today.'

'Oh man . . .'

'Well, maybe there's still a chance he didn't get rid of the old ones. We're working on a search warrant for his place. Oh, and our luck ain't so bad, either. Jerry, tell her about the spray.'

Edgar leaned forward on the table.

'I went back to the supply post, took a look at the sheet. On Sunday Powers signed out an OC cartridge. Only I then went and looked at the fifty-one list in the watch loo's office. No use-of-force reported by Powers in this deployment period.'

'So,' Billets said, 'he somehow used his pepper spray, because he had to get a refill cartridge but he never reported using the spray to his watch commander.'

'Right.'

Billets thought about things for a few moments before speaking again.

'Okay,' she said, 'what you've come up with quickly is all good stuff. But it's not enough. It's a circumstantial case and most of this can be explained away. Even if you could prove he and the widow have been meeting, it doesn't prove murder. The fingerprint on the trunk can be explained by sloppy work at the crime scene. Who knows, maybe that's all it really was.'

'I doubt it,' Bosch said.

'Well, your doubts aren't good enough. Where do we go from here?'

'We still have some things in the fire. Jerry's going for a warrant based on what we've got so far. If we get inside Powers's house, maybe we find the shoes, maybe we find something else. We'll see. I also have an angle in Vegas working. We figure that for them to have pulled this off, Powers had to have followed Tony over there once or twice, you know, to know about Goshen and pick him to hang it all on. If we're lucky, Powers would've wanted to stay right on Tony. That would mean staying at the Mirage. You can't stay there without a trail. You can pay cash but you've got to give a legit credit card imprint to cover room charges, phone calls, things like that. In other words, you can't register under any name you don't have on a credit card. I've got a guy checking.'

'Okay, it's a start,' Billets said.

She nodded her head, cupped a hand over her mouth and lapsed into a contemplative silence for a long moment.

'What it all comes down to is that we need to break him, don't we?' she finally asked.

Bosch nodded.

'Probably. Unless we get lucky with the warrant.'

'You're not going to break him. He's a cop, he knows the angles, he knows the rules of evidence.'

'We'll see.'

She looked at her watch. Bosch looked at his and saw it was now one o'clock.

'We're in trouble,' Billets said solemnly. 'We won't be able to contain this much past dawn. After that I will have to make proper notification of what we've done and what we've got going. If that happens, you can count on us not being involved, and worse.'

Bosch leaned forward.

'Go back home, Lieutenant,' he said. 'You were never here. Let us have the night. Come back in at nine tomorrow. Bring a DA back with you if you want. Make sure it's somebody who will go to the edge with you. If you don't know one, I can call somebody. But give us till nine. Eight hours. Then you come in and we either have the complete package tied up for you or you go ahead and do what you have to do.'

She looked carefully at each one of them, took a deep breath and exhaled slowly.

'Good luck,' she said.

She nodded, got up and left them there.

Outside the door to interview room three, Bosch paused and composed his thoughts. He knew that everything would turn on what happened inside the room. He had to break Powers and that would be no easy task. Powers was a cop. He knew all the tricks. But somehow Bosch had to find a weakness he could exploit until the big man went down. He knew it was going to be a brutal match. He blew out his breath and opened the door.

Bosch stepped into the interview room, took the chair directly across from Powers and spread out the two sheets of paper he carried with him in front of Powers.

'Okay, Powers, I'm here to tell you what's what.'

'You can save it, asshole. The only one I want to talk to is my lawyer.'

'Well, that's what I'm here for. Why don't you take it easy and we'll talk about it?'

'Take it easy? You people arrest me, hook me up like a goddamn criminal and then leave me in here for a fucking hour and a half while you sit out there and figure out how fucked up this is, and you want me to take it easy? What planet are you on, Bosch? I'm not taking anything easy. Now cut me loose or give me the goddamn phone!'

'Well, that's the problem, isn't it? Deciding whether to

book you or cut you loose. That's why I came in, Powers. I thought maybe you could help us out on that.'

Powers didn't appear to pick up on that. His eyes dropped to the center of the table and they were working – small, quick movements, looking for the angles.

'This is what is what,' Bosch said. 'If I book you now, then we call the lawyer and we both know that is going to be that. No lawyer is gonna let his client talk to the cops. We'll just have to go to court and you know what that means. You'll be suspended, no pay. We'll go for no bail and you'll sit in the can nine, ten months and then maybe it gets straightened out in your favor. And maybe not. Meantime, you're all over the front page. Your mother, father, neighbors . . . well, you know how it goes.'

Bosch took out a cigarette and put it in his mouth. He didn't light it and he didn't offer one to Powers. He remembered offering one to the big cop at the crime scene and being turned down.

'The alternative to that,' he continued, 'is that we sit here and try to get this straightened out right now. You've got two forms there in front of you. The good thing about dealing with a cop like this is I don't really need to explain this stuff to you. The first one's a rights form. You know what that is. You sign that you understand your rights and then you make your choice. Talk to me or call your lawyer after we book you. The second form is the attorney waiver.'

Powers stared silently down at the pages and Bosch put a pen down on the table.

'I'll take the cuffs off when you're ready to sign,' Bosch said. 'See, now the bad thing about dealing with a cop is that I can't bluff you. You know the game. You know if you sign that waiver and talk to me, you'll either talk yourself out of this or right into it . . . I can give you more time to think about it, if you want.'

'I don't need any more time,' he said. 'Take off the cuffs.'

Bosch got up and went around behind Powers.

'You right or left?'

'Right.'

There was barely enough room between the back of the big man and the wall to work on the cuffs. It was a dangerous position to be in with most suspects. But Powers was a cop and he probably knew that the moment he became violent was the moment he lost any chance of getting out of this room and back to his life. He also had to assume someone was watching and ready behind the glass in room four. Bosch unhooked the right cuff and closed it around one of the metal slats of the chair.

Powers scribbled signatures across both forms. Bosch tried to give no indication of his excitement. Powers was making a mistake. Bosch took the pen from him and put it in his pocket.

'Put your arm behind you.'

'Come on, Bosch. Treat me like a human. If we're going to talk, let's talk.'

'Put your arm behind you.'

Powers did as he was told and blew out his breath in frustration. Bosch recuffed his wrists through the metal slat at the back of the chair and then took his seat again. He cleared his throat, going over the last details in his mind. He knew his mission here. He had to make Powers believe he had the edge, that he had a chance to get out. If he believed that, then he might start talking. If he started talking, Bosch thought he could win the fight.

'Okay,' Bosch said. 'I'm going to lay it out for you. If you can convince me that we have it wrong, then you'll be out of here before the sun's up.'

'That's all I want.'

'Powers, we know you have a relationship with Veronica Aliso predating her husband's death. We know you followed him to Vegas on at least two occasions prior to the killing.'

Powers kept his eyes on the table in front of him. But

Bosch was able to read them like the needles of a polygraph machine. There had been a slight tremor in the pupils when Bosch mentioned Las Vegas.

'That's right,' Bosch said. 'We've got the records from the Mirage. That was careless, Powers, leaving a record like that. We can put you in Vegas with Tony Aliso.'

'So I like goin' to Vegas, big deal. Tony Aliso was there? Wow, what a coincidence. From what I heard, he went there a lot. What else you got?'

'We've got your print, Powers. Fingerprint. Inside the car. You got a refill of pepper spray on Sunday, but you never filed a use-of-force report explaining how you used it.'

'Accidental discharge. I didn't file a use-of-force because there wasn't any. You haven't got shit. My fingerprint? You're right, you've probably got prints. But I was in that car, asshole. I'm the one who found the body, remember? This is a joke, man. I'm thinking I better just get my lawyer in here and take my chances. No DA is going to touch this bullshit with a ten-foot pole.'

Bosch ignored the baiting and went on.

'And last but not least, we have your little climb down the hill tonight. Your story is for shit, Powers. You went down there to look for Aliso's suit bag because you knew it was there and you thought it had something you and the widow overlooked before. About a half million dollars. The only question I really have is whether she called you up and told you or if that was you in her house this morning when we dropped by.'

Bosch saw the pupils jump again slightly but then they went flat.

'Like I said, I'll take that lawyer now.'

'I guess you're just the errand boy, right? She told you to go and get the money while she waited at the mansion.'

Powers started laughing in a fake way.

'I like that, Bosch. Errand boy. Too bad I barely know the woman. But it's a good try. Good try. I like you, too, Bosch, but I gotta tell you something.'

He leaned across the table and lowered his voice.

'I ever run across you again on the outside, you know, when it's just me and you, head to head, I'm going to seriously fuck you up.'

He straightened up again and nodded. Bosch smiled.

'You know, I don't think I was sure until now. But now I'm sure. You did it, Powers. You're the man. And there is never going to be an outside for you. Never. So tell me, whose idea was it? Was she the first one to bring it up or was that you?'

Powers stared sullenly down at the table and shook his head.

'Let me see if I can figure it out,' Bosch said. 'I guess you went up there to that big house and saw all that they had, the money, maybe heard about Tony and his Rolls, and it just went on from there. I'm betting it was your idea, Powers. But I think she knew you would come up with it. See, she's a smart woman. She knew you would come up with it. And she waited . . .

'And you know what? We've got nothing on her. Nothing. She played you perfect, man. Right down the line. She's going to do the walk and *you*' – he pointed at Powers's chest – 'are going to do the time. Is that how you want it?'

Powers leaned back, a bemused smile on his face.

'You don't get it, do you?' Powers said. 'You're the errand boy here, but look at yourself. You've got nothin' to deliver. Look at what you've got. You can't tie me to Aliso. I found the body, man. I opened the car. If you found a print, then that's when I left it. All the rest is a bunch of bullshit adding up to nothing. You go in to see a prosecutor with that, they're going to laugh your ass out onto Temple Street. So go get me the phone, errand boy, and let's get it on. Just go get me the phone.'

'Not yet, Powers,' Bosch said. 'Not just yet.'

*

Bosch sat at his spot at the homicide table with his head down on his folded arms. An empty coffee cup was near his elbow. A cigarette he had perched on the edge of the table had burned down to the butt, leaving one more scar on the old wood.

Bosch was alone. It was almost six and there was just the hint of dawn's light coming through the windows that ran high along the east wall of the room. He'd gone at it for more than four hours with Powers and had gained no ground. He hadn't even made a dent in Powers's cool demeanor. The first rounds had assuredly gone to the big patrol cop.

Bosch wasn't asleep, though. He was simply resting and waiting and his thoughts remained focused on Powers. Bosch had no doubts. He was sure that he had the right man sitting handcuffed in the interview room. What minimal evidence they had certainly pointed to Powers. But it was more than the evidence that convinced him. It was experience and gut instinct. Bosch believed an innocent man would have been scared, not smug as Powers had been. An innocent man would not have taunted Bosch. And so what still remained now was to take away that smugness and break him. Bosch was tired but still felt up to the task. The only thing that worried him was time. Time was against him.

Bosch raised his head and looked at his watch. Billets would be back in three hours. He picked up the empty cup, used his palm to push the dead cigarette and its ashes into it and dropped it into the trash can under the table. He stood up, lit another cigarette and took a walk down the aisle between the crime tables. He tried to clear his mind, to get ready for the next round.

He thought about paging Edgar to see if he and Rider had found anything yet, anything at all that could help, but decided against it. They knew that time was important. They would have either called or come back if they had something.

As he stood at the far end of the squad room and these thoughts travelled through his mind, his eyes fell on the sex crimes table, and he realized after a moment that he was looking at a Polaroid photo of the girl who had come into the station with her mother on Friday to report that she had been raped. The photo was on the top of a stack of Polaroids that were paper-clipped to the outside of the case envelope. Detective Mary Cantu had left it on the top of her pile for Monday. Without thinking about it, Bosch pulled the stack of photos from beneath the clip and began to look through them. The girl had been badly mistreated and the bruises documented on her body by Cantu's camera were a depressing testament to all that was wrong with the city. Bosch always found it easier to deal with victims who were no longer living. The live ones haunted him because they could never be consoled. Not fully. They were forever left with the question why.

Sometimes Bosch thought of his city as some kind of vast drain that pulled all bad things toward a spot where they swirled around in a deep concentration. It was a place where it seemed the good people were often outnumbered by the bad. The creeps and schemers, the rapists and killers. It was a place that could easily produce someone like Powers. Too easily.

Bosch put the photos back under the clip, embarrassed by his thoughtless voyeurism of the girl's pain. He went back to the homicide table, picked up the phone and dialed his home number. It was nearly twenty-four hours since he had been to his house, and his hope was that Eleanor Wish would answer – he had left the key under the mat – or there might be a message from her. After three rings the line was picked up and he heard his own voice on tape tell himself to leave a message. He punched in his code to check for messages and the machine told him he had none.

He stood there a long moment thinking about Eleanor, the phone still at his ear, when suddenly he heard her voice.

'Harry, is that you?'

'Eleanor?'

'I'm here, Harry.'

'Why didn't you answer?'

'I didn't think it would be for me.'

'When did you get there?'

'Last night. I've been waiting for you. Thanks for leaving the key.'

'You're welcome . . . Eleanor, where'd you go?'

There was a beat of silence before she answered.

'I went back to Vegas. I needed to get my car . . . clear out my bank account, things like that. Where have you been all night?'

'Working. We have a new suspect. We're holding him here. Did you go by your apartment?'

'No. There was no reason to. I just did what I had to do and drove back.'

'I'm sorry if I woke you.'

'That's okay. I was worried about where you were, but I didn't want to call you there in case you were in the middle of something.'

Bosch wanted to ask her what came next for them, but he felt such a sense of happiness that she was there in his home that he didn't dare to ruin the moment.

'I don't know how much longer I'll be tied up,' he said.

Bosch heard the heavy doors in the station's rear hallway open and bang shut. Footsteps were coming toward the squad room.

'Do you have to go?' Eleanor asked.

'Um . . .'

Edgar and Rider walked into the squad room. Rider carried a brown evidence bag with something heavy in it. Edgar carried a closed cardboard box across which someone had stenciled *Xmas* with a Magic Marker. He also had a broad smile on his face.

'Yeah,' Bosch said, 'I think I better go.'

'Okay, Harry, I'll see you.'

'You'll be there?'

'I'll be here.'

'Okay, Eleanor, I'll see you as soon as I can.'

He hung up and looked up at his two partners. Edgar was still smiling.

'We got your Christmas present here, Harry,' Edgar said. 'We got Powers right here in this box.'

'You got the boots?'

'No. No boots. We got better than boots.'

'Show me.'

Edgar lifted the lid off the box. Off the top he took out a manila envelope. He then tilted the box so that Bosch could look in. Bosch whistled.

'Merry Christmas,' Edgar said.

'You count it?' Bosch asked, his eyes still on the stacks of currency with rubber bands around them.

'Each bundle has a number on it,' Rider said. 'You add them all up, it equals four hundred eighty thousand. It looks like it's everything.'

'Not a bad present, eh Harry?' Edgar said excitedly.

'No. Where was it?'

'Attic crawl space,' Edgar said. 'One of the last places we looked. Box was just sitting there in front of me as soon as I stuck my head up.'

Bosch nodded.

'Okay, what else?'

'Found these under the mattress.'

From the envelope Edgar withdrew a stack of photos. They were six by four in size and each had the date of the photograph digitally printed on the bottom left corner. Bosch put them on the table in front of them and looked through them, carefully picking them up by the corners. He hoped Edgar had handled them the same way.

The first photo was of Tony Aliso getting into a car at the valet stand in front of the Mirage. The next was of him walking to the door of Dolly's talking to the man Aliso knew as Luke Goshen. It was dark outside in these shots and they were taken from a distance, but the neon-glutted entrance of the club was lit as brightly as daylight and Aliso and Goshen were easily recognizable.

Then there were photos from the same location but the date at the bottom corner had changed. They showed a young woman leaving the club and walking to Aliso's car. Bosch recognized her. It was Layla. There were also pictures of Tony and Layla poolside at the Mirage. The last shot was of Tony leaning his deeply tanned body over Layla's lounge chair and kissing her on the mouth.

Bosch looked up at Edgar and Rider. Edgar was smiling again. Rider wasn't.

'Just like we thought,' Edgar said. 'He cased this guy over there in Vegas. That shows he had the knowledge to set this whole thing up. Him and the widow. We got 'em, Harry. This shows premeditation, lying in wait, the works. We got 'em both, nine ways to Sunday.'

'Maybe.' He looked at Rider. 'What's up with you, Kiz?'

She shook her head.

'I don't know. It just seems too easy. The place was very clean. No old boots, no sign that Veronica ever even set foot in that place. Then we find these so easy. It was like we were supposed to find it all. I mean, why would he take the time to get rid of the boots but leave the photos under the mattress? I can see him wanting to hang on to the money, but putting it in the attic seems pretty lame.'

She moved her hand toward the photos and the cash in a dismissive gesture. Bosch nodded his agreement and leaned back in his chair.

'I think you're right,' he said. 'He's not that stupid.'

He thought about the similarity to the gun being planted on Goshen. That, too, turned out to be too easy.

'I think it's a setup,' Bosch said. 'Veronica did this. He took the photos for her. He probably told her to destroy them, but she didn't. She hung on to them just in case. She probably snuck them back in under his bed and put the cash up in the attic. Was it easy to get to?'

'Easy enough,' Rider said. 'Fold-down ladder.'

'Wait a minute, why would she set him up?' Edgar asked.

'Not from the start,' Bosch said. 'It was like a fall-back position. If things started to go wrong, if we got too close, she had Powers out there ready to take the fall. Maybe when she sent Powers after the suitcase she went to his place with the photos and the cash. Who knows when it started? But I bet when I tell Powers we found this stuff in his house, his eyes are going to pop. Whaddaya got in the bag, Kiz, the camera?'

She nodded and put the bag on the table without opening it.

'Nikon with a telephoto on it, credit card receipt for his purchase of it.'

Bosch nodded and his thoughts strayed a bit. He was trying to think about how he was going to work the photos and money with Powers. It was their shot at breaking him. It had to be played right.

'Hold on, hold on,' Edgar said, a look of confusion on his face. 'I still don't get this. What makes you say it was a setup? Maybe he was holding the cash and the photos and they were going to split it all after the heat died down. Why does it have to be that she set him up?'

Bosch looked at Rider and then back at Edgar.

''Cause Kiz is right. It's too easy.'

'Not if he thought we didn't have a clue, if he thought he was clear right up to the moment we jumped out of the bushes up there in the woods.'

Bosch shook his head.

'I don't know. I don't think he would have played it the way he did when I was just talking to him. Not if he knew he had this stuff back at his place. I go with it being a setup. She's putting it all on him. We pull her in and she'll feed us some story about the guy being obsessed with her. Maybe, if she's any kind of actress, she tells us, yes, she had an affair with him but then she broke it off. But he wouldn't go away. He killed her old man so he could have her all to himself.'

Bosch leaned back and looked at them, waiting for their response.

'I think it's good,' Rider said. 'It could work.'

'Except we don't believe it,' Bosch said.

'So what's she get out of this?' Edgar asked, refusing to drop his disagreement. 'She's givin' up the money puttin' it in his pad. What's that leave her?'

'The house, the cars, insurance,' Bosch said. 'Whatever's left of the company – and the chance to get away.'

But it was a weak answer and he knew it. A half million dollars was a lot of cash to use to set somebody up. It was the one flaw in the theory he had just spun.

'She got rid of her husband,' Rider said. 'Maybe that was all that was important to her.'

'He'd been screwing around on her for years,' Edgar said. 'Why now? What was different this time?'

'I don't know,' Rider said. 'But there was something different or something else we don't know about. That's what we have to find out.'

'Yeah, well, good luck,' Edgar said.

'I've got an idea,' Bosch said. 'If anyone knows what that something else is, it's Powers. I want to try to scam him and I think I know how. Kiz, you still got that tape, the one with Veronica in it?'

'*Casualty of Desire?* Yeah. It's in my drawer.'

'Go get it and set it up in the lieutenant's office. I'm going to grab some more coffee and I'll meet you there.'

Bosch stepped into interview room three with the box of cash so that the side that said *Xmas* on it was held against his chest. He hoped it looked like any common cardboard box. He watched Powers for a sign of recognition and got none. Powers was sitting just as Bosch had left him. Ramrod straight, his arms behind him as if by choice.

He looked at Bosch with deadpan eyes that were ready and waiting for the next go-round. Bosch put the box on the floor where it would be shielded from view, pulled out the chair and sat across from him again. He then reached down, opened the box and took out a tape recorder and a file folder. He put them on the table in plain sight.

'I told you, Bosch, no taping. If you got the camera on the other side of the glass going, then you're ripping off my rights, too.'

'No camera, no tape, Powers. This is just to play you something, that's all. Now, where were we?'

'We were to the point of put up or shut up. You cut me loose or you get my lawyer in here.'

'Well, actually, a couple of things have come up. I thought you might want to know about them first. You know, before you make a decision like that.'

'Fuck that. I'm through with this shit. Get me the phone.'

'Do you own a camera, Powers?'

'I said get – a camera? What about it?'

'Do you own a camera? It's a pretty straightforward question.'

'Yes. Everybody owns a camera. What about it?'

Bosch studied him for a moment. He could feel the momentum and control start to maybe shift just a bit. It was coming across the table from Powers. He could feel it. Bosch played a thin smile on his face. He wanted Powers to know that from this point on it was slipping away from him.

'Did you take the camera with you when you went to Vegas last March?'

'I don't know. Maybe. I take it on all my vacations. Didn't know it was a crime. The fucking legislature, what will they think of next?'

Bosch let him have his smile but didn't return it.

'Is that what you called it?' he said quietly. 'A vacation?'

'Yeah, that's exactly what I called it.'

'That's funny, because that's not what Veronica is calling it.'

'I don't know anything about that or her.'

His eyes momentarily looked away from Bosch. It was the first time, and again Bosch felt the balance shifting. He was playing it right. He felt it. Things were shifting.

'Sure you know about it, Powers. And you know her pretty good, too. She just told us all about it. She's in the other room right now. Turns out she was weaker than I thought. My money had been on you. You know the saying, the bigger they are the harder they fall, all of that. I thought you'd be the one but it was her. Edgar and Rider broke her down a little while ago. Amazing how crime scene photos can work on somebody's guilty conscience. She told us everything, Powers. Everything.'

'You're so full of bullshit, Bosch, and it's getting pretty old. Where's the phone?'

'This is how she tells it. You—'

'I don't want to hear it.'

'You met her when you went up there that night to take the burglary report. One thing led to another and pretty soon you two were having a little romance. An affair to remember. Only she came to her senses and broke it off. She still loved ol' Tony. She knew he travelled a lot, strayed a lot, but she was used to that. She needed him. So she cut you off. Only, and this is according to her, you wouldn't be cut off. You kept after her, calling her, following her when she'd leave the estate up there. It was getting scary. I mean, what could she do? Go to Tony and say this guy I had an affair with is following me all the time? She—'

'This is so much bullshit, Bosch. It's a joke!'

'Then you started following Tony. You see, he was your problem. He was in the way. So you did your homework. You followed him to Vegas and you caught him in the act. You knew just what he was up to and how to put him down in a way that we'd go down the wrong path. Trunk music, they call it. Only you couldn't carry the tune, Powers. We're on to you. With her help, we're going to put you down.'

Powers was looking down at the table. The skin around his eyes and his jawline had drawn tight.

'This is so much crap,' he said without looking up. 'I'm tired of listening to it and to you. She's not in the other room. She's sitting up there in that big house on the hill. This is the oldest trick in the book.'

Powers looked up and a twisted smile cracked his face.

'You try to pull this shit on a cop? I can't believe it. This is really weak, man. You're weak. You're embarrassing yourself here.'

Bosch reached over to the tape recorder and pushed the play button. Veronica Aliso's voice filled the tiny room.

'It was him. He's crazy. I couldn't stop him until it was too late. Then I couldn't tell anyone because it . . . it would look like I—'

Bosch turned it off.

'That's enough,' he said. 'It's out of line for me to even play *that* for you. But I thought, cop to cop, you should know where you stand.'

Bosch silently watched Powers as he did a slow burn. Bosch could see the anger boiling up behind his eyes. He didn't seem to move a muscle, yet he seemed all at once to become as hard as a stack of lumber. He finally was able to hold himself back, though, and compose himself.

'It's just her word,' he said in a quiet voice. 'There's no corroboration of anything. It's a fantasy, Bosch. Her word against mine.'

'It could be. Except we have these.'

Bosch opened the file and threw the stack of photos in front of Powers. Then he reached across and carefully fanned them on the table so they could be seen and recognized.

'That backs up a good part of her story, don't you think?'

Bosch watched as Powers studied the photographs. Once again Powers seemed to go to the edge with an interior rage, but once more he contained it.

'It doesn't back up shit,' he said. 'She could've taken these herself. Anybody could have. Just because she gives you a stack of . . . She's got you people wrapped up, doesn't she? You're buying every line she feeds you.'

'Maybe that would be so, only she didn't give us the photos.'

Bosch reached into the file again and pulled out a copy of the search warrant. He reached over and put it on top of the photos.

'Five hours ago we faxed that to Judge Warren Lambert at his home in the Palisades. He faxed it back signed. Edgar and Rider have been in your little Hollywood bungalow most of the night. Among the items seized was a Nikon camera with telephoto lens. And these photos. They were under your mattress, Powers.'

He paused here to let it all sink in behind Powers's darkening eyes.

'Oh, and one other thing we found.' Bosch reached down and brought the box up. 'This was in the attic with the Christmas stuff.'

He dumped the contents of the box on the table and the stacks of cash tumbled every which way, some falling to the floor. Bosch shook the box to make sure it had all come out and then dropped it to the floor. He looked at Powers. His eyes were wild, darting over the thick bundles. Bosch knew he had him. And he also knew in his gut that he had Veronica Aliso to thank for that.

'Now, personally, I don't think you are this stupid,' Bosch said quietly. 'You know, to keep the pictures and all this cash right in your house. Of course, I've seen crazier things in my time. But if I was betting, I'd bet that you didn't know all of this was there because you didn't put it there. But, hey, either way it works fine for me. We've got you and we'll clear this one, that's all I care about. It would be nice to grab her, too, but that's okay. We'll need her for you. With the photos and her story and all the other stuff we've talked about here, I think we got you for the murder easy. There's also lying-in-wait to tack on. That makes it a special circumstances case, Powers. You're looking at one of two things. The needle or LWP.'

He pronounced the last acronym *el-wop*, knowing that any cop, just as any criminal in the system, would know it meant life without parole.

'Anyway,' Bosch continued, 'I guess I'll go get that phone brought in here so you can call your lawyer. Better make it a good one. And none of those grandstanders from the O.J. case. You need to get yourself a lawyer who does his best work outside of the courtroom. A negotiator.'

He stood up and turned to the door. With his hand on the knob he looked back at Powers.

'You know, I feel bad, Powers. You being a cop and all, I was sort of hoping you'd catch the break instead of her. I feel like we're hitting the wrong person with the hammer. But I guess that's life in the big city. Somebody's got to be hit with it.'

He turned back to the door and opened it.

'*Bitch!*' Powers said with a quiet forcefulness.

Then he whispered something under his breath that Bosch couldn't hear. Bosch looked back at him. He knew enough not to say a word.

'It was her idea,' Powers said. 'All of it. She conned me and now she's conning you.'

Bosch waited a beat but there was nothing else.

'Are you saying you want to talk to me?'

'Yeah, Bosch, have a seat. Maybe we can work something out.'

At nine Bosch sat in the lieutenant's office, Billets behind the desk, bringing her up to date. He had an empty Styrofoam cup in his hand, but he didn't drop it in the trash can because he needed something to remind him that he needed more coffee. He was beat tired and the lines beneath his eyes were so pronounced they almost hurt. His mouth tasted sour from all the coffee and cigarettes. He'd eaten nothing but candy bars in the last twenty hours and his stomach was finally protesting. But he was a happy man. He had won the last round with Powers and in this kind of battle the last round was the only one that mattered.

'So,' Billets said, 'he told you everything?'

'His version of it,' Bosch said. 'He lays everything on her and that's to be expected. Remember, he thinks she's in the other room laying everything on him. So he's making her out to be the big bad black widow, like he never had an impure thought in his life until he ran across her.'

He brought the cup up to his mouth but then realized it was empty.

'But once we get her in here and she knows he's talking, we'll probably get her version,' he said.

'When did Jerry and Kiz leave?'

Bosch looked at his watch.

'About forty minutes ago. They should be back with her any time.'

'Why didn't you go up to get her?'

'I don't know. I figured I took Powers, they should have her. Spread it around, you know?'

'Better be careful. You keep acting like that and you'll lose your rep as a hardass.'

Bosch smiled and looked down into his cup.

'So what's the gist of his story?' Billets asked.

'The gist is pretty much how we figured it. He went up there to take a burglary report that day and it went from there. He says she put the moves on him and next thing you know they had a thing going. He started taking more and more patrol swings through the neighborhood and she was stopping by his bungalow in the mornings after Tony went to work or while he was in Vegas. The way he describes, she was reeling him in. The sex was good and exotic. He was hooked up pretty good.'

'Then she asked him to tail Tony.'

'Right. That first trip Powers took to Vegas was a straight job. She asked him to tail Tony. He did and he came back with a bunch of photos of Tony and the girl and a lot of questions about who Tony was meeting with over there and why. He wasn't stupid. He could tell Tony was into something. He says Veronica filled him in, knew every detail, knew all the OC guys by name. She also told him how much money was involved. That was when the plan came together. She told Powers that Tony had to go, that it would be just them afterward, them and a lot of money. She told him Tony had been skimming. Skimming off the skim. For years. There was at least a couple million in the pot plus whatever they took off Tony when they put him down.'

Bosch stood up and continued the story while pacing in front of her desk. He was too tired to sit for very long without being overcome with fatigue.

'Anyway, that was what the second trip was for. Powers went over and watched Tony one more time. It was research. He also tailed the guy Tony made the pickups from. Luke Goshen, who he obviously had no idea was an agent. They decided Goshen would be the patsy and worked out the plan to make it look like a mob hit. Trunk music.'

'It's pretty complicated.'

'Yeah, that it is. He says the planning was all hers, and I kind of think he might be telling the truth there. You ask me, Powers is smart but not that smart. This whole thing was Veronica's plan and he became a willing player. Only she had a backdoor built into it that Powers didn't know about.'

'He was the backdoor.'

'Yeah. She set him up to take the fall, but only if we got

too close. He said he'd given her a key to his place. It's a bungalow over on Sierra Bonita. She must've gone over there sometime this week, shoved the photos under the mattress and stuck the box of money in the attic. Smart woman. Nice setup. When Jerry and Kiz get her in here, I know just what she'll say. She's going to say it was all him, that he became infatuated with her, that they had an affair and that she broke it off. He went ahead and knocked off her husband. When she realized what had happened, she couldn't say anything. He forced her to go along with it. She had no choice. He was a cop and he told her he could pin it all on her if she didn't go along.'

'It's a good story. In fact, it still might work with a jury. She could walk on this.'

'Maybe. We still have some things to do.'

'What about the skim?'

'Good question. Nothing like the kind of money he's talking about showed up on Aliso's bank accounts. Powers said she said it was in a safe deposit box but she never told him where. It's got to be somewhere. We'll find it.'

'If it exists.'

'I think it does. She planted a half million in Powers's place to put him in the frame. That's a lot of money to spend on setting him up, unless you happen to have a couple million more stashed someplace. That's what we—'

Bosch looked through the glass into the squad room. Edgar and Rider were walking towards the lieutenant's office. Veronica Aliso was not with them. They came into the office with urgent looks on their faces and Bosch knew what they were going to say.

'She's gone,' Edgar said.

Bosch and Billets just stared at them.

'Looks like she split last night,' Edgar said. 'Her cars are still there but there was nobody at the house. We slipped in a back door and it's empty, man.'

'She take her clothes, jewelry?' Bosch asked.

'Doesn't look like it. She's just gone.'

'You check the gate?'

'Yeah, we checked at the gate. She had two visitors yesterday. First was a courier at four-fifteen. Legal Eagle Messenger Service. Guy was there about five minutes, in and out. Then a visitor last night. Late. Guy gave the name John Galvin. She had already called the gate and given the same name and told them to let him through when he showed up. They took his plate down and we ran it. It's Hertz out of Vegas. We'll put a call in. Anyway, Galvin stayed until one this morning. Just about the time we were in the woods hooking up Powers, he split. She probably went with him.'

'We called the guard on duty at the time,' Rider said. 'He couldn't remember if Galvin left alone or not. He doesn't specifically remember seeing Mrs Aliso last night, but she could have been down in the backseat.'

'Do we know who her attorney is?' Billets asked.

'Yes,' Rider said, 'Neil Denton, Century City.'

'Okay, Jerry, you work the trace on the Hertz rental and, Kiz, you try to run down Denton and see if you can find out what was so important that he had to messenger it over to her on Saturday.'

'All right,' Edgar said. 'But I got a bad feeling. I think she's in the wind.'

'Well, then we have to go into the wind to find her,' Billets said. 'Go to it.'

Edgar and Rider went back out to the homicide table and Bosch stood silent for a few moments, thinking about this latest development.

'Should we have put people on her?' Billets asked.

'Well, looking back, it seems that way. But we were off the books. We didn't have the people. Besides, we didn't really have anything on her until a couple hours ago.'

Billets nodded, a pained expression on her face.

'If they don't get a line on her in the next fifteen minutes, put it out on the air.'

'Right.'

'Listen, getting back to Powers, you think he's holding anything back?'

'Hard to say. Probably. There's still the question about why this time.'

'What do you mean?'

'I mean Aliso had been going over to Vegas for years and bringing back suitcases full of money. He'd been skimming for years, according to Powers, and also had been having his share of the women over there. Veronica knew all of this. She had to. So what was it that made her do it now, rather than last year or next year?'

'Maybe she just got fed up. Maybe this was just the right time. Powers came along and it clicked.'

'Maybe. I asked Powers and he said he didn't know. But I think maybe he was holding back. I'm going to take another run at him.'

Billet didn't respond.

'There's still some sort of secret we don't know about,' Bosch continued. 'There's something there. I'm hoping she'll tell it. If we find her.'

Billets dismissed it with a wave of her hand.

'You have Powers on tape?' she asked.

'Audio and video. Kiz was watching in room four. As soon as he said he wanted to talk she started it all rolling.'

'Did you advise him again? On the tape?'

'Yeah, it's all on there. He's sealed up pretty good. You want to watch it, I'll get the tape.'

'No. I don't even want to look at him if I can help it. You didn't promise him anything, did you?'

Bosch was about to answer but stopped. There was the sound of muffled yelling that he could tell was coming from Powers, still sequestered in room three. He looked through the glass of the lieutenant's office and saw Edgar get up from the homicide table and go down the hall to check it out.

'He probably wants his lawyer now,' Bosch said. 'Well, it's a little late for that . . . Anyway, no, I made no promises. I did tell him I'd talk to the DA about dropping special circs, but that's going to be tough. With what he told me in there, we can take our pick. Conspiracy to commit, lying in wait, murder for hire maybe.'

'I guess I should get a DA in here.'

'Yeah. If you don't have anyone in mind or anybody you owe a hot case to, put in a request for Roger Goff. This is his kind of case and I've owed him one for a while. He won't blow it.'

'I know Roger. I'll ask for him . . . I have to call out the brass, too. It's not every day you get to call a deputy chief and tell him not only have your people been running an investigation they were specifically told to stay away from, but that they've arrested a cop to boot. And for murder, no less.'

Bosch smiled. He would not relish having to make such a call.

'It's really going to hit the fan this time,' he said. 'One more black eye for the department. By the way, they didn't seize any of it because it's not related to this case, but Jerry and Kiz found some scary stuff in Powers's place. Nazi paraphernalia, white-power stuff. You might alert the brass about that, so they can do with it what they want.'

'Thanks for telling me. I'll talk to Irving. I'm sure he won't want that to see the light of day.'

Edgar leaned in through the open door.

'Powers says he's got to take a leak and can't hold it any longer.'

He was looking at Billets.

'Well, take him,' she said.

'Keep him hooked,' Bosch added.

'How's he gonna piss, his hands behind his back? Don't be expecting me to be taking it out for him. No way.'

Billets laughed.

'Just move the cuffs to the front,' Bosch said. 'Give me a second to finish in here and I'll be right there.'

'Okay, I'll be in three.'

Edgar left and Bosch watched him through the glass as he walked to the hallway leading to the interview rooms. Bosch looked back at Billets, who was still smiling at Edgar's comical protest. Bosch put a serious look on his face.

'You know, you can use me when you make that call.'

'What do you mean?'

'I mean, if you want to say you didn't know about any of this until I called you this morning with the bad news, that's cool with me.'

'Don't be ridiculous. We cleared a murder and got a killer cop off the street. If they can't see that the good in this outweighs the bad, then . . . well, fuck 'em if they can't take a joke.'

Bosch smiled and nodded.

'You're cool, Lieutenant.'

'Thanks.'

'Anytime.'

'And it's Grace.'

'Right. Grace.'

Bosch was thinking about how much he liked Billets as he walked down the short hallway to the interview rooms and into the open door of room three. Edgar was just closing the cuffs on Powers's wrists. His hands were in front of him now.

'Do me a favor, Bosch,' Powers said. 'Let me use the can in the front hallway.'

'What for?'

'So nobody'll see me in the back. I don't want anybody to see me like this. Besides, you might have a problem if people don't like what they see.'

Bosch nodded. Powers had a point. If they took him to the locker room, then all the cops in the watch office would likely see them and there would be questions, maybe even anger from some of the cops who didn't know what was going on. The bathroom in the front hallway was a public rest room, but this early on a Sunday morning it would likely be empty and they could take Powers in and out of there without being seen.

'Okay, let's go,' Bosch said. 'To the front.'

They walked him past the front counter and down the hallway past the administration offices, which were empty and closed for the day. While Bosch stayed with Powers in the hall, Edgar checked the rest room out.

'It's empty,' he said, holding the door open from inside.

Bosch followed Powers in and the big cop went to the furthest of three urinals. Bosch stayed by the door and Edgar took a position on the other side of Powers by the row of sinks. When Powers was finished at the urinal, he stepped toward one of the sinks. As he walked, Bosch saw that his right shoelace was untied and so did Edgar.

'Tie your shoe, Powers,' Edgar said. 'You trip and fall and break your pretty face, I don't want any cryin' 'bout *po*-lice brutality.'

Powers stopped and looked down at the shoelace on the floor and then at Edgar.

'Sure,' he said.

Powers first washed his hands, used a paper towel to dry them and then brought his right foot up on the edge of the sink to tie his shoe.

'New shoes,' Edgar said. 'Laces on 'em always come undone, don't they?'

Bosch couldn't see Powers's face because the cop's back was turned toward the door. But he was looking up at Edgar.

'Fuck you, nigger.'

It was almost as if he had slapped Edgar, whose face immediately filled with revulsion and anger. He looked over at Bosch, a quick glance to judge whether Bosch was going to do anything about his plan to hit Powers. But it was all the time Powers needed. He sprang away from the sink and threw his body into Edgar, pinning him against the white-tiled wall. His cuffed hands came up and the left one grabbed a handful of the front of Edgar's shirt while the right pressed the barrel of a small gun into the stunned detective's throat.

Bosch had covered half of the distance to them when he saw the gun and Powers began to shout.

'Back off, Bosch. Back off or you got a dead partner. You want that?'

Powers had turned his head so that he was looking back at Bosch. Bosch stopped and raised his hands away from his body.

'That's it,' Powers said. 'Now this is what you're going to do. Take your gun out real slowly and drop it in that first sink there.'

Bosch made no move.

'Do it. Now.'

Powers spoke with measured force, careful to keep his voice low.

Bosch looked at the tiny gun in Powers's hand. He recognized it as a Raven .25, a favored throw-down gun among patrol cops going back to at least his own time in a uniform. It was small – it looked like a toy in Powers's hand – but deadly and it fit snugly into a sock or boot, virtually unseen with the pants leg pulled down. As Bosch came to the realization that Edgar and Rider had not completely searched Powers, he also knew that a shot from the Raven at point-blank range would certainly kill Edgar. It was against all his instincts to give up his weapon, but he saw no alternative. Powers was desperate and Bosch knew desperate men didn't think things out. They went against the odds. They were killers. With two fingers he slowly removed his gun and dropped it into the sink.

'That's real good, Bosch. Now I want you to get on the floor underneath the sinks.'

Bosch did as he was told, never taking his eyes off Powers as he moved.

'Edgar,' Powers said. 'Now your turn. You can just go ahead and drop yours on the floor.'

Edgar's gun hit the tile.

'Now, you get under there with your partner. That's it.'

'Powers, this is crazy,' Bosch said. 'Where're you going to go? You can't run.'

'Who's talking about running, Bosch? Take out your cuffs and put one on your left wrist.'

After Bosch had complied, Powers told him to loop the cuffs through one of the sink trap pipes. He then told Edgar to put the free cuff around his right wrist. He did so and then Powers smiled.

'There, that's good. That ought to hold you guys for a few minutes. Now, give me your keys. Both of you, throw 'em out here.'

Powers picked Edgar's set up off the floor and unlocked the cuffs around his wrists. He quickly massaged them to get the circulation going. He was smiling but Bosch wondered if he even knew it.

'Now, let's see.'

He reached into the sink and grabbed Bosch's gun.

'This is a nice one, Bosch. Nice weight, balance. Beats mine. Mind if I borrow it for a couple minutes?'

Bosch knew then what he was planning to do. He was going for Veronica. Bosch thought of Kiz sitting at the homicide table, her back to the front counter. And Billets in her office. They wouldn't see him until it was too late.

'She's not here, Powers,' he said.

'What? Who?'

'Veronica. It was a scam. We never even picked her up.'

Powers was silent as the smile dropped away and was replaced with a serious look of concentration. Bosch knew what he was thinking.

'The voice came from one of her movies. I taped it off the video-tape. You go back to those interview rooms and it's a dead end. There's nobody back there and no way out.'

Bosch saw the same tightening of skin around Powers's face that he had seen before. His face grew dark with blood and anger, then, inexplicably, the smile suddenly creased across it.

'You smart fucker, Bosch. Is that so? You 'spect me to believe she's not there? Maybe this is the con, and not before. See what I'm saying?'

'It's no con. She isn't there. We were going to pick her up with what you told us. Went up the hill an hour ago but she's not there either. She left last night.'

'If she's not already here, then how . . .'

'That part was no scam. The money and pictures were in your house. If you didn't put them there, then she did. She's setting you up. Why don't you just put the gun down and let's start this over. You apologize to Edgar for what you called him and we drop this little incident.'

'Oh, I see. You drop the escape but I still get hit with the murder.'

'I told you, we're going to talk to the DA. We got one coming in right now. He's a friend. He'll do right by you. She's the one we really want.'

'You fucking asshole!' Powers said loudly. He then brought his voice back into check. 'Don't you see that I want her? You think you beat me? You think you broke me down in there? You didn't win, Bosch. I talked because I wanted to talk. I broke you, man, but you didn't know it. You started trusting me because you needed me. You should've never moved the cuffs, brother.'

He was silent a moment, letting that sink in.

'Now I've got an appointment with that bitch that I'm going to keep no matter what. She ain't here, then I'll go find her.'

'She could be anywhere.'

'So could I, Bosch, and she won't see me coming. I have to go.'

Powers grabbed the plastic bag out of the trash can and emptied it on the floor. He put Bosch's gun into the bag, then turned the faucets in all three sinks on full blast. The cascading water created a cacophony as it echoed off the tile walls. Powers picked up Edgar's gun and put it in the bag. He then wrapped the bag around itself several times, concealing the two guns inside. He put the Raven in his front pocket for easy access, threw the handcuff keys into one of the urinals and flushed each one. Without even looking at the two men handcuffed under the sink, he headed to the door.

'Adios, dipshits,' he threw over his shoulder and then he was gone.

Bosch looked at Edgar. He knew that if they yelled, it was likely they wouldn't be heard. It was a Sunday, the administration wing was empty. And in the bureau there were only Billets and Rider. With the water running, their shouts would probably be unintelligible. Billets and Rider would probably think it was the normal yelling from the drunk tank.

Bosch swiveled around and braced his feet on the wall beneath the sink counter. He grabbed the trap pipe so that he could use his legs as leverage in an attempt to pull the pipe free. But the pipe was burning hot.

'Son of a bitch!' Bosch yelled as he let go. 'He turned the hot water on.'

'What are we going to do? He's getting away.'

'Your arms are longer. See if you can reach up there and turn off the water. It's too hot. I can't grab the pipe.'

With Bosch feeding his arm almost up to the elbow through the pipe loop, Edgar was barely able to touch the faucet. It took him several seconds to turn the water down to a trickle.

'Now turn on the cold,' Bosch said. 'Cool this thing down.'

It took another few seconds, but then Bosch was ready to try again. He grabbed the pipe and pushed against the walls with his legs. As he did this, Edgar squeezed his hands around the pipe and did the same. The added muscle broke the pipe free along the seal beneath the sink. Water sloshed down on them as they threaded the cuffs chain through the pipe break. They got up and slid along the tile to the urinal, where Bosch saw his keys on the bottom grate. He grabbed them up and fumbled with them until he had the cuff off. He handed the keys to Edgar and ran toward the door, sloshing through the water that had completely spread across it.

'Turn off the water,' he yelled as he hit the door.

Bosch ran down the hallway and vaulted over the detective bureau front counter. The squad room was empty and through the glass he saw the lieutenant's office was vacant. He then heard a loud pounding and the muffled shouts of Rider and Billets. He ran down the hallway to the interview rooms and found all the doors open but one. He knew Powers had checked for Veronica Aliso anyway after locking Billets and Rider in room three. He opened the door to three and then quickly ran back through the squad room into the station house's rear hallway. He slammed through the heavy metal door and into the back parking yard. Instinctively reaching to his empty shoulder holster, he scanned the parking lot and the open bays of the garage. There was no sign of Powers, but there were two patrol officers standing near the gas pumps. Bosch focused on them.

'You seen Powers?'

'Yeah,' said the older of the two. 'He just left. With our fucking car. What the fuck's going on?'

Bosch didn't answer. He closed his eyes, bowed his head and cursed silently to himself.

Six hours later, Bosch, Edgar and Rider sat at the homicide table, silently watching the meeting taking place in the lieutenant's office. Huddled in the small office like people on a bus were Billets, Captain LeValley, Deputy Chief Irving, three IAD investigators including Chastain, and the chief of police and his administrative aide. Deputy District Attorney Roger Goff had been consulted on the speaker-phone – Bosch had heard his voice through the open door. But then the door was closed and Bosch was sure the group was deciding the fate of the three detectives sitting outside.

The police chief stood in the middle of the cramped room with his arms folded and his head down. He was the last to arrive, and it looked as if he was getting the run-down from the others. Occasionally he nodded, but it didn't look to Bosch as though he was saying much at all. Bosch knew that the main issue they were discussing was how to handle the problem with Powers. There was a killer cop on the loose. Going to the media with that would be an exercise in self-flagellation, but Bosch saw no way around it. They had looked in all the likely places for Powers and had not found him. The patrol car he had commandeered had been found abandoned up in the hills on Fareholm Drive. Where he had gone from there was anyone's guess. Surveillance teams stationed outside his bungalow and the Aliso house, as well as the lawyer Neil Denton's house and office, had produced nothing. It was now time to go to the media, to put the rogue cop's picture on the six o'clock news. Bosch guessed that the reason the police chief had showed up was that he planned to call a press conference. Otherwise he would have left the whole thing for Irving to deal with.

Bosch realized Rider had said something.

'Excuse me?'

'I said what are you going to do with your time?'

'I don't know. Depends on how much we get. If it's just one DP, I'll use it to finish work on my house. If it's longer than two, I'll have to see about making some money somehow.'

A DP, or deployment period, was fifteen days. Suspensions were usually handed out in such increments when the offense was serious. Bosch was pretty sure the chief wouldn't be handing out minor suspensions to them.

'He isn't going to fire us, is he, Harry?' Edgar asked.

'Doubt it. But it all depends on how they're telling it to him.'

Bosch looked back at the office window just as the chief was looking out at him. The chief looked away, not a good sign. Bosch had never met him and never expected that he would. He was an outsider brought in to appease the community. Not because of any particular police administrative skills, but because they needed an outsider. He was a large black man with most of his weight around his waist. Cops who didn't like him, and there were many, often referred to him as Chief Mud Slide. Bosch didn't know what cops who liked him called him.

'I just want to say I'm sorry, Harry,' Rider said.

'Sorry about what?' Bosch asked.

'About missing the gun. I patted him down. I ran my hands down his legs but somehow I missed it. I don't understand it.'

'It was small enough that he could fit it in his boot,' Bosch said. 'It's not all on you, Kiz. We all had our chances. Me and Jerry fucked up in the rest room. We should've been watching him better.'

She nodded but Bosch could tell she still felt miserable. He looked up and saw that the meeting in the lieutenant's office was beginning to break up. As the police chief and his aide, followed by LeValley and the IAD dicks, filed out, they left the bureau through the front entrance. It would make for an out-of-the-way walk if their cars were parked in the station lot out back, but it meant they didn't have to walk by the homicide table and acknowledge Bosch and the others. Another bad sign, he thought.

Only Irving and Billets remained in the office after it cleared. Billets then looked out at Bosch and signaled the three of them into her office. They got up slowly and headed in. Edgar and Rider sat down but Bosch stayed on his feet.

'Chief,' Billets said, giving Irving the floor.

'Okay, I'll give it to you the way it was just given to me,' Irving said.

He looked down at a piece of paper on which he had taken a few notes.

'For conducting an unauthorized investigation and for failure to follow procedure in searching and transporting a prisoner each of you is suspended without pay two deployment periods and suspended *with* pay for two deployment periods. These are to run consecutively. That's two months. And, of course, a formal reprimand goes into each of your jackets. Per procedure, you can appeal this to a Board of Rights.'

He waited a beat. It was heavier than Bosch had expected, but he showed nothing on his face. He heard Edgar audibly exhale. As far as the appeal went, disciplinary action by the police chief was rarely overturned. It would require two of the three captains on the Board of Rights to vote against their commander in chief. Overruling an IAD investigator was one thing, overruling the chief was political suicide.

'However,' Irving continued, 'the suspensions are being held in abeyance by the chief pending further developments and evaluation.'

There was a moment of silence while the last sentence was computed.

'What does he mean, abeyance?' Edgar asked.

'It means the chief is offering you a break,' Irving said. 'He wants to see how things fall out over the next day or two. Each of you is to come to work tomorrow and proceed with the investigation where you can. We talked with the DA's office. They're willing to file on Powers. Get the paperwork over there tomorrow first thing. We've put the word out and the chief will take it to the media in a couple hours. If we're lucky, we'll get this guy before he finds the woman or does any other damage. And if we're lucky, you three will probably be lucky.'

'What about Veronica Aliso, aren't they going to file on her?'

'Not yet. Not until we have Powers back. Goff said that without Powers, the taped confession is worthless. He won't be able to use it against her without Powers on the stand to introduce it or her being able to confront a witness against her.'

Bosch looked down at the floor.

'So without him, she walks.'

'That's the way it looks.'

Bosch nodded his head.

'What's he going to say?' he asked. 'The chief, I mean.'

'He's going to tell it like it is. You people will come out okay in some parts, not so okay in others. Overall, it's not going to be a good day for this department.'

'Is that why we're getting hit for two months? Because we're the messengers?'

Irving looked at him a long moment, his jaw clenched, before answering.

'I'm not going to dignify that with a reply.'

He looked at Rider and Edgar and said, 'You two can go now. You're finished here. I need to discuss another matter with Detective Bosch.'

Bosch watched them go and prepared for more of Irving's ire about the last comment. He wasn't sure why he had said it. He knew it would bait the deputy chief.

But after Rider closed the door to the office, Irving spoke of another matter.

'Detective, I wanted you to know that I've already talked to the federal people and we're all squared away on that.'

'How is that?'

'I told them that with today's developments it has become pretty clear – make that crystal clear – that you had nothing to do with planting evidence on their man. I told them it was Powers and that we were terminating that particular aspect of our internal investigation of your conduct.'

'Fine, chief. Thanks.'

Thinking that was it, Bosch made a move toward the door.

'Detective, there is one other thing.'

Bosch turned back to him.

'In discussing this matter with the chief of police, there is still one other aspect that bothers him.'

'And what is that?'

'The investigation started by Detective Chastain brought in ancillary information about your association with a convicted felon. It's troubling to me, too. I'd like to be able to get some assurance from you that this is not going to continue. I'd like to take that assurance to the chief.'

Bosch was silent a moment.

'I can't give you that.'

Irving looked down at the floor. He was working the thick muscles of his jaw again.

'You disappoint me, Detective Bosch,' he finally said. 'This department has done a lot by you. So have I. I've stood by you through some tough spots. You've never been easy, but you have a talent that I think this department and this city certainly need. I suppose that makes you worth it. Do you want to possibly alienate me and others in this department?'

'Not particularly.'

'Then take my advice and do the right thing, son. You know what that is. That's all I'm going to say on that.'

'Yes, sir.'

'That's all.'

When Bosch got to his house, he saw a dusty Ford Escort parked at the curb out front. It had Nevada plates. Inside the house, Eleanor Wish was sitting at the table in the small dining room with the classified ads section of the Sunday *Times*. She had a lit cigarette in the ashtray next to the paper and she was using a black marker to circle want ads. Bosch saw all of this and his heart jumped into a higher gear. What it meant to him was that if she was looking for a job, then she might be digging in, staying in L.A. and staying with him. To top it all off, the house was filled with the aroma of an Italian restaurant, heavy on the garlic.

He came around the table and put his hand on her shoulder and tentatively kissed her on the cheek. She patted his hand. As he straightened up, though, he noticed she was looking at ads for furnished apartments in Santa Monica, not the employment section.

'What's cooking?' he asked.

'My spaghetti sauce. You remember it?'

He nodded that he did but he really didn't. His memory of the days he had spent with her five years before were all centered on her, the moments they were intimate, and what happened afterward.

'How was Las Vegas?' he asked, just to be saying something.

'It was Vegas. The kind of place you never miss. If I never go back that will be fine with me.'

'You're looking for a place here?'

'I thought I might as well start looking.'

She had lived in Santa Monica before. Bosch remembered her apartment with the bedroom balcony. You could smell the sea and if you leaned out over the railing, you could look down Ocean Park Boulevard and even see it. He knew she couldn't afford a place like that now. She was probably looking at the listings east of Lincoln.

'You know there's no hurry,' he said. 'You can stay here. Nice view, it's private. Why don't you . . . I don't know, take your time.'

She looked up at him but decided not to say what she was about to say. Bosch could tell.

'Do you want a beer?' she asked instead. 'I bought some more. They're in the fridge.'

He nodded, letting her escape from the moment, and went into the kitchen. He saw a Crock-Pot on the counter and wondered if she had bought it or brought it back with her from Las Vegas. He opened the refrigerator and smiled. She knew him. She had bought bottles of Henry Weinhard's. He took two out and brought them back to the dining room. He opened hers and gave it to her, then his own. They both started to speak at the same time.

'Sorry, go ahead,' she said.

'No, you.'

'You sure?'

'Yeah, what?'

'I was just going to ask how things went today.'

'Oh. Well, they went good and bad. We broke the guy down and he told us the story. He gave up the wife.'

'Tony Aliso's wife?'

'Yeah. It was her plan all along. According to him. The Vegas stuff was just a misdirection.'

'That's great. What's the bad part?'

'Well, first of all, our guy is a cop and—'

'Oh, shit!'

'Yeah, but it's even worse. He got away from us today.'

'Got away? What do you mean got away?'

'I mean he escaped. Right out of the station. He had a pistol, a little Raven, in his boot. We missed it when we hooked him up. Edgar and me took him into the can, and he must've stepped on his shoelace while we were going over. You know, on purpose. Then, when Edgar noticed it and told him to tie his shoe, he came up with the Raven. He got away from us, went into the back lot and just took a squad car. He was still in uniform.'

'Jesus, and they didn't find him yet?'

'That was about eight hours ago. He's in the wind.'

'Well, where could he go in a patrol car and in a uniform?'

'Oh, he dumped the car – they already found that – and I doubt, wherever he is, he's in the uniform. It looks like he was into the far-right, white-supremacy thing. He probably knew people who'd get him clothes, no questions asked.'

'Sounds like a helluva cop.'

'Yeah. It's funny. He was the guy who found the body, you know, last week. It was on his beat. And because he was a cop, I didn't give him a second thought. I knew that day he was an asshole, but I didn't even look at him at all as anything other than the cop who found the stiff. And he must've known that. And he timed it so that we'd be in a rush out there. He was pretty smart about it.'

'Or she was.'

'Yeah. More likely it was her. But, anyway, I feel more, I don't know, upset or disappointed about that first day, that I didn't take a look at him, than I do about letting him get away today. I should've looked at him. More often than not the one who finds the body is the one. His uniform blinded me to that.'

She got up from the table and came over to him. She put her arms around his neck and smiled up at him.

'You'll get him. Don't worry.'

He nodded. They kissed.

'What were you going to say before?' she asked. 'When we both talked at once.'

'Oh . . . I don't remember now.'

'Must not have been important, then.'

'I wanted to tell you to stay here with me.'

She put her head down against his chest so that he couldn't see her eyes.

'Harry . . .'

'Just to see how it works. I feel like . . . it's almost like all this time hasn't gone by. I want – I just want to be with you. I can take care of you. You can feel safe and you can have all the time you need to make a new start here. Find a job, whatever you want to do.'

She stepped back from him and looked up into his eyes. The warning Irving had given him was the furthest thing from his mind. Right now all he cared about was keeping her close and doing whatever it took to accomplish that.

'But a lot of time has gone by, Harry. We just can't jump in like this.'

Bosch nodded and lowered his eyes. He knew she was right but he still didn't care.

'I want you, Harry,' she said. 'Nobody else. But I want to take it slow. So that we're sure. Both of us.'

'I already know I'm sure.'

'You just think you are.'

'Santa Monica is so far away from here.'

She smiled and then laughed and shook her head.

'Then you're just going to have to sleep over when you come visit.'

He nodded again and they embraced for a long moment.

'You can make me forget a lot of things, you know that?' he whispered into her ear.

'You, too,' she said back.

While they made love the phone rang, but whoever was calling did not leave a message when the machine picked up. Later, after Bosch got out of the shower, Eleanor reported that another call had come in but no message was left.

Finally, while Eleanor was boiling water for the pasta, the phone rang a third time and Bosch got it before the machine picked up.

'Hey, Bosch?'

'Yeah, who's this?'

'It's Roy Lindell. Remember me, Luke Goshen?'

'I remember. Was that you who called a couple times before?'

'Yeah, why didn't you pick up?'

'I was busy. What do you need?'

'So, it was the bitch, huh?'

'What?'

'Tony's wife.'

'Yeah.'

'Did you know this guy Powers?'

'Not really. Just to see around.'

Bosch didn't want to tell him anything he didn't already know.

Lindell exhaled in a bored way loudly into the phone.

'Yeah, well, Tony once told me that he was more afraid of his wife than he was of Joey Marks.'

'Yeah?' Bosch said, suddenly interested. 'He said that? When?'

'I don't know. One night we were talking in the club and he just said it. I remember the place was closed. He was waiting for Layla and we were talking.'

'Lindell, thanks a lot for telling me this. What else did he say?'

'Hey, I'm telling you now, Bosch. Anyway, I couldn't before. I was in character, man, and in that character you don't tell the cops shit. And then after, I . . . well, then I thought you were trying to fuck me over. I wasn't going to tell you shit then, either.'

'And now you know better.'

'Yeah, right. Look, Bosch, most guys you would've never heard from. But I'm calling. You think you'll hear from anybody else from the bureau saying maybe we made a mistake about you? No way. But I like your style. I mean, you get pulled off the case and what do you do, you turn around and get right back on it. Then you solve the fucker. That takes balls and style, Bosch. I can dig that.'

'You can dig it. That's great, Roy. What else did Tony Aliso tell you about his wife?'

'Nothing much. He just said she was cold. He said that she had him by the short hairs. Hooked and snooked and that was that. He couldn't get a divorce from her without losing half his wad and then having her running around out there with all that she knew about his business and his business associates. If you know what I mean.'

'Why didn't he just go to Joey Marks and ask for a whack on her?'

'I think on account that she knew Joey from way back and he liked her. It was Joey who introduced her to Tony way back when. I think Tony knew that if he went to Joey, it would get KO'd pretty quick and it might get back to her. And if he went to somebody else, he'd have to answer to Joey. Joey had the final say on that kind of stuff, and he wouldn't want Tony getting involved in a freelance job like that and possibly endangering the wash operation.'

'How well do you think she knew Joey Marks? You think she could've gone back to him now?'

'No way. She killed the golden goose. Tony made Joey legitimate money. His first allegiance is always to the money.'

Bosch was quiet for a few moments and so was Lindell.

'So what happens with you now?' Bosch finally said.

'You mean with my thing? I go back to Vegas tonight. I sit down in front of the grand jury in the morning. I figure I'll be talking to them at least a couple weeks. I've got a pretty good story to tell 'em. We should have Joey and his crew tagged and bagged by Christmas.'

'Hope you're bringing your bodyguards.'

'Oh, yeah. I'm not alone.'

'Well, good luck, Lindell. All the bullshit aside, I like your style, too. Let me ask you something, why'd you tell me about the safe house and the Samoans? That wasn't in keeping with your character.'

'I had to, Bosch. You scared me.'

'You thought I'd actually clip you for them?'

'I wasn't sure, but that didn't really worry me. I had people watching over me that you didn't know about. But I *was* sure that they'd clip her. And I'm an agent, man. It was my duty to try to stop that. So I told you. I was surprised you didn't guess I was undercover right then.'

'Never crossed my mind. You were good.'

'Well, I fooled the people I had to fool. I'll see you around, Bosch.'

'Sure. Oh, Lindell?'

'Yeah.'

'Did Joey Marks ever think that Tony A was skimming off him?'

Lindell laughed.

'You don't give up, do you, Bosch?'

'I guess not.'

'Well, that information would be part of the investigation and I can't talk about it. Officially.'

'What about unofficially?'

'Unofficially you didn't hear it from me and I never talked to you. But to answer your question, Joey Marks thought everybody was skimming off him. He trusted no one. Every time I wore a wire with the guy, I was sweating bullets. Because you never knew when he was going to put his hand down your chest. I was with him more than a year and he was still doin' that every now and then. I had to wear the bug in my armpit, man. You try pulling tape out of your armpit sometime, man. It hurts.'

'What about Tony?'

'That's what I'm getting at. Sure, Joey thought Tony was skimming. He thought I was, too. And you gotta understand, a certain amount of that was permissible. Joey knew everybody had to make a buck to be happy. But he mighta felt Tony was taking more than his share. He never told me that's what he thought, but I know he had the boy followed a couple times over here in L.A. And he got to somebody in Tony's bank in Beverly Hills. Joey was being copied on the monthly statements.'

'Yeah?'

'Yeah. He would've known if there were any deposits that were outta line.'

Bosch thought a moment but couldn't think what else to ask.

'Why'd you ask that, Bosch?'

'Oh, I don't know, something I'm workin' out. Powers said the wife told him Tony had a couple million he skimmed. It's hidden somewhere.'

Lindell whistled over the line.

'Seems like a lot to me. Seems like Joey would've caught that and put the hammer down on Tony pronto. That's not what you call permissible.'

'Well, I think it accrued over the years, you know. He could have piecemealed it. Also, he was washing money for some of Joey's friends in Chicago and Arizona, remember? He could've skimmed them, too.'

'Anything's possible. Listen, Bosch, let me know how it all shakes out. I have to catch a plane.'

'One more thing.'

'Bosch, I gotta get to Burbank.'

'You ever heard of anybody in Vegas named John Galvin?'

Galvin was the name of the man who had last visited Veronica Aliso on the night she disappeared. There was a beat of silence before Lindell finally said the name was not familiar. But that silence was what Bosch really heard.

'You sure?'

'Look, I never heard of the guy, okay? I gotta go.'

After hanging up, Bosch opened his briefcase on the dining room table and took out a notebook so he could write down a few notes about what Lindell had said. Eleanor came out of the kitchen with utensils and napkins in her hands.

'Who was that?'

'Lindell.'

'Who?'

'The agent who was Luke Goshen.'

'What did he want?'

'I guess to apologize.'

'That's unusual. The bureau usually doesn't apologize for anything.'

'It wasn't an official call.'

'Oh. Just one of those macho male bonding calls.'

Bosch smiled because she was so right.

'What's this?' she asked as she put the silverware down

and took the tape of *Casualty of Desire* out of his briefcase. 'Oh, was this one of Tony Aliso's movies?'

'Yeah. Part of his Hollywood legacy. It's one of the ones Veronica was in. I was supposed to give it back to Kiz.'

'You already saw it?'

Bosch nodded.

'I would've liked to see it. Did you like it?'

'It was pretty bad, but we can put it on tonight if you want.'

'You sure you wouldn't mind?'

'I'm sure.'

During dinner Bosch updated her in detail about the case. Eleanor asked few questions and eventually they lapsed into a comfortable quiet. The Bolognese sauce and linguini Eleanor had made was fantastic and Bosch broke the silence to tell her so. She had opened a bottle of red wine and that tasted good, too. He told her about that as well.

Afterward, they left the dishes in the sink and went out to the living room to watch the movie. Bosch sat with his arm on the back of the couch, his hand lightly touching Eleanor's neck. He found it boring to watch the film again and his mind quickly drifted away as he thought over the day's events. The money was what held his attention the longest. He wondered if Veronica already had it in her possession or if it was in a place where she had to go to get it. Not a local bank, he decided. They had already checked the local bank accounts.

That left Las Vegas, he concluded. Tony Aliso's travel records showed that in the last ten months he had not been anywhere but Los Angeles and Las Vegas. If he had been operating a skim fund, he'd have to have had access to it. If the money wasn't here, then it was over there. And since Veronica had not left the house before today, Bosch also concluded that she didn't have the money yet.

The phone rang and interrupted these thoughts. Bosch climbed up from the couch and answered the phone in the kitchen so he wouldn't disturb Eleanor's viewing of the movie. It was Hank Meyer calling from the Mirage but it didn't sound like Hank Meyer. It sounded like a scared boy.

'Detective Bosch, can I trust you?'

'Sure you can, Hank, what's the matter?'

'Something's happened. I mean, something's come up. Uh, because of you I know something I don't think I should know. I wish this whole thing . . . I don't know what to—'

'Hold on, hold on, Hank. Just calm down and tell what it is that's wrong. Be calm. Talk to me and we'll fix it. Whatever it is, we'll fix it.'

'I'm at the office. They called me at home because I had a flag on the computer for that betting slip that belonged to your victim.'

'Right.'

'Well, somebody cashed it tonight.'

'Okay, somebody cashed it. Who was it?'

'Well, you see, I put an IRS flag on the computer. Meaning that the cashier was supposed to request a driver's license and get a Social Security number, you know, for tax purposes. Even though this ticket was worth only $4,000 I put the flag on it.'

'Okay, so who cashed the slip?'

'A man named John Galvin. He had a local address.'

Bosch leaned over the counter and pressed the phone tightly to his ear.

'When did this happen?' he asked.

'At eight-thirty tonight. Less than two hours ago.'

'I don't understand, Hank. Why is this upsetting to you?'

'Well, I left instructions on the computer for me to be contacted at home as soon as this slip was cashed. I was contacted. I came in and got the information on who cashed the slip so I could get it to you ASAP and then I went directly to the video room. I wanted to see this John Galvin, you know, if we got a clear picture of him.'

He stopped there. It was like pulling teeth getting the story out of him.

'And?' Bosch said. 'Who was it, Hank?'

'We got a clear picture. It turns out I know John Galvin but not as John Galvin. Uh, as you know, one of my duties is to interface with law enforcement, maintain relations and help when I can whenever there—'

'Yes, Hank, I know. *Who* was it?'

'I looked at the video. It was very clear. John Galvin is a man I know. He's in Metro, a captain. His name is—'

'John Felton.'

'How'd—'

'Because I know him, too. Now listen to me, Hank. You didn't tell me this, okay? We never talked. It's best that way. Safest for you. Understand?'

'Yes, but . . . but what is going to happen?'

'You don't have to worry. I'll take care of it and no one at Metro will ever know about this. Okay?'

'Okay, I guess. I—'

'Hank, I've got to go. Thanks, and I owe you a favor.'

Bosch hung up and called information for the number of Southwest Airlines at the airport in Burbank. He knew Southwest and America West handled most of the flights to Las Vegas and they both flew out of the same terminal. He called Southwest and had them page Roy Lindell. While he waited, he looked at his watch. It had been more than an hour since he had talked to Lindell, but he didn't think the agent was in as much of a hurry as he had intimated on the phone. Bosch thought he had just said that to get off the phone.

A voice came on the line and asked who he was holding for. After Bosch repeated Lindell's name, he was told to hold and after two clicks Lindell's voice was on the line.

'Yeah, this is Roy, who's this?'

'You son of a bitch.'

'Who is this?'

'John Galvin is John Felton and you knew it all the time.'

397

'Bosch? Bosch, what are you doing?'

'Felton is Joey's man in Metro. You knew that from being on the inside. And when Felton does things for Marks, he uses the name John Galvin. You knew that, too.'

'Bosch, I can't talk about this. It's all part of our in—'

'I don't give a shit about your investigation. You have to figure out whose side you're on, man. Felton has got Veronica Aliso. And that means Joey Marks has got her.'

'What are you talking about? This is crazy.'

'They know about the skim, don't you see? Joey wants his money back and they're going to squeeze it out of her.'

'How do you know all of this?'

'Because I know.'

Bosch thought of something and looked out through the kitchen door to the living room. Eleanor was still watching the movie and she looked over at him and raised her eyebrows in a question. Bosch shook his head to show his dissatisfaction with the person on the other end.

'I'm going to Vegas, Lindell. And I think I know where they'll be. You want to get your people involved? I sure as hell can't call Metro on this.'

'How are you so sure she's even there?'

'Because she sent up a distress signal. Are you in or out?'

'We're in, Bosch. Let me give you a number. You call it when you get over there.'

After Bosch hung up, he went into the living room. Eleanor had already turned off the tape.

'I can't watch any more of that. It's terrible. What's going on?'

'That time you followed Tony Aliso around in Vegas, you said he went to a bank with the girlfriend, right?'

'Right.'

'Which bank? Where?'

'I, uh . . . it was on Flamingo, east of the Strip, east of Paradise Road. I can't remember the name. I think it was Silver State National. Yes, that's it. Silver State.'

'The Silver State on Flamingo, are you sure now?'

'Right, yes.'

'And it looked like she was opening an account?'

'Yes, but I can't be sure. That's the problem with a one-man tail. It's a small branch bank and I couldn't hang around inside too long. It looked like she was signing account papers and Tony was just watching. But I had to go out and wait outside until they were done. Remember, Tony knew me. If he even saw me, the tail would be blown.'

'Okay, I'm going.'

'Tonight?'

'Tonight. I have to make some calls first.'

Bosch went back into the kitchen and called Grace Billets. While filling her in on what he had learned and his hunch about what it all meant, he got a pot of coffee going. After getting her approval to travel, he next called Edgar and then Rider and made arrangements to pick them up at the station in one hour.

He poured himself a cup of coffee and leaned against the counter in deep thought. Felton. There was a contradiction, it seemed to Bosch. If the Metro captain was the Joey Marks organization's inside man, why had he moved so quickly to go after Goshen when he got the match on the fingerprints Bosch had provided? Bosch played with this for a while and finally decided that Felton must have seen an opportunity in moving Goshen out of the way. He must have believed that his position in the Las Vegas underworld would rise if Goshen were out of the picture. Perhaps he even planned to arrange Goshen's assassination, thereby insuring the indebtedness of Joey Marks. Bosch realized that for this plan to work, Felton either didn't know that Goshen knew he was the organization's inside man, or he planned to get rid of Goshen before he got a chance to tell anyone.

Bosch took a sip of the scalding coffee and put these thoughts aside. He went back into the living room. Eleanor was still on the couch.

'Are you going?'

'Yeah. I've got to pick up Jerry and Kiz.'

'Why tonight?'

'Got to be there before the bank opens tomorrow.'

'You think Veronica is going to be there?'

'It's a hunch. I think Joey Marks finally figured out just like we did that if he didn't whack Tony, then somebody else did and that person had to have been close to him. And that that person now has his money. He knew Veronica from way back and would figure she was up to it. I think he sent Felton over to check into it and to get his money back and take care of her if she was dirty on it. But she must've talked him out of it somehow. Probably by mentioning she had two million in skim in a safe deposit box in Vegas. I think that's what stopped Felton from killing her and instead made him take her with him. She's probably only alive until they get into that box. I think she gave Felton her husband's last betting slip because she knew he might cash it and we'd be watching for it.'

'What makes you think it's at the bank where I saw him go?'

'Because we know about everything he had over here, all his accounts. It's not over here. Powers told me Veronica had told him that Tony dropped the skim into a safe deposit box that she wouldn't have access to until he was dead. She wasn't a signatory on it. So my guess is that it's in Vegas. It's the only place he's been outside of L.A. for the last year. And that if one day he was taking his girlfriend to open a bank account somewhere, he'd just go ahead and take her to the same bank he used.'

Eleanor nodded.

'It's funny,' Bosch said.

'What is?'

'That what all of this really came down to was a bank caper. It's not really about Tony Aliso's murder, it's about the money he skimmed and hid. A bank caper with his murder sort of a side effect. And that's how you and I met. On a bank job.'

She nodded, her eyes going far off as she thought about it. Bosch immediately wished he hadn't brought the memory up.

'Sorry,' he said. 'I guess it's not really that funny.'

Eleanor looked up at him from the couch.

'Harry, I'm going with you to Las Vegas.'

VIII

The Silver State National Bank branch where Tony Aliso had taken his girlfriend while Eleanor Wish had watched was in the corner of a small shopping plaza between a Radio Shack and a Mexican restaurant called La Fuentes. The parking lot was largely empty at dawn on Monday morning when the FBI agents and LAPD detectives came to set up. The bank didn't open until nine and the other businesses would follow beginning at ten.

Because the businesses were closed, the agents had a problem in locating their surveillance points. It would be too obvious to stick four government cars in the lot. They would be too noticeable because there were only five other cars in the entire block-long parking lot, four parked on the outer fringes and an old Cadillac parked in the first row nearest the bank. There were no license plates on the Caddy, which had a spider web crack in the windshield, its windows left open and the trunk sprung and held closed by a chain and padlock through one of its many rusted-out spots. It had the sad appearance of having been abandoned, its owner probably another Las Vegas casualty. Like someone lost in the desert and dying of thirst just a few feet from an oasis, the Caddy had stopped for the final time just a few feet from the bank and all the money inside it.

The agents, after cruising by the location a few times to get the lay of the land, decided to use the Caddy as a blind, by popping the hood and sticking an agent in a greasy T-shirt under it and ostensibly working on the dead engine. They complemented this agent with a panel van parked right next to the Caddy. Four agents were in the van. At seven that morning they had taken it to the federal utilities shop and had a painter stencil *La Fuentes Mexican Restaurant – Established 1983* on the side panels in red paint. The paint was still drying when they drove the van into the lot at eight.

Now at nine, the lot was slowly beginning to fill, mostly with employees of the stores and a few Silver State customers who needed to take care of business as soon as the bank opened its doors. Bosch watched all of this from the backseat of a federal car. Lindell and an agent named Baker were in the front seat. They were parked in the service bay of a gas station across Flamingo Road from the shopping center where the bank was located. Edgar and Rider were in another bureau car parked further up Flamingo. There were two other bureau cars in the area, one static and one roving. The plan was for Lindell to move his car into the bank parking lot once it became more crowded with cars and the bureau car would not stand out. This plan included a bureau helicopter making wide arcs around the shopping center.

'They're opening up,' a voice from the car radio reported.

'Gotcha, La Fuentes,' Lindell said back.

The bureau cars were each equipped with a radio pedal and overhead mike on the windshield visor, meaning the driver of each car simply depressed the foot pedal and spoke, avoiding having to raise a microphone to his mouth and possibly being noticed and identified as law enforcement. Bosch had heard that the LAPD was finally getting such equipment, but the narcotics units and specialized surveillance teams were getting it first.

'Lindell,' he said, 'you ever go to talk on the radio and slam on the brakes by mistake?'

'Not yet, Bosch. Why?'

'Just curious how all this fancy equipment works.'

'It's only as good as the people who work it.'

Bosch yawned. He couldn't remember the last time he had slept. They had driven through the night to get to Las Vegas and then spent the rest of the time planning for the bank surveillance.

'So what do you think, Bosch?' Lindell asked him. 'Sooner or later?'

'This morning. They'll want their money. They don't want to wait.'

'Yeah, maybe.'

'You think it's later?'

'If it was me, I'd do it later. That way if there were people out there watching and waiting – whether it's the bureau or LAPD or Powers or whoever – they'd get cooked in the sun. Know what I mean?'

'Yeah. We sit out here all day and we aren't going to be very sharp when the time comes.'

Bosch was quiet for a little while after that. From the backseat he studied Lindell. He noticed that the agent had gotten a haircut. There was no sign of the spot where Bosch had hacked off his ponytail.

'You think you're going to miss it?' Bosch asked.

'Miss what?'

'Being under. The life, I mean.'

'No, it was getting old. I'll be happy to go straight.'

'Not even the girls?'

Bosch saw Lindell's eyes take a quick swipe at Baker and then look at Bosch in the rearview mirror. That told Bosch to let that subject go.

'Whaddaya think about the lot now, Don?' Lindell said, changing the subject.

Baker scanned the lot. It was slowly filling up. There was a bagel shop on the far end from the bank, and that was responsible for most of the autos at the moment.

'I think we can take it in, park it by the bagel place,' Baker said. 'There's enough cover now.'

'Okay, then,' Lindell said. He tilted his head slightly so that he was projecting his voice toward the visor. 'Uh, La Fuentes, this is Roy Rogers. We're going to take our position in now. We'll check ya from the bagel shop. That will be to your posterior, I believe.'

'Roger that,' came the return. 'You always wanted to be on my tail end, didn't you, Roy?'

'Funny guy,' Lindell said.

An hour went by while they watched from their new position and nothing happened. Lindell was able to move their car in closer, parking in front of a card-dealing school about half the parking lot's length from the bank. It was class day and several would-be dealers had been pulling in and parking. It was good cover.

'I don't know, Bosch,' Lindell said, breaking a long silence. 'You think they're going to show or not?'

'I never said it was anything more than a hunch. But I still think it all fits. It even fits better since we got here. Last week I found a matchbook in Aliso's room at the Mirage. It was from La Fuentes. Whether they show or not, I say Tony's got a box in that bank.'

'Well, I'm thinking about sending Don here in to ask about that. We might be able to call an end to this and stop wasting our time if we find out there's no box.'

'Well, it's your call.'

'You got that right.'

A couple more minutes of tense silence went by.

'What about Powers?' Lindell asked.

'What about him?'

'I don't see him here, either, Bosch. When you got here this morning, you were all hot and heavy about him comin' out here to find her and blast her full of holes. So where is he?'

'I don't know, Lindell. But if we're smart enough to figure this out, so is he. I wouldn't doubt it if he knew from

408

tailing Tony where the box was all along and just left that out of our little conversation.'

'Wouldn't surprise me, either. But I still say it'd be stupid for him to come here. He's got to know we have a fix on this.'

'Stupid isn't the word. It's suicidal. But I don't think he cares. He just wants her to go down. And if he takes a bullet, too, then that's the way it goes. Like I told you before, he was ready to do the kamikaze scene at the station when he thought she was there.'

'Well, let's just hope he's cooled down a little since—'

'There!' Baker barked out.

Bosch followed his pointing finger toward the far corner of the lot, where a white limousine had just pulled in and was moving slowly toward the bank.

'Jesus,' Lindell said. 'Don't tell me he is this stupid.'

All limos looked basically the same to Bosch but somehow Lindell and Baker had recognized the car.

'Is that Joey Marks?'

'It's his limo. He likes those big whitewalls. It's the wop in him. I just can't – he can't be in there. He's not going to waste two years of my fucking life making this pickup, is he?'

The limo stopped in the lane in front of the bank. There was no further movement.

'You got this, La Fuentes?' Lindell asked.

'Yeah, we got it,' came a whispered reply, though there was clearly no way anyone in that van could be overheard by someone in the limo.

'Uh, one, two and three, standby,' Lindell continued. 'Looks like we might have the fox in the henhouse. Air Jordan, you take five until further. I don't want you swinging over and spooking anybody.'

This brought a chorus of rogers from the three other ground units and the helicopter.

'On second thought, three, why don't you come on up by the southwest entrance and stand by there for me,' Lindell said.

'Roger that.'

Finally, the door to the limo opened, but it was on the side blocked from Bosch's view. He waited, not breathing, and after a beat Captain John Felton emerged from the limo.

'Bingo,' the whisper came over the radio.

Felton then leaned back into the open door and reached in. Veronica Aliso now emerged, Felton's hand tightly around her arm. Following her, another man emerged at the same time the trunk opened automatically. While this second man, who was wearing gray pants and a shirt with an oval name tag sewn above the breast pocket, went to the trunk, Felton bent down and said something to someone still inside the limo. He never took his hand off Veronica's arm.

Bosch caught only a glimpse of Veronica's face then. Though he was an easy thirty yards from her, he could see the fear and weariness. It had probably been the longest night of her life.

The second man pulled a heavy red toolbox from the trunk and followed behind as Felton walked Veronica toward the bank, his arm still gripping her and his head swiveling as he looked about. Bosch saw Felton's focus linger on the van and then finally look away. The paint job had probably been the deciding factor. It had been a nice touch.

As they walked alongside the old Cadillac, Felton bent down to look at the man working under the hood. Satisfied he was not a threat, Felton straightened up and went on to the glass doors of the bank. Before they disappeared inside, Bosch saw that Veronica was clutching a cloth bag of some kind. Its dimensions were not discernible because it appeared to be empty and folded over on itself.

Bosch didn't breathe again until they were no longer in sight.

'Okay,' Lindell said to the visor. 'We've got three. Felton, the woman, and the driller. Anbody recognize him?'

The radio was silent for a few seconds and then a lone voice answered.

'I'm too far away but I thought it looked like Maury Pollack. He's a safe-and-lock man who's worked for Joey's crew before.'

'Okay,' Lindell said. 'We'll check him later. I'm sending Baker in now to open a new account. Wait five and then, Conlon, you go in next. Check your sets now.'

They went through a quick check of the radio sets Baker and Conlon were wearing under their clothes with wireless earpieces and wrist mikes. They checked out and Baker got out of the car and walked briskly along the sidewalk in front of the other stores toward the bank.

'Okay, Morris,' Lindell said. 'Take a walk. Try the Radio Shack.'

'Roger.'

Bosch watched as an agent he recognized from the predawn meeting started crossing the lot from a car parked near the southwest entrance to the lot. Morris and Baker crossed paths ten feet apart but didn't acknowledge each other or even glance at the limo, which still sat with its engine idling in the lane in front of the bank.

It took about an hour for the next five minutes to go by. It was hot out but Bosch was mainly sweating from the anxiety of waiting and wondering what was going on. There had been only one transmission from Baker once he was inside. He had whispered that the subjects were in the safe deposit vault.

'Okay, Conlon, go,' Lindell ordered at the five-minute mark.

Bosch soon saw Conlon walking along the storefronts from the direction of the bagel shop. He went into the bank.

And then there was nothing for the next fifteen excruciating minutes. Finally, Lindell spoke just to break the silence.

'How we doin' out there. Everybody chipper?'

There was a chorus of microphone clicks signaling an affirmative response. Just as the radio had gone silent again, Baker's voice came up in an urgent whisper.

'They're coming out, coming out. Something's wrong.'

Bosch watched the bank doors and in a moment Felton and Veronica came out, the police captain's hand still firmly on her arm. The driller followed behind, lugging his red toolbox.

Felton didn't look around this time. He just walked with purpose toward the limo. He carried the bag now and it did not appear to Bosch to have grown in size. If Veronica's face looked fearful and tired before, it now looked even more distorted by fright. It was hard for Bosch to tell at this distance, but it looked like she was crying.

The door to the limo was opened from within as the threesome retraced their path alongside the old Cadillac and were getting near.

'All right,' Lindell said to the listening agents. 'On my call we go in. I'll take the front of the limo, three, you are in behind me. One and two, you got the back. Standard vehicular stop. La Fuentes, I want you people to come up and clear the limo. Do it quick. If there's shooting, everybody watch the cross fire. Watch the cross fire.'

As the rogers were coming in, Bosch was watching Veronica. He could tell she knew she was going to her death. The look on her face was vaguely reminiscent of what Bosch had seen on her husband's face. That certain knowledge that the game was up.

As he watched, he suddenly saw the trunk of the Cadillac spring open behind her. And from it, as if propelled by the same taut steel, jumped Powers. In a loud, wild-animal voice that Bosch heard clearly and would never forget, Powers yelled one word as he hit the ground.

'*Veronica!*'

As she, Felton and the driller turned to the origin of the sound, Powers raised his hands, both of them holding weapons. In that instant Bosch saw the glint of his own gun, the satin-finished Smith & Wesson, in the killer cop's left hand.

'*Gun!*' Lindell yelled. '*Everybody in! Everybody in!*'

He jerked the car into gear and slammed his foot on the gas pedal. The car jerked forward and started screaming toward the limo. But Bosch knew there was nothing they could do. They were too far away. He watched the scene unfold with a grim fascination, as if he were watching a slow-motion scene from a Peckinpah movie.

Powers began firing both guns, the shells ejecting and arcing away over both his shoulders as he stepped toward the limo. Felton made an attempt to go inside his jacket for his own gun but he was cut down in the fusillade, the first to drop. Then Veronica, standing perfectly still, facing her killer and making no move to run or shield herself, was hit and went down, dropping to the pavement, where Bosch couldn't see her because the limo blocked his view.

Powers kept coming and firing. The driller dropped his toolbox, raised his hands and started stepping backward away from the line of fire. Powers apparently ignored him. Bosch couldn't tell if he was shooting at Veronica's fallen body or into the open door of the limo. The limo took off, its tires spinning at first without purchase before it finally started to move, the rear door still open. But almost immediately, its driver failed to negotiate the left turn in the parking lane and the big car crashed into a row of parked cars. The driver jumped out and started running in the direction of the bagel shop.

Powers seemed to pay the fleeing driver no mind. He had reached the spot where Felton had fallen to the ground. He dropped Bosch's gun on the police captain's chest and reached down for the bag, which was on the ground next to Felton's hand.

It seemed that Powers did not realize that bag was empty until he had actually picked it up off the ground and held it. And as he was making this discovery, the doors of the van behind him were opened and four agents carrying shotguns were coming out. The agent in the T-shirt was coming around the side of the Cadillac, the handgun he had hidden in the engine compartment now pointed at Powers.

A squealing tire from one of the approaching bureau cars drew Powers's attention away from the empty duffel bag. He dropped it and turned on the five agents behind him. He raised both his hands again, though he only had one gun this time.

The agents opened fire and Bosch watched as Powers was literally lifted off the ground by the force of the impact and onto the front hood of a full-sized pickup truck that probably belonged to a bank customer. Powers landed on his back. His hand lost its grip on the remaining gun and it clattered off the hood to the ground. As loud as the eight seconds of shooting had been, the silence that followed the gun falling to the ground seemed even louder.

Powers was dead. Felton was dead. Giuseppe Marconi, aka Joseph Marconi, aka Joey Marks, was dead – his body sprawled and awash in blood on the soft leather seats in the back of his limousine.

When they got to Veronica Aliso, she was alive but dying. She had been hit with two rounds in the upper chest, and the bubbles in the froth of blood in her mouth indicated her lungs had been shredded. While the FBI agents ran about securing and containing the scene, Bosch and Rider went to Veronica.

Her eyes were open but losing their moisture. They were moving all around as if searching for someone or something that wasn't there. Her jaw started to work and she said something but Bosch couldn't hear. He crouched down over her and turned his ear to her mouth.

'Can you . . . get me ice?' she whispered.

Bosch turned and looked at her. He didn't understand. She started to speak again and he turned his ear to her mouth again.

' . . . the pavement . . . so hot. I . . . I need ice.'

Bosch looked at her and nodded.

'It's coming. It's coming. Veronica, where's the money?'

He bent over her, realizing that she was right, the pavement was now burning the palms of his hands. He could barely make out her words.

'At least they don't . . . they don't get it.'

She started coughing then, a deep wet cough, and Bosch knew her chest was full of blood and it wouldn't be long before she drowned. He couldn't think of what to do or say to this woman. He realized they were probably his own bullets in her and that she was dying because they had fucked up and let Powers get away. He almost wanted to ask her to forgive him, to say she understood how things could go so wrong.

He looked away from her and across the lot. He could hear sirens approaching. But he had seen enough gunshot wounds to know she wasn't going to need the ambulance. He looked back down at her. Her face was very pale and going slack. Her lips moved once more and he bent to listen. This time her voice was no more than a desperate rasp in his ear. He could not understand her words and he whispered in her ear to say it again.

' . . . et my gergo . . .'

He turned his head to look at her, the confusion in his eyes. He shook his head. An annoyed expression crossed her face.

'Let,' she said clearly, using the last of her strength. 'Let . . . my daughter go.'

Bosch kept his eyes locked on hers as that last line ran through his mind. Then, without thinking about it, he nodded once to her. And as he watched, she died. Her eyes lost their focus and he could tell she was gone.

Bosch stood up and Rider studied his face.

'Harry, what did she say?'

'She said . . . I'm not sure what she said.'

Bosch, Edgar and Rider stood leaning against the trunk of Lindell's car, watching as a phalanx of FBI and Metro people continued to descend on the crime scene. Lindell had ordered the entire shopping center closed and marked off with yellow tape, a move that prompted Edgar to comment, 'When these guys throw a crime scene, they really throw a crime scene.'

Each of them had already given a statement. They were no longer part of the investigation. They were merely witnesses to the event and now observers.

The special agent in charge of the Las Vegas field office was on the scene directing the investigation. The bureau had brought in a motor home that had four separate interview rooms in it and agents were taking statements in them from witnesses to the shooting. The bodies were still there, now covered in yellow plastic on the pavement and in the limo. That splash of bright color made for good video for the news helicopters circling overhead.

Bosch had been able to pick up pieces of information from Lindell on how things stood. The ID number on the Cadillac in which Powers had hidden for at least the four hours it was under observation by the FBI was traced to an owner in Palmdale, California, a desert town northeast of Los Angeles. The owner was already on file with the bureau. He was a white supremacist who had held antigovernment rallies on his land the last two Independence Days. He was also known to have sought to contribute to the defense funds of the men charged with bombing the federal courthouse in Oklahoma City two years before. Lindell told Bosch that the SAIC had ordered an arrest warrant for the owner on charges of conspiracy to commit murder for his role in helping Powers. It had been a nice plan. The trunk of the Caddy was lined with a thick carpet

416

and several blankets. The chain and padlock used to hold it closed could be unhooked from the inside. Through rusted-out spots on the fenders and trunk it had been possible for Powers to watch and wait for the right moment to come out, guns ready.

The driller, who it turned out was indeed Maury Pollack, was only too happy to cooperate with the gents. He was just happy he wasn't one of the ones wearing a yellow plastic blanket. He told Lindell and the others that Joey Marks had picked him up that morning, told him to wear a working-man's outfit and to bring his drill. He didn't know what the situation was because there was little talking in the limo on the ride over. He just knew the woman was scared.

Inside the bank Veronica Aliso had presented a bank officer with a copy of her husband's death certificate, his will and a court order issued Friday in Las Vegas Municipal Court granting her, as sole heir to Anthony Aliso, access to his safe deposit box. Access was approved and the box was drilled because Mrs Aliso said she had not been able to locate her husband's key.

The trouble was, Pollack said, when he drilled the box open, they found it was empty.

'Can you imagine that?' Lindell said as he related this information to Bosch. 'All of this for nothing. I was hoping to get my hands on that two mil. Of course, we'd've split it with L.A. Right down the middle, Bosch.'

'Right,' Bosch said. 'Did you look at the records? When was the last time Tony went into his box?'

'That's another thing. He was just in on Friday. Like twelve hours before they killed him, he went in and cleared the box. He must've had a premonition or something. He knew, man. He knew.'

'Maybe.'

Bosch thought about the matchbook from La Fuentes that he had found in Tony's room at the Mirage. Tony didn't smoke but he remembered the ashtrays at the house where Layla had grown up. He decided that if Tony had cleared his box out on that Friday and eaten at La Fuentes while he was here, the only likely reason he would have ended up with matches from the restaurant in his room was that he had been at the restaurant with someone who needed them.

'Now the question is, where's the money?' Lindell said. 'We can seize it if we can find it. Ol' Joey's not going to need it.'

Lindell looked over at the limo. The door was still open and one of Marconi's legs stuck out from under the yellow plastic. A powder blue pants leg, a black loafer and white sock. That was all Bosch could see of Joey Marks now.

'The bank people, are they cooperating or do you need a warrant for every move you make?' Bosch asked.

'No, they're on board. The manager's in there shaking like a leaf. Not every day you get a massacre outside your front door.'

'Then ask them to check their records and see if there's a box in there under the name Gretchen Alexander.'

'Gretchen Alexander? Who's that?'

'You know her, Roy. It's Layla.'

'Layla? Are you fuckin' kidding me? You think he'd give that bimbo two million duckets while he goes off and gets himself killed?'

'Just check, Roy. It's worth a shot.'

Lindell went off toward the bank doors. Bosch looked at his partners.

'Jerry, you going to want your gun back? We should tell them now so they don't destroy them or file them away forever.'

'My gun?'

Edgar looked at all of the yellow plastic with a pained look on his face.

'No, Harry, I don't think so. That piece is haunted now. I don't ever want it back.'

'Yeah,' Bosch said. 'I was thinking the same thing.'

Bosch brooded about things for a while and then heard his name being called. He turned and saw Lindell beckoning him from the door of the bank. He headed over.

'Bingo,' Lindell said. 'She's got a box.'

They walked back into the bank and Bosch saw several agents conducting interviews with the branch's stunned employees. Lindell led him to a desk where the branch manager sat. She was a woman of about thirty with brown curly hair. The nameplate on her desk said Jeanne Connors. Lindell picked up a file that was on her desk and showed it to Bosch.

'She has a box here and she made Tony Aliso a signatory on it. He pulled the box at the same time he pulled his own on the Friday before he got nailed. You know what I'm thinking? I think he emptied his and put it all in hers.'

'Probably.'

Bosch was looking at the safe deposit entry records in the file. They were handwritten on a three by five card.

'So,' Lindell said, 'what we do is we get a warrant for her box and drill the sucker – maybe get Maury out there to do it, since he's being so cooperative. We seize the money and the federal government is that much ahead. You guys'd get a split, too.'

Bosch looked at him.

'You can drill it, if you've got the probable cause, but there isn't going to be anything in it.'

Bosch pointed to the last entry on the box card. Gretchen Alexander had pulled the box herself five days earlier – the Wednesday after Tony Aliso was killed. Lindell stared at it a long moment before reacting.

'Jesus, you think she cleared it out?'

'Yeah, Roy, I do.'

'She's gone, isn't she? You've been looking for her, haven't you?'

'She's in the wind, man. And I guess so am I.'

'You're leaving?'

'I gave my statement, I'm clear. I'll see you, Roy.'

'Yeah, okay, Bosch.'

Bosch headed to the door of the bank. As he opened it, Lindell came up behind him.

'But why'd he put it all in her box?'

He was still holding the box card and staring at it as if it might suddenly answer all his questions.

'I don't know but I've got a guess.'

'What's that, Bosch?'

'He was in love with her.'

'Him? A girl like that?'

'You never know. People can kill each other for all kinds of reasons. I guess they can fall in love with each other for all kinds of reasons. You gotta take it when it comes, no matter if it's a girl like that or . . . someone else.'

Lindell just nodded and Bosch stepped through the door.

Bosch, Edgar and Rider took a cab to the federal building and picked up their car. Bosch said he wanted to stop by the house in North Las Vegas where Gretchen Alexander had grown up.

'She isn't going to be there, Harry,' Edgar said. 'Are you kidding?'

'I know she won't be there. I just want to talk to the old lady for a minute.'

He found the house without getting lost and pulled into the driveway. The RX7 was still there and didn't look like it had moved.

'This will only take a minute, if you want to stay in the car.'

'I'll go in,' Rider said.

'I'll stay and keep the AC going,' Edgar said. 'In fact, I'll drive the first leg, Harry.'

He got out as Bosch and Rider exited and came around and took Bosch's place behind the wheel.

Bosch's knock on the front door was answered quickly.

The woman had heard or seen the car and was ready.

'You,' she said, looking through the two-inch crack she had allowed in the door. 'Gretchen still isn't here.'

'I know, Mrs Alexander. It's you I want to talk to.'

'Me? What on earth for?'

'Would you please let us in? It's hot out here.'

She opened the door with a resigned look on her face.

'Hot in here, too. I can't afford to put the thermostat lower than eighty.'

Bosch and Rider entered and moved into the living room. He introduced Rider and all three of them sat down. This time Bosch sat on the edge of the sofa, remembering how he had sunk in last time.

'All right, what's this about? Why do you want to talk to me?'

'I want to know about your granddaughter's mother,' Bosch said.

The old woman's mouth went slack and Bosch could tell Rider wasn't much less confused.

'Her mother?' Dorothy asked. 'Her mother's long gone. Didn't have the decency to see her own child through. Never mind her mother.'

'When did she leave?'

'Long time ago. Gretchen wasn't even out of diapers. She just left me a note saying good-bye and good luck. She was gone.'

'Where'd she go?'

'I have no earthly idea and I don't want to know. Good riddance, is what I say. She turned her back on that beautiful little girl. Didn't have the decency to ever call or even send for a picture.'

'How did you know she was even alive?'

'I didn't. She could be dead all these years for all I know or care.'

She was a bad liar, the type who got louder and indignant when she lied.

'You know,' Bosch said. 'She sent you money, didn't she?'

The woman looked sullenly down at her hands for a long moment. It was her way of confirming his guess.

'How often?'

'Once or twice a year. It wasn't near enough to make up for what she did.'

Bosch wanted to ask how much would have been enough but let it go.

'How did the money come?'

'Mail. It was in cash. I know it came from Sherman Oaks, California. That was always the postmark. What does this have to do with anything now?'

'Tell me your daughter's name, Dorothy.'

'She was born to me and my first husband. My name was Gilroy back then and that was hers.'

'Jennifer Gilroy,' Rider said, repeating Veronica Aliso's true name.

The old woman looked at Rider with surprise but didn't ask how she knew.

'We called her Jenny,' she said. 'Anyway, you see, when I took over with Gretchen I was remarried and had a new name. I gave it to Gretchen so the kids at school wouldn't bother her about it. Everybody always thought I was her momma and that was fine with the both of us. Nobody needed to know diff'rent.'

Bosch just nodded. It had all come together now. Veronica Aliso was Layla's mother. Tony Aliso had gone from the mother to the daughter. There was nothing else to ask or say. He thanked the old woman and touched Rider on the back so that she would go through the door first. Out on the front step, he paused and looked back at Dorothy Alexander. He waited until Rider was a few steps toward the car before speaking.

'When you hear from Layla – I mean, Gretchen – tell her not to come home. Tell her to stay as far away from here as she can.'

He shook his head.

'She shouldn't ever come home.'

The woman didn't say anything. Bosch waited a couple moments while looking down at the worn welcome mat. He then nodded and headed to the car.

Bosch took the backseat behind Edgar, Rider sat in the front. As soon as they were in the car and Edgar was backing out of the driveway, Rider turned around and looked at Bosch.

'Harry, how did you ever put that together?'

'Her last words. Veronica's. She said, "Let my daughter go." I just sort of knew then. There's a resemblance there. I just didn't place it before.'

'You've never even seen her.'

'I've seen her picture.'

'What?' Edgar said. 'What's going on?'

'Do you think Tony Aliso knew who she was?' Rider asked, ignoring Edgar.

'Hard to say,' Bosch said. 'If he did, it makes what happened to him easier to understand, easier to take. Maybe he was flaunting it with Veronica. Maybe it's what sent her over the edge.'

'And Layla-slash-Gretchen?'

Edgar's head was swiveling back and forth between them and the road, a look of confusion on his face.

'Something tells me she didn't know. I think if she did, she would have told her grandmother and the old lady didn't know.'

'If he was just using her to get to Veronica, why'd he move all the money into her box?'

'He could've been using her but he also could've been in love with her. We'll never know. Might've just been coincidence that it happened on the day he got killed. He could've just transferred the cash because he had the IRS on him. Maybe he was afraid they'd find out about the box and freeze his access to it. It could've been a lot of things. But we'll never know now. Everybody's dead.'

'Except for the girl.'

Edgar made a hard stop, pulling to the side of the road. Coincidentally, they happened to be across the street from Dolly's on Madison.

'Is somebody gonna tell me what the hell is going on?' he demanded. 'I do you people a favor and keep the car cool while you two go inside for a chat and then I'm left in the dark. Now what the hell are you two talking about?'

He was looking at Bosch in the rearview mirror.

'Just drive, Jed. Kiz will tell you when we get to the Flamingo.'

They drove into the front circle of the Hilton Flamingo and Bosch left them there. He moved quickly through the football field-sized casino, dodging rows of slot machines, until he reached the poker room, where Eleanor had said she would be when they were done. They had dropped her at the Flamingo that morning after she had shown them the bank she had once seen Tony Aliso going into with Gretchen Alexander.

There were five tables going in the poker room. Bosch quickly scanned the faces of the players but did not see Eleanor. Then, as he turned to look back across the casino, she was there, just as when she had appeared on the first night he'd gone looking for her.

'Harry.'

'Eleanor. I thought you'd be playing.'

'I couldn't play while thinking about you out there. Is everything okay?'

'Everything is fine. We're leaving.'

'Good. I don't like Las Vegas anymore.'

He hesitated for a moment before saying anything. He almost faltered but then the resolve came back to him.

'There is that one stop I'd still like to make before we

424

leave. The one we talked about. That is, if you've decided.'

She looked at him for a long moment and then a smile broke across her face.

IX

osch walked across the polished linoleum on the sixth floor of Parker Center, purposely driving his heels down with each step. He wanted to put scuff marks on the carefully tended finish. He turned into the alcove entrance to the Internal Affairs Division and asked the secretary behind the counter for Chastain. She asked if he had an appointment and Bosch told her he didn't make appointments with people like Chastain. She stared at him a moment and he stared back until she picked up a phone and punched in an extension. After whispering into the line, she held the phone to her chest and looked up at Bosch and then eyed the shoebox and file he held in his hands.

'He wants to know what it's about.'

'Tell him it's about his case against me falling apart.'

She whispered some more and then Bosch was finally buzzed through the counter's half door. He went into the IAD squad room, where several of the desks were occupied by investigators. Chastain stood up from behind one of these.

'What are you doing here, Bosch? You're on suspension for letting that prisoner escape.'

He said it loudly so that the others in the squad room would know that Bosch was a guilty man.

'The chief cut it down to a week,' Bosch said. 'I call that a vacation.'

'Well, that's only round one. I still got your file open.'

'That's why I'm here.'

Chastain pointed to the interview room Bosch had been in the week before with Zane.

'Let's talk in there.'

'No,' Bosch said. 'We're not talking, Chastain. I'm just showing.'

He dropped the file he was carrying on the desk. Chastain remained standing and looked at it without opening it.

'What is this?'

'It's the end of the case. Open it.'

Chastain sat down and opened the file, exhaling loudly, as if he were embarking on a distasteful and worthless chore. On top was a copy of a page from the department's manual of procedure and officer conduct. The manual was to IAD dicks what the state penal code was to the rest of the officers and investigators in the department.

The page in the file pertained to officers associating with known criminals, convicted felons and members of organized crime. Such association was strictly forbidden and punishable by dismissal from the department, according to the code.

'Bosch, you didn't need to bring me this, I've got the whole book,' Chastain said.

He was trying out some light banter because he didn't know what Bosch was doing and was well aware that his peers were watching from their desks while trying to act as if they weren't.

'Yeah? Well, you better get your book out and read the bottom line there, pal. The exception.'

Chastain looked down at the bottom of the page.

'Says, "Exception to this code can be established if the officer can show to the satisfaction of superior officers a family relationship through blood or marriage. If that is established, the officer must—"'

'That's enough,' Bosch said.

He reached down and took the page so that Chastain could see what was in the rest of the file.

'What you have there, Chastain, is a marriage certificate issued in Clark County, Nevada, attesting to my marriage to Eleanor Wish. If that's not good enough for you, beneath it are two affidavits from my partners. They witnessed the marriage. Best man and maid of honor.'

Chastain kept his eyes on the paperwork.

'It's over, man,' Bosch said. 'You lose. So get the fuck out of my life.'

Chastain leaned back. His face was red and he had an uncomfortable smile on his face. Now he was sure the others were watching.

'You're telling me you got married just to avoid an IAD beef?'

'No, asshole. I got married because I love somebody. That's why you get married.'

Chastain didn't have a reply. He shook his head, looked at his watch and shuffled some papers while trying to act as though this was just a minor interruption in his day. He did everything but look at his nails.

'Yeah, I thought you'd run out of things to say,' Bosch said. 'I'll see you around, Chastain.'

He turned to walk away but then turned back to Chastain.

'Oh, and I almost forgot, you can tell your source our deal is done with, also.'

'What source, Bosch? Deal? What are you talking about?'

'I'm talking about Fitzgerald or whoever you get your information from at OCID.'

'I don't—'

'Sure you do. I know you, Chastain. You couldn't have come up with Eleanor Wish on your own. You've got a pipeline over there to Fitzgerald. He told you about her. It was him or one of his people. Doesn't matter to me who. Either way I'm out of a deal I made with him. You can tell him that.'

Bosch held the shoebox up and shook it. The videotape

and audiotapes rattled inside it, but he could tell Chastain had no idea what was in the box or what it meant.

'You tell him, Chastain,' he said again. 'See you around.'

He finally left then, pausing only at the counter to give the secretary a thumbs-up sign. In the hallway, rather than turn left toward the elevators, he took a right and headed through the double doors of the chief of police's office suite. The chief's adjutant, a lieutenant in uniform, sat behind the reception desk. Bosch didn't know him, which was good. He walked up and put the shoebox down on the desk.

'Can I help you? What's this?'

'It's a box, Lieutenant. It's got some tapes the chief will want to watch and listen to. Right away.'

Bosch made a move to leave.

'Wait a minute,' the adjutant said. 'Will he know what this is about?'

Bosch left then, not turning around when the adjutant called after him for his name. He slipped through the double doors and headed down to the elevator. He felt good. He didn't know if anything would come of the illegal tapes he had given the police chief, but he felt that all decks were cleared. His show with the box earlier with Chastain would ensure that the word got back to Fitzgerald that this was exclusively Bosch's play. Billets and Rider should be safe from recriminations by the OCID chief. He could come after Bosch if he wanted, but Bosch felt safe now. Fitzgerald had nothing on him anymore. No one did.

X

It was their first day on the beach after spending two days almost exclusively in their room. Bosch couldn't get comfortable on the chaise longue. He didn't understand how people did this, just sit in the sun and bake. He was covered with lotion and there was sand caked between his toes. Eleanor had bought him a red bathing suit that he thought made him look foolish and that made him feel like a target. At least, he thought, it wasn't one of those slingshot things some of the men on the beach were wearing.

He propped himself up on his elbows and looked around. Hawaii was unbelievable. So beautiful it was like a dream. And the women were beautiful, too. Especially Eleanor. She lay beside him on her own chaise. Her eyes were closed and there was a small smile on her face. She wore a one-piece black bathing suit that was cut high on her hips and showed off her tanned and nicely muscled legs.

'What are you looking at?' she said without opening her eyes.

'Nothing. I just . . . I can't get comfortable. I think I'm going to take a walk or something.'

'Why don't you get a book to read, Harry? You have to relax. That's what honeymoons are about. Sex, relaxation, good food and good company.'

'Well, two out of four isn't bad.'

'What's wrong with the food?'

'The food's great.'

'Funny.'

She reached out and hit him in the arm. Then she, too, propped herself up on her elbows and gazed out at the shimmering blue water. They could see the spine of Molokini rising in the distance.

'It's so beautiful here, Harry.'

'Yes, it is.'

They sat in silence for a few moments, watching the people walking by at the water's edge. Bosch brought his legs up, leaned forward and sat with his elbows on his knees. He could feel the sun burning into his shoulders. It was beginning to feel good.

He noticed a woman walking languidly along the edge. She had the attention of every man on the beach. She was tall and lithe and had long brownish-blond hair that was wet from the sea. Her skin was copper and she wore the smallest of bathing suits, just a few strings and triangles of black cloth.

As she passed in front of him, the glare dropped off Bosch's sunglasses and he studied her face. The familiar lines and tilt of the jaw were there. He knew her.

'Harry,' Eleanor whispered then. 'Is that . . . it looks like the dancer. The girl in that photo you had, the one I saw Tony with.'

'Layla,' Bosch said, not answering her but just to say the name.

'It's her, isn't it?'

'I didn't used to believe in coincidences,' he said.

'Are you going to call the bureau? The money's probably right here on the island with her.'

Bosch watched the woman moving away. Her back was to him now and from that angle it was almost as if she were naked. Just a few strings from her suit were visible. The glare came back on his glasses at this angle and his vision of her was distorted. She was disappearing in the glare and the mist coming in from the Pacific.

'No, I'm not calling anybody,' he finally said.

'Why not?'

'She didn't do anything,' he said. 'She let some guy give her money. Nothing wrong with that. Maybe she was even in love with him.'

He watched for another moment, thinking about Veronica's last words to him.

'Anyway, who's going to miss the money?' he said. 'The bureau? The LAPD? Some fat old gangster in a Chicago suburb with a bunch of bodyguards around him? Forget it. I'm not calling anybody.'

He took one last look at her. She was far away now and as she walked she was looking out to sea, the sun holding her face. Bosch nodded to her, but of course she didn't see this. He then lay back down on the chaise and closed his eyes. Almost immediately he felt the sun begin penetrating his skin, doing its healing work. And then he felt Eleanor's hand on top of his. He smiled. He felt safe. He felt like nobody could ever hurt him again.

If you have enjoyed *Trunk Music*
here is a taste of another Michael Connelly
bestseller

CITY OF BONES

Published in Orion paperback
ISBN 978-0-7528-0903-8
Price: £6.99

1

The old lady had changed her mind about dying but by then it was too late. She had dug her fingers into the paint and plaster of the nearby wall until most of her fingernails had broken off. Then she had gone for the neck, scrabbling to push the bloodied fingertips up and under the cord. She broke four toes kicking at the walls. She had tried so hard, shown such a desperate will to live, that it made Harry Bosch wonder what had happened before. Where was that determination and will and why had it deserted her until after she had put the extension cord noose around her neck and kicked over the chair? Why had it hidden from her?

These were not official questions that would be raised in his death report. But they were the things Bosch couldn't avoid thinking about as he sat in his car outside the Splendid Age Retirement Home on Sunset Boulevard east of the Hollywood Freeway. It was 4:20 P.M. on the first day of the year. Bosch had drawn holiday call-out duty.

The day more than half over and that duty consisted of two suicide runs — one a gunshot, the other the hanging. Both victims were women. In both cases there was evidence of depression and desperation. Isolation. New Year's Day was always a big day for suicides. While most people greeted the day with a sense of hope and renewal, there were those who saw it as a good day to die, some — like the old lady — not realizing their mistake until it was too late.

Bosch looked up through the windshield and watched as the latest victim's body, on a wheeled stretcher and covered in a green blanket, was loaded into the coroner's blue van. He saw there was one other occupied stretcher in the van and knew it was from the first suicide — a thirty-four-year-old actress who had shot herself while parked at a Hollywood overlook on Mulholland Drive. Bosch and the body crew had followed one case to the other.

Bosch's cell phone chirped and he welcomed the intrusion into his thoughts on small deaths. It was Mankiewicz, the watch sergeant at the Hollywood Division of the Los Angeles Police Department.

"You finished with that yet?"

"I'm about to clear."

"Anything?"

"A changed-my-mind suicide. You got something else?"

"Yeah. And I didn't think I should go out on the radio with it. Must be a slow day for the media — getting more what's-happening calls from reporters than I am getting service calls from citizens. They all want to do something on the first one, the actress on Mulholland. You know, a death-of-a-Hollywood-dream story. And they'd probably jump all over this latest call, too."

"Yeah, what is it?"

"A citizen up in Laurel Canyon. On Wonderland. He just called up and said his dog came back from a run in the woods with a bone in its mouth. The guy says it's human — an arm bone from a kid."

Bosch almost groaned. There were four or five call outs like this a year. Hysteria always followed by simple explanation: animal bones. Through the windshield he saluted the two body movers from the coroner's office as they headed to the front doors of the van.

"I know what you're thinking, Harry. Not another bone run. You've done it a hundred times and it's always the same thing. Coyote, deer, whatever. But listen, this guy with the dog, he's an MD. And he says there's no doubt. It's a humerus. That's the upper arm bone. He says it's a child, Harry. And then, get this. He said . . ."

There was silence while Mankiewicz apparently looked for his notes. Bosch watched the coroner's blue van pull off into traffic. When Mankiewicz came back he was obviously reading.

"The bone's got a fracture clearly visible just above the medial epicondyle, whatever that is."

Bosch's jaw tightened. He felt a slight tickle of electric current go down the back of his neck.

"That's off my notes, I don't know if I am saying it right. The point is, this doctor says it was just a kid, Harry. So could you humor us and go check out this humerus?"

Bosch didn't respond.

"Sorry, had to get that in."

"Yeah, that was funny, Mank. What's the address?"

Mankiewicz gave it to him and told him he had already dispatched a patrol team.

"You were right to keep it off the air. Let's try to keep it that way."

Mankiewicz said he would. Bosch closed his phone and started the car. He glanced over at the entrance to the retirement home before pulling away from the curb. There was nothing about it that looked splendid to him. The woman who had hung herself in the closet of her tiny bedroom had no next of kin, according to the operators of the home. In death, she would be treated the way she had been in life, left alone and forgotten.

Bosch pulled away from the curb and headed toward Laurel Canyon.

2

Bosch listened to the Lakers game on the car radio while he made his way into the canyon and then up Lookout Mountain to Wonderland Avenue. He wasn't a religious follower of professional basketball but wanted to get a sense of the situation in case he needed his partner, Jerry Edgar. Bosch was working alone because Edgar had lucked into a pair of choice seats to the game. Bosch had agreed to handle the call outs and to not bother Edgar unless a homicide or something Bosch couldn't handle alone came up. Bosch was alone also because the third member of his team, Kizmin Rider, had been promoted nearly a year earlier to Robbery-Homicide Division and still had not been replaced.

It was early third quarter, and the game with the Trail Blazers was tied. While Bosch wasn't a hardcore fan he knew enough from Edgar's constant talking about the game and begging to be left free of call-out duty that it was an important matchup with one of the Los Angeles team's top rivals. He decided not to page Edgar until he had gotten to the scene and assessed the situation. He turned the radio off when he started losing the AM station in the canyon.

The drive up was steep. Laurel Canyon was a cut in the Santa Monica Mountains. The tributary roads ranged up toward the crest of the mountains. Wonderland Avenue dead-ended in a remote spot where the half-million-dollar homes were surrounded by heavily wooded and steep terrain. Bosch instinctively knew that searching for bones in the area would be a logistical nightmare. He pulled to a stop behind a patrol car already at the address Mankiewicz had provided and checked his watch. It was 4:38, and he wrote it down on a fresh page of his legal pad. He figured he had less than an hour of daylight left.

A patrol officer he didn't recognize answered his knock. Her nameplate said Brasher. She led him back through the house to a home office where her partner, a cop whom Bosch recognized and knew was named Edgewood, was talking to a white-haired man who sat behind a cluttered desk. There was a shoe box with the top off on the desk.

Bosch stepped forward and introduced himself. The white-haired man said he was Dr. Paul Guyot, a general practitioner. Leaning forward Bosch could see that the shoe box contained the bone that had drawn them all together. It was dark brown and looked like a gnarled piece of driftwood.

He could also see a dog lying on the floor next to the doctor's desk chair. It was a large dog with a yellow coat.

"So this is it," Bosch said, looking back down into the box.

"Yes, Detective, that's your bone," Guyot said. "And as you can see . . ."

He reached to a shelf behind the desk and pulled down a heavy copy of *Gray's Anatomy*. He opened it to a previously marked spot. Bosch noticed he was wearing latex gloves.

The page showed an illustration of a bone, anterior and posterior views. In the corner of the page was a small sketch of a skeleton with the humerus bone of both arms highlighted.

"The humerus," Guyot said, tapping the page. "And then we have the recovered specimen."

He reached into the shoe box and gently lifted the bone. Holding it above the book's illustration he went through a point-by-point comparison.

"Medial epicondyle, trochlea, greater and lesser tubercle," he said. "It's all there. And I was just telling these two officers, I know my bones even without the book. This bone is human, Detective. There's no doubt."

Bosch looked at Guyot's face. There was a slight quiver, perhaps the first showing of the tremors of Parkinson's.

"Are you retired, Doctor?"

"Yes, but it doesn't mean I don't know a bone when I see —"

"I'm not challenging you, Dr. Guyot." Bosch tried to smile. "You say it is human, I believe it. Okay? I'm just trying to get the lay of the land here. You can put that back into the box now if you want."

Guyot replaced the bone in the shoe box.

"What's your dog's name?"

"Calamity."

Bosch looked down at the dog. It appeared to be sleeping.

"When she was a pup she was a lot of trouble."

Bosch nodded.

"So, if you don't mind telling it again, tell me what happened today."

Guyot reached down and ruffled the dog's collar. The dog looked up at him for a moment and then put its head back down and closed its eyes.

"I took Calamity out for her afternoon walk. Usually when I get up to the circle I take her off the leash and let her run up into the woods. She likes it."

"What kind of dog is she?" Bosch asked.

"Yellow Lab," Brasher answered quickly from behind him.

Bosch turned and looked at her. She realized she had made a mistake by intruding and nodded and stepped back toward the door of the room where her partner was.

"You guys can clear if you have other calls," Bosch said. "I can take it from here."

Edgewood nodded and signaled his partner out.

"Thank you, Doctor," he said as he went.

"Don't mention it."

Bosch thought of something.

"Hey, guys?"

Edgewood and Brasher turned back.

"Let's keep this off the air, okay?"

"You got it," said Brasher, her eyes holding on Bosch's until he looked away.

After the officers left, Bosch looked back at the doctor and noticed that the facial tremor was slightly more pronounced now.

"They didn't believe me at first either," he said.

"It's just that we get a lot of calls like this. But I believe you, Doctor, so why don't you continue with the story?"

Guyot nodded.

"Well, I was up on the circle and I took off the leash. She went up into the woods like she likes to do. She's well trained. When I whistle she comes back. Trouble is, I can't whistle very loud anymore. So if she goes where she can't hear me, then I have to wait, you see."

"What happened today when she found the bone?"

"I whistled and she didn't come back."

"So she was pretty far up there."

"Yes, exactly. I waited. I whistled a few more times, and

8

then finally she came down out of the woods next to Mr. Ulrich's house. She had the bone. In her mouth. At first I thought it was a stick, you see, and that she wanted to play fetch with it. But as she came to me I recognized the shape. I took it from her — had a fight over that — and then I called you people after I examined it here and was sure."

You people, Bosch thought. It was always said like that, as if the police were another species. The blue species which carried armor that the horrors of the world could not pierce.

"When you called you told the sergeant that the bone had a fracture."

"Absolutely."

Guyot picked up the bone again, handling it gently. He turned it and ran his finger along a vertical striation along the bone's surface.

"That's a break line, Detective. It's a healed fracture."

"Okay."

Bosch pointed to the box, and the doctor returned the bone.

"Doctor, do you mind putting your dog on a leash and taking a walk up to the circle with me?"

"Not at all. I just need to change my shoes."

"I need to change, too. How about if I meet you out front?"

"Right away."

"I'm going to take this now."

Bosch put the top back on the shoe box and then carried it with two hands, making sure not to turn the box or jostle its contents in any way.

Outside, Bosch noticed the patrol car was still in front of the house. The two officers sat inside it, apparently writing out reports. He went to his car and placed the shoe box on the front passenger seat.

Since he had been on call out he had not dressed in a suit. He had on a sport coat with blue jeans and a white oxford shirt. He stripped off his coat, folded it inside out and put it on the backseat. He noticed that the trigger from the weapon he kept holstered on his hip had worn a hole in the lining and the jacket wasn't even a year old. Soon it would work its way into the pocket and then all the way through. More often than not he wore out his coats from the inside.

He took his shirt off next, revealing a white T-shirt beneath. He then opened the trunk to get out the pair of work boots from his crime scene equipment box. As he leaned against the rear bumper and changed his shoes he saw Brasher get out of the patrol car and come back toward him.

"So it looks legit, huh?"

"Think so. Somebody at the ME's office will have to confirm, though."

"You going to go up and look?"

"I'm going to try to. Not much light left, though. Probably be back out here tomorrow."

"By the way, I'm Julia Brasher. I'm new in the division."

"Harry Bosch."

"I know. I've heard of you."

"I deny everything."

She smiled at the line and put her hand out but Bosch was right in the middle of tying one of the boots. He stopped and shook her hand.

"Sorry," she said. "My timing is off today."

"Don't worry about it."

He finished tying the boot and stood up off the bumper.

"When I blurted out the answer in there, about the dog,

I immediately realized you were trying to establish a rapport with the doctor. That was wrong. I'm sorry."

Bosch studied her for a moment. She was mid-thirties with dark hair in a tight braid that left a short tail going over the back of her collar. Her eyes were dark brown. He guessed she liked the outdoors. Her skin had an even tan.

"Like I said, don't worry about it."

"You're alone?"

Bosch hesitated.

"My partner's working on something else while I check this out."

He saw the doctor coming out the front door of the house with the dog on a leash. He decided not to get out his crime scene jumpsuit and put it on. He glanced over at Julia Brasher, who was now watching the approaching dog.

"You guys don't have calls?"

"No, it's slow."

Bosch looked down at the MagLite in his equipment box. He looked at her and then reached into the trunk and grabbed an oil rag, which he threw over the flashlight. He took out a roll of yellow crime scene tape and the Polaroid camera, then closed the trunk and turned to Brasher.

"Then do you mind if I borrow your Mag? I, uh, forgot mine."

"No problem."

She slid the flashlight out of the ring on her equipment belt and handed it to him.

The doctor and his dog came up then.

"Ready."

"Okay, Doctor, I want you to take us up to the spot where you let the dog go and we'll see where she goes."

"I'm not sure you'll be able to stay with her."

"I'll worry about that, Doctor."

"This way then."

They walked up the incline toward the small turn-around circle where Wonderland reached a dead end. Brasher made a hand signal to her partner in the car and walked along with them.

"You know, we had a little excitement up this way a few years ago," Guyot said. "A man was followed home from the Hollywood Bowl and then killed in a robbery."

"I remember," Bosch said.

He knew the investigation was still open but didn't mention it. It wasn't his case.

Dr. Guyot walked with a strong step that belied his age and apparent condition. He let the dog set the pace and soon moved several paces ahead of Bosch and Brasher.

"So where were you before?" Bosch asked Brasher.

"What do you mean?"

"You said you were new in Hollywood Division. What about before?"

"Oh. The academy."

He was surprised. He looked over at her, thinking he might need to reassess his age estimate.

She nodded and said, "I know, I'm old."

Bosch got embarrassed.

"No, I wasn't saying that. I just thought that you had been somewhere else. You don't seem like a rookie."

"I didn't go in until I was thirty-four."

"Really? Wow."

"Yeah. Got the bug a little late."

"What were you doing before?"

"Oh, a bunch of different things. Travel mostly. Took me a while to figure out what I wanted to do. And you want to know what I want to do the most?"

Bosch looked at her.

"What?"

"What you do. Homicide."

He didn't know what to say, whether to encourage her or dissuade her.

"Well, good luck," he said.

"I mean, don't you just find it to be the most fulfilling job ever? Look at what you do, you take the most evil people out of the mix."

"The mix?"

"Society."

"Yeah, I guess so. When we get lucky."

They caught up to Dr. Guyot, who had stopped with the dog at the turnaround circle.

"This the place?"

"Yes. I let her go here. She went up through there."

He pointed to an empty and overgrown lot that started level with the street but then quickly rose into a steep incline toward the crest of the hills. There was a large concrete drainage culvert, which explained why the lot had never been built on. It was city property, used to funnel storm water runoff away from the homes on the street. Many of the streets in the canyon were former creek and river beds. When it rained they would return to their original purpose if not for the drainage system.

"Are you going up there?" the doctor asked.

"I'm going to try."

"I'll go with you," Brasher said.

Bosch looked at her and then turned at the sound of a car. It was the patrol car. It pulled up and Edgewood put down the window.

"We got a hot shot, partner. Double D."

He nodded toward the empty passenger seat. Brasher frowned and looked at Bosch.

13

"I hate domestic disputes."

Bosch smiled. He hated them too, especially when they turned into homicides.

"Sorry about that."

"Well, maybe next time."

She started around the front of the car.

"Here," Bosch said, holding out the MagLite.

"I've got an extra in the car," she said. "You can just get that back to me."

"You sure?"

He was tempted to ask for a phone number but didn't.

"I'm sure. Good luck."

"You too. Be careful."

She smiled at him and then hurried around the front of the car. She got in and the car pulled away. Bosch turned his attention back to Guyot and the dog.

"An attractive woman," Guyot said.

Bosch ignored it, wondering if the doctor had made the comment based on seeing Bosch's reaction to Brasher. He hoped he hadn't been that obvious.

"Okay, Doctor," he said, "let the dog go and I'll try to keep up."

Guyot unhooked the leash while patting the dog's chest.

"Go get the bone, girl. Get a bone! Go!"

The dog took off into the lot and was gone from sight before Bosch had taken a step. He almost laughed.

"Well, I guess you were right about that, Doc."

He turned to make sure the patrol car was gone and Brasher hadn't seen the dog take off.

"You want me to whistle?"

"Nah. I'll just go in and take a look around, see if I can catch up to her."

He turned the flashlight on.

available from
THE ORION PUBLISHING GROUP

———

☐ **Echo Park** £6.99
MICHAEL CONNELLY
978-0-7528-7734-1

☐ **The Black Echo** £6.99
MICHAEL CONNELLY
978-0-7528-1000-3

☐ **The Black Ice** £6.99
MICHAEL CONNELLY
978-0-7528-1541-1

☐ **The Concrete Blonde** £6.99
MICHAEL CONNELLY
978-0-7528-1542-8

☐ **The Last Coyote** £6.99
MICHAEL CONNELLY
978-0-7528-0944-1

☐ **The Poet** £6.99
MICHAEL CONNELLY
978-0-7528-0926-7

☐ **Trunk Music** £6.99
MICHAEL CONNELLY
978-0-7528-0903-8

☐ **Angels Flight** £6.99
MICHAEL CONNELLY
978-0-7528-2694-3

☐ **A Darkness More
Than Night** £6.99
MICHAEL CONNELLY
978-0-7528-4404-6

☐ **The Brass Verdict** £6.99
MICHAEL CONNELLY
978-1-4091-0228-1

☐ **The Lincoln Lawyer** £6.99
MICHAEL CONNELLY
978-0-7528-7779-2

☐ **City of Bones** £6.99
MICHAEL CONNELLY
978-0-7528-4834-1

☐ **Chasing the Dime** £6.99
MICHAEL CONNELLY
978-0-7528-4980-5

☐ **Lost Light** £6.99
MICHAEL CONNELLY
978-0-7528-4256-1

☐ **The Narrows** £6.99
MICHAEL CONNELLY
978-0-7528-6380-1

☐ **The Closers** £6.99
MICHAEL CONNELLY
978-0-7528-6464-8

☐ **Blood Work** £6.99
MICHAEL CONNELLY
978-0-7528-1676-0

☐ **Void Moon** £6.99
MICHAEL CONNELLY
978-0-7528-3716-1

☐ **The Overlook** £6.99
MICHAEL CONNELLY
978-0-7528-8273-4

All Orion/Phoenix titles are available at your local bookshop or from the following address:

Mail Order Department
Littlehampton Book Services
FREEPOST BR535
Worthing, West Sussex, BN13 3BR
telephone 01903 828503, *facsimile* 01903 828802
e-mail MailOrders@lbsltd.co.uk
(Please ensure that you include full postal address details)

Payment can be made either by credit/debit card (Visa, Mastercard, Access and Switch accepted) or by sending a £ Sterling cheque or postal order made payable to *Littlehampton Book Services*.
DO NOT SEND CASH OR CURRENCY

Please add the following to cover postage and packing

UK and BFPO:
£1.50 for the first book, and 50p for each additional book to a maximum of £3.50

Overseas and Eire:
£2.50 for the first book plus £1.00 for the second book and 50p for each additional book ordered

---

BLOCK CAPITALS PLEASE

name of cardholder _____

address of cardholder _____

delivery address
(if different from cardholder)
_____
_____
_____

postcode _____   *postcode* _____

☐ I enclose my remittance for £_____

☐ please debit my Mastercard/Visa/Access/Switch (delete as appropriate)

card number ☐☐☐☐☐☐☐☐☐☐☐☐☐☐☐☐☐

expiry date ☐☐☐☐   Switch issue no. ☐☐

signature _____

prices and availability are subject to change without notice